*Imagine a World
where Legends run free
and Nightmares seek power.
Where Slaves endure . . .
and a living Myth
brings Hope*

The adventure continues with
Freefight
Available now!

The saga resumes with
Freefall
Available 2017

Tales from

Heart of a Warrior
The Turning of the Tide
Sleeping with the Enemy
Double Jeopardy
A Shot in the Dark

Coming Soon!

www.thegryphonsaga.com

Freeform

Book One of the Gryphon Saga

By L.E. Horn

COPYRIGHT © 2016 L.E. HORN
All Art Copyright © 2016 L.E. Glowacki
Sherrington Publishing 2016
Canada

Third Edition
ISBN: 978-1-988431-07-9 (Hardcover); 978-0-9949059-2-5 (Paperback); 978-0-9949059-3-2 (Electronic Book)

All rights reserved. The use of any part of this publication, reproduced, transmitted in any form or by any means electronic, mechanical, photocopying, recording or otherwise, or stored in a retrieval system without the prior written consent of the publisher—or, in the case of photocopying or other reprographic copying, a license from the Canadian Copyright Licensing Agency—is an infringement of the copyright law. All characters and character likenesses are the property of L.E. Horn and cannot be reproduced without the written consent of the author.
Disclaimer: This book is a work of fiction. Any references to historical events, real people or places are used fictitiously. The persons, places, things, and otherwise animate or inanimate objects mentioned in this novel are figments of the author's imagination. Any resemblance to anything or anyone living (or dead) is unintentional.

Library and Archives Canada Cataloguing in Publication Pending

Printed in Canada

To Myste and Wendy, who inspired.

PROLOGUE

THOSE BOUND TO THEIR HOME planets envision space as eternal blackness relieved only by the serene blaze of stars, a place of infinite mystery and careful exploration. It beckons to sentient species with frosted fingers, an invitation to examine every comet, asteroid, or planet.

For those who know better, space is dynamic and evolving. Although planets supporting life are not common, within the vastness of the universe there are many that can and do. There are as many that once did and can no longer. The apparent emptiness of the universe is, in reality, not empty at all.

If space could speak, it would whisper, "Beware. Trespass at your own risk."

A particular green and gold planet hangs like a jewel in a remote little corner of space, with only two small moons and the stars to keep it company. The planet is unassuming and unremarkable; most expect it to go unnoticed. Yet the space above the planet is bristling with activity.

BORN OF THE OPEN OCEAN, waves either begin as gentle swells hardly noticeable beneath a ship's hull, or as white capped monsters when storms whip the water into a frenzy. Regardless of their origin, as they approach the shore they are forever altered by the grip of rock beneath, the offshore currents along, and the winds that rise above the land.

Today, the breeze off the dunes was creating some cracking waves for the handful of surfers braving the cold spring currents along the beach. After weeks of torrential rain, the coast was experiencing unseasonably warm weather that created a pleasant sunny morning for lying on the sand. Many people were out celebrating the early glimpse of spring. Most of the beach bunnies were early tourists, not locals. The locals favored being sheathed in insulated neoprene while riding the waves.

Under a sunshade, a burly man sighed before leaning back in his beach chair. His body was so muscular that every time he moved, his chair creaked in protest. Sweat ran down his skin and dampened his shirt. Even shaded, the humid air was almost stifling enough to encourage a swim. Almost. He'd spent enough time here to know the water looked far more appealing than it would feel.

Here on the sand it seemed like high summer. The fact he wore clothing and not swimming attire might have revealed him as a local, but it didn't make him any more comfortable. The smaller man seated next to him wore similar clothes. Although his partner's mouse-like face appeared engrossed in an e-book, he knew his companion was just as focused as him.

The burly man shifted again. He hated the surveillance phase. The final stalk and pounce was more his thing, but with experience came the patience to wait for just the right moment. His superiors placed him in charge of special acquisitions because he was so efficient.

Dark glasses prevented the other beachgoers from noticing where his eyes lingered. This was deliberate; it disguised the rigid focus devoted to one particular young man playing in the surf. The target appeared unaware he was potential prey. The predator considered the youth's oblivious nature a wasted opportunity since this location was unpromising for any kind of ambush.

At the moment, his object of interest was riding an enormous cresting wave. The burly man watched as the wave tanked, the youth easily stepping off the board before dropping into the water. His equally youthful friend followed. The two excited voices carried over the waves to the intent ears of the stalker.

"Those two are stuck together like glue." The smaller man didn't look up from his e-book while he spoke. "Mr. Sociable isn't alone often. He's a tough one unless we grab him while he's in the can."

His muscular companion grunted. "This place is far too public anyway. Even after peak hours, the houses on the rise have a direct sightline. Unfortunately, we might have to resign ourselves to collaterals on this one." He looked at his watch. "We've got to split. Dan's due in from the airport with our latest parcel."

"The one you grabbed in Illinois? I hear she's a real pistol." To those watching, the little man appeared engrossed in his book, but his bigger friend could sense his sudden interest.

"Yeah. Matty got it good from her. If I hadn't been there, the whole thing would have gone bust," the big man said. "Those guys have a lot to learn. They're lucky the boss didn't find out how it went."

"Sounds as though Juke will like her." The little man packed away his e-reader, stood, and folded up his chair.

"I hope so. We don't have much for him this quarter." The chair was already slung under the burly man's arm as he shook the sand from the umbrella.

"Anything else coming from the Great White North?" The mousey man hefted his chair.

The burly man nodded. "We've got our prize winner arriving here in a week, booked at the little inn on the bay. She's coming with a girlfriend, but it will be an easy grab."

"What about the guy farther south?"

"I've decided he's going to have a terrible hit-and-run accident. Being out on the water alone is risky, especially in such a remote location. We'll use the boat with backup on the shore."

"What evidence are we leaving?" The little man shifted his chair to the other arm as he entered the parking lot.

"They'll find the surfboard—destroyed by the prop," the hulking man cracked a smile.

"So you think two weeks here before we collect out east?"

"As long as prop boy and prairie girl go smoothly," the burly man said as he tossed the chair and umbrella into a dark green SUV. He glanced out to the ocean where the youth and his friend caught another wave. "If we waited this long for all of them, we'd be out of business."

WINTER ON THE CANADIAN PRAIRIES is a test of resilience for even the sturdiest of specimens. By March, even those that enjoy winter are ready to see the snow disappear. Sometimes, Mother Nature blesses them with an early melt, bringing the trees to leaf in April. In other years she is not so obliging.

Lianndra stared out her apartment window, watching a stray snowflake float toward the ground. *Another gray evening in Saskatchewan. Winter just won't let go this year.*

The setting sun was a photographer's dream, painting the clouds vivid hues of pink. Sitting on her windowsill with her phone to her ear, Lianndra was immune to its charm.

"It's okay," Lianndra said into the phone while attempting to push her hair back from her face. It refused to cooperate, and a few strands fell right back to where they'd started. The light from the dying sun streamed through the window of her tiny apartment. It lit the strands of her hair a lovely pale blonde.

If only my hair was actually that color, she thought.

Her friend's concerned voice brought her back from her musings.

"No, Jayne, really, I'll be fine on my own," Lianndra said.

"I still wish I was going with you," Jayne said. "I hate wasting the other ticket. Have you booked the flight?" Jayne's cheerfulness seemed forced.

"I'm leaving in a week. I've barely enough money to cover food for the trip. My mom expects me home in a few weeks."

"California would be so nice right now. We could sit around on the beach and swap bad boyfriend stories." Jayne's voice sounded resigned.

Bad boyfriends were a popular topic between the two of them. Jayne had recently suffered a nasty breakup, and Lianndra's two-year relationship dissolved partway through her university term. Since she'd been living with Scott, it had been a messy split with ill feelings on both sides.

Jayne was good company, but Lianndra didn't want to talk about boyfriends. *I want to escape the drama and be on my own for a while.* She'd never taken a solo vacation, and the notion appealed to her. Considering nothing caught her interest lately, she thought it might be a sign it was the right thing to do. *As long as I don't upset my best friend.*

"We can do retail therapy when I get home," Lianndra said.

"Yeah," Jayne replied sadly. "Maybe it's for the best. They keep cutting back my hours at the library. If I booked that much time off, I might not have a job."

Lianndra stifled a sigh of relief. *She's okay with it. Just disappointed.* "You have been there a long time. I doubt they would lay you off."

"Oh well, never mind about me. This is your vacation, and you deserve it." Jayne's voice took on a brisk, serious tone. "You be careful down there. Don't get mugged or anything."

Lianndra smiled. "I'll be careful. You be good while I'm gone and don't do anything I wouldn't do."

She heard an indelicate snort from the other end. "As if. Stay in touch." The phone disconnected.

Lianndra put her phone down on the cardboard box beside her. The windowsill wasn't comfortable to sit on, but packed or almost packed boxes covered every other flat surface.

The apartment was tiny, a far cry from the spacious condo in which she and Scott used to live. Student loans alone could not have paid for the rented condo, even with both contributing. Scott's family's money helped them.

One of the things I took for granted about him, Lianndra thought. *I don't think I'll ever know what he saw in me.* She'd always considered herself average, unlike the more ornamental women that hung out with him. Lianndra seldom wore makeup and preferred sneakers and jeans to heels. *He had his pick of them, and he chose me.*

Lianndra remembered her astonishment when Scott first approached her during a lab they shared. He was tall, with shaggy brown hair and dark, puppy dog eyes. He wouldn't have looked out of place in a fashion magazine. Girls flocked to his gregarious nature and good looks.

As time passed, they moved in together. Lianndra told herself he must be attracted to her natural, unsophisticated look. Their differences were soon clear, starting with the fact Scott loved to socialize while she preferred to curl up with a good book. The relationship lasted two years before turning sour.

If it was meant to be, our uniqueness would have enhanced us and not torn us apart, Lianndra thought.

Lianndra picked up the unwieldy packing tape dispenser to seal up a few more boxes.

I will not think about ex-boyfriends, she told herself.

The tape fell off the roller for the umpteenth time, getting tangled in itself. The air in her apartment turned blue with increasingly inventive expletives. After the tape made a determined grab for the end of her ponytail, Lianndra abandoned the dispenser. One more poorly sealed box later, and she succumbed to cardboard claustrophobia. Unearthing her parka from under a pile of books, she headed out into the chilly evening air.

It was April, yet winter still had Saskatoon in its frigid clutches. Most of the snow had melted but she could see her breath. The slush underfoot was more ice than water, reflecting the streetlights off the slippery sidewalk. Lianndra focused on her senses, examining her surroundings in an effort to not think about Scott. Her enlarged shadow crept along the brick walls as she picked her way around the frozen puddles. She looked up at the mature trees lining the street. They arched like umbrellas overhead, their delicate network of branches glowing in the overhead lights.

The cold and exercise helped clear her head, pushing back the depression sometimes threatening to overwhelm her since Scott left. It was fortunate her studies took up so much of her time. Studying veterinary medicine was almost as intense as studying human medicine, and in some ways, even more so. *At least humans can tell you where they hurt.*

Lianndra sensed a prickling sensation on the back of her neck and turned. Under the large trees was a line of parked vehicles. They looked empty. She noticed a dark pickup with tinted windows a few cars back; she couldn't tell if anyone was inside it but felt as though someone was watching her.

Great. Now I'm getting paranoid. Lianndra faced forward once again, pulling her parka up around her neck. *Should've worn a scarf.* She shivered. *When will spring arrive?*

A young couple stepped out of the apartment building she was approaching. She nodded to them. They were obviously in love, and Lianndra stifled a stab of envy.

Her heart lurched. *Time to go home.*

LIANNDRA WAS STILL UP AT midnight. The boxes sat in stacks closer to the door. This left enough of her old couch free for her to curl up on with her laptop.

Time to check the tickets, she thought. *That will cheer me up.*

Lianndra had never won anything of value. When they'd first notified her of the free flights to San Francisco, including reduced rates at hotels and amenities in Bodega Bay, she'd been skeptical. A quick call to the airline, however, confirmed the prize was legitimate. The tickets had to be redeemed within a certain time frame, but they coincided nicely with the end of the term. All she was responsible for were accommodations and food. As a student, she had limited funds available for such an adventure. *I can use the rest of the money Mom sent me at Christmas, plus the bit I have left in savings*, she thought. *How many opportunities like this am I likely to have?*

Lianndra had always wanted to visit California. The flight would take her to the San Francisco airport. From there, the prize provided a rental car for the drive up along the coast. She'd booked a room at a reasonably priced inn right in Bodega Bay. There wouldn't be much money for sightseeing, but the parks and beaches were within walking distance.

The coast has rain in the spring, but a little rain doesn't bother me, she thought. *Much better than snow.*

Feeling better, she put aside her laptop before walking to her window and staring out into the darkness. Tiny white flakes drifted over the long rows of cars parked under the street lights. *For Pete's sake, it's snowing.*

Glancing down, she noticed it had been snowing for a while; the white fluffy stuff blurred the outlines of the cars parked on the street. With a prickle of unease, she noticed a dark pickup. It wasn't yet covered in snow, and it looked a lot like the one she'd just seen two streets over. As she stared at it, a tiny light appeared behind the tinted glass as if someone inside had just lit a cigarette.

A sudden chill ran down the back of her neck. *Paranoid, that's me. Probably just waiting for someone. One truck pretty much looks like another, and everyone is driving them these days.* Lianndra stepped back, letting the curtain fall across the window before turning her mind to happier thoughts. *Bodega Bay, here I come!*

THE SKINNY MAN BEHIND THE wheel lit his fifth cigarette of the evening, glancing up at the window just in time to see the curtain close. He turned to his companion, who was hunched over a laptop.

"So the friend isn't coming with her? That's great. Certain people will be very happy," the skinny man said.

"Yeah. Mr. Big is having issues with one of the targets. It's making him touchy. I don't like it when he's touchy." The passenger was as thin as the driver and possessed a high-pitched voice to match his fine features. Curled into his parka, his pointed nose poked out of the fur-lined hood. Fingerless gloves helped with his accuracy as he tapped on the keyboard but did little to keep him warm. He paused, rubbing fingers together before he closed the computer and pulled a phone out of his pocket. Selecting a number, he conducted a brief conversation with someone on the other end as he passed on the new development.

He disconnected. "Things are dovetailing nicely. If they solve the one issue down there, they can collect three within two weeks."

"Excellent," the driver said. "This one's not leaving for a week. It should give them time to set up the target in North Dakota and wrap up the job in Wyoming."

"Wyoming will be easy if Dan comes through. There's no backup plan if they have to wait for him." The passenger slid his phone back into his pocket. "But the girl will be vacationing for two weeks, so they have time. It sounds as though California will be lucrative with three targets within shouting distance."

"So long as we get paid on time. I hate these Canadian jobs." The driver stubbed his cigarette in the ashtray.

The passenger shivered again, pulling at his hood. "Yeah, well, we're off to Southern Ontario next. Should be warmer, I hope."

"Ah, yes, Toronto. The center of the universe, right?" The man behind the wheel sounded pleased. He boosted the heat before pulling out into the quiet street.

A WEEK LATER, LIANNDRA STEPPED out of the busy airport terminal. She turned her face toward the bright California sunshine, shaking her long, dark blonde hair clear of her light jacket.

Closing her eyes, she let the sun's warmth soak into her skin. *The warm air feels so good. I can already sense the cold leaching out of my bones.*

Lianndra looked down at the plastic fob attached to the rental car keys and walked to where the shuttle bus waited. After the short ride to the parking lot, she stepped off the bus while throwing the bored driver an enthusiastic, "Thank you."

Her small suitcase easily towed along behind her, its size a testament to her ability to pack light. As she walked, Lianndra noticed the pavement was wet and puddles were along the curb. *Water, not ice. Of course, it's spring in California.*

The coast recently received huge amounts of rain; she remembered seeing headlines about the mudslides. It didn't worry Lianndra as it was warmer than back home, and the sun was peering through the fast-moving rain clouds.

With a surge of good humor, she noticed the local people wearing sweaters and coats. Lianndra felt warm in her T-shirt.

Wimps! she thought, laughing, which earned her a curious glance from someone walking past. *Wouldn't last a day in a Canadian winter.*

Her car was a subcompact in a cheerful yellow. Lianndra dug through the outer pocket of her suitcase, retrieving her phone before sliding behind the wheel. Lianndra activated the map, tapped in the address, and placed it on the seat beside her.

Emerging from the airport was nerve-wracking enough; getting out of San Francisco was terrifying for a country girl like herself. *Where do all these people live?* She managed with a minimum of honking horns and missed exits, and in no time found herself on the coastal highway heading for Bodega Bay.

Lianndra opened the windows and synced music from her phone to the car's speakers. Soon she was singing her way along the coast, feeling liberated from entanglements.

The hilly terrain made the effects of March's heavy rains obvious. At one point, she pulled over to the side of the road to gawk at the pasture fences hanging in midair on the steep hillsides. The rain had washed away the soil from underneath the fence posts until they hung suspended from their linked wires.

I hope the cows didn't wash away with it, she thought.

Lianndra noticed the highway showed signs of recent work, necessary because in places the road margins had eroded away. The ocean views were spectacular, and Lianndra often stopped at the little lookouts.

I'd better get a move on if I'm going to make Bodega Bay by evening, she thought.

Closer to the bay, the highway hugged the shore. Lianndra admired the sandy beaches and the wild dune ecosystem while she drove. She'd read about plants uniquely adapted to survive the ocean winds, the heat of the dry summers, and the drifting sands. The wildflowers here were spectacular, vivid dots of color among the sparse foliage. The air was redolent with the fishy, saltwater smell unique to the ocean.

As she arrived at Bodega Bay, the land rose to form tall, grassy bluffs between her and the water. Feeling adventurous, she drove around until her little inn came into view. It was easy to find as it was at the northern end of the bay, an elegant place with historical charm.

The desk clerk helped her to her room. Furnished with antiques, it was as though she'd taken a trip back in time. Her spirits high, she pulled the antique brocade curtains as wide as possible, drinking in the view. The inn perched on the bluffs overlooking the bay so she could see the ocean. It was heaven for a prairie girl.

As she adjusted her watch to local time, Lianndra noticed there were only a couple of hours until dark. She placed her suitcase with care on the ancient table as she considered using her phone to find a nice restaurant. Thumbing it, she saw there were five texts and one voicemail awaiting her attention. With a grimace, she turned it off before tossing it on the bed and heading out unaided in search of supper. Freedom meant being unchained from everything, especially her phone.

I am going offline this vacation, she thought.

The pleasant woman behind the desk recommended a restaurant a short drive south. Lianndra hopped back in the car, and in moments found herself seated near a large expanse of windows with a nice view of a golf course and the ocean. Tonight, she saw only one other couple seated for supper.

This place is likely packed during the summer months, she thought.

After perusing her coupons as well as the menu, she blew the budget on the seafood platter.

The tide looked as though it was on its way in, but even at high tide, she figured there would be plenty of exposed beach to stroll. At this time of year, the beaches were not busy; the cool ocean breeze kept people from sunbathing or swimming.

While waiting for her meal, she watched a couple strolling along with their two dogs. The man laughed before reaching out and pulling the woman close. Lianndra looked away toward waves that now looked leaden.

She'd optimistically brought her swimsuit. Lianndra loved swimming in real water, shunning the chemical soup in swimming pools. *Perhaps renting a kayak is more sensible. The water might be too cold for a swim. As long as I can get out in the bay, alone, I'll be happy.*

Her food arrived, a sumptuous plate full of varied local seafood. As she ate, she spotted a surfer catching a small wave. He was fully sheathed in a wet suit. *Hmmm . . . kayaking. Tomorrow. Definitely.*

THE TWO MEN WATCHED THE small plane taxi into the gathering darkness.

"Glad that's over with," the mousey man said in disgust. "I'm still not sure this one was worth the trouble."

"He's on the list." His burly companion shrugged as he headed for the vehicle. "Although we will have to dry dock him before he goes in with the group, which will be more work than I have time for. We've got to get moving. We need to be stalking the prairie girl in Bodega Bay by sunset tomorrow."

"Maybe we should've hitched a ride with Dan." The smaller man rubbed his hands together. Spring had not yet arrived in Wyoming.

"We have to check on another candidate on the way back, so we need a vehicle," his big friend replied. "Besides, I don't want to come back here to collect it." He slid into the passenger side of the SUV. "You take first shift. Wake me up in two hours." The mousey man sighed as he started the vehicle. The moment his companion started to snore, he turned up the heat.

LIANNDRA SPENT THE NEXT DAY scouting near her inn, deciding what to explore during her holiday. She walked to the marina, admiring the sleek yachts moored at the docks. A local outfit rented kayaks she could pick up at the marina.

She noticed there were a few tourists walking the beaches despite the earliness of the season.

Lianndra went to a nearby deli, buying enough food to help sustain her. It was one way to decrease the bills; eating at restaurants would drain her resources in no time. She stuffed the tiny fridge in her room with her recent purchases, eating the pizza that wouldn't fit in it as an early supper.

Afterward, she headed back to the marina. Land virtually enclosed the bay which made it safe for kayaking.

The man at the rental hut advised her to stick to the shoreline if she chose to leave the bay. He showed her a map of Bodega Bay, pointing to the harbor entrance near Doran Park.

"Past the flashing buoy, the currents can get you into trouble if you don't have a motor," he said, pointing until he was sure her eyes locked on it. He gestured elsewhere on the map. "Farther outside the bay, you'll run into the surf zone, and that's trouble, too. Within the bay, the water stays quiet, plus there's lots to see." He turned to look at the clock. "Have the boat back in three hours as it will be dark soon afterward." He fit her with a life jacket and found her a paddle.

Twenty minutes after arriving at the hut, she pushed off from the small dock in a plastic kayak that had seen better days. It had been a few years since she last kayaked. Lianndra had never been on the open ocean in one, only on lakes and rivers. Following directions, she headed south of the marina, familiarizing herself with the small craft.

The cool water permeated the thin hull. *Definitely too cold for swimming.*

The water was crystal clear along this stretch of the bay so she peered over the side of the kayak. In places, she spotted small crabs going about their business while darting fish flashed where the evening light penetrated the shallow water. The scenery was beautiful; in response to the recent rains, the plants were in riotous bloom. They painted the hillsides with brilliant color.

As she paddled, the life jacket became hot and uncomfortable. Glancing around to see if she was still in view of the rental shack, Lianndra removed it.

I'll just keep it on my lap, she thought. *I can grab it if I need it.*

Although she heard motorized craft in the distance, all was peaceful here in the bay. The occasional sailboat cruised by on its way back to the marina. Even those disappeared as the sun sank lower on the horizon. Seals were everywhere, in the water and hauled up on the shore. Their round heads popped up out of the water to stare at her with huge liquid eyes as she went by. Enjoying herself, Lianndra lost track of the time until she noticed the light was fading. She glanced at her watch and decided, with under an hour of daylight left, she wanted to explore around the other side of Doran Park before heading back.

She was close to the harbor entrance. As she paddled through it, she saw the buoy the rental attendant mentioned. It was just past the harbor mouth between her and the larger landmass forming the western boundary of the bay.

As she left the protected harbor, the power of the tidal current pushed against her. The wind was increasing, creating waves that bobbed her like a cork.

Not too bad, I can manage, she thought.

Being raised on a farm, her muscles were no stranger to hard work. Her poor father had likely hoped for sons. *It made for strong daughters,* she thought with a smile. Still, she was out of shape after a long winter at school.

Doran Beach was on her left. It offered nice picnic spots to check out in the next couple of days. *If the weather held.* A glance at her watch showed there was still time before she had to return the kayak.

I'll be sore tomorrow, but it sure feels good now. Time to head back. Once she turned the craft around, she became aware the wind was picking up, with dark clouds lining the horizon. The buoy bobbed in the water ahead of her as she paddled back toward the harbor mouth. The gusting wind carried the whine of a high-pitched engine above the sound of the waves. *Likely one of those single person watercraft things. Kayaking is so much more relaxing. Plus, you get to see the wildlife.*

Halfway to the buoy she paused, catching her breath. Doran Beach appeared deserted, and the peninsula of Doran State Park hid the marina from her view. She dared not stop paddling for long as the wind pushed her kayak sideways. Luckily, the harbor mouth was nearby.

Looks like stormy weather for tonight. Lianndra glanced again at her watch. *I might be late getting the kayak back.*

At that moment, something bumped the kayak.

Although the craft barely lifted out of the water, the vibration running through the hull was substantial. The bump threw her balance off, and she flung out a hand to grab the side of the kayak. Her fingers got pinched between the paddle and the craft. Holding the paddle under her arm, she shook her injured hand, sending drops of blood flying.

Lianndra examined the small cut. *Nothing a future veterinarian can't handle. But what the heck bumped me?*

Something broke the water twenty feet away, a swift swirl of dark motion that vanished into the crest of a wave as soon as she spotted it. Her stomach sank and the hair on the back of her neck rose. Then the adrenaline kicked in. Lianndra dug her paddle deep into the water, sprinting the kayak faster than she thought possible.

The second hit came before she'd completed three strokes of the paddle. It lifted the back of the kayak clear of the water and flipped it in a twisting motion that spilled her out into the cold ocean.

Lianndra struggled in the water's depths before she surfaced, gasping. Even with the surge of adrenaline flooding her system, the intense cold felt like it would stop her heart. She blinked salt water from her eyes just in time to see a triangular dorsal fin slide under the water from the far side of her flipped boat. It was followed by a long stretch of flank and a huge tail fin.

Faint vertical stripes along its sides caught the evening light as the tail fin disappeared.

Oh my God. Her mind raced in panic. She'd seen enough shark specials on television to recognize her attacker—a tiger shark. Her mind, always an information sponge, now raced with adrenaline-fueled possibilities. *Great white sharks often bite people by accident, spitting them out when they realize they are a bony human and not a fat seal. But tiger sharks and bull sharks eat anything and everything they think looks tasty. Which, right now, is me!*

Treading water, she scanned the waves for her life jacket. Her paddle floated beside her, so she grabbed it with one hand. Already, her arms were sluggish. Lianndra knew she needed to get out of the water if she was to have any chance. Her clothing was as heavy as stone. She kicked off her runners, but the jeans clung to her legs so she couldn't get free of them. She headed for her flipped kayak, dragging the paddle behind her.

The water beneath her swelled and receded as something large passed. *That was not a wave!* Trying not to panic, she attempted to keep her movements smooth and splashing to a minimum. *The last thing I need is to mimic an injured animal by panicking. The shark must still be in taste test mode or it would have attacked me already.* Like all predators, it probably was cautious and didn't want to risk an injury. Even something minor could affect its ability to survive. More nature documentary facts popped into Lianndra's head as she stroked toward the kayak. *Tiger sharks often eat sea turtles. Their powerful jaws can penetrate the turtle's tough outer shell.*

Lianndra paused, treading water again. Her right arm, the one holding the paddle, was threatening to cramp. Even from her limited perspective, the overturned kayak looked like a turtle. Sprawled on top, her hanging limbs would make it look even more like one with tasty flippers dangling.

Damn! She turned around, pushing herself out of the water, trying to see above the waves. The wind whipped foam off their tops as she bobbed. The land was within reach but the shark was between her and it. When she spun around, the next lift of a wave revealed a blinking light—the buoy was nearer than she thought. The beacon flashed against the fading daylight. Lianndra noticed it was a large buoy, with openings between the lower spars.

I might be able to climb up on it if I can reach it, she thought. *Maybe I can wave someone down from there.*

The kayak thumped again as the shark bumped it. Floating on the crest of a wave, she saw the broad snout come out of the water. Clutching the paddle as a potential weapon or sacrificial limb, she struck out for the buoy, trying to keep her strokes smooth. Lianndra could barely feel her legs and her arms were like lead.

The buoy appeared closer with each stroke. Lianndra shivered; she clenched her teeth to keep them from chattering. She strove to keep her mind off the huge predator, who might soon suspect her soft, juicy body would be a better snack than the kayak.

There's also the blood, she reminded herself, hoping the cut on her hand wouldn't lead the creature straight to her.

Lianndra felt the current from the outgoing tide. At that moment the ocean gave her a huge break—it pushed her toward the buoy. Lianndra lengthened her strokes and kicked harder to keep in line with her target. She thrashed out with one hand, grabbing one of the support spars. A wave lifted her body and crashed it hard up against sharp barnacles which shredded clothing and skin alike.

More blood in the water. Any pretense of calm deserted her. *It will attract the shark!* Lianndra tried heaving herself onto the buoy, the barnacles ripping her jeans and the skin of her toes straight through her socks as she scrambled for a toehold. The paddle went flying, splashing down a few feet away. Even as she struggled, inane thoughts ran through her head. *Isn't this like a scene out of a movie?* Her other hand connected with the spar and she gained a precious few inches up the buoy's side. *A girl, a buoy, and a shark . . .* She wiped the thought from her head. The movie hadn't ended well for the girl. *That will not happen to me!* The thought spurred her onward. With a final heave, she pulled her body from the water. The buoy lurched to one side, and the next lift of a wave almost spilled her off again. Gritting her teeth, Lianndra pushed across the buoy until her body was lying sideways between the spars. *Where's a superhero when I need one?* On the heels of hysteria, an image of a favorite comic book character popped into her head. *I sure wish Axiom-man would come to my rescue!*

This far from the harbor mouth, the waves and the ocean currents were more turbulent. The buoy didn't just bob but swayed on its tether. Lianndra nervously scanned the water; she wasn't far above the surface. If the shark became more committed to this project, who knew what it would do. The kayak floated on the harbor side of the buoy. She craned her neck over her shoulder, looking out to sea.

Nothing.

Where is the Jet Ski I heard earlier? With the sun barely over the horizon, the rise and fall of the waves could hide such a small craft.

Looking landward again, Lianndra scanned the deserted beach and vacant picnic tables. The Coast Guard station was on the other side of the Doran Park peninsula, so it was out of her sightline. What were the chances someone would see her? The solid upper part of the buoy prohibited her from standing upright.

I need something to wave, she thought.

Letting go of a spar with one trembling hand, she peeled her soaked T-shirt off of her torso. She tried waving the shirt, hoping to attract someone's attention with the unusual motion. After a few minutes, she lowered her aching arm. She needed more reach.

Nothing on the buoy was loose enough to pry off as a staff. She startled as something banged against the base—it was just the paddle, pitching with the water against the side of the buoy.

Lianndra squirmed around on the rocking buoy until the paddle was within her grasp. She squinted into the ocean depths, wondering if the shark had given up or if it was still somewhere beneath the surface. Right on cue, she spotted the briefest glimpse of the dorsal fin above the water, skimming away from the buoy.

"He was right here," she muttered. Her heart felt as though it would pound its way out of her chest.

She grabbed for the paddle, splashing in her hurry. The fin changed course before it disappeared. *Had it turned back this way?* Heart in her throat, her fingers locked on the paddle and she swung it up out of the water before backing her body as far into the buoy's center as possible.

Lianndra sat hunched for a few moments, shaking with fear and cold, wondering if the shark would make a try for her. She knew killer whales washed seals off ice floes by generating waves to cascade over the ice. Wrapping an arm around a spar, she tied her shirt to one end of the paddle. Sitting up as much as possible, she waved the makeshift flag. It was just tall enough to extend past the top of the buoy. The light pink shirt looked red in the setting sunlight.

Looking toward the beach, she signaled, her arm quivering like Jell-O. The wind helped her flag wave but its howl drowned her cries for help. Her entire body shivered as her fingers cramped around the paddle's shaft. When her arm muscles seized as well, she collapsed back on the buoy. Gasping, she laid her head on the base. The crash of the waves against the metal echoed beneath her ear. Penetrating the waves was the electronic hum of the flashing beacon, a hum rising in pitch until it became a whine loud enough to drown out the wind.

Her exhausted mind was slow to process the significance of the sound. When the buoy lurched, visions of sharks rearing out of the water flashed through her brain. Lianndra screamed, clutching at the spars while dropping her precious flag.

From the side of the buoy nearest her feet, the whine dropped to a gurgling rumble. A human voice shouted above the wind and waves. "You look like you need help. What on earth are you doing way out here?"

Lianndra twisted around to see a dark-haired man sitting on a sleek Jet Ski. He wore a skintight wet suit that did little to hide his lanky frame. The young man was having difficulty holding his position along the lurching buoy. He gave the craft a boost of power, moving it so the current kept it pinned against the base. The grating sound of the barnacles scraping the Jet Ski's side made him wince.

Stiff with cold, she disentangled herself from the spars and grabbed his hand. With a strong heave, he pulled her off the buoy and onto the seat behind him, standing up on the foot wells until she sat. Although the small craft bucked a little, he kept it stable by expertly shifting his weight to compensate.

Fortunately for all concerned, it seated two. Shaking, Lianndra could only stammer one word: "Sh-shar-k."

He obviously heard her since his glance scanned the ocean's surface before kicking the craft into gear. She grabbed at his waist as he accelerated, wrapping her arms tightly around him. His spine pressed up through the neoprene suit.

He steered around the peninsula and headed into the bay. They passed the Coast Guard station, which looked deserted as there wasn't even a boat at the dock. She noticed him glance that way before arrowing straight for the marina.

Lianndra took in the Jet Ski. *This little beauty is likely a rental,* she thought. She wondered what he'd been doing with such a small craft out on the open ocean. *He's good at piloting this thing.* She glanced at the water rushing below them. *I wonder if we still look like a turtle from below?*

Lianndra shivered. She was sure he felt her shake through the wet suit.

He slowed as they approached the dock then nestled the craft between the platform and a small rowboat. Balancing again, he offered her his arm to help her step off.

Lianndra could barely untangle her fingers from the grip around his waist. When he saw how much she was trembling, he stepped off first, reaching over to interlock his arm with hers and lift her onto the dock.

The deserted marina was quiet this far from the surf. Lianndra was suddenly aware she was topless except for her bra. It was not only soaking wet but transparent. Her frozen condition was also having some embarrassing side effects.

He finished tying the craft and regarded her with concern in his eyes. He seemed to do his best not to notice her near topless condition but appeared both relieved and disappointed when she crossed her arms over her chest.

The marina was deep enough into the bay to break the gathering wind, but enough of it swirled around her to keep her shivering. He placed a hand on her shoulder, guiding her out of the wind along a small fishing vessel. Stripping off the top part of his two-piece wet suit, he helped her feed first one shaking arm, and then the other, into the sleeves.

While it was too big across the shoulders it wouldn't zip up around her full hips. Lianndra gave up after the second try, pinning it closed with her arms. The suit top was warm from his body and smelled of male sweat. She didn't think she'd ever experienced anything so comfortable.

Although he was now naked from the waist up, he didn't look cold. His torso was long and lean, the bones barely covered with muscle.

His dark brows dropped, shading his eyes. "We went by the Coast Guard but their boat wasn't there," he said. "They must have been out on another call so I didn't stop. Should I call an ambulance?" He looked worried. His wet hair was so dark it was almost black, and his skin showed evidence of many hours out in the sun. In vivid contrast, his eyes were light—not blue—but more silver-gray.

Unusual and becoming, she thought. Then she realized he was waiting for a reply, obviously wondering if she was too much in shock to speak.

"No, no," she said. Then she looked at herself. Her jeans were in shreds, and bloody lacerations ran across her bare feet. She straightened. "No, I'll be fine. It was the barnacles on the buoy." She felt warmer; the tremors were lessening. "I don't know how to thank you. The shark thought I was a turtle."

He looked confused at this last statement, clearly wondering if she was delusional.

Humor the crazy woman, Lianndra thought with a smile.

He still stared at her as though undecided whether he should insist on an ambulance. She thought he was even younger than she'd first assumed, maybe eighteen or nineteen. He was tall. Scott was six feet, but this gangly youth was even taller. Like a Great Dane puppy, he was all bones and lacked muscle. Lianndra could count every one of his ribs and his chest showed only the barest amount of dark hair. Still, he had promising breadth to his shoulders, and the bones of his face were settling into pleasing shapes.

Give him a few years and he'll be lining 'em up. She smiled again, craning her neck to look him in the eye.

His eyes were open, unguarded—unblemished by life.

Sheltered life, she guessed. It made her seem so much older, even though likely only five years separated them. At this stage in their lives, it seemed a world of difference.

Reassured by her smile, he placed a tentative hand on her arm and guided her along the floating dock toward the rental hut.

"I'll have to pay for the kayak." Lianndra wondered just how much a plastic kayak was worth.

He laughed. "I wouldn't worry. You've had quite a scare. He'll be happy you are okay. The kayak will likely wash up on the tide line by morning." He squeezed her arm. "By the way, my name is Michael Laughlin."

"Well, Michael, I don't know what I would have done if you hadn't come along," Lianndra said. "The tiger shark was thinking of making me its dinner."

His eyebrows rose. "Tiger shark? What makes you think it was a tiger shark? Are you sure?"

"I saw the stripes," she replied, and shuddered, pulling the wet suit closer around her shoulders.

At the mention of her identifying observation, Michael was immediately on board. "I'll have to let the Harbor Master know there's one around. They usually stick to the warmer water farther south of here. Those guys are bad news . . . even if you're not a turtle." They were just outside the rental hut when he stopped her. "Did you want to stop by my place until you warm up? My friend and I are renting a house near here. It's right along the beach."

Michael seemed nice enough, and she likely owed him her life, but Lianndra wasn't about to chance becoming part of some all-night beach party. "No, really, I'm fine. My inn is close." She tugged at the wet suit with one hand. "Is there somewhere I can drop this off tomorrow?"

"We're the third place on the left, just down the road from here." He pointed to where the top of a contemporary house was just visible past a tall bluff. "Drop it off anytime. I have another one."

Lianndra smiled with relief. She didn't want to seem ungrateful. Although this holiday was off to a rocky start, getting entangled in any social scene was not her idea of a solution. *I would feel like an old woman hanging with his friends anyway.*

Michael smiled at her as he held the marina office door open.

He has a nice smile. Down girl. He's too young, too uncomplicated. Besides, you've sworn off men for the foreseeable future.

As Michael suggested, the rental man expressed relief she'd survived the experience and reassured her the kayak would wash up on shore. If not, she was only liable for the deductible.

"You sure it was a tiger shark?" he asked, echoing Michael's skepticism. "We're too far north for them."

"She saw the stripes," Michael said.

The smaller man shrugged. "With this climate change stuff going on, who knows what's normal anymore." He pushed papers across the counter to her. "If you can just fill out this form, we will only charge your credit card with the deductible if it doesn't show."

Michael stayed until she finished filling everything out. It was dark by the time they emerged from the hut and Lianndra accepted his offer to walk her back to the inn. *Last thing I need is a mugging on the same day I almost get eaten by a shark.*

There were people everywhere, mostly couples enjoying the warm spring evening. As they walked, Michael chatted about the local tourist sites. He fell silent as they approached the foyer door. Lianndra slowed and halted, unsure of how to say goodbye to someone who'd rescued her from a hungry tiger shark.

Michael cleared his throat, rattling off a long jumble of words that exposed an underlying, somewhat endearing, nervousness. "You know, there is a little cove up the coast from here. It's beautiful for snorkeling—private, and the fish are extraordinary. If you like, I could take you there before you leave. I have friends we could go with. I'd hate to think you won't go back in the water. Sharks usually mind their own business and don't bother people."

Peering at him in the light of the inn sign, Lianndra recognized his nervousness. She felt a stab of guilt. *He really saved my skin today.* She was flattered he wanted to see her again. Although she wasn't a lot older than him in years, she was far older in life experience. *He is kind of hot, and I would love to enjoy the water before I go.*

"I don't have a wet suit," she said.

"My friend's got a spare." He was smiling now as he scanned her body. "Should fit, I think."

Much to her surprise, Lianndra blushed as she heard herself saying, "Okay." She was grateful for the dim lighting. *I am on holiday after all. Why am I even fighting this? It sounds like fun.* "I'm staying in room fourteen."

He positively beamed at her, white teeth flashing in the darkness.

As he was leaving he called to her. "By the way," he said, "what's your name?"

She laughed, amused her name hadn't come up in conversation. "Lianndra . . . Lianndra Ross," she called back to him.

He mouthed her name to himself before waving and disappearing into the night. As he strode off, he whistled a tune vaguely familiar to her.

She'd taken three steps before it popped into her head—it was the theme song to one of her favorite movies.

Shaking her head, Lianndra skirted the front desk and jogged to her room, suddenly feeling exhilarated.

Well. Who would have thought?

THE NEXT DAY WAS STORMY, with dark clouds sweeping in off the ocean.

Lianndra lazed in bed for most of the morning before deciding that waiting around for Michael's phone call was juvenile. *Why on earth didn't I give him my phone number? I hope he can find the one to the front desk, or he'll be sending smoke signals.*

Lianndra dressed in her spare jeans, carefully sliding her hiking boots over her sore feet. *I must pick up sneakers to replace the ones I lost.*

The inn's tiny foyer featured many local brochures; she selected one for an art gallery. The helpful inn clerk provided directions.

The gallery was interesting, but Lianndra's feet were too sore to do much walking. It was still pouring rain when she was ready to leave. Returning to the inn, she checked for messages; went out to dinner, returned to her room—checked for messages, scolded herself for being such a ditz . . . and then once again checked for messages.

He's likely thought better of a scuba date with a hysterical woman he rescued off a buoy. Forget him. I would have enjoyed today if he hadn't suggested we get together. I am supposed to appreciate my solitude. She sighed. It wasn't a good sign she was so ready to leap at the slightest offer. *Rebound big time. If he calls, I should just make excuses.*

The television was the only modern thing in the room, and she spent the evening watching pay-per-view. Halfway through the movie, she realized she'd lost track of the plot because she was listening for the phone and thinking about Michael.

He rescued me. Turning off the light, she slipped under the covers, and buried her head in the pillow. *Just white knight syndrome; I've got to pull it together.*

No matter how she tried to distract herself, her thoughts kept returning to Michael and his charming smile. She took a long time to fall asleep.

THE ROOM'S LANDLINE RANG EARLY the next morning.

"Hi, Lianndra! It's Michael."

The introduction was unnecessary, she thought groggily. *There's no mistaking his enthusiastic voice.*

She sat up, talking to him on the phone from a lying position made her feel uncomfortable. "Hi, Michael. How are you?" She winced at her bubbly tone. *Pull it together girl!* "I haven't been outside yet. Is it nice out?" She was stalling. *Okay, now. Get ready to let him down gently.*

"No, dreadful actually," he said. "Thought you might like someone to show you the sights. At least the indoor ones." He sounded so hopeful.

Lianndra's spirits lifted. *This is what my holiday is about; I'm supposed to have fun. Plus, it's raining.*

All thoughts of turning him down fled. She made arrangements to pick him up in her car at his rental home. Right on time, she pulled up at a gorgeous house that looked at least twice the size of her family's home. Michael jogged out in the pouring rain, wearing jeans and a heavy cable sweater with a windbreaker over top. He carried a cooler which he tossed into the back seat.

The art gallery she'd seen the day before was first on his list to visit, but there were others in town. They chose one, strolling through it while taking advantage of every opportunity to sit and talk. At first, Lianndra assumed the tall young man was taking his time to peruse the art. But after the third bench, she suspected he'd noticed her limping and was accommodating her sore feet.

Score one more point for Michael, she thought with a smile.

After touring the galleries, they returned to the car. He directed her to an ocean lookout that took her breath away. A few carloads of people shared the same idea, gazing out to sea from the shelter of their cars as the raindrops fell.

"A good spot for lunch," Michael said. Twisting to reach between the front seats, he stretched one long arm for the cooler. In the confines of the little car, his movements brought his shoulder up against hers. He was so close Lianndra could smell him, a mixture of soap and warm male skin making her pulse bound.

Down girl! By the time Michael settled himself back in his seat, Lianndra's expression was one of calm, revealing interest in nothing more than lunch. Glancing at her self-appointed guide, she noticed his face was flushed. *Exertion? Or something else?*

He kept his gaze focused on food. Once they'd each selected a sandwich, he discussed the prevalence of great white sharks in northern California.

Michael was Canadian. "Grew up on a sheep farm," he said after swallowing a big bite of ham and cheese. "Lucky enough to have a wealthy friend who can rent a big house."

"Nice! Wish I had those kinds of friends." Lianndra laughed. "I won a prize to pay for most of this, otherwise I wouldn't be here."

He flashed her a smile. "Well, I'm glad you are. As the proverbial third wheel, I'm bored with my roommates. Luckily, I'm good at keeping myself entertained." He shrugged. "We're basically runaways. Runaways from farm chores, future career decisions, and Trent's rich parents, who don't want him underfoot for more than a week at a time."

Lianndra grinned while selecting another sandwich from the pile teetering on the dash. As she munched, she listened to him talk about the wildflowers on the coast and the manta rays he'd seen in the ocean. By the time they finished eating, the rain was easing up. When Michael offered to take over the driving, Lianndra considered insurance policies and rental agreements but gave in after only a moment's consideration.

It's easier to sightsee if you aren't worried about staying between the lines. I'm sure they'd rather have their car back in one piece with him driving than ditched with me, she thought as she relaxed into the passenger seat.

Michael was a good driver; careful but not nervous. As they cruised along the highway, he narrated the trip like a nature guide. He loved the flora and fauna of the bay. Lianndra listened, asking questions from time to time, content to stare out the window at the beautiful scenery.

The terrain changed as they swung away from the coast; there were more trees interspersed with open farmland. Inland and north of Bodega Bay, the road passed into massive redwoods.

Lianndra couldn't wait to get out and touch them. They paused at the head of the path while Michael picked up a dead branch lying beside the parking lot and measured it against Lianndra's body. Breaking it over his knee to the right length, he handed her the makeshift walking stick. She claimed she didn't need it, but after three strides, recognized its value while negotiating the uneven path with sore feet. With a crooked grin, Michael selected one for himself, and they hiked inland along the marked trail.

The redwoods were the most impressive living things she'd ever seen. Each massive trunk provided homes for a plethora of life, from leafy ferns and thick mosses to birds flitting through the upper canopy. The textures of the place fascinated her: the soft mosses and bristly fern leaves, the rough tree bark folding into deep ridges, and the spongy soil beneath their feet.

"The largest of these are over two thousand years old," Michael said, his silver-gray eyes shimmering in the dim light.

It was like standing in an ancient cathedral, with trunks as living pillars stretching well beyond where their eyes could follow. Thick mosses muffled sounds except for the occasional drip of water. The forest smelled of decaying leaves and rotting wood.

Death and rejuvenation, part of a cycle as old as time itself. Lianndra was rapt, staring around her with eyes wide.

Despite the silence, they weren't alone on the trail. The primal energy of the place kept an entire busload of tourists standing in equally awed silence around them. Other than the steady dripping, the only other sound was the soft clicking of their digital cameras.

By the time Lianndra and Michael returned to the car, the rain had stopped altogether. Another big tour bus pulled up with eager faces pressed to the tinted windows. When they'd left on their hike, the lot contained only their car plus one bus. Now it was full of vehicles.

As she and Michael approached their car, Lianndra noticed two men leaning on the hood of a dark green SUV. One of the men possessed a thick, muscular body. His eyes were so intense they made her uncomfortable. The other man was small and thin. A tendril of fear wormed its way through her, making her grateful for the cheerful chatter of the tourists disembarking from the bus. Michael seemed oblivious to their presence, so she did her best to ignore the men. *Must be waiting for someone. Although they don't know what they missed by not taking the walk to the giant trees. Mind you, they don't look like tourist types.*

Michael unlocked the doors to their little car, and she dismissed the men from her mind. Sliding behind the wheel, Michael looked thoughtful, a smile tugging at the corners of his mouth.

"What is it?" Lianndra asked, shaking drops of water from her hair. *I must look like a wet dishrag by now.* She wondered why it mattered to her.

Before she could muse any longer on his expression, Michael asked, "Do you like horses?"

Lianndra smiled. "I owned one before I went away to university."

It turned out he knew the trainer at the local riding stable. Lianndra grinned, shaking her head. *I am not surprised.*

After heading back to the bay, Michael commandeered a pair of horses for them. The trainer took a few minutes to chat with Lianndra about her riding experience before allowing the two of them to head out unescorted.

"I ride here often, so Susan lets me go out on my own," Michael said. "I have a horse at home, and I miss her. Somehow, surfing just isn't the same." He laughed. "I guess it's because your surfboard doesn't talk back to you."

Having seen the way a couple of the female stable hands were acting around him, Lianndra wasn't sure it was his riding ability that scored him the horses. Once mounted, she noticed the animals were nicely trained and responsive. It had been at least two years since she'd ridden but her body quickly picked up the familiar rhythms.

It was late in the afternoon. The horses must keep to approved pathways through the dunes, but once they were on the beach, they were free to go where they liked. The stirrups soon made the cuts on her feet ache so she kicked loose of them.

Lianndra always wanted to ride on a beach. Her heart soared as she asked her horse for a canter straight into the onrushing water. Michael followed her lead. Their laughter rose above the sound of the waves as they splashed through the surf. Even the horses got into the spirit of it, snorting and striking out at the water as they ran.

I love riding. For Lianndra, horses were creatures of the elements; intelligent animals kind enough to let her into their world, one of keen senses and powerful muscles that reacted to the whims of each moment. They were alive in a way she often wished she could be. When she was on their backs, they talked to her through their bodies. For a few precious seconds at a time, she saw the world through their eyes and felt their power. Looking over at Michael, she could tell he felt it too: the sensation of oneness with his horse as they enjoyed the scents of the brisk evening wind, the feel of the water on their skin, and the rhythm of the hoof beats.

The horse Michael rode was a tall gray gelding with big bones. The young man sat the horse's antics easily, keeping his balance without ever having to grab the saddle or even the mane.

His long legs help, Lianndra thought as her horse took a leap over a wave and her body absorbed the movement. Michael was a good rider, at least her equal and maybe better.

Her horse was a chestnut mare with the refined face of an Arabian and a lean body built for speed. Seeming to sense Lianndra was an experienced rider, she was up for fun and wanted to go. Lianndra held back the mare to allow Michael's heavier horse to keep pace. Finally, she relented, letting the animal run. The red mare flattened out until she flew along the sand. The wind forced tears from Lianndra's eyes, whipping her damp hair into a tangled mess, but she loved every second. When she slowed the mare, Michael's horse was far back. The gelding's big feet splatted on the sand with each stride.

They pulled up, both horses and humans soaked to the skin. The horses' necks arched and nostrils flared while the humans sported wide grins.

Michael looked at the sinking sun and turned his horse around, patting its wet neck. "We'd better walk them back, or Susan will take a strip off of me."

As she snuck a glance at his silver eyes and big smile, Lianndra couldn't remember the last time she'd felt this happy.

Careful, she thought. *He's been pushing the right buttons, but one day of fun does not a connection make.* The horses opened her heart and soul. She was vulnerable, coming so recently off a failed relationship. Michael had turned on the charm all day. *Is there anything about him that isn't appealing?* He seemed carefree, untouched by the world. *Or maybe it's just his magic. If so, it's a real gift.*

The horses dried off by the time they got back. Although one of the staff offered to do it, Michael and Lianndra waved her off, preferring to strip the horses of their tack themselves. They brushed them until both animals were content and left them munching on hay.

It was dark when they left the stable. Lianndra was tired but in a fulfilled, happy way.

A few days like this and I'll feel as though I can climb Mount Everest, she thought as Michael pulled up at the beach house.

She got out of the car to switch sides, and he closed the driver's door after her. He folded his arms and leaned on the window frame as she adjusted the seat for her shorter legs.

To her horror, Lianndra heard herself babbling. "I can't tell you how much I enjoyed this day." She was suddenly unsure of how to say goodbye to him. *But it's true. I had a great time.*

He grinned, but she thought he looked uncomfortable as well. Then he took her hand, pitching his deep voice even lower as he bowed. "That's me, rescuer of damsels from sharks and general boredom." Giving her a huge smile, he lightly kissed her hand. "I'll call you tomorrow. If the weather's good, we can go snorkeling."

Maybe he's more together than I thought. A tingling sensation moved up her arm from her hand. *Nicely done, Sir Michael.* He was at the door when Lianndra remembered the cooler. *Oh well, I'll bring it tomorrow.*

As she pulled onto the road, her thoughts returned to the wonders of the day. *I enjoy his company. I'm looking forward to tomorrow even if we are spending the day with his friends.* She bit her lip. *As long as we don't run into any hungry sharks.*

IN THE SUV PARKED DOWN the road from the beach house, they watched her pull away from the driveway.

The hulking man behind the wheel looked pleased, puffing on his cigarette. "This is working out better than expected."

The smaller man beside him tapped on his laptop. He made a sound of satisfaction. "Well, you're right. I owe you a beer. While these two were traipsing around visiting the tourist traps, his friend booked a cabin cruiser for tomorrow. Four passengers. He's listed the destination as 'touring the coastline.'"

"I was sure they mentioned diving when they were at the redwoods." Flicking the ash out the window, the driver looked satisfied. "Any problem getting the boat's GPS beacon frequency?"

"Nope. Everything's right here." He tapped a little longer, then hesitated. "What are we going to do with the collaterals?"

The driver shrugged. "Steph hasn't made quota yet on the norm females. I got a glimpse of her last night. She's a looker so she'll do. We'll toss the boy in with Juke's lot. We're short on males for him." He sucked on the cigarette, making the end glow. "Contact Jerry. Tell him we'll need the truck tomorrow."

The small man nodded, digging out his phone.

"Tomorrow," the bulky man continued, smiling, "we go fishing."

THE LANDLINE IN LIANNDRA'S ROOM rang at 7am. The patient inn clerk put a familiar voice through to her.

"It's still cloudy this morning, but it's clearing fast. It'll be sunny by the time we get there." Michael's voice was a dose of good cheer first thing in the morning. "We've booked the boat for nine. Cassidy's bringing her extra suit and gear. It will be great!" His tone was so infectious, Lianndra smiled. She was still nervous about meeting his friends, but in the face of his enthusiasm, it was rapidly dissolving.

"No problem," she replied. "See you at nine."

"GUYS NEVER CAN TELL SIZES!" Cassidy laughed. She was an attractive pale blonde with blue eyes enhanced by her tanned skin.

The typical Californian beach bunny. Lianndra gave herself a mental slap. Cassidy seemed friendly, and it was nice of her to lend Lianndra her wet suit. *I don't know if it will ever be the same again.* Lianndra glanced down at her obvious curves.

Cassidy possessed a trim figure, including small hips and suspiciously perky breasts. Lianndra put the suit on but only with Cassidy's substantial help. *Lord help me if I sneeze. Wet suits always fit snug but this is ridiculous.*

Every pound she'd gained while at university must show. *With any luck, they're flattened into submission. Now I know how women in whalebone corsets felt.* Her full hips pushed the rubbery fabric to its stretchable limits. The zipper refused to close the last eight inches of the top, leaving an impressive stretch of exposed cleavage. *I'd make a great advert for a certain magazine.*

"I can't go out there like this!" Lianndra made one last attempt to zip the top before giving up in disgust. "I look ridiculous!"

Cassidy laughed. "Trust me, ridiculous is not the first thing the guys will think. Or the last. Or at all, actually." She traced an hourglass in the air with her fingers. "Your shape is feminine, so don't be ashamed."

Easy for you to say, Lianndra thought. *You're like something Hollywood created. Maybe he'll take one look at me and run for the hills.*

Cassidy pulled out a few towels from an overhead cupboard in the small cabin of the rented boat. Tossing one to Lianndra, she opened door and headed up the stairs.

Putting on her best nonchalant face, Lianndra arranged the towel around her neck before following. *The guys better not think this exposure is deliberate.* She let the cabin door swing shut behind her. *It's nothing he hasn't seen before, I guess. I was all but naked from the waist up the other day.*

Trent, Cassidy's boyfriend, glanced at Lianndra as she emerged on deck. His eyes slid to his girlfriend's face, and he grinned before looking away. Michael, already in his wet suit, was busy sorting through flippers and masks. He looked up when he heard the cabin door swing closed, and his jaw dropped when he saw Lianndra. She hesitated before forcing herself to walk over and stand near him.

"Uh, the suit doesn't fit very well," she said. *Damn, I sounded apologetic.*

Michael seemed to tear his gaze away from her cleavage with effort. He looked at her, his grin wide. "I think you look fantastic." His eyes glowed.

Cassidy walked up, wiggling her eyebrows at Lianndra behind Michael's back. Lianndra blushed as she bent to pick up a pair of flippers. Too late, she realized the move caused the weight of her confined breasts to fall forward as though contemplating freedom from the wet suit.

Lianndra noticed Michael standing frozen in front of her as she snatched up the flippers. Cassidy gave him a vicious poke in the ribs with her elbow. She deftly untangled two masks and snorkels before handing one set to Lianndra. The lithe blonde then grabbed Lianndra by the arm and led her away.

"Let him compose himself." Cassidy giggled. "Our Michael's a Boy Scout. Honestly, I don't know what he and Trent ever had in common." She trailed a hand through Trent's shaggy brown mop as the two women passed. He ignored her, continuing to struggle into his wet suit.

With a stab of envy, Lianndra recognized the ease of a long-term relationship in Trent's nonchalant acceptance of Cassidy's intimate touch.

Their boat was the only one on the water. The cove was beautiful and secluded; it featured a strip of deserted beach lined with trees warped by the ocean's wind. Within her wet suit, Lianndra found the water comfortable. At first, the salt water stung the cuts on her ankles and feet, but eventually, the pain faded.

The life of the little cove was so beautiful that she soon stopped expecting sharks to pop out of every crack and crevice. Michael's knowledge carried through underwater as he escorted her from one area to another. Every time they surfaced to catch their breath, he pulled out his snorkel and gave her a rundown of the species she'd seen.

He's a living guidebook, Lianndra thought. Her head was soon swimming with Latin fish names.

After a few hours of snorkeling in the shallows, they settled on the beach for lunch. Lianndra brought the cooler; Michael deemed the sandwiches still edible. As he stuffed his mouth full of tuna, he explained the cove was part of a new nature preserve, not yet developed for visitors.

"By this fall, they'll have pathways through the trees, and scuba divers will be everywhere," he said, before he shrugged, looking grim. "It's a shame, but a better alternative than tearing it apart and building condos."

Lianndra nibbled on her sandwich, considerate of the stresses placed on Cassidy's poor wet suit. She was growing fond of Michael's friend, finding her a refreshing, outspoken contrast to her more reserved university friends. Cassidy wasn't shallow as Lianndra first assumed with the beach bunny exterior.

Stereotypes work both ways, she reminded herself. *She probably has me pegged as a nerdy bookworm.*

They sat on the beach, eating their lunch as they traded stories about the morning's swim. The talk circled around to Lianndra's shark experience. Trent and Cassidy expressed their amazement at just how much Lianndra knew about sharks.

Lianndra laughed. "I watch a lot of documentaries. Haven't you guys seen the shark specials?"

Michael snorted. "These two? Television? Never. They have apps to keep them up on the latest Hollywood rumors."

Trent threw a shell fragment at him, and Michael expertly deflected it.

"Hey!" Trent said. "At least I don't sit on my butt in front of the television or computer."

Michael kicked sand at him, most of which landed across Cassidy's legs. She gave him a dirty look as she leaned forward to brush herself clean. "I for one would have nightmares watching anything featuring sharks. Honestly, Lianndra, I don't know how you kept your cool. I would have been a hysterical mess."

Lianndra shrugged. "It's amazing how calm you are when your body kicks into survival mode." She pushed a strand of wet hair out of her eyes. "To tell the truth, I lost it. I don't know what I would have done if Sir Galahad here hadn't stumbled upon me."

Michael grinned. "Yeah, you were hard to miss, clinging half-naked to a flashing buoy and screaming like a banshee while waving a shirt on the end of a pole. If it'd been later in the season, everyone on the beach would have headed out to rescue you."

"Certainly all the guys, anyway." Trent smiled as he received a brisk elbow in the ribs from Cassidy. "Seriously, though, did you learn the shark info from watching TV?"

Lianndra confirmed with a nod. "Exam prep avoidance. It's amazing the things one will do to avoid studying Advanced Animal Nutrition. For instance, due to my passion for documentaries, I know the implications of the ocean suddenly retreating from a beach, how part of Hawaii is falling into the ocean, that the Pacific Northwest is long overdue for the big one, and trusting anyone who tells you not to panic is unwise."

"The big one what?" Cassidy was laughing, choking on her drink.

"Earthquake, silly. Even I know that one," Trent replied, handing her a piece of paper towel.

Cassidy poked him again which led to a wrestling and tickling match. Lianndra hoped it wouldn't escalate into anything embarrassing.

She settled for ignoring the flying sand and wriggling bodies, pretending to examine the beautiful scenery around them. *In reality, not difficult to do. It's gorgeous out here.*

Lianndra stuffed the last of her sandwich into her mouth. She swallowed. "I wouldn't mind going for a hike except I must get changed. I can't hike in this getup." She dusted crumbs and sand from her cleavage.

Trent disentangled himself from Cassidy and stood. He looked ruefully at his sand encrusted form. "I'll swim out to bring the dinghy in for you," he said. "You guys can take it back to the boat to get changed. If you touristy types want to stomp about, go ahead. I wouldn't mind lying on the beach in the sun."

He looks as though he often worships the sun between bouts of lifting weights, Lianndra thought. *Trent is the perfect match for Cassidy. They both look like beach volleyball champs, and future skin cancer patients.*

She watched Trent wade into the water, doing the duck walk in his flippers.

On one side of her, Cassidy sighed, shaking sand out of her hair. "He has such a nice butt." She flashed a smile as Michael groaned. "Well, he does."

"How long have you been together?" Lianndra asked her.

"Almost two years now. Our parents are getting antsy." Cassidy shrugged. "I met Trent in high school. His dad runs a huge cattle ranch. They are filthy rich. When I heard the guys were heading to California, I tagged along."

Although Lianndra knew Trent was Michael's friend, he and Cassidy blended in with the locals. *Not their first winter holiday here, obviously.* "I didn't think there were any rich cattle farmers left."

"Trent's dad doesn't just farm cattle, they have oil on their land," Cassidy said before repositioning herself into the sunlight and bunching up Lianndra's unused towel for a pillow.

Michael rolled backward onto his elbows, squinting to where Trent's snorkel was just visible above the water. "Trent and I have been friends for years," he said. "My parents' sheep farm is near his family's spread." He grinned. "No oil, though. I live vicariously off my friend's wealth." He reached around behind Lianndra to retrieve an escaped sandwich wrapper. "For that matter, so do you," he said to Cassidy.

Cassidy didn't open her eyes, merely shrugged, and said, "Somebody has to spend it."

"We've been spending it for weeks now." Michael ran his hand through his dark hair, shaking out grains of sand. Cassidy sniffed in response but still didn't open her eyes. Michael grinned before continuing. "Gotta go home eventually, I guess. I'm spending the summer helping my folks at the farm; hoping to go to university in the fall. We took a year off after high school." He laughed. "I'm supposed to figure out what I want to do with my life, but all I've figured out is that I hate beach volleyball."

Aha! Nineteen. I thought so. Lianndra laughed and turned her gaze back to the ocean. Then she frowned. "Looks like we're not alone in paradise." She nodded toward the waves.

From around one side of the cove came a rather dilapidated old fishing vessel. As soon as it appeared, it seemed to stop moving forward and rocked in the small waves of the cove. It was towing a smaller boat behind it.

"Are they fishing?" Lianndra asked.

Beside her, Michael straightened. He was frowning. "They're not supposed to; these are protected waters." He squinted into the sun. "Besides, I don't see any gear out."

Movement closer to the beach revealed Trent pulling himself out of the water into the dinghy. They saw him notice the fishing boat and stare at it for a moment before rowing the dinghy to shore.

Lianndra felt uneasy. *We're awfully isolated out here.* She sensed Michael's tension and guessed he felt the same way. There were four of them, but who knew how many were on the strange boat. The fishing boat just sat there, rocking in the waves.

Trent obviously shared their concerns. He didn't leave the dinghy. Instead, he rowed it straight up to the beach before calling to them, "I think we should go back to the boat."

Cassidy sat up, shading her eyes with one hand. "It's just a fishing boat. What's the big deal?"

"Cassidy." Trent's tone brooked no argument. Cassidy sighed theatrically before giving in by rolling upright and grabbing her towels. Michael stood, helping Lianndra to her feet with a single fluid movement.

They'd rowed the dinghy halfway to their boat when the other vessel moved. They could hear the engine throttle up, the bow wave splashing white against the hull. It was heading straight for them.

Trent hesitated in his rowing for only a second and then stroked faster.

"We're not going to make it," Michael yelled to him over the roar of the approaching vessel. "Get us back to shore!"

Thoroughly alarmed now, Lianndra glanced at Cassidy. The younger woman was pale beneath her tan, her eyes wide and frightened.

Whatever those guys are up to, it isn't good, Lianndra thought.

With only one set of oars in their little dinghy, all they could do was watch the boat grow ever larger. Trent strained to get them turned around and back to shore.

It was soon obvious the boat would intercept them before they made the beach.

Michael grabbed Lianndra by the arm, pulling her closer to him. "We'll have to swim for it. With any luck, they'll just take the boat. Anyway, they can't go after four of us at once," he said, shouting over the sound of the approaching vessel.

"But why do they want to go after us at all?" Cassidy sounded scared and bewildered.

"Pirates!" Trent said, abandoning the oars to slide closer to Cassidy.

Thoughts of one of Lianndra's favorite movie stars in piratorial hair extensions flashed through her mind. *Pirates?* She couldn't shake the image. *What do pirates want with us? I can see them wanting the boat, but us? Ransom. That's it. Trent is filthy rich.*

Michael lifted her over the side. The cold water shocked her back to reality. Beside her, Cassidy spluttered as an incoming wave swamped her. Michael dove over the other side of the dinghy, surfacing a few feet away.

"Split up and swim!" he yelled.

Lianndra kicked her feet to swim for shore. Behind her, she heard Cassidy call out to Trent, followed by the splash of him diving overboard. The roar of the engines drowned out all else. Adrenaline took over.

The tight wet suit immediately caused issues. Swimming slowly with fins was one thing; swimming fast without them quite another. The tight suit hampered the depth and strength of her kicks, making her arms ache with fatigue after only a few strokes.

Then she heard a change in the boat's engines as it throttled down, followed by the shrill sound of Cassidy's scream. The sound of a smaller motor penetrated the din, and out of the corner of her eye, Lianndra saw movement. A second, smaller craft, arrowing between her and the beach.

She paused, treading water, tired and confused. When she looked back over her shoulder, the fishing vessel loomed behind her. She could make out a knot of human figures struggling on the deck. She couldn't see any sign of Michael, Cassidy or Trent in the water.

Left with few options, she took a deep breath and dove.

Something crashed into the surrounding water. She kicked and tried diving past it, but it moved toward her, enveloping her in its slimy embrace. Thrashing in panic only entangled her further.

Lianndra gasped as she broke the surface, enmeshed in an old fishing net. The many rips spoke to it not being used in a long while, at least certainly not for fish. Although the worn spots would have been good news for a small tuna, none of the holes were large enough to help her escape. As the net winched up, it swung inward, depositing her in a puddle of slime on an old rusty steel deck.

Lianndra barely registered the complete strangers around her when someone grabbed her by the hair. She screeched in pain as something jabbed her in the side of her neck.

Everything went dark.

My holiday isn't working out exactly as planned, Lianndra thought.

She sat on a rusty bench made of corrugated metal which poked through the wet suit into her butt. Lianndra tugged at hands cuffed together behind her back, something fastened her ankles to the floor. Her head ached. *I think I'm going to puke.*

Also bound, Cassidy lay unconscious to one side of her, twisted awkwardly on the ugly metal. Seated across from them, the guys were groaning their way awake.

The surrounding walls were bare, rusted to match the benches. Wood sawdust covered the floor; it looked disgusting and smelled worse.

Trent woke first. His face was ashen. "Ugh," he said with a grimace. "I feel sick."

Michael answered without opening his eyes. "Well, for God's sake, don't barf. I'll spew for sure if you do." He moved as though his head hurt him.

Lianndra saw a livid bruise along one side of his face. She remembered the struggling figures she'd glimpsed on the deck.

"Are you okay?" She asked, surprised at how hoarse her voice sounded. The seat beneath her lurched. Lianndra realized they were no longer on the ocean—they were inside a truck.

"I'm fine." Michael opened his silvery eyes, forcing a smile. "Kidnapped at sea, slugged in the head, drugged, trussed like a turkey before being carted off to God knows where, but otherwise, I'm good." He rolled his head on his neck and flexed his shoulders, testing the restraints, then swung his long legs, tugging at the manacles on his ankles. Chains hidden in the sawdust clinked as he moved. Frowning, he assessed his friend's progress as Trent tried the same maneuvers with as little success. Michael then looked back at Lianndra. "How are you?"

"About the same, except add a disgusting fishing net and subtract the slugging." She strove for a light tone, but her shaking voice betrayed her.

Trent gingerly rested his head against the side of the truck. "What is this? Are we being held for ransom?" He looked across at Lianndra. "I don't suppose you are independently wealthy?"

Lianndra grimaced, wincing as her headache flared. "Sorry. Independently poor. My parents have a dairy farm in Saskatchewan. No oil."

Trent sighed. "Then it's about me. But why take all of us?"

Michael shook his head. "I don't know; it doesn't add up. Only the rental guy knew we were at the cove today. Unless he told these guys. Why wouldn't they just take the boat? It's worth a fair bit. But taking all of us and leaving the boat?" Confusion showed in his eyes. "If they were after Trent, I wouldn't think grabbing us all constitutes your typical kidnapping. Not that I know a lot about it. But it was as though they stumbled on us and took advantage of an opportunity."

"Yeah, but what opportunity?" Trent looked over to Cassidy, who was now sitting up to listen. "Cass, are you okay?"

"No," she replied before vomiting.

The sight and the smell set them all off. In the end, although everyone felt better, the truck was much worse for wear. The sawdust soaked up the liquid which made Lianndra wonder if that was its intended purpose. If the state of it was anything to go by, they weren't the first occupants of this truck. She hated to have her bare feet in the mess, although she tried not to think about it. *I must sterilize those cuts after this. If there is an after this!*

Lianndra raised her eyes to Michael's. He'd been staring at the shavings, and there was a flash of a shared thought between them: *whoever these people are, they have done this before. Recently.*

Michael glanced at Cassidy. She was sitting up, looking scared.

"What the heck do they want us for?" Trent's expression was angry, no doubt fueled by his helplessness. Likely, he hadn't run into many situations in his life where he'd felt powerless. Trent tugged at his ankle restraints. The resulting dull clunk drew Lianndra's attention down to his feet. The restraints were metal, with a chain running from them to a bar extending the full length of the seats. Her eyes traced the bar along the floor, observing a set of manacles welded every three feet.

She glanced at her ankle restraints, noticing they were the same. *This truck is designed to carry human captives. Slavers!* Lianndra knew slavers operated in North America, but that was the extent of her knowledge.

Lianndra met Michael's eyes again. It was amazing how much information they could share in a look, and she could tell his thoughts were following the path of her own. She saw him decide not to reveal their shared realization with the others.

Michael merely shrugged, then said, "I guess we'll find out."

Lianndra focused on the chances of rescue. "Did you guys tell anyone other than the rental guy we were going to the cove today?"

Trent and Michael shared a quick glance before Trent shook his head. "I finalized the outing yesterday. You file a simple trip log with the rental company each time you go out, but no one knew exactly where we were going. The rental guy might notice we didn't come back today. He would assume we were overnighting somewhere along the coast. No one keeps close track of these things."

"The boat has a GPS tracker on board." Michael was obviously trying to sound hopeful. "They'll look for it once they realize we're missing."

If these guys were after us, and it seems they were, they would have been wise to blow the boat to pieces once we were all clear. Lianndra didn't say it out loud. There wasn't any point. The only one who might not realize their predicament was Cassidy. *She doesn't need any more stress.*

Lianndra glanced at the woman beside her. Cassidy was motionless, her head down, her blonde hair hanging over her face.

They sat in troubled silence, each lost in their own thoughts. Lianndra's arms in the tight wet suit ached from being pulled behind her back; she'd lost sensation in her hands. It was amazing the suit still contained her front half at all, what with the manhandling she'd experienced. *Great, more skin. I'm barely decent.*

There were more important concerns than her state of undress. Lianndra's head throbbed. *I would love to lie down.*

Upon closer examination of the bench, she decided it wasn't worth exposing herself to whatever disgusting debris was clinging to it.

The first urgings of needing to pee opened another world of embarrassing possibilities. *No way I'll be able to wiggle out of this uncooperative wet suit with my hands bound behind me.*

Lianndra was contemplating the dynamics of peeing inside her suit when the truck slowed. The ride became rough as though they'd turned onto a poorly maintained road. The potholes threatened to solve Lianndra's problem for her. She exchanged a frightened look with Cassidy, recognizing there was a certain comfort in not knowing their fate. The primitive instincts of a trapped animal created a wild surge of panic within her. She wondered if this was how cattle felt when their transports pulled into the slaughterhouse yard.

Why am I comparing us to livestock? she thought. *At least I'm sure they didn't go to this trouble just to eat us!*

"Lianndra, I'm so sorry I got you into this," Michael said, his gaze intense and direct.

She forced a smile. "Michael, don't be ridiculous. None of this is your fault." *I'm perfectly capable of getting into trouble all by myself.*

"Besides, you got us all into trouble, not just her." Trent's attempt at levity fell short, but Lianndra appreciated it.

The truck turned before slowing to a halt. The tension among the captives was palpable as eyes focused on the door to their prison. All too soon they heard the unmistakable sounds of rusty latches being freed.

The door opened to reveal four male figures armed with handguns. The only thing that distinguished them from the average person on the street was their cold, uncaring gaze. Two of them entered the truck; one held the barrel of his gun up against Michael's temple, while the other bent to release Cassidy's manacles.

Trent moved to protest, and one of the men nearest the door pushed his gun close to the young man's angry face. "Don't!" The voice was harsh.

"Trent, please," Cassidy said, her voice a hoarse imitation of her usual robust self. "Don't do anything dumb." Her face shone with tears but her eyes locked with his. "I love you." Cassidy's voice shook

She's figured it out. Lianndra's panic rose in waves throughout her body, making her tremble. She'd have bolted if she could.

"Cassidy . . ." Trent's voice broke; his entire body shook with what was no doubt suppressed emotion.

"Shut up!" The man with the gun in Trent's face shoved the barrel hard into his cheek.

Trent swallowed and subsided, but his eyes looked sick and angry. The gunman's cohort finished releasing Cassidy's legs, marching her past them before handing her down to the fourth man. He then returned to unfasten Lianndra.

Lianndra could barely stand. *So much for adrenaline enabling you to do amazing feats in the face of danger. I feel more like a rabbit about to die of a heart attack.* She struggled to walk as the thug grabbed her with one arm to push her out the door.

"Where are you taking them?" Michael leaned forward against the gun barrel as if daring the man to shoot him.

Instead, the man punched him, compounding the bruised cheekbone. Michael's body rocked with the blow but his silver eyes glared back. The tension in him didn't subside even when their captor pressed the gun barrel into the darkening bruise, making him wince.

"Worry about yourself, kid," the man said.

He handed Lianndra into the fourth man's less than sterling custody. The man doing the unfastening turned, and with a casual air shot Michael first, and then Trent.

"No!" Lianndra screamed, but the man laughed. Then she saw the darts sticking out of the wet suits; Michael's in his arm, Trent's in his thigh. Trent started to rise from his seat before he lost strength and collapsed across the bench. Michael struggled for consciousness, but his eyes glazed over.

"Dammit. Now we gotta carry 'em," said the man holding the gun on Michael.

"Yeah, well, better that than take any more crap from Adams about beating up the merchandise."

Lianndra turned from the scene inside the van, her stomach lurching as the words confirmed her suspicions. Cassidy's wide, frightened gaze caught hers for a fraction of a second before their captor poked her forward with his gun.

"Move!" he said.

They were inside a vast, ancient warehouse. Solid walls partitioned the truck bay off from the rest of the building. The men forced the two women to march on trembling legs up a set of stairs that appeared as though they shared an ancestry with the bench in the truck. The ragged metal cut into Lianndra's bare feet.

When the door opened, noise and an overwhelming stench assailed them. Lianndra realized the partition wall must be insulated. Cries, screams, sobs—she heard almost every sound of human misery. The stench was appalling: human sweat mixed with urine and feces. Stepping through, she could see one entire wall of the huge warehouse lined with metal enclosures. The iron bars resembled something she would see in an ancient zoo long before they used less visible physical barriers to restrain animals. The cages housed women bunched together, their numbers impossible to estimate. Each woman wore a dingy yellow tunic covering the essentials. Sawdust with a familiar consistency bedded the floors of the cages.

At the sight of their captors, the sound level declined. Some of the caged women glanced at the new arrivals before dropping their gazes and turning away. Many showed no interest, standing or sitting with heads bowed.

The men escorted the newcomers to a nearby room. Waiting at the door were two men familiar to Lianndra—she'd last seen the burly man and his smaller friend leaning on the hood of an SUV at the redwoods parking lot.

Were they watching us yesterday too? Lianndra's thoughts raced. It put a very different complexion on things. Their kidnapping was not random but planned.

Without a word, the dart gun holder retreated. Lianndra stared at one of the SUV men; she struggled to put the pieces together.

None of it made any sense. Her mind went numb, overwhelmed by what was happening to her. The two men pushed Lianndra and Cassidy into the windowless room, locking the door behind them.

There were tables and cabinets lining two walls, and across from them was another door.

The smaller man unfastened their wrist manacles. "Strip," he said.

It was too much. The adrenaline finally kicked in. Lianndra bolted to the other door to find it locked. The two men laughed at her. Lianndra whirled with her back to the door, an animal at bay, chest heaving, glaring at them. Cassidy stood in the center of the room. With her head hanging and eyes glazed over, she seemed lost in another world.

"Look." The hulking burly man shrugged his shoulders, waving a hand in the air. "You've got two choices here. Either you strip, or we strip you." His eyes trailed along her body. "Although messing with the merchandise is frowned upon, we find the stripping process highly entertaining." His velvet voice belied his crude words.

Cassidy heard him. She made a small moaning sound and began to strip. Her arms shook as she peeled off the wet suit. One of the men sat on a table to enjoy the show. The hulk crossed his arms, waiting for Lianndra to decide.

Lianndra felt Cassidy's humiliation. A burst of pure rage rescued her. *How dare they do this to us!* Chin up and eyes narrowed in anger, she unzipped her top.

"Atta girl." The smaller man purred. "Much better."

Lianndra locked her eyes with his, glaring as she took off her top. *Be damned if I am going to let these thugs turn me into a hysterical female.* She tossed it straight at him, forcing him to catch it with one hand. The swimsuit followed, leaving her stark naked before them. *I will not cower before lowlife monsters.*

Oddly, the hulk seemed to respect her rage. Dropping her clothing into a bin behind him, he considered her thoughtfully. While Cassidy stood with her hands covering herself as best as she was able, Lianndra stood straight and unashamed with her fists clenched at her sides.

The hulk ambled to the wall and pushed a button. A buzzer prompted two unknown men to enter the room. They grabbed Cassidy.

More thugs. The operation's size shocked Lianndra. *How does it support so many employees?* She moved to follow her new friend, but the hulk stepped between them.

"Don't," Cassidy said in a hoarse voice. "I'll be okay. Just don't make it worse." Then they took her away.

Some of Lianndra's courage went with Cassidy, but she tried not to show it. The hulk was still watching her.

The smaller man in the corner spoke. "This one's got spunk. I think Juke will like her."

"He should, considering he requested her. The one with gray eyes looks promising, too. Hope he's happy with them. We don't have much else to offer him this time."

Lianndra's mind froze at the hulk's words. Not just targeted but requested? Her and Michael? What the heck?

The hulk walked to the cabinet on the wall. He opened it to withdraw a slim rod made from a shiny silver metal. It was about sixteen inches long, with rounded edges. As he handled it, it reflected the overhead lights and Lianndra thought she could see something etched on it. Her attention diverted as the other man slid off the table, approaching her with the manacles he'd removed earlier. Lianndra backed away from him.

The hulk made a "tsk" sound. "Now, now, we've had this discussion." His voice was that of a father scolding a naughty child, and it penetrated her growing panic.

She froze, wincing as they firmly fastened her hands behind her back. The less these guys touched her, the happier she would be.

The man grabbed her arm and moved her toward an unusual table. Iridescent metal, with a long, flat, top and shaped like an hourglass, the table had four sturdy legs bolted to the floor. The hulk laid the metal rod into a groove at one end of the platform as the smaller man, holding her arm, marched her up to the frame.

"Bend forward," he said, pushing her torso over the contraption, her neck arching to fall directly across the metal bar.

Panic surged from deep within, making her push backward.

"I thought we had an understanding," the hulk said in a sad voice. He grabbed her by the hair and hauled her onto the framework until her entire upper body was on the smooth metal top. His accomplice strapped her down while the hulk held her in place. From beneath the table he swung up a rounded mesh cage, which he snapped over the back of her head.

This was obviously an established routine between the two of them. Lianndra found herself held immobile with little effort on their part. She bit back a sob, struggling to find the anger that had sustained her so far.

Her bladder ached with the pressure of the table on her pelvis. *Be damned if I will lose control in front of these jerks!* The rage helped her to focus, to suppress the fear. *I'm not livestock even though they're treating me like I am.* She felt exposed and vulnerable in this position. *If they try anything, I'll pee on them.* An image shot into her mind: a sheep recruited for one of their vet classes that urinated on her as she'd fastened it into a restraint chute.

Neither of the men seemed interested in taking advantage of her current situation. They focused on adjusting her head and neck position with minute cranks of handles attached to the mesh restraint. Finally, the hulk gave a grunt of satisfaction, dropping his hands to the rod lying in the groove. He put a hand on both ends before squeezing, handling it with surprising dexterity for one with such large fingers.

The rod hummed. With her head restrained, all Lianndra could see out of the corners of her eyes was a pale glow as it seemed to light up from within.

What the hell? Heat came from the metal beneath her neck.

"Don't even swallow," the hulk said, removing his fingers from the rod. "Remain still. Take small, slow breaths. Believe me, this advice is for your own good."

Immediately, Lianndra wanted—no, needed—to swallow. She fought the urge, believing he was serious.

"When I tell you, take a deep breath and hold it." He was silent for a few moments. "Now," he said.

She gulped as big a breath as she could.

The metal moved. It rose from the groove on each side of her neck, sliding along her skin like a warm, smooth snake. Lianndra was so shocked a tremor ran through her entire body.

"Hold still," the hulk snapped at her, just in time.

Lianndra's eyes strained to see what she could only feel. The warm metal enclosed her neck, continuing to move in a rolling motion. Then she experienced a crawling sensation from deep inside, and a sharp pain as something penetrated her skin, moving deep into her skull behind her ear. She wanted to scream, the lack of oxygen causing spots to swim before her eyes.

I'm going to black out! Lianndra waited for the darkness to come.

"You can breathe now." The words were barely out of his mouth before she gasped for air. She heard the sound of catches releasing, freeing her from the restraints. The hulk helped her to stand on wobbly legs. The metal rod felt warm—alive—against the skin of her throat, and her skull ached. Beyond the physical sensation was a deep-rooted horror of what just transpired.

My God, I'm wearing a collar!

Before she could recover, the smaller man grabbed her arm and pulled her through the same doorway as Cassidy. Dazed, Lianndra stumbled along beside him through a second door and down a long hallway. She barely registered the manacles being removed from her wrists before he shoved her through a heavy, barred door. Sawdust scratched the soles of her feet.

She was in a small enclosure, with a solid back wall except for a single steel door in the center. Lianndra turned to face the men through the bars just as the hulk wandered up, holding something in his hand. He swung the barred door shut and locked it before addressing her.

"I will demonstrate the restraint device on your collar, in case you are entertaining any rebellious thoughts." With no further warning, he raised the device in his hand and squeezed.

Pain lanced through her neck. It reverberated through her entire body with no beginning or end. When it stopped, Lianndra was lying in the sawdust, gasping. In dismay, she noticed she no longer needed to pee.

The inner metal door swung open. From where she lay, Lianndra could see women staring at her. They had collars just like her own and wore simple tunics doing little to hide their bodies from prying eyes. Unlike the ones the other captives wore, these were red and seemed clean.

The room's walls were solid and not barred. Compared to the other quarters she'd glimpsed; this room was pristine.

"We'll see you again soon." With the parting remark, the hulk turned and strode off with his cohort.

Lianndra staggered to her feet, swayed, then stepped forward into what could only be a new, darker future.

MICHAEL DID NOT CONSIDER HIMSELF to be a slow learner. He'd always been quick to comprehend concepts, could extrapolate on theory, and possessed no problem with grasping hands-on experiences. Yet nothing in his life to date could prepare him for being a slave.

He regained consciousness in a solid metal cage, surrounded by men he did not know, with Trent lying on the sawdust only a few feet away from him. One of the men helped Michael to his feet, and together they moved a groaning Trent to a cot along one wall. The walls of their room were featureless metal, except for one door and rows of cots. In the corner was a small commode, walled off with a curtain.

The collar was Michael's first hurdle. So far, he wasn't proud of his learning curve. His first experience with the collar came three seconds after he realized he was wearing it, when he tried to remove it. It zapped him so hard it knocked him off his feet and left him panting in pain.

"Don't try that again," a tall, sandy-haired man about Michael's age advised, offering him a hand back onto his feet. "The zaps get more intense every time you grab it. Eventually, they knock you senseless, and when you come to, you ache for a week."

Another man added, "He should know. He was the one who tried it. He was moving like an old man for a long time afterward."

Leaving the collar alone wasn't easy. Part of Michael objected to it on an instinctual level, like a wild horse objects to a lasso. The first night he received two more corrections when he tried to pull it off while falling asleep. Only then did his body learn to avoid touching the collar.

Michael slept little that night for many reasons. His thoughts swirled between grim reality and nightmares. He worried about Lianndra and Cassidy.

Where are they? He thought of his family. *Surely the authorities will search for us?* Yet logic intervened: this was a slave ring. His captors would be experienced in covering up the disappearances. In Michael's case, eliminating the boat would go a long way to explaining their theoretical demise. *Tow the boat out to sea and sink it. It goes down, bodies washed away by the ocean. Happens just often enough to be possible.*

His family would think he was dead.

Despair wasn't part of Michael's usual repertoire of emotions. He spent the first night alternating between trying to sleep and pacing, checking for any chinks in the room's armor.

"Trust me when I tell you there is no way out," the sandy-haired man told him as he watched Michael pace.

"You can't just give up!" Michael said, frustrated.

The man's brown eyes flared, but his voice remained even. "I haven't given up. I am biding my time."

His name was Brendan. Brendan introduced Michael to his cellmates: Max, Tyler, and Justin. Although the room held twenty cots, there were just the six of them.

Trent was still sick from the drug injected into him by the dart gun. He laid on the cot with one arm flung over his eyes, unresponsive to questions. Michael stopped trying to get his friend to talk, so he lay down. Moments later, his restless thoughts got him up to resume pacing.

He must find a way out. Then they could find Lianndra and Cassidy, break them out, and get the hell out of there.

"NOW CLOSE YOUR EYES AND let your mind drift." Andrea's voice was soft, hypnotic.

Lianndra followed her suggestion, shifting on the cot, searching for the comfort zone the lotus position theoretically provided.

On the narrow cot next to hers, Andrea folded long legs to keep them from spilling off the thin mattress as the only other seating option was the floor. Neither of them wanted to sit there even though the sawdust here was cleaner than elsewhere in the facility.

Lianndra snuck a sideways peek from lowered eyelids at the other woman. Andrea's skin was the color of dark chocolate, her black hair cropped short. She was an Amazon of a woman at close to six feet in height. She'd been a life coach, plus a yoga and fitness instructor before she'd become merchandise.

Lianndra's first impression of Andrea was a friendly, open, outgoing person, someone who was supportive and whom you could trust. As time passed in such intimate quarters, she came to understand that the face the African-American woman showed the world differed from what lay underneath. Beneath the cheerful façade was a person who was hiding deep inner pain. Lianndra only caught the briefest glimpses of the agony within her.

We all have secrets, Lianndra thought with a mental shrug. *The secrets are hers to keep.* She enjoyed the woman's company. *She's an excellent coach. It's not her fault I can't do a lotus.*

Lianndra thought her new friend was beautiful in an unusual and exotic way. Andrea's body rippled with muscle, the veins popping out with a minimum of encouragement. Yet she remained feminine, with expressive eyes, broad shoulders, large breasts, and curved hips below a narrow waist with legs that went on forever. She fit every interpretation of the Amazon vision, right down to her jaded—often humorous—opinion of the opposite sex. The tall woman had a natural presence, making her the leader of their group.

Lianndra finally settled for an approximation of the lotus position and tried to enter a meditative state. As usual, she had a hard time stopping her mind from drifting down familiar corridors.

Michael. Cassidy. Trent. They were never far from her thoughts. She did not know their fate; she'd neither seen nor heard anything about the guys since she'd walked out of the truck. Lianndra also wondered if her ex-boyfriend Scott ever thought of her, or if her friend Jayne missed her. Lianndra wondered about her family. *They must all think I'm dead.*

It amazed Lianndra that a slavery ring could be so established in such a privileged country. The women she now lived with must have people who cared for them, families who missed them after they vanished, and who searched for them. The slavers obvious success spoke of an intelligent organization at the top-level. *They're good at covering their tracks.* In her case, sinking their rented boat could proclaim the four young people the victims of the ocean currents. Lianndra hated that her family was likely grieving for her. She tried not to think of them too often.

The room in which she lived was nothing like the cages she'd seen upon first entering the warehouse. This seemed separated from the main body of the building. The walls were solid steel, not barred, with a row of cots lining one of them. A single toilet and sink resided in the corner, with a ragged old curtain providing a modicum of privacy. She hadn't noticed such accommodations in the cages in the other part of the warehouse. They were cruder affairs than this.

Other than the door, the only break in the metal walls was the slot through which they received their meals. The door along the one wall of their room led to a hallway. Every day the guards escorted the women through it, down the hall, and into a large room where they took part in strength and aerobics training. Aged equipment, everything from treadmills to gymnastic rings, filled the room.

After hours of exercising, the next stop was the showers where they stripped out of the simple tunics and dressed in fresh ones afterward. Guards armed with collar remotes guided them back to the room where they whiled away the remaining hours of the day.

Although she could not see out from her prison, Lianndra often heard the passage of people outside their room.

At first, Lianndra tried calling out to the people she heard in the hall, but no one answered her. She theorized the guards wouldn't allow the slaves to respond. The size and scope of the slave operation was intimidating. That it could function so effectively in a civilized society was both baffling and terrifying.

The lights were on twenty-four hours a day, but for half the time reduced lighting made sleep easier. If she faced the wall and tented her blanket over her head, Lianndra found it blocked most of the existing light. It made her feel less like a fish in a bowl. Sleep was often elusive, offering only nightmares. During the day they could keep busy, so it was possible to ignore whatever fate awaited them. At night the fear and uncertainty crept in.

During those times, Lianndra thought of Michael. It surprised her that she thought about him and not the other people in her life. She worried about him, as well as Cassidy and Trent. When she thought or dreamed of Michael, it was different. In their brief time together he'd showed a level of openness and honesty that touched her. Lianndra chided herself for being hopeful in a hopeless situation, but she couldn't help it.

If Michael finds a way to free himself, he won't rest until he finds me. As silly as it sounded, something deep inside her believed it was true.

The days rolled into weeks without a break in routine. Lianndra wondered if they would ever be moved from this facility. The familiarity became comforting, in a way. *Better this than whatever the future might hold.*

Then came a day when all was quiet. The women in her room did not go to the exercise room or showers, despite the fact they were due. In the morning, she heard commotion and heavy trucks moving. Then nothing but silence.

Their usual routine resumed the next day. The lack of traffic in the hallway along their room pointed to a marked reduction in the number of slaves in the warehouse. It led to a discussion among the captive women as to when and to whom they might be sold. Their captors seemed in no rush to move Lianndra's group anywhere. The days continued to slip by with their routine unchanged.

Why not us? Lianndra thought. *Is it worse or better to be left behind?*

Although there were twenty bunks in her room there were only six women in with her. There was Muriel, a tiny blonde woman who was strong for her stature. Lacey was Lianndra's height, but built like an athlete; her shoulders and arms bulged with muscle. Beth was almost as tall as Andrea; she was graceful and talkative. Michelle was small like Muriel, although not as strong; she struggled daily with the exercise regimen set out for them. The last woman, Chia, barely spoke English, but she was always ready to flash a smile.

Lianndra questioned her cellmates, trying to find at least one common denominator. It turned out they had little in common. The women were from different areas of North America, possessed different racial and ethnic backgrounds, different physical characteristics, and different interests.

Other than being female, there seemed only three things they shared: the situation, the collars, and the fact they refused to let captivity overwhelm them. At night, Lianndra could sometimes hear soft sobbing muffled by the blankets. During the day, they kept their game faces intact. No tears. No hysterics. They complied with the guards' wishes because of the collars. The women followed Andrea's lead—chins up, faces impassive no matter what the day held in store for them.

At three months, Andrea had been there the longest. In the nine weeks since Lianndra's capture, she learned little about her eventual fate, but a lot about her sisters in slavery. All her cellmates stood up to the hulking man and his companion during processing, rather than succumbing to their fear. Three of the women tried to attack the men, not that it had done them much good. The men forcibly stripped two of them. A seventh woman hadn't even made it to the cage but died during the collaring procedure. One of the other women saw the gory accident. The new captive moved at the wrong time, and the metal bored right through her neck.

The collars were a hot topic among her fellow captives. They tried to determine how they worked. There were no obvious buttons or controls on the metal, only indecipherable etchings. Some of the etchings were common to all the collars, but each one possessed unique characters, indicating they acted as a visual identification. Every woman showed a spidery network of raised lines beneath the skin, just behind the left ear. The lines penetrated deeper into the flesh where their skull met the necks. The collars were warm to the touch, feeling alive against their skin, as if they flexed and contracted with each breath they took. It was an eerie sensation, making the hair on the back of Lianndra's neck stand on end. At night, the bump beneath her neck led to many nightmares about choking to death.

It soon appeared as though the collars performed another function—they suppressed the women's monthly cycles. None of the woman had experienced a menstrual cycle since being collared. At first, each captive ignored the issue, considering the interruption as a sign of the trauma they'd suffered during capture. Then the women compared notes. Once the topic was out in the open, it started another flurry of discussion about the collars and how it could have such an effect on them. The sophisticated pieces of technology seemed out of place in this low-tech outfit.

One thing was certain: the collars were effective at instilling obedience. The pain the devices inflicted was immediate and incapacitating. Even knowing it wouldn't permanently harm them was no help. No one could fight the pain.

MICHAEL SLASHED AT TRENT WITH the blunt training sword, making the smaller man leap back in an awkward parry. Trent was a physical person, and for the duration of their long friendship, Michael had seen him absorb many new skills. Sword fighting wasn't one of them.

Not that I'm any Knight of the Round Table, Michael thought, *but my control over the sword is miles ahead of Trent's.*

Both young men sported bruises over most of their bodies. Fighting was not something Michael wanted to learn, but the collar convinced him otherwise. The guards had shocked him four times before he gave in and picked up the sword.

He told himself the skill might be useful if he could ever bust out of here. In the mornings, their captors escorted the six male captives to a room where they exercised using machines. They rested over the midday. In the late afternoon, they transferred to the area he was now in which was large enough for fight practice.

"What modern war uses swords?" Michael asked, but the expressionless men who stood at the edges of the room weren't interested in conversation. The four of them carried revolvers, dart guns, and the collar remotes. More than enough to keep six men under control, especially as the fifth man was the fighting coach. He possessed a real sword plus a long knife and watched the men as they sparred. The man moved like a martial arts expert. Michael had little doubt he was a lethal weapon, even when unarmed.

Each one of the reluctant students received corrections from the collars more than once, and two even required darting. So far, the real guns had stayed in the holsters.

I guess shooting the merchandise is frowned upon, Michael thought.

He struck again, ducking under Trent's swing, feeling another twinge of worry at his friend's blank face. Michael knew Trent wasn't coping well with the enslavement; he wasn't sleeping and was only eating or exercising under threat of being shocked. Despite Michael's efforts to keep his friend's spirits up, Trent only spoke when asked a question. He also suffered from shaking fits, during which he seemed to tune out his new reality. Even more disturbing were the increasingly frequent fits of rage. These often ended with Trent screaming when the guards activated his collar.

In Michael's opinion, his friend was close to losing it forever. *He is concerned about Cassidy. But it's more than that.*

All of them cared about something other than just themselves. Michael worried about Lianndra. In the short time they'd spent together, he'd felt something life-changing taking place between them. He thought of her all the time and feared what was happening to her.

But with Trent, each passing day seemed to sink his friend deeper into a despair Michael couldn't shift. Where Michael kept his thoughts occupied with the potential for escape, Trent just appeared defeated by the situation.

It was understandable. Yet the other four men who shared their incarceration seemed to cope. The daily fight sessions appeared to help. It gave them an opportunity to vent their anger and frustration in a physical manner.

Michael noticed one final thing. Although of average height and in good physical shape, Trent was the smallest of the six men. Michael was taller than average, and the other four men in their group were just as tall. They had the same build despite having different hair, coloring, and features. The five men were naturals at fighting whereas Trent struggled.

There is a selection process, although I have no idea what it involves, Michael thought. *How do they prejudge fighting ability?* The possibility he was the principal target for the kidnapping bothered him. *Was I responsible for us getting grabbed? Were the others collateral damage?* It made him even more determined to help Trent through this ordeal.

Their fight master blew a whistle, telling the men to shift partners. This time, they picked up a training knife in one hand while keeping the sword in the other. Max now sparred with Trent which relieved Michael. Max would pull his punches enough so Trent could cope. The trick was to do it subtly, so neither got zapped from the watching guards.

Michael looked across to Tyler, his new sparring partner. A large bruise spread along the side of Tyler's face, resulting in the left eye swelling shut.

Feint right, strike left. Michael dropped to a crouch, watching for the telltale eye movements and muscle shifts showing which way Tyler would move.

The fighting came easily, and it shocked him. *Whether I want to admit it or not, these bastards are tapping into a talent I would rather not be developing. What scares me is the use to which I will put this new skill. I do not want to become a killer.*

Out of the corner of his eye, Michael saw a guard watching him; the man's hand was never far from the pain button on the remote. The tendons of Michael's throat tensed beneath the collar, bracing against the coming onslaught.

As things stand, I might not have much choice.

RIGHT ON TIME, A HARSH clank interrupted Lianndra's meditation. The metal door leading to the hallway opened, revealing Brown in the doorway.

They didn't know the men's real names. The women labeled them with nicknames corresponding to a physical characteristic of each individual. Eye color designated Brown and Blue. Hulk was the burly man who processed the women. His cohort became Mouse because he was comparatively tiny and rarely spoke. There was also Goldie, who possessed one gold canine tooth, and Pug, who featured a snub nose.

"Get moving." Brown's hand waved the remote in the air.

Andrea sighed, unfolding her long legs.

Brown was always a man of few words and no sense of humor. He was fair though: no one got zapped unless they disobeyed. Blue was nasty, his finger never far from the pain button.

As they entered the hall, Goldie was Brown's partner for the day. Both men carried remotes and dart guns. Once all six women were in the hall, the men fell in behind them to follow the slaves to the exercise room.

Although providing daily exercise made sense if confining people for any length of time, it seemed as though there was more to it than just keeping them fit. They could never back off. They now spent a minimum of three hours in the room, their captors making it clear they must exercise the entire time. The exercises changed both in intensity and aptitude, using different equipment. As well as being a life coach, Andrea was a trained fitness instructor. The men chose the equipment they must use but before long allowed Andrea to coach the other women, only meddling in minor ways with her program.

With the intensity of the training, Lianndra was so stiff some mornings she moved like an old woman. Captured after Lianndra, poor Michelle had a difficult time keeping up with the exercise. She'd lived a sedentary life doing books for a small business. The woman struggled every day to complete her regimen.

Still, Lianndra was in better physical shape than she'd been in her entire life, even with the farm chores she used to do. She would feel better if she understood why they needed such extreme fitness and why they had to perfect certain exercises.

Today, as she moved into the exercise room ahead of Lianndra, Andrea stopped in the entryway. Peering past her friend, Lianndra's heart froze. Blood soaked the sawdust just inside the door. The women stopped in shock.

"Get moving," Brown said, giving one woman a shove.

Andrea folded her fingers into fists before planting them on her hips. "What happened here?"

Goldie moved into the room. "Nothin' involvin' you."

For the first time, Lianndra noticed both he and Brown showed signs of having been in a scuffle. They had abrasions on their knuckles, and there were dark specks on their clothing resembling dried blood.

Goldie waved his remote at Andrea. "No questions. Get going with your exercisin'."

Goaded by the remotes, the women moved into the room, stepping wide to avoid the stained sawdust. Lianndra stepped onto a treadmill and walked to warm up, but her mind was in turmoil. This was the first sign of real violence she'd seen since arriving here. Her thoughts roiled with questions, searching for an answer. The collar shocks were brutal but did not draw blood.

Do all the slaves have collars? Do they ever fail? Without the debilitating effects of the pain collars, she wondered how they would keep control of captives if they revolted. *Please tell me the blood isn't Cassidy's, or Trent's, or please not Michael's.* The amount made her wonder if the person survived the assault. *Not Michael.* The thought of his tall young body broken and bleeding was making her almost frantic.

The images stayed fixed in her mind, torturing her during the workout. After the three-hour allotment they moved on to the showers. Lianndra normally hated this time of day; she could not adjust to taking a shower in full view of their captors. As usual, the guards occupied themselves by heckling the women.

"Mighty fine asses on these women," Goldie said as he walked along in front of the line of showers. He stopped to slap Chia's rear.

Brown ran a hand along Michelle's back. The woman flinched, but did not meet his eyes. Getting shocked while under water was not a pleasant experience.

Rude and crude the guards may be, but Lianndra noticed that they rarely touched Andrea. They confined themselves to lewd suggestions about the tall African-American woman.

Lianndra usually did her best to ignore them as if they were so insignificant they did not matter. Today it was no effort to do so as thoughts of Michael preoccupied her.

After they returned from the showers, the last meal of the day arrived on trays slid through slots in the wall. Lianndra picked at her food. She noticed the others were much the same, each lost in grim thoughts brought on by the day's events. That night, she lay in the shelter of her blanket and felt the surge of an emotional overload.

Is Michael okay? She wondered at the prevalence of the tall young man in her thoughts. *How could he get such a hold of me in such a short time?* Lianndra brushed away tears of anxiety. *Or is it our shared situation doing this?*

She stifled a sob, struggling to get ahold of herself. If she lost control now, she might never regain it. She wondered if it was better to die than to live like this. Did such a decision explain the blood? Was someone desperate enough to push their captors until they made an example of him?

Did they choose to die rather than live in captivity? The thought calmed her. *If it was their choice, at least someone didn't make it for them.*

She pulled the thin pillow farther under her chin. The collar pushed into her neck, a continual reminder of what she now was.

A slave. Is it better to be dead? she thought. *Some might think so. But, please, let it not be Michael making that decision.*

THEY WERE LATE. EXCEPT FOR the single day when the hallways went silent, there'd been no variation in their routine.

With no clocks in the cell, there were three methods of telling time. The first was the twelve-hour light cycle, the second was their meals, and the third was their internal clock. The body noticed any deviations in such regular schedules.

Today, all the methods coalesced into one verdict: their captors were late.

It had been three months since Lianndra's capture. There were seven of them living in relative harmony in the isolated room. Considering the cost of feeding them, Lianndra wondered how much each was worth on the slave market.

The change in routine made the women uneasy, and they found it hard to sit still. Most were up and pacing in the sawdust. Andrea perched in her usual lotus position on the cot. Lianndra noticed the tall woman's breathing wasn't slow enough to show she was meditating. After a few moments, Andrea obviously sensed Lianndra staring and gave up with a sigh. "I wonder what the hell is up," she said in her husky voice.

Lianndra could tell her friend was having problems disguising the concern she felt, and the other women were picking up on it.

In one corner, Muriel, Beth, and Chia played a game they'd made up to pass the time. The tokens consisted of sawdust blended with oatmeal salvaged from their breakfasts and sculpted into rough shapes. The women cleared the sawdust from one area of the concrete floor, laying out their chosen tokens in a set pattern. Many spent hours playing games they'd created themselves. Lianndra would rather meditate, going inward for her entertainment, although sometimes she played the games when boredom overwhelmed her.

Not far from where Lianndra sat, Lacey and Michelle leaned up against one wall, discussing the things that might've caused their captors to change the routine. The women were now fit, and the delay in their daily exercise was making them jittery.

The sound of the lock disengaging on the door made many of them flinch. By the time Hulk entered the room, all seven were on their feet and in a group at the far end of the room.

Hulk's presence was itself a sign of change. They'd only seen rare glimpses of the burly man. Whatever position he held, he was high enough up the pecking order to not be involved in the daily routine of the place.

Lianndra's heart thumped so hard she was sure the others could hear it. As Hulk's gaze traveled over to her, she forced herself to raise her chin and glare back at him. He seemed to find her defiance amusing.

"Well, ladies, our time together is at an end." He gave them a grin, more a sneer than a genuine smile. "It has been a pleasure."

He walked back into the hall where Blue, Pug, Brown, and Goldie assumed positions to guide the women out of their room.

Lianndra was shaking, and she thought she noticed an answering tremble in Andrea's legs as the tall woman led the way out of the room. One by one, they followed her.

Their escorts turned them in the opposite direction to the one they traveled every day. The women passed through a reinforced door into the main body of the warehouse. The cages on each side were now empty save for one at the far end. Inside, a small group of women huddled together. Lianndra looked at them. She didn't think they had collars on, and she didn't see Cassidy, although she might be hard to recognize under the dirt. The smell was not as overpowering as the first time Lianndra was in this area, perhaps due the cleaning of the cages. She noticed the bare concrete floors were still damp as though just washed.

They moved out of the main body of the warehouse. Another heavy metal door led to a corridor which opened into a strange room. The metal walls were so shiny they could see themselves in them, and the floor revealed a series of stainless steel grates placed over a trench that spanned the room. It looked like an animal containment system designed for easy sterilization and the knot in her stomach tightened.

The men ordered them to strip, and the nervous women obeyed the familiar command. Brown gathered the garments under his arm.

The men backed out of the room.

Blue smirked before throwing them one last snide remark. "I'd say have a good time, but I'm afraid that isn't likely."

A heavy sliding door closed between the women and their captors.

They looked at each other, eyes wide with uncertainty.

Andrea spoke, obviously doing her best to reassure them. "Whatever this is about, we will survive it." she made an apparent effort to stay composed, she then continued. "They haven't kept us all this time to harm us now."

That's true. Lianndra fought to slow her pulse even as a faint hiss came from overhead. *It doesn't mean whatever they have planned will be pleasant.*

And it wasn't pleasant. Not at all. The room filled with a noxious substance that caused the women to empty first their stomachs—followed by their bowels—over and over again. Lianndra thought she would turn inside out. Soon, the emptying became nothing more than gut-wrenching contortions as they dry heaved, their bodies refusing to give up any more. Time passed. Could have been a day. Lianndra didn't know.

When completely purged, jets doused the sweaty, trembling, and filthy women with a chemical spray. Hair fell off their bodies in clumps until they were bald. The fluid noticeably changed to a detergent, applied with a high-pressure spray system so powerful it knocked them about the room. Lianndra shielded her eyes, but the viscous concoction found its way past her tightened fingers. It forced itself into every crack and crevice of her body, burning as it went. Finally, they received a hosing of what seemed like clear water, but it tasted salty. It continued until both the women and the rooms were spotless.

Lianndra's skin felt scoured raw. She was sore everywhere, inside and out. When the exit door opened, she and the others crowded into the hall beyond, eager to just get away.

Not since her capture had she been so afraid. She recognized their wretched experience as a sterilization procedure. Even with expecting something awful in their future, Lianndra hadn't expected this. She'd assumed their slavery would be sexual in context which required a certain level of attractiveness in physical form. Their captors' emphasis on physical fitness and the fact all seven of them were decent looking helped to reinforce this theory. With their skins raw, stripped of every vestige of hair and scoured clean, a more terrifying reality occurred to her.

Human experimentation.

Andrea placed a shaking hand on Lianndra's arm and she welcomed the comfort.

A voice came from a speaker overhead. "Please proceed to the room at the end of the hall." Lianndra recognized Hulk's deep tones and turned with Andrea in time to see another door farther down slide open as the one behind them slid shut.

They're moving us like they move livestock, Lianndra thought.

When the women hesitated, their collars tingled a warning. Andrea cursed, dragging Lianndra forward by the arm. The others followed. As they paced down the long corridor to the open door at the end, giant blowers blasted the last of the water from them. It left their skin flushed a fiery red.

They assembled inside another shiny room. Running along the center of the room was a waist-high metal bar.

"Stand before the bar." Hulk's voice sounded bored as if he'd done this millions of times. Perhaps he had.

Andrea suddenly snapped. She screamed obscenities and backed away from the bar. Shocked, the six other women stared at the always stoic Amazon. Hulk's disembodied voice let the outburst run until she denigrated his lineage—then he must have leaned on the collar remote. Andrea's entire body lifted off the floor in an agonized spasm before crashing back down hard.

"Enough!" Lianndra screamed at the speaker near the ceiling and grabbed the nearest woman, dragging her to the bar. "All right, we're doing it, stop!"

Andrea moaned. The other women stepped close to the bar. Lianndra supported Andrea as she stood, and walked her up to the polished metal.

Nothing happened at first. Lianndra felt the cold metal against her belly. Then there was a pulse of warmth through it. Before anyone could recoil, something invisible pinioned their wrists against the bar. Beneath their feet, the floor seemed to reach up to capture their ankles with no obvious sign of restraint.

Oh God. Lianndra closed her eyes, thinking about the blood on the floor of the exercise room. *If only I'd known. Death might have been preferable to this.*

She wondered if the collars had a lethal setting; maybe she should have supported Andrea's outburst instead of stopping it.

Was Michael already part of some sick experiment? She tried not to think of him sliced to pieces or rotting from within as a human guinea pig in a twisted third world laboratory.

The thought made her so angry adrenaline flooded her with essential strength and urged her to run, to fight—to do anything other than just stand there. Her brain argued with her body. She knew there was no escape; the best she could do was channel the adrenaline into passive defiance, striving to act as though nothing they did affected her.

I am above it all.

Lianndra wasn't the only one who flinched when the wall ahead of them slid up into the ceiling. Her eyes dropped from following its progress to a line of five naked men standing before a metal bar matching her own. With astonishment, she scanned the line, noticing the men wore familiar collars. The second on the left lifted his bald head to lock his silvery gaze with hers.

The bolt of pure energy shooting through her body as their eyes connected was unlike anything she'd ever felt. She saw the effect echoed within him. Michael straightened to his full height. He was a mess. Every bone of his skull was visible beneath his skin. A massive bruise covered the entire left side of his face, including his swollen left eye. He had a series of welts across his chest as though someone had whipped him. His smile was all Michael though, even if it was lopsided with a cut lip. Despite the injuries, Lianndra noticed new lines of muscle covering his still lanky frame. She was sure he noticed changes in her body as his eyes drifted over her.

"Liann . . ." he started.

His voice cut off as an unseen guard activated the remote. Rage enveloped her as Michael's tall form crumpled over in pain. She almost cried his name out loud but caught herself in time. Shaking with the effort of not speaking, she tried to make her eyes speak for her as Michael straightened from the collar's pulse. She saw the relief and joy in his gaze and returned it tenfold.

The smile was fleeting lest their watching captors object. Her eyes skipped over his nakedness, trying to give him a modicum of modesty as she assessed his injuries. When she met his gaze again, he shrugged ever so slightly, like a boy caught fighting. Lianndra's lips twitched; she couldn't help it. Then his face grew serious, his eyes asking questions as they roamed back and forth before returning to hers.

Sadly, she closed hers, making the tiniest shake of her head. She asked a question with her expression and saw his face cloud over in pain. She remembered the blood on the exercise room floor. Her heart clenched in denial as her eyes filled with tears.

Damn them all! She'd only known Michael's friends for an afternoon, yet she felt the pain of Cassidy and Trent's possible fates as if she'd known them for years. But Michael—Michael was alive. Ridiculous to feel hope when he was beaten, naked, and trussed up as helpless as a newborn baby. Yet something about him made her feel as if anything was possible, anything at all.

They would soon know their fate. The adrenaline rush faded, taking her anger with it. Suddenly, she was aware of her helplessness again, of the humiliation of standing naked among others. Trembling, she fought to remain calm as she saw an echo of her feelings in Michael's eyes.

Beside her, Andrea shifted closer to offer as well as receive comfort.

If only we all go together, she thought. *I think I could deal with anything if Michael was there, or even Andrea. I don't want to be alone.*

A sound drew Lianndra's attention to the other end of the room. The door closed behind two figures. One was a tall man in an orange environmental suit, his silver hair and chiseled features visible through the clear face shield. Clothed entirely in black, the other figure wore a draped fabric hanging from the wrists and forming a hood over the head. It was impossible to tell whether the figure was male or female under the cloth.

The two stepped forward, the black figure moving with slow, ponderous steps.

Old? Lianndra thought, *or disabled?*

Veterinarians were trained to interpret pain in movement since animals couldn't tell you where they hurt. She found she couldn't read this movement. Even the walking stride was odd, each step deliberate. She glanced at Michael and noticed he was frowning as he studied the dark figure. As they drew nearer, more characteristics became obvious. The figure in the dark draping was less than six feet tall and broad, with wide shoulders. The hooded head seemed large for the body and the arms were long, almost like an ape's.

Male, Lianndra decided based on the shoulder width and the strength in the frame. She squinted into the darkness framed by the loose hood, but she couldn't make out anything but deeper shadows. The figure drew near and passed by her to the far end of the line of women, guided by the man in the orange suit. As they moved past her, Lianndra caught the faintest whiff of a scent. Not unpleasant but unexpected—aftershave?

The mystery figure stopped at the last woman in the line and turned to face her. Lianndra thought she felt Muriel's trembling along the metal pipe as a gloved hand emerged from the folds of cloth. The hand was strange: there were only three fingers opposing the thumb, and the fingers seemed too thick. The tiny woman flinched as those fingers closed around her bicep before squeezing—at first a little, and then bearing down—until she cried out in pain. They released Muriel's arm to grab her jaw. The figure held on for a moment, the dark hood contemplating her features. It released her and stepped back as though he was assessing her body. But for what? It was strange. The examination seemed asexual, almost as if the hooded man was considering a horse he might buy.

Are we just livestock to him? An image of the small woman pulling a cart flashed through her brain, leaving Lianndra even more confused. *Livestock to do what? If they need us for experimentation why does individual assessment matter as long as we are healthy? One guinea pig is pretty much the same as another.*

A glance showed Michael staring at the hooded man. He was obviously as confused as she was. His shoulder muscles subtly flexed as he tested the invisible shackles.

Don't do it, she thought. *Don't be a hero. There's nothing any of us can do about this.*

He wasn't the only one who glared at the hooded man and everything he represented. She noticed the men stood straighter in their shackles despite their injuries and nakedness. It was obvious they experienced a rougher time in captivity than the women.

Lianndra wondered how strong these invisible manacles really were. *There's a lot of muscle behind that anger.*

So far, the threat of the collars kept them at bay. Michael continued to glower. His frustration was obvious.

The hooded man stepped to the next woman in line and then the next, repeating his bizarre tests with each one. Lianndra wished the lighting in the room was not so directly overhead. No matter how the dark figure moved, the light failed to expose the face within the hood. The figure finished tormenting Beth and stepped in front of Lianndra. He reached out to seize her arm.

Lianndra fought hard not to flinch, move or cry out as the fingers squeezed until she was sure he would snap the bone. She was at the point of cracking when the figure hissed and released her arm. She almost collapsed from the sudden release of pain, but it further challenged her resolve when the fingers seized her jaw.

Anger swelled within her like a wave.

The figure twitched, the head lifting as she tried to drill a hole in his face with a fiery stare. She heard a choking chortle that trailed off to a hiss. An exhalation, followed by a nod that lifted the edge of the hood.

The lights briefly illuminated the face within: dark violet-black skin mottled with gray; slits for nostrils within a small bump of a nose; an elongated jaw with thin black lips; widely spaced eyes that swirled orange and were absent of visible pupils.

Lianndra jerked her head, tearing her jaw free from the pressing fingers. Like lightning, the other hand shot out of the dark folds of the cloth to grab the other side of her jaw in a pincer grip. With a tearing sound, the fingertips of the glove gave way and claws dug into the thin skin of her jawbone. There was a stabbing pain as blood trickled down her neck and over her breast.

Dimly, she heard the solid thud of a body bouncing off metal. Michael howled as the pain surge from his collar jolted through him. Andrea made a strangled sound when she saw the claws against Lianndra's skin and the tall woman tugged at her invisible bonds.

The creature's free hand traced the path of the blood ever so gently with a fingertip down Lianndra's neck, across her collarbone, over her heart, and paused at the swell of her breast. It raised the bloody glove to its lip which parted in a sharp-toothed smile. As a purple tongue lapped the thick red fluid, Lianndra's world spun away into the realm of nightmares.

Seen from the deceptively peaceful blackness of space, the green and gold planet hung like a gleaming solitary jewel. Normally, it had two small moons in orbit. For some time now, not far beyond the planet's atmosphere, there hovered four surplus bodies. Roughly spheroid in shape, the alien artifacts—for they were clearly not natural phenomena—were massive. The dark metal of their hulls spoke of a long, violent history. These were patchwork giants, bristling with panels and beams replaced, reshaped or otherwise altered over time. Even when new, it was unlikely the ships were ever attractive. Now, the aged hulls exuded the primary characteristics of their creators: intelligence, determination, and domination.

A female descendant of those creators contemplated two of these ancient behemoths. It was rare for Motherships to remain gathered at one location for any length of time. Their presence was a clear indication of the value of the prize awaiting them on the planet below. From this portal she saw two of the vast ships. The third hovered on the other side of her fortress in space. In all, four Motherships. It was inspiring to bear witness to this event.

She was well aware the creatures who called this particular planet their home were not likely to share her sentiments about this gathering of alien power. At this very moment, the inhabitants of the planet below her fought for their freedom. The battle should have been over in the blink of an eye given her species' superior firepower and intellect.

Yet the planet, and its inhabitants, proved resilient. Protected by a sophisticated planetary shield prohibiting the use of heavy weaponry, the enemy had reduced the invasion to a foul, crawling, ground war. But the observer had faith in her people. Once they set their sights on an objective, they rarely failed.

Her species specialized in slaves. Not just acquiring them to sell, but breeding and developing them. In some cases, their geneticists worked for extended periods of time, generations even, to develop a particularly talented species. The eventual price they commanded for these slaves was well worth the extra time.

She tapped on the datapad in her hand, contemplating the list before her. The species represented by the numbers beneath her claws was just such an example. For five of these creatures' generations, her people harvested embryos, altered them, and returned them to the host mothers. The resulting Tier-5 offspring would procreate a sixth, more advanced, generation.

This war is accelerating everything and demanding resources from every level, she thought.

Not long ago, the orders came from the Chamber of Elders to harvest some of these Tier-5 humans early for use in the war effort.

It was a sacrifice as the Tier-5s were not yet finished. They required further genetic modification to fulfill their goals as slaves. The elders gambled on these individuals being far enough advanced to assist in the war.

The alien knew it was not her decision to make, just as it was not for her to question the will of the elders. It was her responsibility to see the orders carried out.

She turned to the console in front of her to send the information on to those collecting the required specimens from Earth. It was only the latest of many similar messages. As with the other requests, there would be a fast turnaround; the individuals would be quickly harvested from their home planet.

The Tier-5 males had already proved their suitability for use in the war as soldiers. The females weren't as advanced, but they could be genetically tweaked as adults until they fulfilled the desired niche. As long as they survived the mutations, the slaves would have value, and there would be no long-term loss to her people.

With the message sent, she contemplated the list of humans under her fingers. She admired versatility, and this species was a classic example of such. Capable of so much, especially with a little genetic tweaking. Intelligent, yet still at least a generation away from roaming their home galaxy. Curious, yet still unaware of their planet's role as a nursery for slaves to serve a superior species.

History dictated they would eventually catch on, as had all the other species in this situation.

When that finally happens, they will discover they are a minor creature in a vast cosmos, she thought. The awareness would change nothing. *Humans will provide us with valuable slaves for a long time to come.*

LIANNDRA'S FIRST AWARENESS WAS one of pain. Her head ached, and it hurt to open her eyes. Every muscle in her body throbbed in time to the beat of her heart.

Where am I? Lianndra felt the cold, hard surface beneath her. As her brain groped for her last relevant memory, she struggled to prop herself up on one elbow. Something buried deep inside her urged her to rise, to run away—from what? Try as she might, she couldn't remember.

Her stomach didn't care about rising or running. It demanded emptying in an immediate kind of way. A few moments later there was a small puddle of yellowish liquid, and Lianndra pushed herself away. The movement brought her up against something that grunted in annoyance.

The noise caused her to move her head too fast. For a moment, she fought with her stomach which threatened to find something else to expel all over her new acquaintance.

Not that new, it turned out. Lianndra blinked to clear her vision and Andrea's face swam into focus. The woman looked decidedly green.

"Look out." The dark woman groaned as she began to heave.

Lianndra shrank away just in time. The small but disgusting puddles now existing on each side of her provided enough incentive to push up to a sitting position.

She and Andrea weren't alone. The room was just large enough to hold the other five women who'd shared their enslavement, along with four others she did not recognize. The other women were in various stages of awakening, all except an unfamiliar woman who lay still. The immobility of her body spoke of something not living, a verdict verified when Beth reached out a hand only to snatch it back.

"She's cold," she said, sliding on her hips farther away from the body.

Lianndra was still too foggy to process the death of someone she didn't know. Blinking, she struggled to clear her eyes of a gumminess that spoke to being knocked out for an extended period. The last thing she remembered was the resulting mayhem when the creature cut her. Her mind skittered away from the memory of the repulsive alien face. Frowning, she groped in the darkness of her mind, remembering a numbness spreading from the metal bar up her hands and wrists. The loss of sensation extended up her arms to her body. As the darkness closed in around her, she caught a brief flash of Michael clutching his own metal bar, struggling to hold himself upright, his eyes locked with hers.

Michael. He was not in this room. Nor were any of the other men.

"Where the hell are we?" Andrea managed a semi-vertical pose resembling a sprawling puppy. Lianndra observed her friend's dazed, dark eyes and mussed short, black, crimpy hair.

Wait. Hair? Lianndra raised a hand to her head. She felt the softness of about a half-inch crew cut all over her scalp. *But we were bald.* Bewildered, she looked around noticing the other women featured similar crew cuts. *How fast does hair grow? For how long were we drugged?* Her eyes dropped to the body lying so still. *Was it too long for some?*

Lianndra noticed they were all still naked, which fit with the state they'd last been in after the horrible sterilization procedure.

"I wonder how long we were out of it? They must have drugged us," she said to Andrea.

The bare, featureless metal room was not one she recognized. There were two shallow indentations on opposite walls. When she squinted, she thought they might house sliding doors.

Beth stood, and Lianndra decided she'd been down for long enough. Bracing herself on Beth's proffered arm, she got to her feet, swaying before bending to help Andrea up as well.

As if in response to their movement, one of the wall indentations did indeed reveal itself as a sliding door when it soundlessly slipped upward. The doorway filled with light from without while the lights in their room dipped into almost total darkness. The invitation was obvious.

Leaning on each other for support, the women stumbled their way through.

After tentatively leaving the room in which they'd awakened, they found themselves in a narrow, lit corridor lined with multiple closed doors. The women followed the lights. The corridor behind them darkened as they passed, discouraging them from turning back. Thinking about the dead woman they left behind, Lianndra wasn't inclined to retreat.

The corridor opened into a group of rooms where food and clothing awaited them. Exhausted, the women dressed, ate, and drank before collapsing onto the beds.

There was no sign of their captors.

The last coherent thought running through Lianndra's mind before sleep claimed her was that her bed didn't seem to have any feet attaching it to the floor.

"I THINK WE WERE OUT for weeks." Andrea grimaced as she talked, rotating one shoulder followed by the other.

Her friend stretched out on a peculiar couch. Strange, in that it lacked visible legs and hovered a few inches above the polished metal floor. It emitted no sound, and the fine hairs on Lianndra's hand stood on end when she waved it underneath.

All the furniture hovered. The seats moved in response to a person's weight, and the tables adjusted their height to stay consistent with the nearest seat.

The two of them sat in a small area forming the central hub of a circle of rooms. With the exception of the foyer, the area around the hub consisted of twelve doorways opening into tiny, private quarters. Each room offered a bed, a compact lavatory, and a storage console that slid out of the wall when one passed a hand over an indent in the metal.

"I wonder when we get to meet them?" Andrea asked for what must have been the tenth time, her tone indicating impatience rather than a request for an answer.

They'd been cooped up in the circle of rooms since they'd arrived. The lights had dimmed and brightened twice which Lianndra assumed meant two days had passed. They were all clad in the yellow tunics waiting for them on the hovering beds when they first explored their quarters. Simple foods such as fruit, unleavened bread, and something resembling meat materialized at regular intervals from a square, waist-high box in the central area. A spout lower down on the device provided water with an unpleasant, slightly metallic taste. The fruits' appearance was familiar, but they didn't taste quite right. In fact, they all pretty much tasted the same. Lianndra also noticed fruit of the same type lacked any variation in shape.

They're mass-produced, somehow. Do they have a mold for apples? How do they make the skin? Are they cloned? She tried to quiet the student within.

Even after two days of waiting for something to happen, she wasn't eager to meet their captors. Memories of the dark face in the hood haunted her. *I'd rather be enslaved by some sicko, third world country drug dealer than by what I glimpsed beneath the hood*, she thought.

While she hoped they were still on Earth, everything from the hovering furniture, to the unit dispensing their food confirmed her worst fears. The very air of the place was alien. It smelled like a sterilant, although there was also an odd odor, one she remembered all too well from her brief brush with the alien.

"Not talking much, huh?" Andrea sat up on the couch, swinging her legs over the edge. She grabbed Lianndra's arm to pull her down beside her. Underneath them, the couch sank before returning to its previous hovering level.

Lianndra let her head drop back against her friend's arm to stare up. The perforated metal ceiling above contained dark, discoid shapes she could see through the holes. Their purpose was a total mystery. She shuddered, her thoughts veering away from the obvious—*alien*.

Her body still ached, but the last two days permitted her to regain some of her strength. Stretching her arms out in front of her,

Lianndra sighed. "I don't know what to say. You saw him too. If that thing is what owns us now, heaven help us."

Andrea grunted. "Well, we can't sit here forever. At least I doubt they've gone to so much trouble just to eat us."

"Maybe we're in a weird zoo." said Muriel. She walked up behind them to lean on the back of the couch, making it bob down and then back up.

A zoo? Lianndra supposed it made as much sense as anything else. Before she could contemplate that any further, the entrance door to their circle of rooms suddenly opened, making them all jump.

If Lianndra hadn't been seated, she would have retreated to the far side of the room. She relaxed a little when she saw the two creatures entering were human females. They seemed to be in their late forties, trim and fit, with grim expressions on their faces. Lianndra noted that even though the women exuded the air of someone in charge, they each wore collars identical to her own.

The taller of the two examined them as the door slid shut. Her face was heavily lined in a permanent frown, perhaps revealing a life without joy. Her dark hair was graying at the temples.

"My name is Marnie," the woman said. "I am one of the ward supervisors on this ship. This is Kath. She is also a ward supervisor. I am here to welcome you to your new life on the Fang Mothership *Gi%ndia*."

No one spoke. Glancing around, Lianndra noticed ten pairs of eyes staring at the women in astonishment. Kath seemed to examine each of them from the inside out, staring at them one at a time. Marnie also watched them after her opening salvo, noticing where each stood in the room as if assessing them.

Andrea was the first to give way to her impatience. "Nice to meet you, Marnie. I have a few questions, like, what is a ward supervisor?"

"And what the heck is a Fang Mothership?" Lianndra surprised herself by speaking. Even though the dour women intimidated her, it seemed the part of her wanting answers was not going to wait for them.

Marnie's eyes flared for a moment. "Your ward supervisor is the one who organizes your sorry asses. These quarters are temporary. You will all be assigned to permanent quarters under the supervision of either Kath or me. As your ward supervisors, we call all the shots for your new lives, including where you live, what you eat, when you train. You will listen and obey."

They paused again. Out of the corner of her eye, Lianndra saw Andrea roll her eyes. She knew the woman was not easily intimidated. "All right, I have to know: or what?" Andrea asked.

Kath grinned. Lianndra thought she'd never seen a less cheerful sight. "For many reasons, the one-year survival rate for new recruits is less than thirty percent. One cause of death is a lack of obedience."

Andrea frowned but didn't respond. She looked thoughtful. Lianndra's heart accelerated. *Thirty percent is pretty low.*

One of the other women asked with a slight tremor to her voice, "What exactly have we been recruited for?"

Instead of answering, Marnie stepped forward to place a small round object on the table in front of them. She pressed something on the side and an image materialized above it.

Lianndra pressed herself deeper into the couch cushions. She didn't have to look at Andrea to know she was tensing up too.

The alien towered over them, only the faintest of flickers betraying it as a holographic image. Lianndra felt a shiver pass through her as she gazed upon the nightmarish image for the second time. The holograph made it impossible to judge the creature's real size. The leathery skin was lighter than Lianndra remembered; more lilac than violet-black. The huge eyes were more orange than red, and the broad, elongated jaws beneath the nostrils seemed narrower. The creature's head was hairless, with large scales coming to thick points.

"The purpose of this recording is to orient new arrivals to their lives on the Tlo%m Motherships." The voice was raspy with some slurring of the consonants, but it was English, and Lianndra could understand the alien. She was also surprised the voice sounded female. Squinting at the image, she saw how the thin skin around the pointed teeth puckered and the tongue contorted as it spoke. The human language was obviously not easy for the alien to speak.

"I am a Tlo%m." The word was almost indecipherable, with double glottal stops obscuring the pronunciation. "I am female or Fara. The males of my species are known as Farr." The image changed to show a male.

Lianndra instantly recognized the darker skin, broader body, and blockier face. Whereas the female had an obvious neck, the male's head flowed via bulky muscles into his massive shoulders. She noticed the hands of both sexes consisted of three thick fingers and a stubby opposable thumb, all terminating in hooked claws.

When the image changed back to the Fara, she continued her speech in her hoarse voice. "You have joined the large population of slaves now calling this ship their home. The Tlo%m collect many species as slaves. We sell most acquisitions to other markets; we breed and genetically alter some to suit specialized purposes. Female slaves of your species, however, are to fulfill a specific task aboard this Mothership. We will train you to perform for our Farr in a competition. Only the best of you will be successful in this endeavor."

The image changed to pan across the expanse of a large room outfitted with platforms suspended in midair. A woman swung between platforms from a cable. A bulky form moving deceptively fast intercepted her, dropping down from above on its own cable.

It was a male—a Farr—and as they watched, the woman vaulted clear over him, landing on a platform above his head. Her leap was astonishing and impossibly high, but the alien moved just as deftly after her. What followed was a series of incredible acrobatic feats by the human, mirrored by some impressive gymnastics on the part of the alien.

"I introduce you," the female's raspy voice said, "to the Blooddance."

BLOODDANCER LIANNDRA SWUNG DOWN TO the platform floor, reeling in the skrin attached to her wrist as she did. She was only stationary for a few moments before calling on the full length of her skrin to snatch a spar far above her and reel her to the next platform.

The skrin would respond to Lianndra's every command. The device looked like a bulky metal cuff encircling her wrist, extending across the back of her hand to her thumb. It contained sensors that responded to nerve signals, extending a whiplike coil acting much like a prehensile tail. It was necessary for navigation of the ever-changing landscape existing around her.

The room was large, the span of its width doubled by the height. The dimensions gave it a palatial quality equaled only by the ancient cathedrals back on Earth. It was lit so even the furthest corners received illumination. Hovering platforms of various sizes and shapes occupied the entire space. They linked to each other as well as to the roof or floor by long narrow vertical spars. Some of the spars were lit from within or outlined completely in light.

Humans named it the Coliseum, after the famous sports arenas of ancient times on Earth. There were only two means of access to it: one door on each opposing wall. One was for the slave to enter, and if all went well, exit. The Fang used the other.

The Coliseum was the home of the Blooddance.

Lianndra was familiarizing herself with the layout in the few seconds granted to her before the Blooddance began. With the skill acquired through experience, she cataloged the location of the platforms and spars with a single, sweeping glance. She would need every advantage available to her against her opponent.

With a blast of noise counting as alien music, her Fang opponent appeared from one of the doorways.

Lianndra recognized the Fang; the human derivative of his name was Tarsk. Like humans, the Fang were bipedal; it was the only real similarity between the two species. Much of Tarsk's muscled bulk wore armor made of interwoven metal, leaving only his head and hands exposed. Like most Fang males, he was less than six feet in height but twice as broad as a human. His limbs were wide in girth while his neck was almost nonexistent, with big shoulder muscles flowing up into his jaw. The points of his teeth showed through the thin-skinned lips.

Like many of the males of his species, Tarsk was as ill-tempered as he was powerful, but as he'd a particular weakness for human females with pale coloring, she could use it to distract him during the Blooddance.

Blooddance, the humans called it. It was a good name. Half-fight, half-dance—it was all brutal. The goal of the Fang was blood; the aim of the human was to survive. The longest Blooddance recorded was seven hours, and it resulted in the death of the human. Many other humans died in Blooddances a fraction as long.

In the eight months since her enslavement by the Fang, Lianndra had developed a reputation as an accomplished Dancer. Luck as much as anything else, she knew.

She crouched on her platform. Tarsk's almost pupilless eyes locked with hers, their orange hue swirling with hints of deep red.

Tarsk bared some of the sharp teeth that earned his species the human nickname: Fang. Their real species name, the Tlo%m, contained queer double glottal stops almost unpronounceable by humans. The Fang language was also difficult. In the time Lianndra had Danced for them, she'd only been able to pick up a few words; most were profane.

The better I Dance, the more they swear, she thought.

Lianndra drew on the strength of her experience to force an inner calm as she focused on Tarsk. She stared down at him and Tarsk grinned, pulling his lips back from his short, sharp incisors. It wasn't those teeth he would ultimately use on her. The feeding fangs—three long, wicked, piercing teeth—would descend from his gums once he had her in his grasp. In one three-fingered, taloned hand he held the only accessory allowed in the Blooddance: his skrin. He unfurled it in one smooth flick of his thick wrist, sending it soaring to the spar above her.

The Blooddance was on.

Blooddance was an accurate description. The Dancers trained to perform athletic leaps, twists, and spins in midair assisted by the skrins attached to their wrists. Although heavily muscled, the Fang were able to move with balance and grace through the air. Humans owned one advantage; the gravity in the ring was less than Earth's. The humans trained using the equivalent of their home planet's gravity in the slave quarters. When they moved to the Coliseum, they could perform with a swiftness that challenged the Fang. Without this advantage, the humans would be easy prey.

Half an hour in, Lianndra was sweating in the hot and dry Fang atmosphere. She spun into the air, releasing her skrin midway to seize another spar. Tarsk seemed committed to swinging to a platform above her, but he unexpectedly released his skrin to plummet toward her. She saw him coming, desperately twisting her torso away from him. His talons still managed to rake her shoulder, drawing first blood.

Tarsk landed with a heavy thud on the floor, a move that would have likely broken human bones but didn't faze the Fang in the slightest. Lianndra, panting in pain, finished her swing to an overhead spar. She felt the blood flowing down her back. She gritted her teeth and kept moving, flinging herself to yet another spar as Tarsk pressed his advantage by coming after her.

Dammit, that's an early tag. Lianndra clenched her jaw before swinging away.

The Farr's claws whistled through the air just past her right thigh. As Fang males went, Tarsk was an able warrior, although in their previous matches she went over an hour before he tagged her. *Lucky shot on his part, or apathy on mine?* She didn't have time to ponder the issue. Tarsk's eyes reddened with bloodlust as he performed a swift change in direction to come at her from below, releasing his skrin in mid-swing.

Once there was the release of human blood, however minor, the Blooddance was usually due to end. Few Fang could resist the scent of human blood for long. Even as Lianndra contorted her body to miss his lethal talons, she saw him clench the fist of his free hand, activating the captive mode.

In response, her skrin turned against her, releasing its hold on the spar above to whip itself around her body, binding her facedown to the nearest narrow platform. Blood dripped from her shoulder. Her body tensed as the platform shuddered under Tarsk's weight. The watching crowd of male Fang began to chant to a primitive beat not so different from the drumbeats of ancient music back on Earth.

He dropped to all fours behind her, climbing up her prone body. Lianndra suppressed a shudder and closed her eyes. No matter how many times she went through this, she could not get used to it. *I suppose the day I get used to it will be the day I no longer care. Then I'm as good as dead.*

Tarsk did not lie down on her since his greater weight would have crushed her. He hovered on all fours just above her, letting his body touch hers. His heavy breathing tugged at her hair, and she winced at the rancid smell. A long, dark violaceous tongue snaked out of his mouth to lap at the blood dripping from her shoulder. This time, Lianndra shuddered. The feel of his hot tongue was repulsive and as it moved up the blood trail to the raked wounds on her shoulder, the revulsion turned to pain.

At this point in the Blooddance, Lianndra used her knowledge of Fang profanity, mentally cursing the Fang licking the blood from her body. She then cursed Fang in general. She particularly cursed the Fang culture which created the Blooddance as a means of keeping their males entertained while the females engaged in more intellectual pursuits.

Tarsk gave a low moan before pushing himself off her. The chanting changed to cheering as he straightened and used his skrin to lower himself to the floor. He shook his fists in the air. The crowd roared.

Lianndra regained control over her skrin once the Fang left the Coliseum. In pain and trembling with rage, Lianndra used it to drop down before exiting the arena through a different door than Tarsk. As always, emotions flooded her. All the Blooddances ended this way, but she could not get used to the feelings of anger and violation. She always left the Coliseum wishing she could kill all the Fang, the entire Mothership full of them.

She knew it was a pipe dream. It was a sad fact no Farr had ever been killed by a Dancer, and a Dancer couldn't escape the gory ritual. Some women even killed themselves rather than continue with the Blooddances. Lianndra's only solace was to extend each Blooddance as long as possible, making the Fang work for their blood.

The Coliseum exit led to a small cube of a room, its smooth walls blemished only with a single vertical bar suspended from the ceiling. The bar sprouted a handgrip, and at her touch, the cube moved. It whisked her through the guts of the enormous ship to the human slave quarters.

Her shoulder ached. *I've had worse, but I should get Tania to fix me up before I crash.*

Lianndra headed for the medical bay which was close to where the transit cube always dropped Dancers. Sometimes the medtechs met her at the cube if the Blooddance was bad enough. The Dancers carried from the Coliseum rarely made it to the medics. Their bodies vanished as though they'd never existed. There were no human funerals on the Motherships.

Tania greeted her with a gentle smile and a shake of her head when she saw the blood on her shoulder. "Not too bad this time, hmm?" The medtech tended to talk at her patients regardless of whether they participated, but Lianndra liked her. Tania's gray hair and wrinkles were rare in the slave quarters where the majority of the women were under thirty-five. She was one of the few women here whose expertise deemed her valuable as something other than a Dancer.

Lianndra sat herself down on the med table, grimacing as Tania cut the remnants of her tunic away from the slashes across her shoulder.

Tania placed her bare arm along a bizarre device hanging from a bracket on the wall. It was the length of a human forearm, flattened and curved to fit with a nozzle-like point on one end. As soon as the medic's arm made contact, it molded to her forearm as though it were a part of her.

"Hold on," Tania said as a small cone with a fine tip extended from the pointed end of the device. She began to trace Lianndra's wounds with the tip as a green beam reached out to stitch the wounds together.

Lianndra's fingernails dug into the soft surface of the table as the technology sealed her wounds. It was always painful as the abused nerves, muscles, and skin repaired. She'd passed out more than once when healing more serious injuries. Without this technology, the women would have to go days, weeks, or months between Blooddances. The apparatus healed the wounds but could not erase the stress of the injury or the blood loss. A few bad injuries, compounded by the strenuous workouts of the Blooddances, often led to the demise of a Dancer.

It seemed like forever before Tania disengaged the healtech to lay it on the shelf behind her.

"Thanks, Tania. Easy one today."

Tania sniffed. "Wish they were all like this one." She picked something up off the counter and approached Lianndra.

"Blood work? Again?"

The medtech shrugged. "Orders. They want blood more often. No idea why." She drew the sample and waved Lianndra on her way. "Off you go. Stay out of trouble."

Lianndra smiled before heading off down the corridor. *I'm hungry as a horse. Time to refuel.*

EVERY LEVEL OF THE MASSIVE Tlo%m Motherships performed a different function. Above the slave quarters was an entire level dedicated to the genetic manipulation laboratories. Within one of these labs, a purple-skinned alien hunched over the console on her desk, the leathery lips of her long snout curled in concentration. Heavy footsteps from behind alerted her to the approach of another, older Fara.

Xoe%san%krin turned as her superior approached and called her name. The older Fara was frowning at her datapad. It was unusual to see her superior frown, and Xoe%san%krin felt a stab of unease.

"We have just received new orders from the elders concerning the next wave of Tier-5 subjects." The forehead of the older female furrowed in concern. "The war coordinator has requested an increased level of genetic manipulation for the new slaves."

Xoe%san%krin experienced a flush of anger. *More unwelcome meddling with my Tier-5 program.* By tradition, the manipulation lab dedicated itself to last-minute tweaking of subpar slave species: those fast-tracked through the system. *Not for the Tier-5s, who represent five generations of human selection and careful genetic manipulation.*

Having the offspring of their genetically enhanced subjects born and raised on their home planet allowed the enhancements to develop in a natural manner. It often took a long time to develop an altered species as diverse and valuable as the humans. They represented a significant investment of time in their development.

Now, they were risking these valued individuals by speeding up the mutation process, altering their adult genes in the manipulation lab. The lab techs could generate individuals much faster by manipulating adult genes to achieve immediate results. The elders had already dictated the Tier-5 human females be harvested ahead of schedule and put through the trials of the Blooddance. The most suitable of the subjects were sent for further genetic modification, attempting to create a slave that ordinarily would have taken another two to three generations of breeding to produce. Such rapid modification was always dangerous for the subject; there was an acceptable loss ratio built into the lab's statistics.

Xoe%san%krin already disagreed with the decisions the elders made for the Tier-5s. *One war does not justify jeopardizing generations of hard work. Now the elders, no doubt speaking for the war coordinator, want even more modifications done to the current round of Tier-5 human subjects.*

It was not just a question of reducing the value of the end products. What concerned Xoe%san%krin was the casual discarding of protocol.

Protocol exists for a reason, she thought.

Genetic meddling on such a large scale and in a tight time frame could backfire, producing undesirable results. The slaves created could be useless, resulting in the entire human generational project being scrapped altogether. The loss of time, effort, and currency could be substantial.

She opened her mouth to object but then recognized this was not the platform from which to do so. Her Tlo%m superior was already turning away, tapping on her datapad, making the necessary scheduling adjustments. Her superior's forehead was still furrowed. Xoe%san%krin knew the older female would not go against orders from the Chamber of Elders even if those orders went against current protocols.

Have the implications of this decision been foreseen by minds greater than hers? she wondered. *Foreseen and approved? Who is making these decisions?*

Xoe%san%krin had many hours of frustrating work to go before she would be able to make contact with someone who might have the answers she sought.

She dutifully turned back to her console to call up the lists of the Tier-5 slaves now scheduled to receive the enhancement serums, the preliminary process for the genetic manipulation. Hasty actions could lead to mistakes.

Perhaps—she felt the first stirrings of hope—*there is an opportunity in this for my new friends.*

THE LARGE ROOM THE BLOODDANCE slaves called the mess hall was not busy today. Lianndra made a selection at the serving counter before perusing those present, searching for a familiar face. Over time, there were fewer slaves she could actually call friends. The realities of Dancing meant slaves died or disappeared all the time.

The Dancers tended to socially arrange themselves based on characteristics they had in common. Lianndra knew everyone needed something familiar to cling to. She'd always been somewhat of a loner so tended to have few friends. Her time as a Dancer whittled her close friends down to one: Andrea.

Lianndra spotted someone who was obviously a new arrival, known by the more experienced Dancers as a newbie. The young woman sat alone at a table, her hair in disarray, eyes huge and frightened, not touching the food in front of her.

Lianndra didn't feel up to a newbie initiation speech today. She spotted an empty chair well away from the girl, but her conscience interfered. Lianndra knew she'd been fortunate to enter her enslavement in a group, enabling them to figure out their new life together. This poor girl looked all alone. With a sigh, Lianndra braced herself before redirecting her steps to the seat across from the newbie. The orientation speech the Fang provided for new arrivals was lacking in information. It was a description of what the Fang expected from the slave, rather than a proper introduction to their new life.

The dark-haired girl didn't look up as Lianndra placed her tray on the table and sat down. It turned out her name was Stacey, although it took Lianndra a while to get it out of her.

"Did you come in alone?" Lianndra asked.

If anything, the girl turned even paler. "There were five of us. When I woke up on the ship, the others were dead." Her eyes never left the table as she spoke.

Wow, Lianndra thought. It was normal to lose a few slaves in transit. The drugs the Fang used were pretty potent. *But to lose so many?* "I'm sorry," she said.

The girl didn't reply.

Lianndra stared down at the top of Stacey's head. After a few moments of silence, she steeled herself and spoke. "Look, I hate being a hardass, but the truth of the matter is, you either develop a backbone and start looking after yourself, or you are going to die."

The girl looked at her, her eyes huge and terrified.

Lianndra sighed. "I don't mean to be cruel. It's the simple truth. I want you to listen to what I'm going to tell you. It'll help you understand your situation. Coping with it will be up to you."

Stacey gulped but held her gaze with Lianndra's which was a hopeful sign.

"All right," Lianndra began, putting her eating utensil down. *So much for a warm meal.* "The humans call these aliens Fang. Their real species name is one most of us humans can't pronounce: Tlo%m." Her tongue staggered through the name, getting tangled in the glottal stop in the middle. "Fang do not have a home planet. It was destroyed long ago in some nasty civil conflict. As a result, they live in these massive vessels they call Motherships. We are in the belly of one now."

Lianndra gestured around her. "The slave quarters are in the lower third of the ship. The Fang have a segregated culture. Males, known as Farr, live a life separate from the females, who are called Fara. Fara are the brains of the outfit— the technicians—the professional experts of the species. Fara rarely visit the lower levels; they live in the upper levels of these ships. They are taller than the males, not as heavily built, and paler in color."

Lianndra knew she had Stacey's full attention now. Ignoring the dark-haired girl's wide stare, Lianndra paused to take a bite of her meal then continued while chewing. "The middle levels contain the Farr's quarters. The Farr are the muscle of the species. Born wicked fighters, they spend most of their growth years engaged in mock battles until they reach maturity when they become part of a vicious fighting force." She took another bite of food. "The two sexes rarely mix. Fang don't use sex to procreate, but rather raise their embryos in incubators."

"The Fang are slavers. They are almost always engaged in war with other alien species, which gives many of the males some outlet for their hormone-induced aggression. Attack, conquer, enslave, move on, seems a typical Fang pattern. Lucky for us, most of the Farr go off to these acquisition wars. We believe they send the male human captives there as well." When she looked at Stacey, the girl's eyes were liquid with tears. Lianndra wondered if she knew any male captives.

Lianndra took a deep breath before continuing. "Fang seem to collect species the way humans collect paraphernalia. I've lost track of the number of alien species I've seen as Fang captives. They seem to reserve the human females for their entertainment." She took a swig of the juice. Stacey returned to staring at the table. Feeling frustrated, Lianndra continued. "The Farr come in from the war in shifts. While on leave, many seek to be entertained and to prove themselves in staged fights. Other than fighting among themselves, their only source of entertainment are the human slave fights or the Blooddance."

Stacey looked up again. Lianndra knew the holographic orientation talked about the human female's role in the Blooddance even if it hadn't explained it.

"Humans seem to occupy a special place in the captive hierarchy for Fang," Lianndra said. "Fang pull humans from Earth in comparative secret without announcing their presence. They treat it as a giant human slave nursery."

Lianndra had no idea how many humans the Fang had enslaved over time; she only knew new slaves came in on a steady basis. Lately, it seemed the influx was increasing. "We see very few human men on the Motherships. Only human females are housed in this slave enclave. But the women all talk of men being taken, so they are likely being used on the front lines of the latest war." As usual, talking of this led to thoughts of Michael. She swallowed a mouthful that suddenly tasted sour. "As you may have guessed, Fang are predators, but enslaving human females is not about food." Lianndra pushed her plate away. As usual, when she thought too hard about the Dance, she abruptly lost her appetite. "They use us in the Blooddance. With the Blooddance, it's about blood. Human female blood seems to trigger a physical release in the Farr. Most slaves liken it to sex for Farr, but it's more likely a way to bleed off the violent energy in the resident Farr population. Otherwise they are so aggressive they might start fights with each other. Not a good thing within the confines of a ship, even one the size of this."

Lianndra tapped Stacey on her arm, willing her to focus. "Although the Fang always win, your goal is to extend the Blooddance for as long as possible. Longer Blooddances burn off the Farr's vicious energy and decrease the brutality of the eventual end. Short ones often end with dead humans. The more skilled the Dancer, the longer the Blooddance. The incentive for becoming skilled is effective as well as brutal—inferior Dancers don't live long. They either die during the Blooddance, or they're taken to the group Blooddances in the private Farr residences. No human slave has ever returned from a private residence summons."

Stacey had already been pale; now she was white.

If the girl can't handle being told this stuff, she's never going to survive it. "Some Dancers are more popular with the Fang than others. The more popular the Dancer, the more they participate. On average, a Dancer is lucky to last for a few years before exhaustion or injuries decrease their success. Many Dancers die while Dancing, and some die in the private group Blooddances. Sometimes even good Dancers in their prime just vanish without an explanation and are never heard from again. We think those get sent somewhere else, maybe to the war."

Stacey was silent until now. Finally, the girl said, "What do I do? I'm only nineteen. I don't want to die. But I don't know if I can do this Dancing thing."

Lianndra stood, picking up her half-filled tray. "I know it's a lot to take in. I'll try to help you, if you're ready to help yourself. Meet me tomorrow morning in the training hall at the third bell. Ask your ward supervisor. She'll give you directions. My name is Lianndra; she'll know me."

She felt the girl's frightened eyes on her back as she walked away. *I've done what I can. The rest is up to her.* The grim truth was the washout rate among the new Dancer population was high. It wasn't lack of skill, but lack of ability to control their fear. *Little did I know that my ability to think clearly during my shark attack would prove such a useful trait.*

Her Bodega Bay memories led to thoughts of being rescued from the shark, riding the chestnut mare on the beach, and—Michael. Giving herself a mental shake, she grabbed a biscuit off her tray before throwing the rest in the compactor. She'd be hungry later. *Might as well save myself another trip to the mess hall.*

IN A CORRIDOR ON A level far above the slaves' mess hall, a Tlo%m Fara paused in the shadow of an overhead beam.

Ewt%mit%fnsk could remember a time when there'd been so many lights in the corridors that shadows did not exist. The latest war had gone on too long, drained many resources, with power cells being one of them. Now the corridors contained shadows.

Just like my thoughts, she mused.

Skulking around like this would have been inconceivable a short time ago. The Fara were proud of their open communication strategies. All voices heard. All voices heeded. This was no longer the case. Ewt%mit%fnsk acknowledged it had not been the case for some time. It was now apparent a few powerful Fara were making decisions for the many. The resources required for the long war revealed her species was under strain in more ways than one.

Ewt%mit%fnsk's awareness of the subterfuge came to her with startling clarity at the last Conglomeration of Ancients. Each Mothership possessed a Chamber of Elders which was responsible for all major decisions on their given ship. They held court regularly so all voices could be heard. Less frequently, the elders from all the gathered Motherships meet as a conglomeration; some were present in person, others as holoimages sent from the other ships farther afield. This system had worked efficiently for many generations.

Sitting in the audience seats of the chamber room, Ewt%mit%fnsk remembered noticing how the rank of elders had recently changed. At one time, the years of experience required to accumulate wisdom would be evident in the clear signs of aging, like blackened, dull and sagging skin, as well as yellow-tinged eyes. Now the elders' ranks glowed with younger members of her species, their skin still flushed with the violets of midlife. She thought it strange she hadn't noticed the changes until now.

The voice being heard at this moment by the Conglomerate of Ancients was Tj%rog%merk, the Fara Superior for Ewt%mit%fnsk's area of expertise. She'd risen to power quite fast. The red blush on her dark skin was vibrant as she stepped before the elders.

Ewt%mit%fnsk knew Tj%rog%merk had collected relevant opinions and data before reporting to the elders. Many of the Fara, including Ewt%mit%fnsk, felt it was time to concede the latest war. They'd passed on these views to Tj%rog%merk.

By ordinary Tlo%m standards, this war was continuing for far too long. It was not unheard of for the Tlo%m to concede defeat and move on if the opponent proved strong or losses were higher than acceptable. It was one of the reasons her species was so successful at plundering the numerous colonies and worlds of the galaxies. For some reason, the elders were pushing the envelope with this war. They were refusing to back down even when forced to engage in a costly, extended battle relying on foot soldiers rather than technology.

Ewt%mit%fnsk stood with her sisters at the latest Conglomeration of Ancients, listening to Tj%rog%merk present to the elders. What emerged from her superior sounded, on the surface, to be what Ewt%mit%fnsk and her sisters discussed. As Ewt%mit%fnsk listened more closely, she realized the information was being subtly manipulated with an overlying message: No concessions. We will pull together to win this war.

Ewt%mit%fnsk still remembered her shock. She'd glanced around at the Fara sitting in the gallery around her. Some sat with glazed eyes like they were hardly listening. Others appeared as though they were listening, but were they? Faith in the system was part of being raised a Fara. The elders would hear the superiors from each area of expertise before they retired to discuss and come to a consensus among themselves. Those discussions were privy to the elders only. The decisions made were final. They were universally accepted among the Fara population as the result of the accumulated wisdom of many generations.

Wisdom based on faulty information, Ewt%mit%fnsk thought.

Within the Tlo%m species, it was the job of the Fara elders to set policy and make the important decisions about the war. The Tlo%m breeding program, which relied on genetic manipulation, generated new Fara capable of making cool, rational decisions about every aspect of Tlo%m life.

Lately, the Chamber of Elders kept the leaders hopping, sending them back to the techs with requests for information and resources, most of which assisted in the current war. Many of the various areas of expertise were feeling the pinch as their dwindling supplies were redirected to the prolonged war effort. The technicians sent progress reports back up the chain; they wanted the elders to know the ramifications of an ailing war.

Ewt%mit%fnsk sighed. In retrospect, she acknowledged the Tlo%m breeding program should have been the first clue all was not well with her people. Physical sex within her species stopped long ago, well before the destruction of their home world in a civil war. All Tlo%m were now born from artificial incubators, although the occasional male was still sacrificed to provide fresh genetic material. In the primitive days, on their dry, sandy home planet, the mated female would have devoured choice parts of him. The resultant surge of nutrition went into egg production.

In modern times, nutrition was artificially provided and the temperature of the incubators altered over the course of the egg's development to dictate the sex of the offspring. Until recent times this worked without any issues.

Artificially controlling reproduction proved an important step in the intellectual advancement of the Tlo%m species. Fara of specific genetic lines were born to predesignated areas of expertise. Thus, young Fara followed in their familial footsteps. Newly generated individuals refreshed positions within the structure by moving older Fara up the responsibility chain until they could join the Chamber of Elders. As the aging Fara retired, a new one supplemented her familial line.

There were several areas of expertise, and several family lines, each referred to as a cluster. The Tlo%m control over the artificial reproduction of new Fara was so fine-tuned, they could forecast when new members would be needed for each cluster and arrange for their creation. Yet the success of the artificial reproduction process had regressed. The first sign of trouble was the artificially generated males attaining smaller size and reduced mental abilities. As they were investigating this problem, a more alarming trend surfaced: an increase in the number of deaths among the Fara embryos. The lab techs were working overtime with little progress made toward a solution.

To make matters worse, it was soon discovered the Fara embryos were dying in a disproportionate fashion. Certain family lines were experiencing greater embryonic losses than others. Without familial replacements, a number of middle-aged Fara held influential positions for a long period of time. Ewt%mit%fnsk now recognized this imbalance was resulting in concentrations of solitary power where it never existed before.

Yet why would these Fara spin the data to favor the war? Ewt%mit%fnsk needed more information. She couldn't understand what they hoped to gain by promoting the war's continuance.

Working for personal gain should have been unnatural for any Fara. Since the earliest times, they'd been selected to perform for the good of the species.

She wondered if a genetic quirk was allowing some Fara to take advantage of a complacent population. *Perhaps smaller Farr and dead Fara embryos were not the only problems within the breeding program?*

Ewt%mit%fnsk's area of responsibility was the maintenance of wards. Her family line looked after the slave quarters in every aspect:

feeding, cleaning, accommodations, training, and medical care. Her personal responsibility was to coordinate with the laboratory technicians overseeing routine medical testing done on the slaves. During such collaborations Ewt%mit%fnsk had befriended one of the lab technicians in the testing area. They sometimes met to share a meal. She'd never, before now, visited her friend's private quarters.

Now, as she paused in the shadows, Ewt%mit%fnsk felt another pang of uneasiness. Technically, she had no reason to skulk in the shadows, but she felt uncomfortable entering the laboratory area's hub. Although nothing outlawed meeting privately, visiting between members of different areas was most often done in the public locales. Her friend seemed a little puzzled as to why Ewt%mit%fnsk couldn't wait until their next scheduled meal date, but she didn't hesitate when Ewt%mit%fnsk requested a meeting in her personal quarters.

Straightening her broad shoulders, Ewt%mit%fnsk stepped out of the shadows and into the light.

"THAT WAS THE LAST EMPTY room." Andrea sat in the lotus position on Lianndra's only chair. She stared out the open doorway as the ward supervisor escorted yet another disoriented newbie to their permanent quarters on the ship.

I don't know how she gets those legs folded onto the chair. Lianndra admired her friend's casual pose. *I can barely squeeze my butt in there.* Even as fit as she was, her form still contained curves that Andrea's body would never see.

Lianndra returned her attention to the central foyer. The space within the slave area was split up into the familiar wards plus communal areas for meals, Blooddance training—derisively called recitals—and exercising. The Fang permitted women to indulge in hobbies as long as they were not disruptive. Many of the possibilities on Earth were available here.

Happy critters perform better, Lianndra thought.

Andrea stared at her, and Lianndra realized she'd not yet answered her question. "Uh, yeah. I think ours is full up now."

The taller woman frowned before unlocking her legs to let her feet drop to the floor. "They're packing us in like sardines. I wonder what's going on?"

"I asked Marnie, and she was her usual communicative self—in other words, I learned nothing." A ward consisted of twelve rooms arranged in a circle with a central foyer. Like all the ward supervisors, Marnie was the rarest of creatures: an old Dancer. She was a taciturn sort. Lianndra always found it hard to get any useful information out of her.

Andrea's ward was a short distance away from Lianndra's and possessed a more talkative supervisor, one who liked to gossip. Andrea listed the ward supervisors, given in reverse order of the grapevine.

"Kath mentioned that Judy overheard Trixie and Lesa talking about the Fang failing in their war efforts," Andrea said.

Lianndra followed the line of names and gossip. "Trix has been here forever. If anyone has an ear on what's going on, it would be her." She waved a hand toward the door. "How they will train these women is beyond me. It's difficult enough now to get prep time."

"Well, I'm hoping it leads to less time Dancing." Andrea reached for her drink and finished it in one gulp. "I wouldn't mind a break in routine. Last week I did two, which is crazy."

Lianndra nodded. Considering how many newbies had arrived in the last few months, the experienced Dancers had a brutal schedule. Slaves were disappearing—far more than were accounted for by the dreaded private parties. *Gone to the war?* They'd always assumed the men went to the front lines, but if the war was going poorly, perhaps they were taking women there as well. Her stomach tightened. The Blooddances were bad enough. But fighting an alien war? *Was that what happened to Michael?*

She knew of another possibility for Michael. While the women slaves participated in the Blooddances, men and captured aliens competed in brutal fights in a place referred to as the Pit. Lianndra watched the Pitfights faithfully every night. So far, she'd not seen Michael.

Is he already dead? she wondered.

Lianndra clamped down hard on her thoughts. She had to believe he was alive, even though she would likely never know. After all this time she still hoped for a way out of this place. As irrational as it may be, Michael's memory was linked to that hope.

And what if the Fang don't win this war?

Lianndra never voiced the last question out loud. The front lines of the war were on a planet called Tarin, a short distance from where the Motherships sat like great bloated fortresses in space. If the Fang were losing, it was possible the war might be brought to the ship itself. They could die without ever leaving the bowels of this cursed Mothership.

Or leave one prison for another, Lianndra thought with a shudder. The Fang were at least a known evil. The aliens in the Pitfights seemed pretty nasty. *Of course, you can't expect to see their softer side when they are fighting for their lives.*

She sighed before stretching out on her bed, adjusting her head position so the collar didn't dig into her neck. Beside her on the chair, Andrea resumed her lotus position and meditated. Lianndra's thoughts continued to turn down darker paths and meditating on them would not bring her any peace.

EWT%MIT%FNSK COULD READ THE CURIOSITY in Xoe%san%krin's face as the latter triggered the door release. She tried to appear casual as she greeted the laboratory technician, but she knew her skin was involuntarily adopting the pale red tint indicating tension. Genetically advanced they might be, but her people still had not conquered the tiny color enhancing pores covering the skin.

Subterfuge is not considered a Tlo%m trait, she thought.

The technician's quarters were even more austere than Ewt%mit%fnsk's own. Xoe%san%krin's cluster was one of those most affected by the Fara embryo deaths. Each technician worked double shifts to keep up with the demands the war put on them. Xoe%san%krin likely spent little time in her quarters.

Ewt%mit%fnsk helped herself to a seat hovering in the central area of the tech's quarters and accepted the drink her friend offered. Uncertain how to best broach this sensitive topic, she decided to first tread on more familiar ground. She began with a work-related issue: the slaves in the multigenerational genetic enhancement project, now headed for the manipulation lab.

"I have authorized the preliminary genetic manipulation of the human female Tier-5s as requested," Ewt%mit%fnsk said. "We injected the first of them with the serum this cycle. I expect we will see results soon. Do you have space to accommodate them in the manipulation lab?"

Polite by nature, Xoe%san%krin didn't reveal any frustration with Ewt%mit%fnsk for delving into a conversation best discussed during work hours. With her increased work schedule, it was probably more unusual to have a casual exchange.

The heftier Fara seated herself and took a sip of her beverage before answering. "We have limited space. Once the subjects show the serum has taken effect, we intend to analyze, inject, and then process them for the front lines as quick as possible. War coordinator Tar%tosk%rask needs to get them trained since the fighting units have experienced heavy losses on all fronts."

Ewt%mit%fnsk had never met the war coordinator. Tar%tosk%rask was one of the few Fara involved directly in the war. At one time, war was the exclusive domain of the Farr. The decline in the quality of the new Farr meant they could not replace any senior commanders lost to the war from within the Farr ranks. The decrease in Farr abilities led to the recent formation of a new Fara initiative: battle strategy. For the first time in Tlo%m history, a Fara was running a war.

Ewt%mit%fnsk liked the direction this conversation was taking. "I pray these new slaves will help turn the tide," she said. She kept her eyes on her drink while striving to keep her pores from flushing the deeper reds of uneasiness. "I attended the conglomerate meeting. The superiors recommend the war continue."

Xoe%san%krin shifted in her chair and Ewt%mit%fnsk caught the barest flush of pink in the skin of her friend's face. "I heard." The pink tones deepened as the technician struggled with her feelings. "I suppose the elders know best."

Ewt%mit%fnsk took a deep breath. "The elders can only act on the information given to them." She met Xoe%san%krin's startled gaze. "During our gathering with the superior, we spoke out against the war." She locked her eyes with the tech's, noting any reaction. "Yet our superior manipulated our information to speak in favor of the war during the conglomerate meeting."

She let the sentence hang as she observed the technician's reaction. Xoe%san%krin looked uncomfortable, but not surprised.

There was a long silence before Xoe%san%krin replied. "We also made it clear in our gathering we cannot meet the demands now placed upon us. The work on the Tier-5 females will take all our resources. We are modifying the genetics so fast that the subjects may not properly adapt to the changes. We are putting individuals in the field that could fail at crucial junctures of time."

"The humans have always been among the more resilient of our subjects." Ewt%mit%fnsk tried to reassure. The obvious discomfort of her friend distressed her, and she had to force herself to continue.

"It is strange the superiors have taken this approach." It was easy to sound concerned. "Of course, they likely have access to information we do not. Perhaps the war situation is not as bleak as rumor indicates."

Ewt%mit%fnsk sensed the conflict within her friend and sat quietly sipping her drink.

Finally, Xoe%san%krin said, "All the reports validate that the war is not going well."

Ewt%mit%fnsk could barely hear her. She sensed opportunity, and with an internal wince, continued. "They must be acting on information sources that we do not have access to." She hesitated before saying, "As we know, private agendas have never been an issue. It is not part of our genetic programming."

Xoe%san%krin placed her beverage on a platform nearby and rose to move to her food console, punching in a code for a popular sweetmeat. Ewt%mit%fnsk followed her, helping to arrange them on a platter. Her hearts were thumping, and she was sure her face was bright pink by now.

The technician took great care placing the sweetmeats, but Ewt%mit%fnsk sensed the turmoil within her friend. Finally, she could wait no longer. "Xoe%san%krin, is there something you know that you are not telling me?" She reached out a taloned hand to touch her friend's. "I wouldn't ask, but this is important."

"Can you give me time?" Xoe%san%krin's gaze seemed resigned. "I have to talk this over with someone. Then I will contact you. I promise."

Ewt%mit%fnsk thought both of her hearts might freeze on the spot. *There is something going on here. I don't believe it, there is something.*

She forced herself to sound much more collected than she felt. "Of course, Xoe%san%krin," she said, accepting a sweetmeat from her.

As they seated themselves again, Xoe%san%krin took control of the conversation. She chatted about one of the newest species additions to their program and the promise it held as slaves able to mine the deepest pits of metal-rich asteroids. Such adaptations would ensure top price in the slave markets, with minimal genetic manipulation.

Ewt%mit%fnsk conversed on yet another species conquest, but her inner thoughts were in chaos. What does Xoe%san%krin know? She felt as if she was standing on a precipice about to step off into the unknown, a feeling she'd never experienced. *I asked for this. Now I have to face up to it.*

THE FANG HAD NOT YET entered the Coliseum. Waiting, Lianndra tested her skrin, unfurling it before winding it back in again. On a platform across from her, the nervous newbie copied her action, twitching her own skrin, so it clung to a spar before she yanked it free. Lianndra winced, wondering how she would cope with this partner. She hadn't trained with her. New girls dominated the training sessions, and Lianndra was coming into this Blooddance much less prepared than usual. She would have to rely on her experience to get them both through it alive.

This was the most recent of Lianndra's many double sessions; consisting of newbies paired with experienced Dancers to facilitate training. Instead, the extra bodies resulted in more injuries among the Dancers. Andrea was just getting off the infirm list after two weeks due to injuries resulting from a double Blooddance gone awry.

The Coliseum had difficulty accommodating the acrobatics of two Dancers against two Farr. To top it off, most of the Farr coming to the Blooddances were hot off the front lines of the war, unpredictable and savage. They often struck with unnecessary force. Many Dancers ended up injured, or worse.

Lianndra used her skrin to swing over to the newbie's platform. She knew this was only the kid's second Blooddance. "Just try to hang back," she told the frightened girl. "Watch me. Stay out of the way. I'll tire them out as much as possible by myself. Move only when you must. Let's just get through this in one piece."

The girl nodded, looking terrified. Lianndra hoped the newbie understood what she'd told her—English was not her first language. She held little hope that once things got going the kid would remember. Lianndra suspected both of them would visit Tania after this one.

She heard the hiss of the Coliseum door and was instantly moving. These war vets didn't pause to pose; they always came in hot. Sure enough, the newbie gave a short shriek of surprise as the Farr's skrins whistled past them, lifting the aliens into the air.

These guys were good. Lianndra swung, climbed and leaped, barely a stride ahead of the panting Farr. To give the newbie credit, she stayed out of the way, hovering on the corner platforms and only moving when necessary. Lianndra taunted the Farr until they both came after her, leaving the new Dancer alone. After an hour, Lianndra acquired several shallow cuts on her limbs, the result of close calls. She was tiring and knew the end was near.

The smaller Farr, featuring an ugly war wound along one arm, broke away from pursuing Lianndra to swing toward the girl watching from a high platform. Startled, the newbie dropped on her skrin, missing the platform she'd intended to swing to, which landed her straight into Lianndra's path.

There was no avoiding the resulting collision. Lianndra tried to roll out of it, sending her skrin searching for a platform two levels below the one originally intended while struggling to free herself from the thrashing girl. The large Farr in pursuit of her was not agile enough to avoid the collision either. He slammed into the newbie. His arm flung wide, raking his claws deep into Lianndra's side.

Her breath left her in a whoosh of expelled air and pain lanced through her. Her Dancer instincts saved her, delivering her to the lower platform while her legs barely held her upright. She locked eyes with the Farr, who'd landed one level farther down.

His lips parted in a grimace, exposing sharp teeth. She knew he smelled the blood coursing down her side. With resignation, she saw his fist clench and felt her skrin wind around her, binding her to the platform.

She couldn't see the newbie. Lianndra could only hope she'd avoided a lethal tumble to the Coliseum floor. She was so dizzy from the loss of blood she barely felt the Farr crawl over her, licking the blood from her wound. Then she realized both Farr were on her, sharing the steady red flow.

That doesn't bode well for the newbie, she thought, shuddering with revulsion. Lianndra started to lose consciousness. *They'll be carrying me out of this one.*

The darkness closed in.

LIANNDRA GRIMACED IN PAIN, GIVING an involuntary moan under Tania's expert administration. The healtech did its work, stitching the muscles closed over her exposed ribs. The claws had missed her lung, or they would not have bothered carrying her here. But it was close this time.

Tania finished her ministrations and patted Lianndra on the shoulder. She moved to her workstation bench, stripping off the healing technology in one fluid movement.

Lianndra frowned as the medic approached her with a small tube filled with orange liquid. "Now what? I don't need anything extra. A few days and I'll be good as new."

Tania blinked and shook her head, tapping the tube against the edge of the table. "This is new. Some kind of vitamins. Only the best Dancers get it."

Lianndra didn't want anything cooked up by the Fang injected into her body. "No thanks," she said, but then yelped as Tania stopped tapping the tube against the table and slapped it against Lianndra's bare thigh instead. "Hey!" The liquid stung as it entered her body.

"Sorry, refusal not an option." Tania turned away. "I have my orders too, you know."

Lianndra boosted herself off the table, rubbing her thigh as it burned. Tania was busy at her medpanel, entering data. Lianndra muttered thanks before leaving the room. She swayed as she walked along the corridor toward her quarters. *Need to sleep. Must have lost even more blood than I thought.*

EWT%MIT%FNSK WAS COLD. IT WASN'T a familiar sensation, but this low in the bowels of the giant ship the environmental controls were at the bare minimum for Tlo%m tolerance. Even the lighting remained dim. The maintenance slaves that serviced the giant pipes and conduits running through these corridors needed neither heat nor light to perform their allotted tasks. Their collars linked to the Central Intelligence Processor, which monitored activities and reported any rare anomalies to their ward supervisors.

As she walked, she watched a large blocky alien hauling a machine behind it. It paused at the intersection of a huge pipe to blast it with sealant before continuing. It ignored her. Ewt%mit%fnsk realized she didn't know if it was capable of independent thought. In fact, she couldn't even remember the name of the species, a detail that bothered her more than it once would have.

She pulled her thick cowl closer around her shoulders. Tlo%m were susceptible to the cold; their scaly skins had no mechanism for maintaining warmth. Her animal skin cowl still retained the heavy fur. She'd snuck it out from under the nose of one of her coworkers, someone who visited the maintenance slaves on the lower levels. It would have been hard to explain why Ewt%mit%fnsk needed such a garment.

A noise made her jump and spin. She relaxed only a little when she recognized Xoe%san%krin's form in the shadows, wearing a cowl made from a glittery synthetic material. The technician wasn't alone. Beside her stood a taller Tlo%m Fara who Ewt%mit%fnsk did not recognize.

As Ewt%mit%fnsk approached them, the older, slimmer Fara retreated even farther into the shadows.

"There will not be an exchange of names," Xoe%san%krin told her, drawing her into the darkness. "My friend has agreed to answer some of your questions. Afterward, you may decide if you wish to proceed any further."

Ewt%mit%fnsk swallowed while forcing herself not to peer too closely at the mysterious Fara. Questions flooded her brain, threatening to overwhelm her. *What am I doing here? This path can lead to nowhere good.*

A movement out of the corner of her eye revealed itself as another enslaved alien trudging along the corridor. This one dragged a section of conduit behind it on a sled. As the alien approached an intersection, its collar lit up, directing him along the correct path.

A sight that should not cause me a moment's thought. Like others of her kind, Ewt%mit%fnsk always believed in her species' right to dominate, based on their superior intellect and abilities. *But what if it is a lie?*

She turned her back on the alien to focus on the Fara who shouldn't exist: a Tlo%m who had rebellion in her heart.

Ewt%mit%fnsk formulated her first question.

LIANNDRA AWOKE TO THE SHIFT in her equilibrium as a weight descended onto her bed.

"Come on sleepyhead," a familiar voice urged, "you'll miss the big event."

Lianndra groaned as she rubbed her eyes, which itched as if someone had poured beach sand into them. She felt sick, which was strange. Slaves didn't get sick on the ship. The health program kept their immune system at peak performance while the air filters screened for any viruses or bacteria. This wasn't just for the slaves' benefit; Fang were susceptible to certain bacteria, which was why human slaves went through sterilization before being brought to the ships.

Her head pounded as she straightened up on her bed to peer at Andrea.

The tall woman surveyed her friend. "What's up? You look like crap. Didn't think you'd lost so much blood with the last bout. Tania got to you quickly."

"I don't know why I feel so lousy." Lianndra reached for the fluid container she kept by her bed and gulped some. "I suspect the vitamins Tania nailed me with are responsible."

"Vitamins? Tania?" Andrea seemed puzzled. "Oh, the orange stuff? She gave me that a while ago." Her expression turned thoughtful. "Come to think of it, I was feeling sick afterward too."

Lianndra felt relieved she wasn't the only one to receive the concoction. Being singled out was never good when you were a slave. However, it did nothing to improve her current state. "What time is it?"

"You've only got ten minutes to curtain." Like most of the slaves, Andrea stuck with the human method of keeping time. The wards provided humans with their familiar methods of measurement. The Fang found such methods effective in keeping peace within the slave colony.

Lianndra rubbed her eyes again. "Maybe I'll just watch from here tonight. I feel I might throw up if I even do as much as look at food."

Andrea frowned at her before sighing. "All right. I had a late lunch. I'll hang out with you."

"You don't have to miss supper on my account," Lianndra said, attempting to swing her legs over the side of the bed.

Andrea blocked her motion, pushing her back. Then she squeezed in beside her. Lianndra noticed the woman was still moving stiff from her recently healed injuries. Andrea played with the bed's folding sequence until the two of them were in a sitting pose. Lianndra gave up her protests and lay back, closing her eyes. Satisfied, Andrea activated the small private console, giving them a ringside seat to the night's festivities. She handed Lianndra her beverage. "Drink. I have no idea what was in the orange junk, but you need to flush it from your system. Don't worry about me, I'll eat later. I'm Dancing tomorrow, and I don't eat much the day before."

Lianndra frowned as she took a long sip of her drink. Andrea was a powerful Dancer and seldom received serious injuries. This last one was an exception; it had taken over two weeks to heal. Lianndra worried Andrea was not ready for another Blooddance. She was one of Lianndra's few remaining friends. Losing her would be devastating.

As they watched the evening's performance begin, Lianndra thought of the friends she'd lost in the last year. Of the seven original women enslaved in her group, only three remained alive. Small, blonde Muriel used her skrin to hang herself a month after their arrival on the ship. She'd excelled in the training and her first Blooddance went well, with only minor injuries. Afterward, she could not stop shaking, despite her friends' best efforts to calm her. She'd excused herself to use the facilities in her room, and by the time the ward supervisor arrived to vaporize the jammed door, it was too late.

Muscular Lacey Danced well for four months before being fatally wounded in a particularly gruesome Blooddance. Long and lithe, Beth was the best of them; a talented Dancer who just vanished after one particular match. The cube whisked her away with no one providing any answers. Poor tiny Michelle never performed well, barely lasting minutes each time before surrendering to the Fang. After a few such disgraces, the Fang sent her to one of the dreaded private parties and she was never seen again.

The last slave from their group, Chia, was a reasonable Dancer who stuck to a small Spanish-speaking clique, shunning others.

The rooms of the dead or disappeared were never empty for long. The wards were full of women, ranging in age from seventeen to thirty-five. Lianndra gave up counting them as a steady stream of newbies came in to replace those lost. Most of the slaves kept to small social groups, treating each other like family and discouraging newcomers. Often based on common culture or language, these cliques reflected the vast cultural variety on Earth. Over time, the individual groups lost their members. Older Dancers often became loners by preference. It was easier on the heart.

A few successful Dancers, those rare ones surviving for many years, gained social status and jobs outside of Dancing. They became ward supervisors, guards, cleaners, cooks, medtechs, or other supporting staff for the huge slave complex. Dancers dying during the Blooddance vanished. Lianndra often wondered if they ended up as part of the food chain or if the Fang disposed of them. Dancers performing poorly never returned from the private Blooddances. The most mysterious disappearances were those of the good Dancers. Often the best ones vanished without a trace right after a Blooddance, never to be seen or heard from again. Despite many attempts to pump the ward supervisors for information, Lianndra hadn't been able to find out anything about them.

Their area contained only human women but Lianndra knew there were other slave zones on the ship. There were separate zones for each species as well as gender, and the zones never mixed. The human females took part most often in the Blooddances, although a few Farr preferred to Blooddance with males. Some human males and many alien prisoners went into Pitfights.

Scheduled after the evening series of Blooddances and held twice weekly, the Pitfights were a duel to the death. Rarely, a Fara the humans called the priestess granted the participants a reprieve.

With her features hidden by a red shroud, the priestess sat flanked by other disguised figures in a box hovering high above the Pit's floor. As the fight neared its grisly end, a strident horn sounded, indicating action should cease. The priestess then used a colored beacon to show whether the bout would be to the death. Most often, it was to the death. But some said the priestess possessed favorites she would protect on a whim. Lianndra noticed a few of the Pit slaves often benefited from the Fara's decisions.

Lianndra hadn't seen Michael since the day in the metal room back on Earth, so every night she watched the assorted Blooddances and Pitfights on the monitors. They piped the events into the wards starting at dinner time. Many of the slaves gathered in the mess hall to watch them and cheer on their favorites. Lianndra always watched, even on those nights after she was Dancing and incapacitated by pain. She would scan the participants for a strapping, tall young man with silver eyes.

She didn't know if she wanted to see him in the Pit. Popular opinion stated most of the male slaves went to the front lines of the war. Only certain ones fought in the Pit, and she didn't know what the Fang used as selection criteria. She didn't want to see Michael enter the Pit only to die in his first fight. Maybe he was already dead, killed fighting a war not his own.

During the day she could keep busy training, socializing or watching the Blooddances. At night, as the wards darkened for the sleep cycle, her tough demeanor eroded, and her thoughts roamed. She dreamed of Michael often. He was her symbol of hope in a hopeless situation. When she couldn't hold back the despair during the last moments before she fell asleep, her thoughts turned to the tall young man she'd known for only a few days. Sometimes, Lianndra thought she didn't want to know what had happened to him. She feared she might lose her fragile hold on her sanity if she was to discover he was dead. Yet part of her longed to see him again. As long as she had hope, maybe someday that would happen and this living hell would come to an end.

This day's first Blooddance was a single, featuring a newbie: a limber Dancer who made a commendable effort avoiding the Farr for twenty minutes before he drew blood. The Blooddance went on for a bit longer before her own skrin attacked her. It wasn't a bad injury; the girl should recover. Some, like Muriel, didn't, and chose to end their own lives. The Fang didn't seem too interested in preventing such deaths, obviously not wishing to provide counseling for those not mentally tough enough to survive on their own.

The rest of the Blooddances offered matches between prominent Dancers and Farr. Everyone had their favorites. Andrea and Lianndra were no exception, cheering when one of their own kept the Farr at bay for nearly three hours. This meant the Pitfight didn't start until late. Lianndra's head was pounding by the time the screen focused on the darkened Pit.

A spotlight shone on the first of the two contestants: an alien the humans called a Gryphon. The creature used a stance much like the mythical centaur, with the trunk and arms held upright while it swiftly traveled on its four powerful legs. When needed, it could drop its torso to the ground to use all six limbs for locomotion. The muscular legs ended in clawed toes and the arms were more delicate and featured humanlike fingers. The dexterous hands could as easily wield weapons as they could calibrate a mechanical device. The arms flowed into broad, powerful shoulders, while the neck arched in a short but graceful curve to a set of long, tufted ears. Oversized violet eyes lay to the sides of the elongated head. The jaws tapered to a hooked beak similar to that of a bird of prey.

Lianndra had seen images of these creatures in their natural state. Normally, the head possessed either a crest or mane of longer feathers. The feathers stood up around the head when the creature was angry. Combined with the beak at the tip of the snout, they had earned the alien the nickname of Gryphon among the human slaves. There were no feathers or fur on the creature in the Pit. The Fang sterilization procedure left it looking like a plucked chicken. The skin featured multicolored patterns that Lianndra theorized mimicked the fur. Elongated spikes started from the back of the head and continued in a single row along the curve of the neck to the shoulders. They became a series of shallow, rounded bumps on the back before flaring up to pointed spikes as a crest along the top of the long, whippy tail.

The Gryphon were the Fang's nemesis, their enemy in the current war. It was common knowledge that captured Gryphon suffered through multiple torture sessions. Eventually, they found their way to the Pit, where they died. Although the Gryphon were fierce fighters, the Fang always ensured the scales tipped to favor their opponents. Forced to fight unarmed, the Gryphon faced the heavy battle-axes and swords their opponents wielded. Even then it was often a close fight. The priestess seldom intervened in Gryphon fights.

As the Gryphon entered the Pit, it reared up on its hind legs, revealing something which surprised Lianndra. It was female. The breasts were clearly visible, two of them in between the forelegs. Lianndra had never seen a female Gryphon. As the light played across the form on the monitor, she noticed the creature was more refined than the males she'd seen, with a narrower body, finer legs, and a sleeker overall appearance. The females obviously had more muted skin color as well: soft golds and purples rather than the vibrant yellows and blues of the opposite sex.

Lianndra detected pride in the Gryphon's stance as she locked her gaze with the priestess. Lianndra thought she saw the hooded form twitch. *Do these two have a history?* she wondered. *If so, it seems the Fara failed to break this Gryphon's spirit.*

The light shifted off the Gryphon to the other side of the Pit, where her opponent appeared. Lianndra stared in astonishment at the creature oozing into the arena. The body was blob-like, translucent, with various dim shapes floating within it. The blob constantly altered color while radiating a soft light. A crown of delicate tentacles probed the air above it, while larger ones dragged it forward from beneath. Lianndra couldn't believe this creature was terrestrial. If so, its home must have much less gravity than what the ship created.

"Jelly," Andrea said. "I've only heard of them. Never seen one."

"It has no weapon," Lianndra noted, "and it can barely move in the sand. This won't be much of a fight. They must like this Gryphon."

Andrea had made a supply run a few hours ago. She shifted on the bed beside Lianndra to reach her beverage and snack. "I've heard the Jellies are nasty. Must have something up its sleeve."

The overhead lights came on, a sign the fight was to begin. The horn sounded. It was obvious the Gryphon agreed with Andrea's assessment. The Gryphon kept her upper torso erect, leaving her arms free. Her spikes rose until they bristled in aggression from her neck and torso. The tip of her long tail twitched, like a cat planning to pounce. But she was circling the Jelly with caution, keeping maximum distance between her and the ponderous blob.

The Jelly crawled toward the center of the Pit, seemingly unaware of the circling Gryphon. The colors shifted from blues through green to yellow.

Mood swings? Lianndra wondered.

A streak of red shot through the body, and faster than the eye could follow, something launched from among the tentacles. The Gryphon reacted wickedly fast, leaping clear as a thin tentacle slapped the Pit's wall where she'd stood moments before. She didn't leap away but rather toward the blob, one foreleg snapping out to strike at the crown. Before she could connect, one of the thicker tentacles slapped her claws aside.

In an instant, both combatants were separate again, having tested their mettle with the opening salvo. The watching Farr howled their approval. Lianndra wondered if they had preferences for who won the match. Likely it didn't matter as long as there was lots of blood spilled.

For over an hour, the two aliens took potshots at each other, doing no damage other than a lacerated tentacle on the part of the Jelly. The Farr grew restless, hissing and shouting insults. Finally, the priestess stood, signaling for silence. She said something in their guttural language. The Farr yelled their support. The Gryphon stared up at the hovering cube. Her neck spikes sagged as the priestess addressed her.

The spotlight picked up movement at one of the Pit's entrances. Another Gryphon entered the arena. Lianndra and Andrea gasped. This one could have been a child; it was only a third the size of the adult, with spikes made up of tiny nubs and a highly patterned hide. It walked toward the big one as if unsure of what to do.

The Jelly flashed red. The adult Gryphon shrieked before launching herself between the flying tentacle and the childlike Gryphon. For the first time, the tentacle struck home, lashing across the muscled hindquarter, leaving a trail of blood in its wake. They heard a high-pitched scream, then the Gryphon was at the far end of the Pit. She had the small one pushed behind her against the wall, well away from the Jelly. The injured hind leg buckled when the Gryphon tried to use it. The wound didn't look serious, so the tentacle must have had venom in its strike.

Hatred for the Fang swelled within Lianndra, and by the tension in Andrea's body beside her, she knew her friend felt the same. For all its brutality, the Pit possessed its own code of honor, kept sacred by the fighters themselves. This battle had just crossed a line obvious to everyone except the Fang. The Jelly seemed willing to win at any cost.

Lianndra would like to think if she was the Jelly, she would choose death over such dishonorable conduct, but was that fair? She knew nothing of the circumstances surrounding the capture of these aliens. *Perhaps Gryphon slaughtered its entire family. Yet does anything justify attacking a child in such a way? I don't want to watch, but how can I not? I need to know if they live.*

The injured hind leg disabled the Gryphon. Out of necessity, she was on all six legs, dragging the one hind as she circled the Pit, keeping herself between the Jelly and the youngster. Her spikes bristled aggression and her tail arched.

This time, when the Jelly flashed red, the small Gryphon reacted to an invisible signal from the adult, leaping away while the adult charged. Screaming, the big Gryphon took the full brunt of the tentacles across her shoulders as she barreled into the Jelly, slashing with her claws. The two aliens disappeared in a maelstrom of dust and flashing color. Both Lianndra and Andrea were on the edge of the bed, clutching each other's hands, horrified eyes locked on the screen. Around the Pit, the Farr erupted, screaming their support of the carnage with their guttural cries.

The dust settled to reveal the forms of the Jelly and the Gryphon so intertwined it was difficult to determine where one started and the other ended. Neither moved. The small Gryphon paced forward into the Pit before beginning to keen, a high-pitched sound of sorrow piercing Lianndra to the heart. Several Farr emerged from the Pit's entrance to corral the grieving Gryphon and begin the cleanup.

Lianndra kept the screen on until the little Gryphon disappeared, presumably taken back to the alien ward. She wiped tears away as she turned off the monitor. *A temporary reprieve only. The Fang* won't hesitate to torture and kill the little Gryphon, even if it is a child. I hate them.

"My God." Andrea's voice sounded strained as she choked back tears. "The Gryphon . . . she sacrificed herself to save the child. It was so, so . . ."

"Human," Lianndra finished quietly. *I am going to have to reassess my opinion of aliens. They are not all like the Fang. It's been so easy to throw them together as unfeeling and essentially evil. Us versus Them. Human versus Alien.* For the first time, she felt a connection between herself and a nonhuman, alien-based life form.

Some of them could be just like us. She rubbed her aching head with both hands. *The universe just got more complicated.*

EWT%MIT%FNSK RAN HER TALONED FINGERS along the list of numbers. Behind each number, she had entered a human name, something she never did before. *Numbers are all that are necessary for identification. Names are superfluous. Or so I used to believe.*

As she perused the list, anger burned within her. It was bad enough to harvest the valuable Tier-5s before they could reach maximum potential. The humans were a valuable species, and the Tier-5s represented generations of hard work. *Now the geneticists are meddling with them as adults,* she thought. *This directive is troubling from many perspectives.*

The latest subjects of this initiative were the ones listed on the console before her, awaiting her approval. Arranging for the last phase of the project fell under her jurisdiction. The plans were at the ready. She was waiting for signs each Tier-5 human subject had responded to the preliminary serum and therefore initiated their mutations. The serum should yield results along a certain genetic plane, with a small margin for error. Although it was risky manipulating a full-grown adult, her people spent lifetimes perfecting mutations on the adults of other species. The recent war was adding impetus to rapid mutation and manipulation in more than a few of the slave species cultured by the Tlo%m.

For some, such manipulation could mimic an evolution taking many generations to occur naturally on their home planets. Or, it might have taken a major evolutionary prod, like a planet-wide cataclysm, to cause a spontaneous mutation.

The Tlo%m geneticists were renowned throughout the universe for their ability to manipulate genes in many diverse ways. The extrapolations and inclusions of new genetic materials were most accurate if the subjects contained similarities at the genetic level. Such genetic similarities often existed between species that share a world. Many of the alterations included in the human genes came from other species on their home planet.

It was no longer an option for the Tlo%m to use related species from their own home world to enhance or repair their genetic makeup—they lost their planet long ago. It had happened well before Ewt%mit%fnsk's time. There were many theories about what went wrong. The history surviving their planet's destruction possessed gaps that time had not filled. In the end, rebel insurgents took the blame for the civil war, supposedly pulling their civilization apart from within. Ewt%mit%fnsk studied enough history to doubt this theory. The extensive modification of the Tlo%m genetic makeup after their planet's death lent credence to other, more insidious, causes. But the cause now mattered less than the permanent effect on the lifestyle of her species.

Condemned to drifting through space in their massive Motherships, the Tlo%m's entire existence centered on the conquest of other species. Respected as slave traders, the Tlo%m ability to genetically manipulate species into specialized roles was appreciated by their customers. They even filled special requests for elite clients that would take generations to achieve.

This ambitious war for one single planet has interfered with our slave trading function, calling on too many of our resources, she thought.

The Tlo%m needed to resolve this war or they would face a crisis not only financial in its nature.

Deep in contemplation, Ewt%mit%fnsk tapped the console before her. Thanks to the rebellion, she now knew something about these Tier-5 humans to which few of her kind were privy. Her job was to watch them closely and wait. When it came time to act she would have to do so smoothly and efficiently to not raise suspicion.

How ironic the fate of my species might rest with a small group of human slaves, she thought.

LIANNDRA DRAGGED HERSELF OUT of bed, groaning. Drenched in sweat, she wondered if she had a fever.

This has been going on too long, she thought. *I wonder if I'm allergic to whatever was in the supplement.* Her next Blooddance was in three days. *At this rate, I won't be able to make it to the lowest platforms.*

It took her a long time to shower and stagger down the hall to the medic's quarters.

Tania didn't seem concerned. "Some people react to the vitamin supplement this way," she said. "I'll take blood just in case, but you should be better by tomorrow." She took the sample, sliding it into the large machine behind her which sucked up the tube. The Fara techs analyzed the blood; Tania was only responsible for administering medicines, healing injuries, and taking samples.

"I'm Dancing in three days," Lianndra said, alarmed.

"You'll be fine by then," Tania replied.

Bloody medic has lost her mind, Lianndra thought as she left the room. A bad performance would not shortlist her for a private party; her reputation would hold her for a while. Permitting the Farr to win too fast might cause worse injuries, not to mention that she hated letting a Farr have easy blood. It wasn't something she wanted to let happen.

Lianndra had just left the medic's office when everything in the hall went kaleidoscopic, radiating colors in a spectrum that drove spikes into her brain. Lianndra staggered and bounced off another woman who smelled of crushed lilacs.

Lilacs?

The heavyset woman cursed before pushing her away. Leaning against the wall, Lianndra closed her eyes and the lilac scent faded. When she opened them, everything was normal. Well, sort of. Were the walls always a sickening shade of puke yellow? Why hadn't she noticed the antiseptic smell of the air before now?

Strange colors and strong smells. Great, I'm turning into a werewolf, Lianndra thought, remembering one of her favorite horror novels. *Perfect.*

LIANNDRA WAITED ON THE HIGHEST platform for the Farr to arrive. For once, she was alone. No doubles today.

She still wasn't quite herself. Her energy came in fits and spurts, and she'd experienced several bouts of vision impairment as well as nauseating incidences of enhanced smell. As a result, she hadn't eaten in over a day. Lianndra should have been weak as a kitten but instead, she felt curiously buoyant.

Normally coated in drab colors, today the Coliseum seemed to have received a new paint job. The reds pulsed with multiple shades, and the metal gleamed with iridescent blue highlights and deep purple shadows. The place was redolent with scent as well; she could tell where each drop of blood shed in the last week had fallen. The coppery metallic reek was obvious.

I am a werewolf, she thought, baring her teeth while picturing herself as a wolf. *Those were some vitamins. Wonder how long it'll last?* The Fang manipulating her body should alarm her, but if it gave her an edge while Dancing, Lianndra guessed she was all for it. *As long as they don't take it too far, a little animal juice doesn't hurt.*

The Coliseum door opened, admitting a large Farr. Lianndra didn't recognize him. He was huge—larger than most—and his torso revealed half-healed scars.

An older generation Farr. Just in from the war, she thought, crouching on the platform. *He'll be particularly dangerous, smarter than most, and have fast reflexes.* Dancers became casualties dueling with Farr still jumpy from the front lines. *I have no intention of becoming one of those.*

The Farr's orange gaze swirled with red as he searched for her, his skrin unfurling. Even from her perch high above, Lianndra saw the clear inner membranes flick across his eyes. It was the Fang substitution for a blink, usually done so fast the human eye couldn't follow it. She also noticed star-shaped pupils, almost invisible within the solid color irises. Lianndra crouched farther down on her platform, her lips peeling back from her teeth in a silent snarl.

Her heart was pounding, but she had no time to consider the weirdness of her new abilities. Lianndra's eyes met the Farr's, and the match was on.

From the first move, everything was different about this Blooddance. The Farr's reflexes were sharp. He came after her with murderous reddened eyes and bared teeth as though out to kill. It was Lianndra's responses, however, that were remarkable. She leaped farther, spun, twisted, and somersaulted as never before. Somehow, she knew what the Farr would do a split second before he did it. The minute twitches of the heavy muscling predicted his moves. She'd never been able to interpret such things before now. Two hours into the Blooddance, a surprising thought zinged through her brain. *I can take this guy.*

At first, the shift was subtle, almost teasing. Lianndra took more chances, cutting the margins of miss to mere inches, and then even closer. The Farr's nostrils flared wide open as he pursued her. Then there came the moment when their eyes met across a platform, and she saw recognition dawn.

He knows I'm playing him.

His fist started to clench, signaling her skrin to betray her. Lianndra leaped straight over him, vaulting over his head and twisting to wrap her arms beneath his big jaws. Instead of binding her to the platform, her skrin spun around both of their bodies, binding her to his back.

Before he signaled the skrin to release again, she sunk her fangs into his neck.

I have fangs?

Blackish blood welled, and she spat the putrid stuff from her mouth. Lianndra tried folding her lips back over the long fangs, but with minimal success. The watching Farr were howling, all of them, and the one beneath her wrestled himself free of the loosening skrin then twisted to glare at her, his claws flexing. Before he acted, an imperious feminine voice sounded through the speakers. The Farr snarled but froze, baring his teeth. He raised one hand to touch the blood running down his chest from his neck.

The voice from above saved her life. Lianndra was so shocked by this latest development she stood frozen on the platform. The Farr could slice her in two. Instead, he backhanded her. Only the instinctive deployment of her skrin saved her from a nasty fall to the Coliseum's floor.

The voice barked again, and the Farr skrinned his way to the floor before stalking from the Coliseum.

Shaking, Lianndra found her way to the cube. It carried her away from the Blooddance, but not from her chaotic thoughts.

The cube changed direction, and something twigged in Lianndra's foggy brain. It took her a few moments to realize it wasn't taking her back to her ward.

EWT%MIT%FSNK WAITED, ARMS HANGING BY her sides and lips folded over her long, pointed teeth. She knew this was the body language to best reassure humans during the rare interactions between Fara and humans.

On each side of her stood Bernaf slaves, a species used by the Fara as bodyguards. Their short, wiry bodies and attenuated limbs possessed soft, pale gray skin. The aliens' heads seemed large for their frames, with bulbous, oversized craniums, enormous, dark, slanted eyes, and mere slits for nostrils and mouth.

The Bernaf were a small species but their stature belied an incredible agility and strength that made them lethal when required. Although demand for Bernaf slaves was high, the Bernaf home world was a secret even the Tlo%m methods of interrogation hadn't been able to pry loose. They pounced on Bernaf ships when they found them. These two served only Ewt%mit%fnsk.

Ewt%mit%fnsk was nervous as she waited in the corridor. This situation was unusual. With her new connections, Ewt%mit%fnsk knew the Tlo%m rebels arranged for the disabling of the monitors in this area for a brief time. The rebels needed her to connect with certain human slaves, and they didn't want anyone knowing about it. That they could shut down the monitors was yet another sign the rebels were both more plentiful and more organized than Ewt%mit%fnsk might have assumed.

Her long, taloned fingers rolled a datachrys between them. If discovered, the information recorded on it could doom many of her fellow rebels to instant termination. Not so long ago, the thought of being part of such a conspiracy would have reduced her to a quivering mass of nerves. A rebellious fire now smoldered deep within her, working to strengthen her resolve.

LIANNDRA'S HEART POUNDED. AROUND HER, the cube's walls shimmered in iridescent hues as it carried her in a different direction than usual. She raised shaking hands to her face, tracing the familiar contours before settling trembling fingers on her lips. Baring her teeth, she searched for a sign of the long fangs.

Was it my imagination? she wondered

They'd retracted, but she felt raised areas just under the gums, extending above her canine teeth. Her canines had always been pointed as far as human teeth went, but now she traced their outlines well up into her jaw.

Retractable teeth? What the hell was in that supplement? Now that she was paying attention to the fangs, she felt how her lips adjusted to fold over them. *How long have they been like this?* Lianndra didn't remember if her mouth had felt funny when her entire body had been off-kilter.

Her hands dropped to her sides as she leaned backward against the cube's wall. Whatever this was about, it couldn't be good. Dancers that disappeared right after a Blooddance never returned. Wherever she was going, she wasn't coming back.

The cube halted. Lianndra flattened against the wall, fighting to get control over her body and stifle the trembling of her extremities. She forced herself to stand erect, to face whatever new horrors fate held in store for her. As the door hissed open, she raised her chin.

Three figures stood before her. The central alien could only be a Fang Fara, although Lianndra had never seen one up close. She was tall and not as muscled as the males of her species. Her head was a different shape with elongated jaws, tapered and speckled with paler dapples over the usual deep violet-black. Judging by the ridges along her lips, her teeth might even be larger than her male counterparts. The Fara's arms were longer in proportion to her body and the fingers more delicate behind the claws.

Lianndra noticed two of those claws filed to mere stubs on each hand. *Perhaps so they can handle things requiring precision, like computers?*

This was a very different beast from the Farr. The eyes, still coldly reptilian, held a gleam that made her more uneasy than the usual bloodlust of the males. Reptilian this Fara might be, but this was an intelligent reptile.

The figures on each side of the Fara were barely three feet in height. They had enormous dark, slanted eyes, large heads on attenuated necks, and pale gray skin. With a shock, Lianndra recognized the aliens were the spitting image of those humans claimed to have encountered on Earth. What was missing from the common description was the whipcord strength they wore like a second skin. Their long arms appeared skinny, but they had an elastic energy about them, an ease in the way they stood, which implied speed and agility. Lianndra wasn't sure she would want to Blooddance with them.

The Fara stepped forward, and Lianndra couldn't suppress a flinch. "Please." The slurred word was clearly English.

Despite her fear, it shocked Lianndra; Farr had trouble with human languages, especially English. Their own language was full of glottal stops. Even though Lianndra adopted a few Fang profanities as her own, she did not know of any human that spoke the language well, although there were some who understood it. Farr mangled English words to a degree where they were almost unidentifiable. She'd always considered it the result of a mouth full of big teeth and a thickened tongue. Yet as this Fara continued to speak, Lianndra understood what she was saying.

Perhaps it's the Fara's refined features and longer jaw, Lianndra thought.

"Do not be afraid." The black lips formed the words with ease despite the tips of the sharp teeth showing as she spoke. "I do not have much time. You must listen."

The Fara waited for Lianndra to come forward to her, which she did, surprising herself. There was something in the demeanor of the Fara that spiked Lianndra's curiosity, something furtive.

When Lianndra stood before her, the Fang raised one taloned hand, opening it to reveal the datachrys. "The information on this will tell you what you need to know about the upcoming trials ahead. I will download it now into your collar. The program will activate once the collar receives final modification at the laboratory."

The huge orange eyes swirled with a burst of red. Lianndra knew the color change meant intensity of emotion for a Fang. She started to speak, but the Fara cut her off with a gesture.

"I do not have time for your questions. Any attempt to talk of this meeting or the data on the datachrys, will result in it being erased from both your mind and the collar. It may harm the cellular matrix of your brain if such occurs."

She reached up toward Lianndra's collar, pausing when the human took a step back from her. The eyes swirled again, meeting Lianndra's for the first time. The lips parted, but the Fara didn't speak for a beat or two as if assessing what words might reassure the human woman.

Finally, the Fara spoke. "This information could lead you to freedom."

The words reverberated through Lianndra. *Freedom. Was she serious? How do I know if she is telling the truth?* The Fara might have an agenda for being so secretive. *She might be hiding something from her people. What have I got to lose? This Fang can do what she wants with me regardless of how I feel. If there is even a hope of freedom ... why not try?*

Lianndra forced herself to step forward. It took courage to stand before the Fara while turning her head to one side, exposing the collar, along with her neck, to the alien. The Fang touched the datachrys to the collar. Lianndra felt warmth pulse through it, and she shuddered. She stepped back to look up at the tall alien.

"I am afraid the next few days will be unpleasant, but be assured, better times are ahead," the Fara said.

There was an air of finality in those sentences, and as Lianndra went to step away from the Fara, the stun feature in her collar activated. As her consciousness faded, she sensed small, gray-skinned aliens step forward to catch her slumping body.

MY LIFE UNTIL NOW HAS been a party. Lianndra hung suspended from the laboratory ceiling. Newly de-haired and disinfected, she felt naked and exposed. The lab techs maintained her in a permanent state of sedation; she faded in and out of consciousness. It kept her unaware of the passage of time but did little to buffer the unpleasant side effects of the stuff they injected.

Sometimes she lost it, fighting the restraints with the intensity of a tiger, only to end up hanging limp, breathless with exhaustion. There were times she tested restraints and imagined they barely held her. Lianndra debated this scenario during one of her rare lucid phases. *I seem to remember the Fang techs running in a panic*, she thought.

Whatever the case, she was now familiar with some of her body's new idiosyncrasies. These included the canines sliding neatly out of her gums to form long fangs and her finger and toenails growing into strong, curved claws instead of wimpy human nails. Her eyesight provided her with a wider spectrum of color than normal human eyes. Her skin itched all over her body as if there were more changes to come.

But by far the strangest offering was the tail.

At first, it was a small bump at the base of her spine. After an excruciating series of injections, it developed into an impressive naked rat's tail measuring about four feet long. It was prehensile, much like a monkey's. Lianndra discovered the grasping ability was functional just before the Fang did. It had led to a fair amount of activity among the techs until they fastened it into a restraint along with the rest of her. The tail had a mind of its own, acting in a subconscious manner rather than under her direct control. Lianndra wondered if all mammalian tails were like this. It felt as though the appendage revealed her every mood. *I once had a cat whose tail twitched when she got ready to pounce on you,* she thought.

During her more lucid periods, Lianndra wondered at what point she'd stopped being human. Her foggy brain could not deal with the concept. She imagined what the reaction would be to her back on Earth if she ever made it home. Her family would not recognize her. Some might run away screaming. Her thoughts switched to one human in particular.

Lianndra doubted Michael wanted to see her like this. *What good is freedom if I look like a monster?* The thought made her fight the restraints which sent one tech running for the sedation controls. Then she slid under again, rescued from thoughts only growing darker with time.

Yet no matter how bad it got, Lianndra did not tell the lab techs about her strange conversation with the Fara outside the cube. Through the tortuous procedures, she held it close to her, clinging to it like a lifeline.

Perhaps they can reverse this one day. Then it'll be worth it to be free.

BEING PINNED INSTEAD OF SUSPENDED woke Lianndra from her stupor. Beneath her was a table; something invisible pressed her down onto it. Visions of dissecting tables flashed through her brain. She rebelled with all her strength. An inhuman scream filled the laboratory, the sound startling her until she realized it was her own voice. Lianndra lifted herself through pure force of will. Techs flew to their consoles, reinforcing the table restraints as she writhed. Lianndra slumped as she was once again pressed down. Her heart pounded.

A hum came from beneath, sucking her body even closer to the table. It held her immobile while her mind raced in panic.

What now? As she woke, logic reasserted itself. *Dissection is not their goal, not after the work they have put into me.* It would be something else. Not pleasant. *But also not deadly.*

The answer became obvious when her collar moved.

Reason left her as she succumbed to the most primitive of instincts: protect the throat. Lianndra was now so accustomed to wearing the collar she rarely noticed it other than the basic annoyance of lying on it when sleeping. Although she could never forget what it represented, in the normal daily routine it didn't bear much thought.

But when it came alive around her throat, she panicked. Held immobile, her soaring heart rate was the only available outlet for her fear.

The collar pulsed as it moved on her neck, reorienting itself. A slim metal arm rose from the table edge, its pointed tip joining forces with the molten collar. She felt something penetrate her skin to insert its way through her skull and into her brain, something far larger than the spidery network that already existed.

The pain was a brutal invasion probing its way into her head. When it paused, Lianndra gasped in relief. Then it exploded, and a flaming starburst pierced every part of her brain.

Lianndra blacked out.

***T**HE COLLARS ARE DESIGNED TO ensure obedience. The simple slave one you wore has now evolved to the more advanced remote model, capable not only of instilling pain to promote obedience but also of killing if necessary. Your controller sends commands to your inner ear via the collar. For most slaves, they either obey those commands or die.*

Your collar is different. This interactive guide, downloaded from the datachrys, has disabled the kill function, but the pain node is still enabled. To disable this might alert your controller to a problem. There is no way we know of to fake a pain impulse reaction.

As a rebel slave, your safety and eventual path to freedom relies on your ability to obey as though the collar was working normally. Bear this in mind.

Lianndra awoke, the Fang voice fading away inside her head. She was sure it was not the voice of the Fara she'd met outside the cube. This one sounded older, raspier.

She became aware she was no longer in the lab and that the restraints had disappeared. Lianndra was lying on a long, narrow bed in temporary quarters. Temporary because she saw places where light showed through at the corners of the room. The walls themselves bore the drag and scuff marks of being reassembled many times.

Other than a headache, she felt good. She smelled something damp and pungent. It took her a moment to recognize it as the smell of decaying vegetation. Unfamiliar sounds reminded her of furtive wild animals in a natural setting.

I don't think I'm still on the ship, she thought. *Where the heck am I?*

Lianndra sat up, flexing her joints. Her body's weight pushing down on the base of her spine made her aware of the thing sprouting from that place. Squirming onto one hip to relieve the pressure, something brushed her leg, and she acknowledged recent events were not just a dream.

I do have a tail.

It twitched as she contemplated first it, and then each finger, turning her hands to examine her claws. Lianndra also noticed her arms were no longer naked but now sported a faint fuzz of golden, dense hair. In fact, as she pushed back the thin single cover, the fuzz covered her whole body. The places usually hairy were still, well, hairy.

Great, she thought, *Now I'm turning into a blonde Bigfoot.*

Lianndra felt naked despite the fur and experienced tremendous relief to see a simple green tunic lying across the foot of the bed. She stood to slide it over her head. The lower hem of the fabric pushed down on her tail, and she worried its twitching might show things she would rather not have revealed. Her fingers trailed over the slave collar, tracing the spot behind her left ear where a thick strand entered her skull. The collar itself was narrower, forming a thinner band across her throat. With a shudder, she snatched the fingers away.

The door along one wall opened without warning.

Could have knocked, Lianndra thought in exasperation, tugging at the hem of her tunic. She looked up into the eyes of a creature that used to be human.

The female—*woman*—Lianndra corrected herself, who stood at the door possessed human features. At first, Lianndra thought she wore clothes, but then she noticed the woman's entire body covered with dark hair. It was thinner on her face and hands and longer on her head, cascading down her back to blend with the short, dense hair covering the rest of her body. It appeared interwoven in areas over the breasts and groin to mask those details.

"Come," the woman said, turning to leave and obviously expecting Lianndra to follow. As she turned, Lianndra noticed the slave had a tail, shorter than her own. Yet the hand left for a moment on the door frame, possessed normal human fingernails and not Lianndra's strong claws.

The woman led her out into a lush jungle. For a second, Lianndra's heart soared, thinking she might be back on Earth. Then she noticed the strange plants. She'd never visited the tropics on Earth but she was sure her planet had never seen a vine writhing like a snake. It dropped from above to trail along her arm before recoiling as if scorched. After that unsettling experience, the more she looked around her, the less like Earth the jungle seemed.

The strange foliage wasn't the only difference. Lianndra noticed the extra bounce in each step which indicated the gravity on this planet differed from Earth's. It seemed closer to the gravity maintained within the Coliseum.

Her companion wasn't the talkative type. *Maybe she's just shy.* "Where are we?" Lianndra asked.

The woman answered without turning around or missing a step. "We are on the planet Tarin," she said in a clipped and unwelcoming tone.

Okay, this will be like pulling teeth. But there is likely only one place they would send me. "I take it we are near the front lines of the Gryphon war?"

"Tarin is the Gryphon home world. These barracks are a long way from the front lines."

Wow, two whole sentences, Lianndra thought.

The pathway opened to a large clearing featuring many dilapidated buildings of various sizes. The clearing bustled with activity. Fang in uniforms walked with purpose between the buildings. There were no vehicles of any kind; everyone was on foot. Looking around with interest, it appeared low-tech to Lianndra, especially for a race as advanced as the Fang. Her guide turned along another pathway. The jungle closed in once more.

"Where are the transports? I don't see any vehicles here," Lianndra said.

There weren't even sounds other than those of the jungle and the harsh murmur of Fang voices behind thin metal walls. No obvious signs of high-tech—no fighter jets, no battle cruisers, not even any all-terrain machines or whatever else they used for planetary warfare.

Lianndra thought she saw a hesitation in the woman's stride, but she might have just been adjusting to step over a giant root—they were everywhere. Lianndra saw the short tail whip back and forth once.

"The Fang have tried to disable the planetary shield but have not met with any success so far. Until the shield falls, they cannot bring in any heavy equipment. It limits them to a foot war," the woman said.

That surprised Lianndra. *Shields preventing heavy equipment use? No wonder this war was not going well for the Fang. The Gryphon are at least as advanced as the Fang if they shielded their planet. Wait a minute.* "Then how did we get here?"

The woman stopped and turned to face her. "Drop ships carry replacements, they follow an entry trajectory to the barracks. The ships do not possess independent drives so are not affected by the shield. The only way off the planet is with simple projectile technology. Now, enough questions." The tail whipped again. It reminded Lianndra again of her annoyed cat.

Glancing behind her, she noticed her tail was waving like a weaving cobra. Lianndra felt it moving but still didn't have any conscious control over it.

The two slaves resumed their trek. Lianndra kept silent but her mind was abuzz. She didn't know what the war between the Fang and the Gryphon was about. She assumed it was an attempt by the Fang to obtain more slaves.

I expected races so advanced would pound away at each other in huge metal space battleships around the planet, or at least with tanks on the ground. A low-tech foot war put a new complexion on things. *They must want these slaves pretty bad for it to go on for so long.*

Lianndra followed the woman along a worn path to a large building which looked just as beat up as the others. As they entered, Lianndra's eyes caught English words scrawled like graffiti along one wall.

"Welcome," she read, "to the rest of your life."

Perfect.

YOU SHALL BE A HEALER and we will use this mutation to further our cause.

The words reverberated in her mind as Lianndra sank her hands deeper into the body before her, past the torn skin and muscle, seeking the vessel pumping the alien's life blood away.

The rebel program installed in her collar activated the voice of the old Fara to her inner ear. Lianndra often repeated the scratchy words within her head. At first, she had no idea what the Fara meant by her reference to Healer. Lianndra soon found out. From her initial day on the alien planet, she trained with other, older Healers. They taught her how to use her new genetically enhanced skills to heal.

Lianndra discovered the Fang geneticists had tapped into the depths of the human brain. They enhanced latent telekinetic abilities in the Tier-5 females. These skills might have evolved naturally on Earth if given enough time. Lianndra heard of people back home that healed with their minds, although it was rare and often discredited.

With this new skill and training, Lianndra manipulated a living body at the cellular level. Once shown the key molecules essential for cell division, she found it easy to identify them again. She used her mind to move the molecules, supplying the cells with nutrients while using the proteins to initiate division. She looked *within* any injury placed before her and knit it back together, one cell at a time.

Lianndra caught on fast; her veterinarian training had schooled her in the basic building blocks of life as well as cellular histology, biochemistry, and animal physiology. Although she was working on aliens, all life forms had things in common; their structure, form, and function could be assessed on this basis. Comparing the damaged cells of the injury site to healthy cells in same individual enabled her to repair almost anything. She flew through the training program and started healing without supervision. Every night, the scratchy Fara voice invaded her mind. At first, Lianndra had been afraid the collar enabled someone to overhear the rebellious thoughts. After a while, she discovered the collars didn't work that way and did not form a telepathic connection. Rather, they worked via computerized nodes implanted in her brain. For her controller to trigger the pain nodes he had to have Lianndra in a direct line of sight. Then he stared at her and clenched his fist. His collar read the nerve impulses of his hand while following his gaze to her, and she would then be shocked. The collar also had the ability to track a slave's location relative to their controller. If they strayed beyond a certain distance, the collar first warned, then caused pain, and if ignored, could kill them.

Lianndra certainly didn't want to give her particular controller any excuse to exact punishment. As it was, he was never far from causing her pain. Perhaps it was because it was so easy for him to do so. All he needed were his eyes, a clenched fist, and a collar.

Controllers were fellow slaves. They could be any species but they shared one thing in common: they served their Fang overlords with unswerving loyalty. Not all of them required the threat of their own collars to do so.

Each controller had responsibility for a number of slaves. Fang commanders supervised the controllers. Controllers transferred slaves to one another by placing a hand-held device against the slave's collar.

In the initial days of the war, the controllers numbered one to every five or so slaves. Now they were often responsible for two to three times that number; the dwindling war resources spread them thin. This was fortunate for the slaves. Many controllers seemed to have a vicious streak, and Lianndra's was no exception. He ruled them with a cruelty bordering on sadism. Only the fact most of his charges were Healers kept him from rendering any permanent harm. As a result of the war not going well, the Fang needed the Healers desperately. They couldn't afford to lose any, particularly to a disgruntled controller.

There were medtechs, and then there were Healers. Medtechs came in many species, but the Healers were human females. Or rather, they'd been humans before being changed by the Fang. Medtechs used Fang technology to diagnose illnesses and heal minor wounds, but much of it remained hampered by the effects of the planetary shield. The humidity of the jungle also affected the accuracy of small electronic devices while the lengthy war stretched the operable tech to the breaking point. The Fang soldiers reserved the surviving technology for themselves, leaving their wounded slaves to the genetically modified Healers.

If only the collars were vulnerable to the effects of the shield. Lianndra continued to hope that someday the wretched thing would just fall off. *As long as it doesn't take part of my brain with it.*

In addition to their enhanced mental abilities, many of the Healers featured some of Lianndra's external modifications, but few showed all of her new features. Their one major similarity was the ability to heal with their minds.

Although I don't know why we need hairy bodies if we spend our time in makeshift hospitals, she thought.

Her tail possessed an annoying tendency to reveal her mood swings, but it was becoming increasingly handy. At the moment, it helped to support her. Lianndra had wound it around a rafter as she balanced on the chest of the huge alien she was healing.

Something pulsed beneath the sensitive finger pads that occupied the space below her claws, and Lianndra brought her mind back to the task at hand. The body she was working on might be alien but all beings needed a circulatory system to move nutrients around and carry away waste products.

Zraph were massive aliens, the size of a standing rhino. Their main contribution to the Fang war was brute strength. Zraph resembled a mudslide come alive: all bulky, rounded muscles, no neck, and bald heads with four eyes. They were bipedal with legs like pillars and rectangular feet ending in thick, stubby toes.

The Zraph that Lianndra was working on suffered from a tear in a major artery leading to one of its seven hearts.

If it wasn't for seven hearts, this one would never have made it, she thought.

Lianndra let her mind follow her fingers. She felt the torn artery at the gross physiological level, and then she moved deeper to the alien cells surrounding the injury.

Mother Nature abhors a vacuum, she thought.

Destroyed tissue created a void in the cells, and the intact ones along the edges automatically went into overdrive to fill in the gap. Lianndra helped with this effort by using her genetically enhanced telekinesis. She redirected essential nutrients, oxygen, and growth factors to the struggling cells. Then she penetrated the cells through pores in the membrane. Identifying the crucial proteins necessary to trigger mitosis, she pushed them into action.

The actions of an experienced Healer accelerated cell division, healing even massive wounds. Some cells divided more willingly than others; organ or nerve cells took considerable encouragement before they divided.

Lianndra's energy depleted as she poured herself into the healing. Under her ministrations, the deepest part of the ugly tear filled in with new cells. She withdrew, healing as she went. Once she reached the external muscle, she pulled out. Zraph were incredibly tough, and they had trained Lianndra not to waste her energy on a complete healing when a few laser staples got him back out to the front line.

Lianndra's tail released the rafter without her conscious thought before she slid down the side of the huge, sparsely haired body of the Zraph. A long shift healing nasty wounds had exhausted her. Two medtechs clambered up behind her, trailing the laser stapler along with them. Lianndra's bare, clawed feet touched the fluid drenched floor of the medic bay. She turned to find herself face-to-torso with her controller.

His species, the Rosk, would not win any beauty contests, which might account for their terrible tempers. Lianndra assumed the females of the species found their mates attractive, but she certainly couldn't fathom it. She'd never seen a female, so maybe they didn't exist. In fact, her controller could be he, she, or a neutral gender.

At any rate, from a human perspective, he'd been hit with a giant ugly stick. He stood eight feet tall, and his warty skin defeated any attempt to clothe him. He settled for a cloth draping over one shoulder that bulged its uneven way to the double-jointed knees on all three of his legs. The few other Rosks she'd seen were also warty, so it seemed a species trait. He had no neck, and a triangular, amorphous head featuring two narrow nostrils and three gummy eyes rimmed with red. His favorite hobby involved setting the Healers up to fail so he could inflict more pain.

As she stood facing him, her neck craned at an uncomfortable angle, Lianndra braced herself for a reprimand. For once the controller seemed preoccupied. He issued a brief command sounding part wheeze, part grunt, before turning to leave. The command carried through her collar to the node implanted within her inner ear, where it was translated into English.

Lianndra turned away to trudge out of the medic bay and along the muddy path to the administration quarters. She'd only been there once before and wondered why they wanted to see her now. Her tail twitched in annoyance. Her body needed food to replace the precious nutrients she lost while healing. Feeling shaky and dizzy, Lianndra hoped whatever this was could be resolved fast.

Lianndra sensed tension as soon as she entered the administration building. The spindly alien in the central cubicle gestured to the third room on the right. Called Wraiths by the Healers, they earned their name due to the wispy, elongated necks and limbs.

Multicolored cables and conduits covered the hallway walls. Lianndra remained surprised at the makeshift look, not to mention the low-tech aspect. The Fang weren't even using wireless technology within the building. Lianndra wondered why. She was certain the slave collars relied on wireless technology to operate between controller and slave.

Why do the collars work on this planet while other devices cannot? she thought. *Do they use different technology? Perhaps the collars are not designed by the Fang, but by someone else.*

Regardless, it was amazing the Gryphon had reduced the Fang to such a crude existence.

Their planetary shield is impressive, she thought as she paused in front of the designated door.

As the door hissed closed behind her, she noticed the Fang they called Jarzak, the commander in chief of the forces on the planet. It surprised Lianndra to see him; only the war coordinator, Tar%tosk%rask, exceeded him in rank. Strategic decisions came from the war coordinator, through Jarzak, then to the Central Intelligence Processor. The CIP then distributed the orders to the frontline fighting forces. It was a direct line of communication from Tar%tosk%rask to Jarzak; he was kept too busy to involve himself in mundane affairs.

Mundane like me, Lianndra thought.

The big Fang's presence made her nervous, and it relieved Lianndra to see she was not the only Healer in the room. A short, redheaded woman she'd never seen before was standing near one wall. Lianndra noticed she and the smaller woman shared the same modifications. Her red hair was very short as if she had recently undergone the sterilization procedure. It reminded Lianndra of how her new body hair was causing her to itch. It was so irritating that she was considering trying life as a hairy nudist. Seeing this woman made her realize just how hairy she'd become, and it made her uncomfortable.

Lianndra's discomfort increased as the Fang commander in chief stepped aside to reveal the other occupant of the room, a stocky human male. His skin was brown, further darkened by many hours in the sun. The man had black, tightly curled, short hair, and his eyebrows were thick over equally dark, piercing eyes. Like all the slaves, he was fighting fit. He dressed in a soldier's camouflage uniform that clung to his muscular body.

Lianndra heard from the other Healers about human males at the front lines of the war, but she'd not seen one until now. These barracks did not receive humans as wounded, and she hadn't seen them on the base. She knew theirs was only one of many Fang barracks on this world so she assumed the men got healed elsewhere. In the beginning, she'd felt deflated when she discovered there were no men at their barracks. A part of her yearned to integrate with other humans, but the obvious physical changes to her body gave her hesitation. She was no longer fully human. The thought of potential rejection by her own species made her insides squirm.

The thoughts coursed through her brain as the human finished examining the redheaded woman from head to foot. He seemed shocked by the woman's appearance. When his eyes skimmed over Lianndra, she wanted to dissolve into the floor.

"They're new recruits?" he asked Jarzak. Lianndra's heart lifted at the sound of a normal human voice even as she detected a slight accent: British or Aussie.

The redheaded Healer had shifted under his scrutiny, and out of the corner of her eye, Lianndra noticed the woman's tail tucked to the back of her legs.

The almost indecipherable voice of Jarzak answered the man. "Both are. One here only a little longer." The Farr had the usual problems speaking English and only an experienced ear permitted her to understand the garbled words.

"Both trained?" His accent was Australian, Lianndra determined. *An Aussie human male slave.* Much higher on the pecking order than her, it would seem.

The Fang nodded, refraining from verbal comment. Lianndra concluded it was the heavier jaw and tongue of the Farr that made the human languages difficult. Certainly, she'd never seen a Farr speaking English like the Fara did.

"Well, we need 'em." He turned to the women, addressing the air between them. "Report here at first daylight tomorrow. Dismissed."

Disappointment stabbed at Lianndra as she and the other woman left. *He didn't even meet my eyes. Am I so hard to look at?*

It wasn't until she was back on the path, trailed by the redhead, that she absorbed what he'd said.

I am leaving the barracks in the morning, she thought. She didn't mind if her life changed yet again, even if it meant following a human to the front lines. *I'm ready to face something more.* It was time. She only hoped the voice in her head agreed and revealed the secrets she knew were there.

"My name is Hannah." The soft voice broke into her reverie as Lianndra turned to face the smaller woman. Their eyes met for the first time and Lianndra felt a mild physical jolt from her collar.

Yes, the voice of the interactive guide came alive in her ear, *she is one of us.*

Lianndra saw the recognition dawn in the tawny eyes of her new friend as the other woman also heard her own version of the Fara's voice. "I'm . . ."

"Lianndra," Hannah said. "I know. I think we have a friend in common."

Wow. Suddenly there were new possibilities. Lianndra's heart skipped a beat. The surrounding jungle seemed more alive than it had mere seconds ago. As they turned to head to the commissary, Lianndra felt empowered by more than mere claws and a tail. *Finally, things are going to happen!*

WITH THE GROUND OVER TWO hundred feet below, Lianndra released her tail's hold on the branch and flew through the air. A mere fifty feet to her left, Hannah paced her through the canopy, a red blur in the dappled light. Claws penetrated rough bark, safely bringing them home against yet another huge trunk. Lianndra had her skrin on her forearm, but she rarely needed it this high in the trees where the huge branches interlocked to form a high-altitude highway. The skrin was most useful for moving up and down in the forest.

It had taken weeks of practice at lower levels before the two Healers tackled the upper canopy. The dense foliage added an element of unpredictability as the jungle flora often possessed distinct fauna characteristics. Staying clear of the mobile predatory plant species was a steep learning curve. In the first week of their deployment, both Healers required rescue by their human caretakers on more than a few occasions.

The Healers learned fast. They were soon traveling beyond as well as above the men who hacked their way through the bottommost foliage. As they moved, the two Healers used special scent glands on their wrists to lay a trail back to the group, a technique that kept them from getting lost. Lianndra found swinging through the canopy invigorating, mimicking the freedom that, in reality, she did not have.

The tropical rainforests of the planet Tarin teemed with life. Lianndra remembered reading about the incredible diversity of Earth's rainforests. If they were similar to Tarin's, they were remarkable.

Every giant tree was a city unto itself, providing a home for vast numbers of plants and entire colonies of animals large and small. The life forms straddling the line between flora and fauna were unique; many were larger than the mobile vines Lianndra noticed her first day on the planet. She'd seen huge, leafy tendrils snatch indigenous critters out of the air. They folded their leathery leaves around the victim until the animal itself was visible only as a bulge along the stems.

The modifications to her human body finally made sense. Claws and a prehensile tail worked better than skrins, enabling the Healers to navigate the upper levels of the enormous jungle trees. They moved ahead of the men, scouting for trouble, searching for sustenance, and looking for the frontline fighting units needing their help.

Lianndra paused, leaning against a branch while tapping a small oval disc she'd woven into her hair. They sent messages back to their controllers using comm units since the collar's communication systems only worked within line of sight.

The Aussie who'd recruited the two Healers from the barracks was their captain and their controller.

He is far and away nicer than my previous controller. Mind you, she thought of the ugly Rosk, *I guess that's not saying much.*

"All clear along this vector. No sign of them yet," Lianndra's soft-spoken words relayed back to the captain. Captain Drake gave her a new vector to search over the comm.

She and Hannah were valuable as trained Healers, but they excelled as mobile scouts. In fact, the two skill sets were not as divergent as they seemed. Drake's small human division searched for and rescued injured or missing frontline soldiers. Their human adaptability meant they could work through any situation while keeping themselves alive. Find, Heal, and Reactivate; the so-called FHR divisions were a new initiative straight from war coordinator Tar%tosk%rask's office, one which was becoming vital to the Fang war effort.

The fact it was the war coordinator's idea explains Jarzak's presence in the office, she thought. *He ensured each group got off to a good start. I've heard it isn't wise to annoy the coordinator.*

The FHR divisions consisted of two Healers plus six human male soldiers overseen by a human captain who was also their controller. The soldiers protected and sustained the Healers because they were valuable assets, capable of healing and reactivating an entire Fang fighting unit within a few hours.

Each FHR division had an assigned patrol area, defined by the fighting units they were to serve and using coordinates fed into the

FHR controller's collar by Jarzak himself. Even Drake must stay within this designated perimeter or face pain and then death via the collar nodes. The slaves reporting to him could only stray a set distance away from Drake or they met the same fate. It was a tidy method for keeping slaves within boundaries without direct Fang supervision.

The permitted area coordinates for each FHR division could be altered by any Fang commander, as long as he possessed the device necessary to do so and was in the FHR controller's presence. So if the fighting units shifted positions, their commanders could reprogram the FHR coordinates to keep pace with them.

The Healers were well within their safe distance from Drake at the moment. Lianndra made the course correction he'd requested and Hannah followed suit. Their enhanced vision, hearing, and sense of smell made it possible for the two women to connect in ways appearing almost telepathic. They moved through the canopy as one, each aware of the other's presence.

Soaring through the jungle lifted Lianndra's spirits, and she knew Hannah felt the same. Away from direct Fang contact, they were the happiest they'd been since their capture back on Earth. The veneer of civilization, Fang or otherwise, fell away with their first leap into the trees and didn't return until the end of the day. From the roughness of tree bark beneath their claws to the sounds and scents of the life around them, the jungle spoke to the Healers. It represented a connection to nature lost long ago, not only by the earthbound humans but also by the technologically advanced Fang. A connection abandoned, yet not forgotten. Deep within the women, something essential was being reborn.

If only we were here by choice and not serving a race as foul as the Fang, Lianndra thought.

As the division patrolled, they hunted. The jungle was rich in protein sources suitable for human consumption. Keeping the Healers in top condition was an important goal for the men. As Hannah and Lianndra moved, they spotted potential food sources, reported them to Drake, who then sent soldiers to collect them. Every night at camp, the women rested while the men set up the sleeping tents and cooked the bounty of the day. As females, the Healers joked to themselves about the role reversal. Some of the men were less than happy with their situation, but Drake was their captain and controller. If he wanted it done in such a manner, that was how it got done.

Drake stayed aloof. If he knew of the occasional resentful glance sent in the women's direction, he did not let on. He treated everyone with the same aura of detachment, expecting each person to perform their duties as assigned. He was quick to verbally correct if someone fell out of line, which resulted in Lianndra being cautious around him. As the FHR division worked its way through a savage jungle on an alien world, Lianndra recognized the captain's attention to detail kept everyone not only focused and efficient but also safe.

One particular thing got under Lianndra's skin: Drake rarely looked at her. She wondered if it was because he saw the Healers as animals and not human, or if she was putting her own spin on things. Lianndra stayed away from him regardless, not wanting to witness him avoid meeting her eyes. The last thing she wanted was to have her suspicions verified.

She mentioned the matter to Hannah while they were on patrol two hundred feet in the air.

The redheaded Healer just shook her head and laughed. "If he feels that way, he's just going to have to suck it up," she said. "We are the only females out here with him in this jungle. If he wants human scenery to ogle, we're the only option going."

This topic was too close to Lianndra's heart for her to treat it lightly. Her genetic changes often made her feel more animal than human. *I wouldn't blame any human male for not wanting to interact with me.*

"Maybe he's not interested in women," Lianndra muttered.

Hannah sobered as if recognizing what was bothering her. "It's too bad if he isn't 'cause we are gorgeous, hairy or not."

Lianndra had to smile. She and Hannah abandoned their clothing weeks ago. Both Healers used their new cellular manipulation abilities to control each body hair. By growing and interweaving the hairs, they could afford themselves the same modesty as clothing without the branch snagging side effects. They could even weave their hair over their slave collars, disguising the bright metal to keep it from catching the sunlight.

When the Fang enslaved her, Hannah had been in first-year medicine. She was a cheerful, outgoing person. After a comparison of their lives as Dancers, it became clear Hannah must have Danced on a different Mothership from Lianndra, which was why they'd never met before. It made Lianndra wonder just how many of the massive ships orbited the Gryphon home world.

Over time, Lianndra came to appreciate that, although the redheaded Healer was carefree on the surface, she had an inner core of steel that revealed itself in brief glimpses. Her new friend even stood up to Drake, politely questioning his more minor decisions. The captain was surprisingly tolerant of such interruptions, answering the questions before issuing his final orders.

Lianndra wouldn't have dared question the dark-haired Aussie captain. She did notice, however, that her friend always picked her questions with care, never commenting on any of Drake's important decisions. Lianndra understood Hannah wasn't undermining Drake's choices, but helping to build the group into an effective team by increasing communication. Hannah seemed to have inexhaustible energy reserves, something which proved useful during the long hours of swinging through the dense forest.

Even without the closeness their situation forced on them, Lianndra and Hannah would have become friends. They often viewed the world in similar ways, although Lianndra was a quieter, more reserved person. Hannah had come through the slave experience with her cheerful, optimistic personality intact. Having Hannah as a friend helped ease Lianndra's loneliness. She missed Andrea.

Back on the Mothership, Andrea mentioned she'd also received the same so-called vitamins triggering the mutation. Lianndra wondered if it turned Andrea into a Healer. It was obviously not a sure thing as Healers were not common. Compared to the thousands of slave soldiers on the front lines, the FHR divisions were not plentiful, and each division possessed only two Healers. It seemed not all women responded to the orange liquid, or perhaps they didn't survive the resulting mutation process.

Or maybe they don't consider all Dancers worthy, so some aren't given the orange gunk to begin with, thought Lianndra.

There weren't many FHR divisions so their ranges never overlapped. As a result, Lianndra and Hannah hadn't met the other FHR Healers. If Andrea was out there in the jungle, Lianndra might never find her.

So far their world revolved around the small group of humans. Although Hannah spoke with the men, Lianndra rarely fraternized with the soldiers and kept to herself. With the Healers in the trees all day, most communications relayed from them through Drake to the men. It created a gulf between the soldiers and the Healers that even Hannah's efforts could not bridge.

Her sensitivity to her appearance made Lianndra aware of how the soldiers sometimes stared at herself and Hannah as they walked through the camp. The looks were not always pleasant. It didn't help that Hannah was more indifferent to nudity than Lianndra. Hannah concentrated on covering the basics and didn't worry about anything else. Lianndra didn't think Hannah's nonchalance to her seminude state reflected the feelings of the men in their unit. The Healers might not appear as typical human females but they were all a long way from Earth.

"Lianndra, you don't like them looking at you, and you don't like Drake not looking at you," Hannah commented to her, keeping it light but sounding mildly exasperated. "Face it—after a while the jungle is not exciting to watch, unless it's trying to kill you. They have to look at something so why not us?"

Hannah had a point. *Maybe I am being too sensitive.* Plus, Drake brooked no nonsense in the camp, intervening if the men tried anything with the Healers.

Drake might be their controller but the Fang controlled him. She did not know how the man felt about being a slave, but he ran things efficiently and fairly despite the Fang influence. She and Hannah might yet have cause to be grateful for Drake as their controller.

ONE OF THEIR EARLY EXPERIENCES with healing a large frontline unit was one made up of Zraph, controlled by a bulky Fang named Harnsk. Zraph were so tough this unit stayed in the fight even with many of them injured. When they heard Drake's FHR division was close, the unit marched to meet them behind the lines.

Zraph were temperamental creatures, even more so when wounded. To protect his Healers, Drake had each one covered by his armed soldiers as the women worked. An injured Zraph was often immune to collar control. The Healers were valuable enough that a Zraph would be sacrificed to protect them.

Lianndra found her agility useful when climbing the huge bodies to reach the injuries and when ducking or dodging to avoid the occasional swing of the club-like arms. Hit with a series of cluster bombs, the unit of Zraph suffered extensive shrapnel damage. Foreign object removal required her to push the objects out of the body as she healed the injury path left behind. The soldiers helped with the larger pieces, pulling them out as the Healers worked.

Such injuries were not as common as knife or sword wounds. The Gryphon seemed to fight with primitive weapons, although they sometimes used lasers, grenades, and bombs salvaged from the Fang fighting units. Lianndra was grateful the bombs, at least, were not commonly used. Shrapnel wounds were difficult to heal.

She was getting better at controlling her patient's pain. Lianndra explained the process to Drake, who questioned her when he first saw her attempt it. He permitted her to continue when he recognized the obvious advantages of a pain-free Zraph while healing.

Now she used the creature's bulky arm to lever herself upward. She flattened her body on the muscled chest of her patient and braced the craggy head between her hands. Looking into the four primary eyes, she wondered how the creature visualized her. Lianndra let herself drift into the mind of the alien. The first time she'd tried this was on Hannah who, as another human, was familiar on a physiological level. It was much more confusing with an alien mind, not to mention dangerous. There was a risk of connecting too deep, getting lost in the maze of alien physiology. Lianndra tried to keep the contact as superficial as possible.

What she was looking for were the pain receivers within the brain. So far, all the creatures she'd worked on possessed them; it was the body's method for preventing physical harm. The actual characteristics of the receivers differed between species. Lianndra located the nerves running from the injuries to the brain first, then she slipped through the cellular barrier encasing the brain's protection system. From there she followed nerves until she found the pain transmitters.

In the case of the Zraph, she'd worked on a few at the barracks so she knew where to look. The creature grew quiet as she blocked the nerve synapses with dams of scar tissue. With the healing complete, she would have to push those cells aside so the transmitters regained their normal function. Then she had only a few seconds to complete another task, the one for which the Fang rebels prepared her.

Her mind raced to the site on the side of the neck where the collar entered the brain. *I must be careful to keep my fingers from tracing the path of my thoughts.* Neither Drake nor the Zraph's Fang commander could know what she was doing.

Quick as lightning, she found the collar's microfiber net in the brain. She sculpted cells, placing a protective buffer of nonconducting scar tissue between the delicate brain network and the nodes. It was one of these nodes located within the wire net that enabled the collar to kill.

Each creature was different. Due to the incredible resilience of the Zraph physiology, the fiber network within their brain was extensive. Lianndra worked to complete the task before anyone grew suspicious.

She removed her hands from the creature's head just as the Fang commander, Harnsk, paced alongside her particular Zraph. Moving past the great chest, Lianndra worked on a huge gash across the creature's arm. Beyond the Fang commander, Drake looked on, his weapon always at the ready. Across the clearing, Hannah finished with her Zraph, glancing Lianndra's way as she slid down the creature's side.

Lianndra caught the barest wink before the redheaded Healer headed off to her next patient, trailing three of the division's soldiers as protective detail.

Mission accomplished, Lianndra thought.

LIANNDRA SAT IN THE NEAR darkness, staring at her arms, focusing on the point where the thick golden hair thinned to the bare flesh of her wrists and hands. When healing others, she used her mind to replicate cells at many times the normal rate. When she healed, her body used nutrients at an accelerated pace. Long sessions of healing drained her resources. Lianndra had yet to have a complete failure of her skills, although she'd heard it was possible.

If I can heal aliens by manipulating cells in such a manner, could I alter my own cells? If I applied myself on a deeper level, what else is possible? The thought was frightening. *Once I alter my body, how do I return to my default self? Could I get caught up in a self-perpetuating healing trance, lost forever in a maze of my own altered cells? If I accidentally altered what makes me a Healer, could I cut myself off from the power enabling me to make the changes?* She gave herself a mental shake to stop herself from descending the spiral of dark thoughts. They led nowhere, discouraging her from trying anything new.

Over the last few weeks, she appreciated the changes the Fang had made in her external appearance. The freedom of swinging through the trees was exhilarating. Every time she returned to the ground, however, the reactions of the men to her presence reminded her of just how different she'd become.

If only I could change my looks as needed, she thought. *I can't alter the fact I am no longer human, but perhaps I can look less like an animal.*

She stared at her arms, battling her uncertainty.

Laying one hand on the opposite arm, she trailed her sensitive finger pads along the area where thick hair gave way to smooth skin. Closing her eyes, she went *within* the hair follicles. Cells multiplied and hair sprouted from the follicles. Compared to the complex healing she'd done with the aliens, it seemed so simple. With a final tweak, Lianndra added curl and used it to weave the hair along her chosen line. Once done it looked like the cuff on a shirt, with a clear division between covered and bare skin.

Lianndra breathed. She didn't feel any fatigue; it was such a simple thing. But now she wanted to try something different, something she'd never done. Adding cells was part of healing. Now she wanted to remove them. With another deep breath, she rested her hand on the cuff of hair and took the plunge.

It took more than a few tries to get it started. She destroyed each cell by breaking the plasma membrane holding it together. This meant tearing apart the molecular bonds of the membranes. The result was free-floating cellular components as debris. Above the skin, she let the leftovers lay inert as a fine powder. Within the depths of the hair shaft itself, she had to mobilize a system for clearing it out. The easiest method would be to divert the tissue's natural fluids, using them to flush the bits and pieces out of the empty shaft. It was messy but seemed the best solution for the moment.

I'll have to think of ways to do it cleanly—perhaps by diverting the debris to the lymphatic system? Or maybe I can figure out a way to store the components for the future?

She opened her eyes to see bare, clammy, and grubby skin instead of the cuff of hair. Grubby, but hairless!

Not very attractive, she thought, feeling elation rise within her, *but better than looking like an ape.*

Lianndra knew this possessed implications beyond her appearance. She'd used her mind to destroy cells rather than rebuild them. Wounds healing imperfectly could now be taken apart and then rehealed. Her mind shied away from the other possibilities inherent in being able to destroy cells. It led to thoughts better left quiet.

A soft crunch of shifting dirt and movement out of the corner of her eye alerted her to Hannah's approach. The smaller woman gave her a questioning glance as she settled beside her. The firelight barely reached the spot where they sat, but Lianndra knew Hannah's enhanced vision could see her hairless arm and the smile in her eyes.

Lianndra grinned. "Do I ever have something to tell you."

NOT ALL DANGER WAS DUE to the war.

A few mornings later, Hannah and Lianndra tracked a unit of Fang retreating from the front lines. Judging by the amount of blood on the trail, the unit had lost a recent battle. Drake was in touch with the commander on his comm; they waited in a dry creek bed nearby. The enemy Gryphon troop they tangled with could also be close, which meant their FHR division must move with caution through the jungle.

Hannah and Lianndra were on a short leash. Drake didn't want them too far ahead in case they required the men's protection. So they crept ahead, always staying within sight.

The system might have kept the Healers safer, but it created the drawback of not giving the women much time to warn the soldiers of any danger. In fact, there were only microseconds between the moment Lianndra scented trouble and the crashing through the underbrush as something descended on the men.

The Razorback got its name from the wicked sharp spikes covering its body. The creature may be vegetarian, but it had the temperament of an injured rhino while possessing an alarming tendency to defend itself by attacking.

It sliced through the soldiers, leaving blood and chaos in its wake; there and gone before anyone got off a shot.

Lianndra and Hannah were instantly among the men, stemming the flow of blood, triaging those needing immediate help and those that could wait. Lianndra helped Drake up from the trampled earth where he lay. He waved her off to help the man just beyond him. The slave's eyes were wild with pain but he still tried to struggle to a sitting position as Lianndra kneeled beside him. "Easy," she said, pushing him down. "Lie back. This might hurt, but I can heal you good as new."

He pulled away from her with a resentful expression. Drake had reprimanded this slave several times for inappropriate behavior around the Healers. The injury was deep. She heard him groan with pain more than once as she knit the tissues together, closing the skin, leaving a half-healed scar. They needed him as whole as possible if the division was to keep moving.

When she opened her eyes, she noticed he stared at her in a strange way. With the heat of the midday jungle and the stress of healing, Lianndra was sweating. Her control over her body hair was now so automatic she seldom paid attention to it. In the heat, she had retracted her hair coverage to keep cool. This left her clad in the hairy equivalent of a bikini. While healing exhausted her, once completed, it often gave the healed a small boost of energy. Judging by the look in the stocky slave's eyes, he was feeling too good.

Lianndra pushed herself upright and away from him. He recognized the movement for the rejection it was. She saw his gaze darken just before he grimaced and spat into the dirt at her feet.

That one was never a winner. She might long for human contact but not the kind he had in mind.

With the dangers posed by the jungle, the soldiers in Drake's division required minor healing on a regular basis. To follow the Fang rebellion's orders, the Healers disabled the kill switches on their collars. Neither Hannah nor she dared to confide in any of the men even though they were human and friendly enough. Their internal Fara guide cautioned them to remain secret. If the Fang got premature wind of what they were doing, it would be for naught. The two Healers covertly worked toward an uncertain goal. They were often unsure how their efforts would result in freedom for themselves and for every slave they touched.

Lianndra traded glances with Hannah, who gave her a thumbs up to show they'd covered the two worst injuries. Then she turned to attend to Drake, who stood cradling what looked like a dislocated shoulder. The injuries of the Fang unit would have to wait until the FHR division was on the move.

OF ALL THE ALIENS LIANNDRA worked on, she hated healing the Fang the most.

The feeling seemed mutual as they preferred using technology and medtechs to heal their wounds. Unfortunately, this unit of Fang commandos ran into a large troop of Gryphon far away from the nearest medic base or its technology.

Fang medic bases resided behind the action. The front line was dynamic, and sometimes the fighting overran the bases. In addition to often being evacuated, the medtechs became overextended dealing with the number of casualties. The FHR divisions alleviated this problem.

As the elite of the Fang soldier's, commandos functioned as special operatives, used by the army to move covertly into enemy territory for a mission, and then retreat before being caught. Essentially, they became accustomed to preferential treatment.

This unit received faulty intel leading them straight into a large troop of Gryphon. Gryphon moved so fast that any information on their whereabouts was often unreliable. Regardless, Lianndra heard the slaves responsible for the bad intel paid for their mistake with their lives.

The old Fang before her was one of the largest Farr she'd ever seen. A body riddled with scars showed many missions completed. He was a veteran. His newest injury would have cost him his life if it had taken Lianndra's unit much longer to reach them. The Fang possessed a circulatory system powered by two hearts. As soon as Lianndra went *within*, she found one of the hearts torn to pieces.

He'd lost a lot of blood which Lianndra could not replace. She could only heal him, leaving the blood replenishment to his own body.

Lianndra fought to keep her fear at bay as she worked on the Farr. Those glowing orange eyes never left her face, and she hoped that the Fang shared his species lack of telepathic ability. She felt as though she had a neon rebel sign written across her forehead. The giant seemed to attribute her nervousness to his mere presence. Fang commandos did not lack ego.

The work was painstaking and difficult. Lianndra trembled by the time she gave his cells the final push to seal up the wound. She sat back from him and closed her eyes, raising an arm to wipe sweat from her forehead.

He caught her by surprise. One moment she was sitting on her heels, the next he'd pinned her against him before sinking his teeth into the juncture of her neck and shoulder.

Fear and revulsion filled her. She raked her claws along his healed skin. Whipping up from behind her, her tail cracked the commando across the face . . . to no avail. Out of the corner of her eye, she saw one of Drake's soldiers level his laser rifle at the Fang, growling something indecipherable.

No, Lianndra screamed in her mind, *they'll kill you!*

She saw Drake grab the rifle by the barrel, shoving it skyward. "No, Sean!" he said. Then she heard Drake's voice yelling for the Fang commander. His voice sounded strange, an unusual combination of anger and desperation. As the teeth chewed deeper, Lianndra realized in panic that Drake lacked authority to stop a Fang. The rules of the Blooddance did not bind this Fang. He could kill her and Drake couldn't do anything about it.

The commander snarled something in the heavy Fang language. The teeth hesitated in their progress toward her jugular. Lianndra took the initiative, tearing herself free, her shoulder soaked in blood. She pushed herself away, stumbling backward. The blond soldier dropped his rifle to catch her as she swayed. Hanging limp in his arms, Lianndra went *within* to stop the bleeding.

The Farr stared at her. His long, thick, pointed tongue licked her blood from his lips as he stood to his full height, his eyes red with bloodlust. Behind him, his commander glared at both Drake and Sean for a moment before shrugging and turning back to clean his weapon.

Just another day at the office for them, she thought, *and a near death experience for me.*

The blond soldier cursed under his breath as he helped her to where Hannah stood, face pale with shock.

"Thanks, Sean." The smaller Healer ushered Lianndra to the far side of the human camp where she could tend to her friend's gashed neck.

Lianndra heard Drake talking to the commander. The Fang pointed to the commandos still requiring the Healers.

Whatever the discussion, Drake was at least able to buy them enough time for Hannah to heal Lianndra before they had to venture back among the Fang.

As Lianndra worked on a Fang commando with a torn leg, Drake passed by, pressing a ration bar into her hand. It was one of the kindest things he'd ever done for her.

Other than saving my life, she thought.

IF WORKING ON FANG FILLED Lianndra with fear, working on the slaves often filled her with despair.

The typical fighting unit contained one Fang commander and fifty to one hundred human slave soldiers, with a ragtag mixture of aliens thrown in for good measure. Units like this were now the norm. During his rare conversations, Drake informed the Healer of his earlier days in the war. At that time, the fighting units were fresh off the ships and made up of phalanxes of elite human soldiers. Now, it seemed if a slave could lift a sword he joined the closest unit.

He'd also told them the numbers of soldiers per unit had decreased from two hundred to less than one hundred. The use of this many slaves in the ground forces was apparently unique to the Gryphon conflict. The Fang lost many Farr during the early part of the war, forcing them to fortify the front line with human slave soldiers. Earth provided the easiest source for the slaves, thus most of the frontline forces were male humans. For years, the Fang harvested humans and trained them as fighting slaves, then sold them to other species. The Gryphon war changed this lucrative business into something else altogether.

Drake's information revealed that at the peak of the war, the Fang used the genetically modified Tier-5 humans to create elite units of slaves. These men possessed a consistency of fighting ability and appearance, which showed the effects of five generations of genetic meddling by the Fang. The naturally athletic Tier-5 elite soldiers were long-limbed, powerfully built, and over six feet tall. Lianndra couldn't help but think Drake was describing Michael. Was he one of the elite Fang slaves?

Lianndra was amazed at the staggering number of humans in the fighting units, taken from Earth over the course of many years.

It's no wonder the slave ring back home was so well established, Lianndra thought. *A few humans were getting wealthy by providing slaves to the Fang.* Her thoughts returned to the here and now. *What on this planet is worth so much to the Fang? The scope and scale of this war are significant. It must be costing them a fortune.*

Although the elite soldiers received weapons training to enhance their natural skill, it was obvious to Lianndra not all the slave recruits were of the same caliber. Many slaves possessed a ragged mixture of physical and mental traits. She noticed these men hadn't received the same level of training and were injured more often. Both Healers noticed obvious signs of strain. Some of the soldiers adopted strange mental quirks to cope with their situation. These slave soldiers were not holding it together emotionally.

Every time a new unit reported to the FHR division, Lianndra's pulse raced. She scanned the face of each soldier, looking for familiar features. Her reaction was so obvious Hannah commented on it.

"I'm looking for a man enslaved with me. I think he might fight in one of these units," Lianndra told her.

As the days slid into weeks, and then into months, Lianndra wondered if she would still even recognize Michael after all this time. *Is he still alive? Would he know me if he saw me under this hair?*

The fighting unit that staggered in on them one afternoon was in rough shape. The slaves in this unit possessed half-healed injuries they'd been carrying with them for days. Healing fresh injuries was one thing but repairing half-healed, infected wounds was difficult and demanded a lot from the Healers.

Both women called on the new talents they'd developed. They reopened the improperly healed tissues by tearing the cells apart. The wound was then flushed clean before being rehealed. Lianndra learned to use the body's natural drainage systems to help flush the cellular debris away. Then they pushed the infected residue out of the injury, an energy-intensive process. This kind of healing would not have been possible if it wasn't for the pain control methods the Healers developed. The pain would have been intolerable for even the most stoic slave.

As Lianndra kneeled beside a young human male with a torn shoulder, he reached up to grab her.

Her first frightened instinct was to yank her arm away. The look in his eyes stopped her cold. They were wild, the pupils shrunk to mere pinpoints which Lianndra thought was due to the fever from an infected wound.

She did a quick internal assessment. He didn't have a fever. The man prattled incoherently to her, at first softly, but then rising in volume.

"We're damned." Those were the first words she could understand. "Damned. They've made us into killers. There's no going back for us now. We're going to Hell." He laughed, the sound rising until it trailed off as a wail. "Doesn't matter if you heal me. I'm in Hell already. I'm a killer now."

Lianndra grabbed his flailing hand, but he wrenched it away. *I can heal their physical injuries, but I can't do a thing for their mental wounds.*

Out of the corner of her eye, Lianndra saw the unit's Fang commander turn around to stare at the slave beneath her hands.

"Shhh." She tried soothing him, stroking his forehead.

The grip on her arm became painful as he continued to babble on about Hell, his voice becoming shriller as he did so. Desperate to stop him, she reached *within* with her mind, pinching off the blood supply to his brain to send him sliding into unconsciousness.

At least it will be easy to heal him now, she thought.

The man's rant hadn't escaped the Fang commander's notice. As Lianndra pulled back to reposition herself, she felt something crackle under her fingers. A massive shock of electricity sparked from the soldier's collar, stabbing into his brain, leaving scorched, useless tissue in its wake. Passed to her through her physical contact Lianndra caught the backlash, enough of a jolt to send her flying. Dazed, she moved back toward him. Before she could touch him, she knew it was too late. Wisps of smoke drifted from the spot where his collar penetrated his brain.

"Lianndra! Are you all right?" Drake strode across the clearing toward her.

She nodded to Drake and glanced over her shoulder at the Fang commander. The Farr's orange eyes met her own for a second before the leathery alien looked away in dismissal. *Just another defective slave cull to the commander. Another eye opener for me. Like I need any more of those.*

Lianndra looked up into Drake's concerned gaze. "I'm okay captain," she told him. For a moment, she saw his piercing eyes smolder and the muscles of his jaw clench as he looked at the body of the soldier. It wasn't like Drake to show emotion, and as Lianndra watched, she saw his coping process revealed: the dark-haired man stifled his emotions, locking them down.

In seconds, he'd schooled his face into his usual stoic, confident self. He glanced at her and gave her a brisk nod before turning away.

Too late captain, I saw you. Lianndra had seen the flash of anger; it wasn't her imagination. Her estimation of the man rose another notch.

She stood to move on to the next slave in line. The slave's gaze met hers, and in them she read a world of pain. This one wasn't babbling out loud but his eyes spoke volumes.

"He was my friend." The slave's voice was hoarse.

Lianndra's vision blurred with tears. *I might live in a nightmare, but these guys are living the nightmare.*

How many of these men could have been doctors, or world leaders, or teachers? The Fang ripped the men from their civilized, structured world and forced them to fight a brutal war on an alien planet.

It was possible some of them might have chosen the life of a soldier. *Back on Earth, there are support systems, but here . . . here if you fall below optimum performance level, you pay for it with your life.* Lianndra wiped her tears away. *How many no longer care? How many would rather die than live one more day like this? This is why the rebellion matters,* she reminded herself while probing the chest wound of the slave under her fingers. *This is why it is worth whatever risk we take. We have to free these men while there is still something left to free.*

11

THE NIGHT WAS FULL OF sound: the hisses, screeches, clicks and hums representing alien life in the jungle.

Lianndra walked through the undergrowth, letting the melodies and smells of nature surround her, each step taking her further from the firelight. The captain allowed them freedom in the area around the camp, so that everyone could relieve themselves. Lianndra started toward the privy pit but veered off as soon as she was clear of prying eyes. Tonight she needed breathing room.

After the Fang's murder of the slave soldier, Lianndra felt exhausted. To top it off, the soldiers had been too busy today to gather any fresh meat or fruit, so supper consisted of dehydrated travel rations. Not tempting at even the best of times.

Lianndra heard Drake's men lounging around the fire, laughing and trading stories with the unit she and Hannah healed today. She moved deeper, leaving the voices behind as the jungle folded around her, enriching her enhanced senses. Lianndra could smell warm-bodied animals, and it made her mouth water. She was hungry for meat, the rich protein necessary to replenish her reserves after intense healing. Large predators made night foraging too dangerous, at least for any normal human. *I'm willing to take the risk.*

A scurrying sound drew her attention to an enormous trunk festooned with vines. Without conscious thought, Lianndra scaled the tree in pursuit. Her claws dug into the furry creepers, while her tail hooked any available protrusions.

Whatever had scurried away sensed her presence, increasing its speed. The frantic sounds spurred on the predator within her. She lunged upward in huge bounds, her claws leaving torn furrows in the bark. As the scent wafted back to her in the creature's wake, she recognized one of the rodent-like tree dwellers they often dined on. Lianndra sensed her pupils widen like a cat's, taking in the ambient light. In mid-leap her vision changed, enabling her to read the thermal signatures of the jungle. The large rodent now registered in brilliant reds and oranges as it disappeared behind the trunk only a few feet beyond her. She twisted to land in the other direction, pushed off with all four limbs, caught the edge of a vine with her tail, and swung around the curve of the tree.

The move surprised the rodent. Lianndra sank her fangs into its throat.

Warm fluid flooded her mouth and snapped her out of her hunger-induced frenzy. She spat out the blood and hair in disgust, wiping the gore off her face with the back of one hand. She clung to the vines with the twitching animal pinned beneath one arm. The scrape of her claws was loud as she descended to the ground, but she was too unsettled to use her usual graceful silence.

Once on terra firma, Lianndra dropped the rodent as she contemplated what she'd done. *Seems there is more animal in me than I might want to admit. Still, here's supper. Now if I can just convince those soldiers to share and not steal it for themselves.*

Distracted by her thoughts, Lianndra didn't hear the footsteps behind her. Something tackled her hard, knocking her into the thick underbrush. Rolling in a daze through the foliage, she pushed ineffectively at hands grabbing her wrists to pin her down. The person—human and male, she identified the pungent smell—was strong. He tried to force her legs apart while using his body weight to hold her down.

A scream she didn't recognize as her own ripped through the night air. It wasn't a sound of fear but of rage. She twisted toward her attacker's arm. Her fangs sank deep, and she heard the man howl. She managed to lift a hip, which freed her tail. It sliced around to whip him across the temple.

His recoil from the blow lifted his torso off of her, freeing one of her arms. Lianndra's head blazed with static as she heaved him off of her just enough to reach between them.

Through her rage-induced haze, she heard voices and the crashing of foliage. The fact rescue was imminent no longer mattered. Bloodsucking Fang were bad enough. This was one of her own!

Her strike was swift and sure. The man above her stiffened in shock. His shock turned to panic. His panic gave way to screaming as she struck not with her claws, but with her mind.

This time, she wasn't stitching flesh together. She was tearing it apart.

The screams had drawn an audience. The jungle was full of shouts and tramping feet. Drake's voice rose above the ruckus, shouting something in an irate tone.

By the time Drake activated the pain nodes attached to her assailant's collar, she'd finished with him. Lianndra shoved hard to get the contorted form off her. She was on her feet in an instant, although her surroundings tilted and heaved before her very eyes. Drake looked furious as he stood over her writhing attacker. He signaled two soldiers to lift the man from the ground. It was then Lianndra recognized her assailant as the soldier who'd made lewd advances to both Hannah and herself.

"Lianndra! Are you okay?" Hannah pushed past the wall of men to run up and grab her arm.

The rage drained from Lianndra's body as she trembled. Attacked many times since becoming a slave, she'd never experienced such violence by another human.

Lianndra knew that fact was more a matter of luck than anything else. She'd heard stories of these kinds of attacks being common among the slaves.

She stepped back into Hannah's comforting arms, trembling. Healing was exhausting, but it couldn't compare to the physical drain of what she'd just done to her attacker. Combined with the lack of food, she swayed on her feet.

Hanging from the arms of two soldiers, the groaning man tried to curl around himself. Drake looked from him to Lianndra, his eyes flooded with questions.

"He won't be siring children. Ever." Lianndra's voice shook. In truth, as the rage subsided, what she'd done sickened her.

Drake looked again at the attacker. Other than the teeth marks in his shoulder, there was not a drop of blood on him, not even seeping from between fingers clutched around his crotch.

The captain shook his head before turning to Hannah. "Get her out of here." His voice was surprisingly soft. "Make sure she's okay."

"Come on." With an arm around her waist, Hannah guided Lianndra.

"Wait." Lianndra extricated herself from Hannah to weave her way past Drake, who was staring at her with an unreadable expression. She went to where the rodent lay hidden in trampled foliage and hoisted it by its hind legs. She turned to stare at the captain, who frowned at the animal before meeting her gaze. Lianndra moved past him, returning to where Hannah waited for her.

"Supper," she said, the *S* slurred by her exposed fangs.

Drake said nothing as she headed back to camp.

THE FIGHTING UNIT CLEARED OUT before dawn, heading back to the front lines. As stealthy as the unit was, both Lianndra and Hannah awakened while they decamped. Drake was up, watching as the other unit packed up their gear. The Healers didn't fall back asleep until the last soldier left.

Lianndra woke a second time when a form loomed over the leafy hollow where she and Hannah slept curled together. Before she opened her eyes, she recognized Drake's distinctive scent. The captain said nothing. Both women rose to follow him to the far side of the clearing.

Behind a mammoth tree was the soldier that attacked Lianndra last night. Tied hand and foot, he sat at the base of the trunk. As the three approached, two of his fellow soldiers cut his ankle ties before hauling him to his feet.

Lianndra knew this man had no friends among the soldiers. His unpleasant behavior ensured he spent most of his time alone. Still, with such a small group and a good captain, they'd worked together smoothly. Lianndra wondered how Drake would punish him when they needed all the manpower they had.

Drake stopped in front of the surly slave. The captain wasn't a particularly tall man, but his natural presence made him seem much taller than the soldier. Lianndra's attacker stood with lowered eyes, but his expression was resentful.

"By now, you all know what this bloke tried to do last night." Drake's lightly accented voice was low and full of disgust. "This was despite my direct order to leave the Healers alone." He stared at the men assembled around the captive. "We're in a lousy situation. I know how hard it is to resist our baser instincts when the Fang treat us as little more than animals. The last thing we should do is prove their point for them."

Lianndra noticed two of the men dropped their eyes, their skin flushing.

A ray of sunlight reflected off the object in Drake's hand, and everyone noted the knife he'd drawn from a sheath at his hip. The soldiers restraining the man—Lianndra knew his name was Jake—tightened their grip as he struggled. Grimacing in disgust, Drake closed one fist to activate the pain nodes on the man's collar until he collapsed to the dirt.

"I spent the night thinking about Jake's punishment. We need the strength of every bloke in this division, and I will not put us at risk due to the actions of one whacker acting like a bloody animal." He kneeled beside the prone captive as he signaled the confused soldiers on each side to pin him down. "It finally dawned on me what Lianndra must have done. All I have to do is show you how attacking a Healer will meet rather unique resistance."

He slashed at the crotch of Jake's threadbare uniform. The fabric parted, and as underwear was not part of the assigned clothing, the prisoner's exposed skin was visible to everyone.

"Look closely, mates. Powers used to heal can also be used to destroy." He straightened, sheathing his knife.

The men gawked. Faces paled. A few shifted and looked uncomfortable.

The wound showed no blood or scar tissue, nothing to disable him either as a functional human or as a useful part of the division. Also nothing that would ever again label him as male.

"Be bloody grateful they are on our side," Drake said. "They work along with us, heal our wounds. Treat them with the respect they are due."

Lianndra stood beside Hannah, feeling sick. Hannah's small hand folded into her own.

"Pack up. We leave in an hour. Dismissed." Drake spun on his heel and strode away.

In silence the soldiers followed him, avoiding each other's eyes. Released, Jake rolled onto his side in a fetal position, lying in the dirt of the jungle floor.

As she and Hannah turned to leave, Lianndra noticed Drake pause by the edge of the clearing. He watched her with a thoughtful expression on his face.

He knew I'd done something to that man, but he didn't know I could remodel—remove—things. In fact, I hadn't known until now just what I'd done either. She was still trying to wrap her head around it.

Hannah gently touched her arm as they moved to pack their few possessions. "Well, those guys won't bother us anytime soon," she said, her voice unsteady. "I don't know if I could have done what you did. You are amazing."

Lianndra gave her a shaky smile. She bent to gather her things. *If you'd asked me yesterday, I would have told you I couldn't either.* Lianndra wasn't proud of what she'd done. Yes, she'd been blazingly angry at the man, but they were on a strange world far from home and living in a nightmare situation. *You can't expect people to act as they normally would.* The violent attack last night still made her tremble. *But I'm not surprised it happened.*

Did she blame him? She didn't know. But it was done. She had to admit she wasn't inclined to undo it.

She remembered Drake's thoughtful expression. *Was he impressed with what I did, or repulsed?*

Drake was aloof and unreadable most of the time, but he was always fair to her, and he had her back on this crazy world.

Because of him our lives are as good as they can get. She wouldn't want that to change, for him not to trust her. They could have just as easily ended up with a cruel captain, or one who had a closer commitment to the Fang. *Drake seems committed to doing his job well. He keeps us alive and off the Fang radar.*

Lately, she even wanted to talk to the captain to get to know him better. She also found herself drawn to the handsome tall blond man named Sean, who was more easygoing than Drake. Lianndra had spoken to Sean a few times, and he seemed genuine. *I keep thinking about Michael, as if I will see him again. He could be dead, and there are other men on this planet. If they could possibly see me as a human other than an animal—I could seek something more.*

I'm so tired of being alone. Hannah was good company; she was thankful for her. But it was impossible to work so closely with other humans and not want more than just a functional relationship. *We are social creatures, after all.*

Still, Lianndra hung back. Her nonhuman differences were too visible, and she remained afraid of being rejected. Now, it was even more likely that there would be fear folded into any social dynamic.

Lianndra shoved her dishes into the small pack and straightened.

Drake was overseeing the striking of the captain's tent. could

She sighed, thinking of the rodent she'd killed just before she'd maimed her human attacker. *I hope when we break free of this, there will be something human left in me. As time goes by, the savage part just keeps getting stronger.*

THE TECHNICIAN WHO SLIPPED THE datachrys into the pocket of Ewt%mit%fnsk's gown was so good Ewt%mit%fnsk didn't realize she possessed it until the Fara disappeared. She waited until the midday meal before she'd an opportunity to listen to it without arousing any suspicions. She retreated to a quiet, remote spot near an exterior portal. Perching on a flotation cushion, Ewt%mit%fnsk plugged the datachrys into her handheld device and sat back, as if enjoying a recorded lecture.

The message was short, a simple update. Long after it finished, Ewt%mit%fnsk sat, gazing out the portal to the peaceful orb of green and gold far below.

Her contact reported a development in their plans. The ripples were spreading.

She sighed. To date, she'd played only a small role in the rebellion. Small, but critical to the entire effort. The regular reports she received indicated her special Healers were doing what they had been designed to do. But progress was slow, one minuscule event at a time. With all the random factors that could intercede, success was far from assured.

There were others in the rebellion who calculated these things. Rebel Tlo%m much higher up the chain had planned for contingencies and for the sequence of events that needed to occur to see their goals through to the end. Except for a few individuals at the hub of the rebellion, no single Tlo%m knew more than what they needed to succeed with their personal contributions. Such compartmentalization was necessary for security reasons, but on a personal level, it made it hard to feel they were accomplishing much.

For the rebellion leadership to risk sending the information on the datachrys to the members, a crucial event must have taken place on the green and gold world.

Ewt%mit%fnsk sighed as she slipped the datachrys into her palm. Seconds after she'd removed it from her device, it disintegrated into a small pile of dust in her scaly hand.

Go, little humans. Use those creative, cunning brains of yours. Save us from ourselves.

LIANNDRA AND HANNAH RESTED HIGH in the canopy of a jungle giant with their tails wrapped around its branches for added security. Below them, their FHR division was setting up camp before preparing dinner. The Healers had time to themselves before the evening routine swung into gear.

As part of her relentless effort to bolster her friend's self-esteem, Hannah encouraged Lianndra to get more creative with her appearance. Today's project was growing the hair on their heads long enough to braid in long cornrows while adding anything perceived as decorative into the braids. Lianndra felt like a teenager primping for a prom date.

Hannah supervised Lianndra through the braiding project on her own red hair. Lianndra's effort led to irregular cornrows decorated with small stones and a few errant metallic feathers. Although it looked rather haphazard, Hannah seemed pleased with the final results. The smaller Healer now hunched over a branch with lovely green inner wood. Her small fingers manipulated a mini-tool she borrowed from Drake to cut the branch into segments. She then drilled holes through them to create beads for Lianndra's braids.

"These will be great in your hair," Hannah said. "They will pick up the color of your eyes."

Lianndra sighed. *What difference does it make what my hair looks like?* She'd become even more withdrawn since the human slave attacked her. Lianndra admitted to herself the assault made her warier, but it wasn't her primary concern. Rage caused her to use healing powers to maim with no conscious thought on her part. *Would I have taken it even further if the others hadn't shown up? What if I'd focused on his brain and not his crotch? Could I have killed him?* The more she explored her healing powers, the more she was capable of, and sometimes it frightened her.

She tried to shake herself loose from her grim thoughts for her friend's sake. Hannah was trying so hard to cheer her up. The redheaded Healer was so obviously enjoying herself that Lianndra was reluctant to stop her. If she tilted her head and squinted, Lianndra admitted her friend's hair looked nice, especially with the beads and feathers woven in.

I wonder if she is trying to get someone's attention? Although Hannah spoke to all the men, the one she spent the most time with was Drake. Lianndra couldn't say she'd ever noticed the captain seeking Hannah. *Of course, I'm always avoiding him, so how would I know?*

Hannah set her finished wooden beads in a crevice in the bark before pulling two metallic feathers from the pouch around her neck. "Okay, now sit still. These cornrows are tricky and I don't want to get them crooked."

As Lianndra submitted to her friend's concentrated ministrations, she smiled. She would value the braids because her friend wanted her to look pretty. *As a symbol of our friendship, they will do just fine. I guess they are making me feel better after all.*

LIANNDRA'S CORNROWS WERE STILL HOLDING

strong the day Drake's command to hold up for new instructions came through loud and clear. She knew it meant he was receiving a comm transmission from a Fang unit needing their help. Lianndra propped a hip in the fork of two large branches, her tail holding her secure as Hannah dropped in from above to sit opposite her.

"Wonder what'll it be this time?" Lianndra said.

They'd been patrolling closer to the front lines than usual over the last few days. In fact, they'd retraced their steps as if waiting for something.

Hannah leaned forward to check her friend's braids. "Hey, you lost a feather."

"Snagged it on a branch and it got lost in the leaves." Lianndra pulled a ration bar from a pocket along her ribs. She had formed the pocket from hair so densely woven it looked like felted cloth. By weaving the hairs of the opening together she could seal it closed.

Hannah noticed the pocket and laughed. "Wow, nice trick. You always come up with new stuff. I'm still carrying them around my neck." She gestured to the ration bar tied to a tether. "Stupid thing keeps trying to string me up. I'm going to try the pocket idea." She frowned at the red hair on her ribs, poking at it with one finger. After a few minutes, she formed something that might hold a ration bar—at least through the first few leaps.

With a smile on her face, Lianndra looked away to survey the open canopy around them. A flock of brightly colored flying creatures ducked and dodged through the branches. She wondered if they were the source of the bright feathers decorating her and Hannah's hair. They often found feathers lying discarded on a branch or leaf.

The reptilian creatures were pretty as long as you didn't see them close up, when their sharp teeth became obvious. The flocks zeroed in on wounded or sick creatures in the upper canopy. Healers were safe as long as they didn't bleed while in the canopy. Whenever she spotted them, Lianndra dropped into the dense foliage of the lower branches just in case.

She kept a wary eye on where the creatures had vanished as Drake's voice dictated new instructions via their comm units. Lianndra and Hannah were to split up to watch for an incoming unit.

"Oh, damn. More Fang commandos." Hannah grimaced, and Lianndra's stomach twisted. The fact they were connecting with them meant commandos needed healing. After her last experience, she was more nervous than ever to heal Fang.

Hannah swung off to her allotted sentry point as Lianndra moved to hers. She caught another glimpse of the flying reptile flock but it continued to move away from them. She settled herself in a tree offering a view of the jungle floor for a good distance around her. View was subjective. Both Healers used their ears and noses to detect activity through the thick undergrowth. The native flora and fauna provided an excellent early warning system for anything moving on the ground.

With one ear on nature's grapevine, Lianndra wrapped her tail around a branch once again as she made good use of her downtime. Lately, she'd used meditation to enter a self-healing trance, permitting her to address any health concerns while they were in the earliest of stages. Adjusting her body until she was comfortable, she went *within*. When she first tried going *within* her own body, she'd been afraid of losing herself. Lianndra discovered if she left one of her senses attuned to the outside world, she could use it as an anchor to draw her back to consciousness. As she gained confidence, she meditated every few days to keep herself in the peak of health and ready for any eventuality.

Today she found little to concern her as she drifted *within*. A slight tear in one muscle, easily mended; the merest trace of congestion in the lobe of one lung, simple to clear. On the periphery of her awareness, she sensed an energy flowing like a river through her body. When first noticed, it had surprised her, and she was unsure as to their purpose. Then she recognized it as the lines of energy corresponding to the meridians used in Chinese medicine.

Lianndra knew little about acupuncture. Curious, she'd experimented by manipulating the tiny concentrations of energy at each point along the meridians while noting their effects.

Sitting on the branch, she followed one of the energy paths and found an interruption in the flow at one point—a spot pulsing erratically. She backtracked to the blockage and then pushed it forward with her mind until she restored the current's flow. She withdrew as carefully as she could and sensed the reestablishment of a smooth flow of energy through her body.

As she awoke from her trance, Lianndra longed for an acupuncture guidebook. *Was the congested meridian point related to the congested lung?* She wished she could have studied the points before attempting to find them, so she could understand the effect of manipulating the energies. *Using the meridians would be a helpful addition to my healing techniques.* For now, she could use her own body as a template while she attempted to learn from it.

The Fang unit didn't come until well after nightfall. Being closer to their approach, Hannah alerted Drake and Lianndra. The Healers flanked the incoming unit, watching and listening for predators in the surrounding jungle.

Drake met them on the way to the camp. Out of a team of fifteen commandos, only five had survived. To Lianndra's horror, the Fang weren't alone; they had a captive.

It turned out their prisoner was the primary reason for meeting with the FHR division. Their captive had received an injury during her seizure.

Drake met Lianndra and Hannah as they swung out of the trees behind the last limping Fang. "We need you both," he said, stalking across the camp to where three burly Fang dropped a bundle on the ground.

In the darkness it was difficult to see what the bundle contained. As Lianndra stepped forward, one of the Fang grabbed her arm to shove her toward the shadowy form lying in the dirt.

It shocked Lianndra to see a small Gryphon, seemingly less than half-grown. She remembered the Gryphon child she and Andrea had seen in the Pitfight. This one possessed its feathery fur, but dark blood covered half its body.

"We need better light," Lianndra said. Behind her, Hannah directed one of their soldiers to fetch it.

Lianndra kneeled beside the small female Gryphon. She was the size of a pony; when standing, her back would be level with Lianndra's waist. The large, violet eyes were dull with pain, the white-feathered crest flattened against her head. Lianndra noticed the fur shone pale blue in the moonlight, marked with white stripes and spots.

I didn't know they were so colorful, she thought.

Lianndra heard the ominous gurgle of a compromised respiratory system.

She'd never worked on a Gryphon. By the dark looks of the surrounding Fang, she'd better do a good job of working on this one.

When the lights arrived, Drake combined diplomacy and brisk commands to back the Fang away from the Gryphon.

Lianndra appreciated his bravery. *It takes balls to stand up to the Fang.*

Hannah kneeled on the other side of the little one's body, holding a lamp in her hand. The light, although dim, allowed Lianndra to assess the most critical injury. A long, deep tear in the Gryphon's side, between its arm and foreleg, bubbled air with each breath.

"I've got this." Lianndra placed one hand into the tear. There was a sharp gasp of pain and the violet eyes widened.

Hannah cushioned the long head between her hands, turning it so one large eye met hers. A newly installed collar on the graceful neck of the Gryphon gleamed in the lamplight. Hannah glanced at Lianndra before closing her eyes and reaching for the pain centers.

With Hannah on pain patrol, Lianndra reached deeper into the wound, casting her mind on a wider swath than normal, trying to get a feel for the Gryphon's physiology. Rather than two lungs as in a human, they had a series of air sacs running through the torso. It was here that the injury had occurred. The air sac system enabled the Gryphon to still breathe even with such massive damage. The equivalent wound in a human would have been fatal. It was fortunate the laser causing the injury partially cauterized it, minimizing the blood loss.

It took a delicate and patient touch to heal the wound. Lianndra sighed with relief as the last air sac inflated. The Gryphon's breathing improved. Lianndra healed the overlying membranes and muscle tissue, withdrawing until the skin reknit over the muscle. Soon, the only sign of the injury was a gap in the blue and white feathery fur along the creature's side.

Lianndra sensed the restlessness of the Fang waiting for her to finish, but she left her hands on the Gryphon's skin for a few moments longer. Going back *within* the creature's body, the Healer unfocused her mental eye, looking for something out of the corner of her vision.

She wasn't too surprised when she found them. The alien possessed energy meridians similar to her own. They followed different pathways, and Lianndra had no idea how they connected to the physical form of the creature, but she traced the energies anyway. She smoothed out any interruptions as best she could. Satisfied at last, she pulled out. Hannah stared at her with questions in her eyes, obviously wondering what she'd done. The instant she and Hannah backed away, the Fang stepped in, attaching restraints to the groggy Gryphon.

Restraints and a collar, this is one important captive, Lianndra thought.

One commando grabbed Lianndra, insisting she heal a gash on his thigh.

It was a long night, and both Healers were shaking with exhaustion by the time the last wound healed. Drake was solicitous as he settled them in a tent with a heaping platter of stewed rodent and a container of fruit cider.

"Eat well and get some sleep," he said. "We leave with them before dawn." Drake left before either Healer could ask questions.

LIANNDRA THOUGHT ABOUT MICHAEL EVERY
night before she slept. Occasionally, those thoughts led to restless dreams of what could have been, if their lives had proceeded in a normal fashion back on Earth.

After Drake departed, Lianndra buried her head in her bedroll to block out the nocturnal animal sounds as well as the grunts and groans of the men settling in for the night. She shook with exhaustion but was too wired to sleep. To calm herself, she mentally traced the planes of Michael's face, drawing an outline from memory, and framing it with a disorganized mop of dark hair. Fighting the panic of not remembering—*it's been so long*—she would mentally draw the arch of his eyebrows, the line of a slightly crooked nose, the wide mouth, and the white-toothed smile. Last, she did the eyes, striking silver irises fringed with dark lashes.

Some nights, she went from there to the physicality of him—his tall body, long legs, and arms; still gawky angles and bones but with the promise of strength to come. This usually led to memories of how he'd looked when she last saw him. Her anger and despair built again when she recalled the bruises. As a result, she often ended up wide awake under the dripping leaves of the jungle. So she'd start again, focusing on the silver of his eyes and his smile.

Tonight she was so exhausted she'd just started thinking of him when she quickly drifted asleep. Perhaps that was what triggered the dream.

Lianndra flew through the jungle, leaping from branch to branch, following a distant sound. She came upon a clearing. What was taking place within it froze her heart.

Michael was there, standing in the center, surrounded by four Fang. Each Fang held a heavy chain in their clawed fingers; the four chains were attached to Michael's collar.

As she watched in horror, the Fang flicked their wrists and skrins unfurled with lightning speed toward Michael. He tried to dodge them, but using the chains, the Fang pulled him into the path of the skrins. Lianndra had never seen the device used as a weapon in this way. They left deep cuts on Michael's smooth skin. Within seconds, every part of his body dripped blood.

Sobbing, Lianndra tried to leap off her branch to claw at the Fang, to stop the carnage. Her body wouldn't obey her; she remained frozen in place and forced to watch as the Fang destroyed him.

In the clearing, Michael collapsed to his knees, streaming blood, with his head bowed beneath his arms. She could see how his entire body shook. Blinded by tears, she screamed his name.

An inhuman cry rose on the echo of her scream, a cry that turned into a roar as Michael surged to his feet. But what stood in the clearing was no longer the Michael of her memory. Covered not just in blood, but in dark hair, he expanded in size and his body rippled with new muscle. His ears elongated to points and his nose lengthened into a snout, with vicious fangs dripping saliva. And his eyes—his eyes shone gold, like the sun.

The Fang cried out in surprise as the monster that had been Michael stood tall, flicking a long, black tail. Clawed hands grabbed at the chains and yanked, pulling his captors within range, slicing through them with the ease of a scythe through tall grass.

As each Fang died, they dissolved away into dust. Soon, only the beast remained. Panting, it stood in the center of the empty clearing. Gold eyes unerringly sought her in the trees, eyes full of pain. The jaws opened.

"Lianndra..."

Lianndra shot up out of her slumber, shaking and soaked in sweat, her heart threatening to pound its way out of her chest. The camp was silent around her. Her scream must have remained only in her mind, but its echoes reverberated within her. With a quick glance at Hannah still wrapped in her bedroll, Lianndra rose to jog off into the jungle. She climbed high into a large tree before finding a spot to sit, staring at the stars through the branches, willing her heart to slow its relentless pounding.

It was only a nightmare, she told herself, *only one of the many I've had.* A very vivid one, but that was all. She leaned back against the trunk, feeling the retained heat of the daylight within the mossy bark. The cool, remote glitter of the stars soothed her, as they always did. The nightmare lost its grip although an uneasy feeling remained.

Lianndra gazed at the stars. So unfamiliar, and yet reassuring. She wondered if one of the lights in the sky was Earth's own sun. *What would lie in store for us if we were free?*

For some of the slaves, the familiar, no matter how horrible, might be preferable to the unknown. Even if they ditched the Fang, what then? Was there a place for humans on this world? For a successful rebellion, they needed a better scenario to fight for. She thought of the little Gryphon. The fates of their two species could be intertwined, and no one knew how things would play out over time.

We are so far from home.

As SHE SWUNG THROUGH THE trees, Lianndra felt compassion for Drake.

The Aussie captain might be a slave but he usually called the shots out in the jungle, far from his Fang superiors. The humans were now at the mercy of the Fang commandos, who'd commandeered Drake's FHR division to help with escorting the Gryphon back to headquarters. It was a risky duty; the first night they camped, a Fang attacked one of the human soldiers. The alien took a long blood meal before throwing his limp body at the feet of the Healers. The Healers sealed his wounds but could do little for so much blood loss. He could barely walk the next day. Drake was livid and protested to the Fang commander, who reprimanded the offending commando, only because the weakened slave compromised their progress.

Drake ordered the Healers to stay well away from the Fang, even insisting they slept in the trees. He also corralled his men into a tight circle at night to keep tabs on each other. Lianndra was sure such obvious measures irritated the hell out of the Fang. She supposed that the reptilian aliens were more tolerant than usual because they needed the humans to help guard and care for the Gryphon until they reached headquarters.

Until then, Drake gets cut some slack, she thought.

Each night, under the pretense of seeing how the small Gryphon was healing, Lianndra insisted on bringing her fresh fruit and nuts. The Fang were feeding the creature meat-based ration bars. Lianndra had been inside the captive's body. She was sure that, like humans, the Gryphon were omnivores and needed other things in their diet to stay healthy. The Fang watched her approach their prisoner with burning orange eyes, making her skin crawl. Drake always followed her and stood near with his strong arms crossed, although Lianndra wasn't sure what he could do if the Fang came after her.

Hannah theorized the small Gryphon was someone important and Lianndra agreed. Why else would they kidnap her? Lianndra's mind was full of questions every time she brought food to the little Gryphon. She felt drawn to the furry alien. The long, tufted ears pricked as she nodded her thanks to the Healer. Lianndra found the large, violet eyes mesmerizing. There was no mistaking the intelligence in them. She sensed the creature wanted to communicate, but there was never the opportunity. The commandos watched their every move.

During the day, it was obvious the Fang viewed humans as disposable inventory. While the commandos kept close to the captive in the center of the column, they sent the slaves around the periphery. The Fang expected the Gryphon to come after them, and they wanted the humans in place as a buffer. Drake countered by keeping Lianndra and Hannah busy as sentries along the perimeter. They were extra alert to any movement in the jungle below and behind them.

Lianndra knew the Gryphon were not jungle dwellers, but creatures of the open grasslands where the big, six-limbed aliens had maximum mobility. Slow moving Fang units were easy prey in the grasslands, but the close confines of the jungle helped to level the playing field. The Fang chose the jungle as their base of operations for that reason. Yet the Fang were certain that despite their difficulty with tight spaces, the Gryphon would come after them.

At one of their check-ins, Drake informed the Healers that another Fang unit was on the way to improve the escort security.

He's hoping the Fang will kick us free then, Lianndra thought. *I'm not counting on it.*

The Healers ran on the edge of exhaustion. Every night, convinced the Gryphon would come from that direction, the Fang commander insisted the women backtrack far along their path to check for pursuit. Drake could not override him.

Lianndra and Hannah were backtracking the night of the attack. It didn't come from behind, but rather in front. The Healers were two miles from camp, carefully swinging through the darkness, when they heard distant laser fire and battle screams. They doubled back, pushing hard, the branches, leaves and vines coming at them far too fast to dodge. They didn't have to rely on their scent trail to find their way back; the sounds of the battle carried for miles.

The jungle was lit up with laser fire. Both women skidded to a halt to survey the chaos below them. For the first time Lianndra saw, up close and personal, the full scope of the aliens the Fang wished to conquer.

The Gryphon were huge, their bodies much broader and taller than a horse's. The stripes and spots on their brightly colored coats helped them blend with the dappled shadows, and they carried everything from aged hand lasers to clubs in their humanlike hands. Their arms sprouted a single line of stiff feathers that rotated so they lay flat along the arm. Lianndra saw one warrior snap the feathers forward to knock a Fang flying. Their four legs kicked in almost any direction, slicing into bodies with their powerful claws. Even their long tails, topped in spikes, thrashed with such speed they cracked like a bull whip, easily able to snap a neck or limb.

They outnumbered the Fang. Movement out of the corner of her eye revealed the commander with one commando pushing the Gryphon captive through the foliage ahead of them. They were trying to escape while their fellow Fang provided a distraction.

"Do what you can for Drake and the men. We've got to get them out of this," Lianndra shouted to Hannah as she swung in pursuit of the escapees. *Oh no you don't,* she thought, her anger flaring. *That little Gryphon is going back to her friends!* She spotted a female Gryphon warrior. Her body was streaked with vivid stripes, and she wielded an imposing battle-axe. Dropping from a tree, Lianndra landed in the Gryphon's path before sprinting ahead. The alien wheeled to give pursuit, weapon raised high. Screaming with a fear that was only half-faked, Lianndra bolted toward the little Gryphon and her captors. In the open, the Gryphon would have caught her in seconds. Hampered as she was by the thick undergrowth, Lianndra kept one step ahead of her. She had a close call when she slowed to change direction, and the axe split the trunk of a small tree right next to her head.

Lianndra and the Gryphon burst upon the fleeing Fang. The little Gryphon kicked through her restraints, bracing all six limbs, screaming through her gag as her two captors gave her shocks from her collar. Both Farr looked up as Lianndra and the Gryphon warrior exploded on them.

Lianndra didn't hesitate to leap for the commander, teeth bared and claws extended. *Time for retribution.*

If Lianndra's actions surprised the Gryphon warrior, she didn't show it. With her goal so clear, she swung her huge axe, splitting the second Fang in two. Lianndra clung to the back of the commander with her fangs buried in his neck when the axe finished its backswing, gutting him. She released the body as it crumpled beneath her.

No more healing for that one, she thought in satisfaction before turning to face the Gryphon.

The warrior removed the restraints on the small one's legs. When she reached toward the collar, Lianndra stepped forward in protest. The big alien turned to contemplate her with its enormous violet eyes. The axe remained holstered on her back, but Lianndra knew it could be readied in a hurry.

Lianndra gestured to her own collar, turning to show the Gryphon how it entered her skull behind her ear. The big creature huffed in dismay. With her gag freed, the little Gryphon talked to the warrior in a high, piping voice, sounding much like a bird. The bigger creature responded. Obviously they were talking about Lianndra as she was the subject of intense scrutiny.

Then the little Gryphon gave the white feathers of her crest a shake and turned to Lianndra. To the Healer's astonishment, she spoke in perfect, accented English. "I believe you can disable my collar?"

She knows what Hannah and I are up to! Lianndra stared for a moment before she replied. "Yes, it will just take a moment."

The little Gryphon stood very still while Lianndra worked. Hannah had disabled the kill node when they healed the wound, but now Lianndra worked to swiftly encase all the nodes in scar tissue. The large warrior watched in silence, but Lianndra was acutely aware of her presence looming over them.

When the Healer finished, the little Gryphon spoke again. "You have proven yourself a friend of our species. We will not forget this." She bowed. "I am here to tell you the Gryphon are aware of the efforts of the Tlo%m rebellion and the Healers' role in those plans." She paused, glancing up at her larger companion, before continuing. "Remember this—the Gryphon are your friends. To respect the rebellion's goal and to protect your best interests, we must treat you as a captive when we rejoin your fellows."

Lianndra stared at her in shock. *How the heck did it speak such perfect English?* It took a few seconds for her to follow the conversation right through to the end and for the words to penetrate. *Oh, they don't want to reveal to the Fang I'm with the rebellion.* She nodded as they headed back toward the camp, marching as if she was a captive in front of the warrior with the small Gryphon following behind.

They walked forward into a silent tableau. One Fang was upright with a damaged leg. Drake stood beside Hannah, his face bloody from a nasty head wound. Behind them, two human slaves lay on the ground, alive but injured. They were the only survivors. Around them, the Gryphon warriors loomed with thunderous looks on their faces, their colorful feathered crests, manes and neck spikes bristled erect while the long tails waved in agitation.

Two of the warriors made Lianndra gawk in awe. She had no idea Gryphon got so large. One of them was a giant even among his own kind, towering over the others with a coat flashing silver and blue in the dappled moonlight. Instead of the smaller crest the female possessed, he featured a thickly feathered mane. Despite his size, the massive Gryphon obviously deferred to the smaller golden male standing beside him. Smaller than the giant, but still larger than the others, this Gryphon radiated confidence. *Leader.* As Lianndra and the small Gryphon emerged from the foliage, she thought she detected a hint of relief in the craggy features.

The leader strode forward to clasp the smaller Gryphon's shoulder. His deep voice trilled something to her in the beautiful, birdlike language, and she replied in high, piping tones.

Lianndra noticed the one remaining Fang slump at the sight of the small Gryphon. Worried about the injured men, Lianndra hurried over to them. With a nervous glance around, Hannah joined her. As Lianndra worked on Sean, she heard the little Gryphon addressing the group of warriors in their own language.

If the Fang understood what the Gryphon were saying, he gave no sign. He didn't flinch when the small Gryphon accepted a long dagger from the biggest warrior and approached him.

Crouched over Sean but watching events unfold out of the corner of her eye, Lianndra was slow to process what was happening. In fact, the movement was so fast she barely registered it. The Farr slumped forward around the dagger buried in his abdomen. Then with one strong shove, the little one sliced the knife up through the leathery skin—tracing the path to the second heart.

The small Gryphon pulled the dagger free as the lifeless body fell to the dirt. Then she offered the knife to the owner who wiped it clean on leaves. The smallest warrior turned to address the humans.

Lianndra found herself standing over Sean, who was struggling to sit up. She pushed the tall blond man back to the ground. Lianndra looked up in time to see the muscles in Drake's back go rigid when the clear English words rolled from the small Gryphon's mouth.

"In appreciation for the services the Healers offered me, we will spare your lives. We understand that as slaves you had no control over the actions you performed against us. If we could free you from Fang control, we would offer it. Unfortunately, the technology inherent in your collars makes such a rescue impossible at this time." She traded a glance with Lianndra before closing one eye.

Did she just wink at me? Lianndra wondered. *She admitted to me that she knows the Healers can deactivate the collars, but she doesn't know if Drake and his men are in on the secret. Or where their allegiances lie.*

The small Gryphon stepped close to Lianndra. Her long head rose to just below that of the Healer's. She reached into the soft blue feathery fur around her neck to remove a necklet, easing it over the gleaming Fang collar. Gently taking Lianndra's hand in her own, the Gryphon dropped the necklet into her palm. The Healer glimpsed a tiny, perfect figurine of a winged Gryphon on a simple leather thong before the little Gryphon folded the Healer's fingers over it. Then she met Lianndra's eyes and shook her head in a curiously birdlike gesture. Her white crest of feathers, not as long as those of the full-sized Gryphon, rearranged itself in a bright cascade around her long face. Then, with a nod to her fellows, she moved off into the underbrush.

One second, fierce multi-limbed warriors surrounded the humans, the next, the big aliens melted with surprising silence into the jungle.

After they disappeared, Drake walked over to stare at the dead Fang commando. Then he turned to look at Lianndra. He raised one hand to touch the wound on his forehead. It was the first time Lianndra had seen Drake at a loss for words.

Standing over the other surviving soldier, Hannah broke the silence. "How's Sean?" she asked Lianndra as she kneeled again beside the other man.

It galvanized Lianndra to action, so she pocketed her gift and met Sean's eyes. His blue gaze fogged with pain.

"Did that Gryphon just give you a present?" he asked, looking confused.

"Uh, yeah. She did." Lianndra placed a hand on Sean's forehead, reaching *within* for the pain receivers. "Just lie still while I take a look at things here." As she worked, her mind raced. *What will Drake do now?*

The man in question stood and watched the Healers for a moment before settling himself with deliberation on a large tree root.

"We should report in." Drake seemed to be thinking out loud, a rare thing for him. He touched his head again and winced before rubbing his eyes. "I honestly don't know what to bloody tell them."

"Just tell them the truth," Hannah said, trading a glance with Lianndra. "They spared us because we healed their friend. As we are only slaves, subject to the whim of our masters, they did not blame us for her capture."

Drake nodded but didn't move.

Every second he hesitates buys the Gryphon time to get the hell out of here. She wondered if he thought that too. *More likely, he's thinking about whether any of us will live through this.*

She knew the Fang would interrogate them; this kidnapping had obviously been an important initiative. The fact they were valuable slaves wouldn't spare them the rigors of the interrogation. Drake was a captain and controller who had lost most of his unit, surviving while the Fang commandos died. Their futures were likely grim.

Lianndra crouched over Sean, who moaned. He drifted in and out of consciousness. She had stopped the bleeding in the deep chest wound and worked on growing the flesh together. She quieted him with a quick touch before meeting Hannah's concerned eyes.

Lianndra took a deep breath before plunging in. "Don't tell them anything," she said. An inner instinct spurred her on. "Don't report. They don't know there were any survivors." Lianndra didn't look at Drake but sensed the intensity of his stare.

"We can't leave our patrol zone without the collars killing us. Any Fang we come across can off us with a single thought." Drake's voice was quiet, as though there were Fang around to hear them.

"No, they can't." Hannah sat back from her patient, who lay unconscious before her. "Not anymore."

Lianndra looked at the captain. He leaned forward, staring at Hannah. The blood on his face enhanced his piercing dark eyes, making him look fierce and unreadable.

Lianndra acted on Hannah's cue, saying, "We disabled the kill nodes on your collar weeks ago when we healed your injured arm. We can do the same for the pain and the communication nodes. We have left the containment and locator nodes active but we can also disable those."

A long silence followed her revelation. He hadn't moved, or even blinked. Apparently, he hadn't breathed either, because when he spoke it was more of an exhalation than real words. "And how long have you been able to do this?"

"Since we started healing." Hannah's voice trembled.

Lianndra knew they were taking a huge risk. If Drake refused to go along with this, he could report them to the closest Fang commander via his collar comm before either Healer did anything about it.

"You are saying you can free us," Drake said.

"Yes." Lianndra turned back to Sean, giving Drake time to assimilate this news. She hoped the gesture would show they trusted him to make the right decision. In fact, Lianndra subtly shifted her weight to balance over her heels. If Drake sided with the Fang, she could act to defend herself and Hannah.

Could I kill him if I had to? One touch—stop his heart, kill him painlessly. I don't want to, but the alternative is worse. Although Lianndra's hands continued to run over the almost closed wound on Sean's chest, it was only a ruse. She focused on Drake, waiting for his decision.

"You can disable every collar? Is this what you have been doing all along?" Drake asked.

I knew he would put it together. He's too smart not to. Lianndra gave up the ruse, rising to watch him.

Hannah stopped healing and stared openly at Drake.

"It could turn the tide of this bloody war." Drake's clasped his hands and Lianndra noticed how white his knuckles were. Suddenly, he started shaking and Lianndra heard him laughing. "Right under my nose the entire time. Who the hell was controlling whom?"

Hannah walked to his side, laying a hand on his arm. "It's not that I didn't trust you. We couldn't tell anybody. What we are doing is vital to the rebellion."

Lianndra stared at her friend's body language as Hannah stood next to Drake. Body language that seemed well received. And reciprocated. How did she not see this? Her mind flicked back in time at snapshots of Drake—when he spoke to them he always hovered nearer to Hannah. With her attention now drawn to it, there was an obvious attraction between them. It gave her a small taste of what Drake was going through—being blindsided by the obvious.

Lianndra relaxed. She now knew what side of the fence Drake would choose.

When she looked down at Sean, his clear blue eyes stared up at her. "In case anyone cares, I vote yes." Then he grimaced. "I'd appreciate it if you'd finish healing me so I can celebrate."

"Let's get these blokes on their feet," Drake said. "We've got to put some serious miles between this camp and ourselves before we can rest again."

Then we can decide our next move, Lianndra thought.

LIANNDRA AND HANNAH SCOURED THE jungle for survivors, their last task before they hightailed it out of the area. If any of the Farr escaped the Gryphon attack, the humans would have to live as hunted fugitives. If none of the Fang were alive to report in, the humans might be considered lost in the battle, enabling them to move freely.

In the end, only one person remained unaccounted for. It was Jake, the man who Lianndra altered.

Drake cursed when they couldn't find him. "He likely bolted at the first opportunity," he growled in an unusual display of emotion. Nodding at Lianndra, he said, "I should have killed the bastard when he attacked you."

"We can only hope they don't believe what he tells them—if he survives to make it back to the barracks," Hannah said. "Chances are good he didn't stick around long enough to know we survived."

"We didn't disable his pain nodes. They'll have him screaming in interrogation," Lianndra said. "Unless they try to terminate him, they won't realize there is anything wrong with his collar."

Drake looked thoughtful as he shifted his backpack. He was carrying an extra load until the other two soldiers were up to strength. To help out, the Healers also carried packs through the trees. The men may be healed, but they were still weak from blood loss.

"Where to now, boss?" Sean asked. His pale blond hair and blue eyes made him stand out starkly against the dark foliage around them. Drake was always reminding him to rub dirt on his skin to better camouflage him in the leafy jungle.

Drake didn't hesitate. He gestured to the Healers. "Go find us a unit. We're going to disable every collar between here and the front line."

Operation freedom has begun, Lianndra thought as she swung up into the trees.

FROM THE OUTSIDE, THE STRATEGIC headquarters for the Tarin war was unremarkable. Inside, it was a maze of technology along with the inherent supporting wires and conduit. Various colors of waterproofing materials wrapped anything electronic, adding a hint of chaos to an otherwise orderly interior.

The length and success of any war can be gauged by the amount of compensatory infrastructure present in its headquarters, Tar%tosk%rask thought in disgust as she looked around the office.

As the war coordinator for the new initiative of battle strategy, Tar%tosk%rask was the link between the Fara elders on the Tlo%m Motherships and the front lines of the Gryphon war. Although the elders set the protocols, it fell to Tar%tosk%rask to make the general decisions determining the fate of the war.

It was a position that set a new precedent for the Tlo%m. The Fara had never involved themselves in battle strategy, until now. Such things were the exclusive domain of the Farr, many of which resented her intrusion on their traditional turf.

Right now, it was a precedent Tar%tosk%rask could do without. Although her tall figure radiated confidence, internally she was anything but. *If only I'd run this war from the beginning. I spend too much time correcting previous errors and enforcing discipline. Progress has been far too slow.*

Tar%tosk%rask sighed, rotating her seat to stare out her office window at the damp jungle surrounding them. Despite her title, she didn't have a hover seat but rather a utilitarian and uncomfortable rotation seat. *The next time I am in Jarzak's office I will examine his chair. If his is more comfortable, there will be consequences.*

The message on the single datachrys sitting on her desk should be of minor consequence. Instead, it was disturbing. A large part of her job was to filter the incoming information, determine its importance, and fold it into a progression plan for each facet of the war. The sheer volume of information was often overwhelming even with the filtration and simulation programs available to screen it. Tar%tosk%rask preferred to see the incoming data as raw as possible.

Several technicians helped with the process. The information came to the techs from the Central Intelligence Processor. Once the war coordinator assimilated the important data, she passed anything pertinent as well as changes in the battle strategy to Jarzak. He then implemented the changes.

With most of the wireless technology hampered by the planetary shield, she requested her techs save messages as hard copies on datachrys before passing them on to her. It was a cumbersome process, but effective. The techs screened out the frequent messages from Farr commanders, whining about lack of resources or inadequate luxuries at the front.

Such time wastage made it clear that the war had eliminated many of the best Farr. Due to the shortage of quality Farr, many substandard specimens were out there leading slave units. In better times, these substandard examples would have been lucky to make it off the Motherships, or they met their end as frontline soldiers where the attrition rates were high.

There just weren't enough Farr to go around. Although reinforcements arrived daily, most consisted of Farr sent to the Motherships for down time to recharge. They were coming back to the war too soon. Unrested Farr were trouble even among themselves. Without recreation, their brawn overcame their brain. Tar%tosk%rask saw the results or, rather, lack of them, on a continual basis.

This latest message stood out for Tar%tosk%rask in that it was unusual. In her experience, unusual things could be an early sign of something going wrong. The trick was to decide which ones were trouble, and which were not.

I'm so tired. Tar%tosk%rask scratched at her arm. *It has been too long since my last crystal scrub.* Sections of her scaly skin were ready for shedding and the itching was a constant distraction.

She pivoted back to her desk, covered in multiple datachrys separated into four piles. Each one held information screened by her trusted techs. The large heap was inconsequential and due for deletion. One pile was the new, as yet unheard, datachrys. A small stack represented those requiring action. The critical pile contained a single datachrys, and it only qualified for that description due to its oddness.

Tar%tosk%rask tapped a long finger on her desk console, bringing up the information. One altered slave. He apparently tried to molest a Healer and paid a heavy price, although the slave survived the experience.

Tar%tosk%rask took pride the Healers were living up to their promise. Her concern was this Healer should not have been able to do what she had done. Healing injuries was one thing, but removing and restructuring tissues, such as this slave had apparently experienced, was unusual. In fact, Tar%tosk%rask was not aware of any such talent. The human could be lying. In theory, the slave could have injured those body parts in a battle or accident and then healed in such a manner to preserve his usefulness.

She sighed. *Why is this bothering me so much? Slaves will say anything to stop the pain of the interrogation. The entire story is suspect.*

Her unease likely involved her personal stake in the Healer's development: rapidly mutating the Tier-5 human females into Healers. The attrition rate at the front lines had overwhelmed the medic bases, so the need for expanded healing talents became urgent. Therefore, Tar%tosk%rask created a new division of Healers with support slaves and made them available for the frontline fighting units.

The FHR divisions had been tremendously successful and performed well beyond her expectations. This was the first sign something could be amiss.

Did the Healer alter him at all? Only careful interrogation would discover the truth.

Interrogation was a skill requiring patience and intelligence. The indiscriminate use of pain during questioning might cause the slave to spin all kinds of creative tales. The Fang commander who found the altered slave wandering alone in the jungle was not one of their best. His methods tended to fall towards the crude side; he wasn't the type to make the appropriate intellectual connections with the information.

Should I use valuable resources to have the slave brought in to headquarters for proper interrogation and examination? Tar%tosk%rask ground her teeth in anger. Her resources were becoming more limited by the day. One of her commando teams recently failed a major initiative to capture a Gryphon strategist to learn more about their war plans. Instead of bringing in their prisoner, they lost an entire unit of their best commandos.

This altered slave was supposedly present for the failure but possessed little useful information. A Gryphon attack. All dead. Tar%tosk%rask suspected the man fled at the first sign of trouble, and his controller failed to use his collar to hold him to his responsibility.

The investigating Fang commander reported that in addition to the escaped slave, they found the commandos dead, but the remaining humans and Healers of the FHR unit had vanished. At least, they did not find their bodies.

Humans are so soft, she thought. The jungle was full of creatures capable of making short work of a human body, whereas the tough, scaly bodies of the Farr would have remained in evidence longer. As there was no response from the collars, the human bodies were likely in the belly of some large jungle beast. *I hope the collars will give the scavengers indigestion.*

The failure of the mission hurt their initiative more than she liked to admit. Any war relied on good information to succeed, and it was in short supply. Gryphon were fierce fighters, and it was a perilous task to capture one. The few successfully captured proved resilient under interrogation and were too willing to die for their cause. Few Farr could interrogate them with any kind of skill and that only compounded the problem. It meant the handful of captured Gryphon must be sent to the nearest Mothership for interrogation, where the aliens died without revealing any of their secrets.

Tar%tosk%rask scratched her head as she regarded the datachrys. Even if the Healer destroyed the man's reproductive organs, it seemed she was now dead. The FHR divisions had been an unqualified success so far, keeping the fighting units up and running against difficult odds. She wasn't about to pull them out of the jungle for examination based on what one expired Healer might have done. Especially not on the word of a human slave.

By all appearances, the Fang should have abandoned this war long ago. Her people remained crippled by the lack of useable technology due to the planetary shield and the surprising intelligence of their enemy. Tar%tosk%rask was one of few that knew the real reason for its continuance. Along with key figures within the political structure, she agreed that such a potential prize was worth almost any price.

With a slight pang of unease, Tar%tosk%rask dropped the datachrys into the deletion pile.

LIANNDRA CROUCHED DEEP IN the undergrowth at the fringes of the camp, with Hannah doing the same somewhere on the other side of the large clearing. The Fang commander's tent was in the center next to a cooking fire. Made up of both humans and aliens, the slaves scattered throughout the clearing. Many of them preferred to throw their bedrolls in the foliage at the edges to achieve some degree of privacy. This provided the Healers with a dangerous opportunity. As the camp descended into their sleep cycle, the Healers could approach those most hidden. The lightest of touches pushed the soldiers into a deeper sleep for the few moments of contact the Healers needed to disable their collars.

They were off program now, so Lianndra no longer heard the voice of the interactive Fara guide in her ear. She assumed her collar's rebel program remained confused by the complete lack of structure defining their days. To further the rebellion's cause, the Healers fully disabled the collar's nodes. Drake told them he wanted the slaves aware of their freedom as soon as the pain impulse failed. With the war going so poorly for the Fang, he felt it would take time for them to connect the collar failures to the Healers' activities. He might well be right; in fact, they were depending on it.

The small rebel band had no control over when, or even if, the freed soldiers mutinied against their Fang commanders. If the slaves were no longer controlled by their collars, at least they would not function as effective soldiers for the Fang.

That alone could be enough to tip the war in the Gryphon's favor, Lianndra thought.

At any rate, Lianndra and Hannah were getting proficient at the sneak approach. They'd even perfected their camouflage, taking advantage of the natural variations in their hair color to mimic the mottled shadows of the jungle. Extending the hair over their faces made them impossible to spot if they froze in the dark.

Lianndra finished working on her first soldier of the night and debated approaching one several meters into the clearing. Some soldiers remained awake, sitting around the scattered fires. By crouching low and keeping to the darkest shadows, she could still move. She crept forward into the shadow of a giant plant, freezing until she was sure she remained unseen. Seconds later she was on the move again, heading even farther in, following the line of bushes. They provided her excellent protection as she visited two humans and a birdlike alien known as a Charlt.

The rest of the rebels had made their way up into the trees to have a good view. Fang unit guards never looked up for invaders since they expected their enemies to come in on foot. Stationed along the camp perimeter, the guards faced out into the jungle. It was easy for the women to use the overhanging trees to drop within the unit's perimeter. As long as they remained undetected while they did their work, everything should go smoothly. The night cooperated with a thick layer of cloud obscuring the double moons. The only light in the clearing was from the firelight and the few torches keeping the area surrounding the commander's tent lit.

A Zraph snored on the other side of the fern clump. Staying within the shadow of the giant alien, Lianndra crept up to him. She would have to stand up to reach both sides of the head at once and didn't dare touch him until she could make sure the big alien remained asleep. Disabling the collar of such a powerful alien was worth the risk. One angry Zraph free of restraints could render an entire unit dysfunctional in moments.

Lianndra straightened, trying to stay within the shadow of the bulky shoulder. Her hand reached the giant's temple just as the two largest of the primary eyes opened.

Lianndra had a split second to put the creature back to sleep before all hell broke loose. She pressed fingers against the bulging temple, reaching for the vessels supplying the creature's brain. She clamped down on them, depriving the brain of oxygen just long enough to plunge the Zraph into a dead faint. The eyes closed again, and Lianndra breathed a sigh of relief.

Disabling the giant's collar took longer than it did with the human slaves, and Lianndra felt exposed as she worked. Lianndra was just pulling her hands away from the Zraph's temples when she sensed something. She looked up, straight into the open eyes of the human soldier lying on the opposite side of the Zraph.

Lianndra froze in shock. The firelight reflected off the planes of his face. Silver eyes. Dark hair. The line of the jaw—wider than she remembered, but the angle was the same.

It was like being struck by a lightning bolt. Electric fire sizzled along every nerve as she crouched motionless, trapped in his silver stare. She'd spent so long searching, thinking and dreaming about him, and now here he was and she couldn't move or speak.

The man said nothing, just lay staring at her as though puzzled.

Is it really him? Why isn't he moving? He doesn't recognize me, she thought in despair. Then reality intruded. *All he can see is a silhouette.* She retracted the hair from her face. Her pale skin reflected the light, if any of the soldiers around the fire looked over she would be exposed. *But I have to take the risk.*

She saw the exact moment when he recognized her. Michael's entire body jolted and then lay still again. Lianndra admired his self-control. *He doesn't want to give me away.*

She trembled, longing to speak to him. Her eyes scanned every possible route, but Michael was just too far away from any leafy cover for her to go to him. She had never felt so torn. *How can I walk away now?* Lianndra had more than herself to consider. At this moment, the fate of the entire initiative they'd embarked upon rested in her hands. With an aching heart, she conceded that the risk was just too great. *I will have to find another way.*

Lianndra closed her eyes and turned away. She retreated into the shadows of the Zraph's body, pushing the hair across her face again. She shook from head to foot. *Tomorrow night*, she promised herself, *we'll figure out a way.*

Feeling as though she was leaving a part of herself behind, she backed into the ferns and crept along in the darkness.

The skies above chose this moment to open up. Being out in the storms of the jungles of Tarin was like stepping into a waterfall. Rain poured from the sky, cascading in a series of steps from leaf to leaf before finally hitting the soil. The entire camp ruffled like a bird shaking its feathers as soldiers awoke to pull their bedrolls to drier sites or merely tugged their waterproof covers higher over their heads.

Heavy rain rolled off Lianndra's hair keeping her skin dry. She could barely see her hand in front of her face through the intense downfall. For a moment, she considered heading for Michael but she knew the rain could end as fast as it'd begun, leaving her vulnerable.

Lianndra promised herself she would not leave this unit until they'd freed Michael. Whether he joined their small rebel group was up to him. She was not the same woman he'd once known. With her modifications, she no longer qualified as human. Lianndra didn't want to see the look in his eyes once the reality of her transformation became apparent to him. However, if she could at least free him, a part of her heart would be at peace.

Lianndra reached the fringes of the clearing, pausing in the dripping undergrowth. She thought she detected movement behind her and jumped as a tall form stepped into the shadows of the dense plants, not twenty feet from where she hid. She caught a whiff of damp male. Her heart leaped when it triggered a familiar, deep-rooted memory. *Michael. But they might be watching him . . .*

He stopped within the trees, and a moment later Lianndra smelled human male urine.

Obviously doesn't suffer from a shy bladder. She couldn't help grinning to herself as she approached him. *Trust Michael to come up with a natural excuse for wandering off.*

Still, the perimeter guards wouldn't be far away. She'd need to be quick and careful.

Creeping close to his chosen tree, she crouched in the shadows of its massive trunk. He finished and paused as if listening for something. Lianndra counted on the heavy rain to keep her hidden from the guards. Closing her eyes, she retracted the hair from her face and arms. Then she stood, moving just to the edge of where the trunk caught the firelight through the foliage.

A strong arm grabbed her, and she was no longer alone. "Lianndra." Michael's long arms pulled her into an embrace hard enough to make her wince. "I couldn't believe my eyes." He stepped back from her to meet her gaze. "I still don't." His voice dropped to a whisper. "What are you doing here sneaking around? If they catch you alone, killing you will seem a mercy."

Michael had grown; he was taller and his body filled out with hard muscle. He was no longer the gawky young man she remembered.

Lianndra gave herself a mental shake. *I have to do this fast. If he's missed, they'll use the collar to see where he is.* She reached up through the pouring rain to touch his face with her soft finger pads before leaning close, prompting him to bend lower to her. "Michael, I don't have time to explain—do you trust me?"

He didn't seem to notice her claws, but he frowned at her question, no doubt wondering where it would lead. "Yes. I do." The tone reassured her. Time might have passed, and they'd been through hell, but he was still his own person, not some Fang lackey.

"I need you to let me do something," she said as he bent closer to her, enabling her to speak more softly. "I can disable your collar."

Lianndra watched as realization dawned on him. "How—" He cut himself off, recognizing they didn't have time for his questions. "That's what you were doing to old Bradley, there. I wondered."

"I won't do it if you don't want me to. If the Fang catch you with a disabled collar, they will kill you." Lianndra said.

Big hands caught her arms before he bent to bring his face closer to hers. He whispered, "Do whatever you have to. Please."

She didn't hesitate and went *within*. He flinched as she did so, his body instinctively rejecting such an intimate foreign invasion. Whatever he was expecting, it wasn't this. She waited as he forced himself to relax, and then continued on as gently as she could, tracing the various nodes and building up the scar tissue rendering them useless. Working on a conscious person was not easy. Even with Michael trying to give her full access, he struggled to allow her to work unhindered.

It was over quickly. She withdrew to the surface. The silver pools of his eyes glimmered at her, astonishment in his expression.

"You're a Healer." His voice was soft and unreadable.

Lianndra wondered what he was thinking. If he knew Healers, and most soldier slaves possessed some knowledge of them, he also knew about the changes. Her mind skittered away from those thoughts. She tried to tell herself she didn't care if he rejected her. It wouldn't matter so much if he was free, free to return home to Earth. *Something I can no longer ever do.*

For now, she had to get him out. "Come with me," she said, unsure how she would make that happen with the perimeter guards surrounding them.

Michael looked torn. "I have friends inside," he said. "How many of the collars have you disabled?"

Good old Michael, loyal to his friends. It was as though he hadn't changed at all. "I am part of a small group of rebels with two Healers. We've only started to work on your unit," she said as quickly as she could. "But we shadow a unit for a few days to disable as many as we can."

He seized on the idea and ran with it. "I can make sure my friends sleep closer to cover for the next few nights. Will that work?"

Risky, and I'm sure Drake won't like it. Even if she had to do it alone, she would. She would not leave Michael here.

"I'll make it work," she said.

The rain was letting up. "You'd better go," Michael told her, but he didn't let go of her shoulders. "I can't tell you . . . I can't believe you're really here."

Before she could react, he pulled her to him, kissing her swift and hard. Everything inside her seemed to melt; she clung to him. She breathed in his musky scent, feeling the racing thump of his heart. Then he pushed her away into the shadows before striding out of the underbrush and toward the firelight.

Seconds later, Lianndra was in the canopy, watching a perimeter guard make his way back to the camp. She waited until he was out of earshot before swinging higher, heading for the forest giant where Drake and the others waited. Her heart still pounded. She wasn't sure what she was going to say to Drake. He was their leader even though the collars no longer worked, but she knew if he ordered her to leave this unit behind, she'd refuse.

Lianndra wouldn't quit until Michael was free. Then she would see where she stood with him.

He kissed me. Lianndra touched trembling fingers to her lips. *He knew I was a Healer, and he still kissed me.*

Michael was Michael. He'd likely kiss a frog if it was his friend and he hadn't seen it in a while.

He kissed me.

WELL, I WAS RIGHT. LIANNDRA sighed. *Drake doesn't like this.*

Shadowing a unit to perform nightly collar raids had become standard practice for the fugitives, but now that Michael knew of them, Drake was nervous about staying in the vicinity.

"We can try to extract him tonight and be miles away by morning," he said, but Lianndra could tell by the tone of his voice he knew she wouldn't go for it.

"We have to disable more collars in this group. And Michael won't leave until his friends are free." Lianndra looked at Hannah, who sat beside the Aussie. "I won't leave until Michael does," she confirmed for him, in case he'd any delusions.

"Lianndra and I are so mobile; they aren't likely to catch us even if someone blows the whistle." Hannah leaned into him as if trying to convince him through physical contact alone. "You and the guys can hang far enough back so you won't get caught if something happens. There are too few of you to help us if things go wrong. Lianndra and I can make a better escape if we aren't worrying about you."

Drake frowned. Lianndra wondered if it was a good move to remind him that if things go wrong, there was little he could do to help them.

"We will never achieve much if we run every time there are risks," Lianndra said. "I'm willing to take this risk, but I don't want anyone else feeling they have to. I can do this alone."

Drake snorted and shook his head. "No. This is a large unit. The more collars we can disable the better. I can't say I like the fact this Michael will tell our story to his friends. We can only hope he picks his friends with care. Be ready to run at the first sign of trouble." He pinned Lianndra with a fierce stare. "And I mean that. Something even smells funny, you get out. Fast. No heroics."

Lianndra nodded, but her eyes slid away from his intense gaze. *As long as Michael gets out too, then we'll be gone so fast cheetahs won't be able to keep up.*

Freeform

THROUGH THE NEXT DAY'S TREK, Michael's thoughts were on Lianndra. Knowing what she and her rebel friends were up to also made for a restless night once they made camp.

Michael had to control his impulse to look for her when he knew the Healers would sneak into camp. He'd cautioned his friends about it as well. The risks were high, but the result would be worth it.

As long as we are free from the Fang, he thought.

Curled up in his bedroll, he faced away from the firelight. He needed to sleep, so he could be ready when the time came to take on the Fang commander. Despite everything he tried, sleep would not come. He closed his eyes and tried counting himself to sleep. Laid on his back and tried to relax. Rolled onto his side and tried to blank his mind of any thoughts. No matter what he attempted, his mind focused on memories of Lianndra. Her green eyes and wide smile. Laughter as she raced a chestnut mare along the beach. Her curves in the tight wet suit. The softness of her lips when he'd kissed her.

Michael had thought of her many times during his captivity, but now that she was close, he couldn't get her out of his mind. He finally let his memory go, reliving the time they'd spent together back on Earth. Sometime during their visit to the giant redwoods, he drifted off.

Perhaps the dream was due to the thoughts evoked by the giant trees or, more likely, because his tired brain followed a long familiar path. The dream, which was not a dream but rather a memory, was relentless; it trapped him within it.

The night air was thick, humid, and still as death. Moisture from the latest storm cascaded from the giant trees overhead onto the dense undergrowth, running along channels in the leaves to the drip edges and off into space.

The only sign of movement was the sound of wet foliage slapping bodies as they forced their way through and the soft squelch of footsteps on soggy ground. The men were shadows, darker than the night, moving forward as one. They were remarkably uniform, about the same age, tall, well-proportioned, and muscular. They carried their weapons and the heavy supply packs with the ease of long practice. Their camouflage clothing blended into jungle flora around them, the uniforms crisp and new.

That was in the beginning, his sleeping brain whispered, *not now.*

The light from the twin moons, sporadic among the swiftly scudding clouds, reflected off of the weapons the men carried across their bodies.

Weapons, therefore, soldiers. In the dream, Michael looked at his hands. He held an old sword the Fang expected him to fight with. Even though he kept it honed, it bore the notches of long, hard use. Michael remembered wondering what had happened to the soldier who used it before him, the stories each notch could tell.

Deep within the dream, Michael felt the stirrings of fear. Wake up, his dream-self spoke, *you know how this ends.*

He sensed rather than saw his fellow slave soldiers moving silently through the vegetation. Any hesitation in their stride meant a slight tingle in the collars around their necks, a warning to push on . . . or else. They knew too well the penalty for disobedience. They'd seen soldiers suffer when the Fang disagreed with a slave's actions.

Their Farr commander stayed behind them, safe between his lethal Bernaf bodyguards. Some Fang units were unlucky enough to have two Farr as part of their group. These slaves felt fortunate to have only one.

The jungle thinned around them, the slaves becoming more cautious in their forward progress. More than once, a slave soldier twitched when his collar gave a minor correction to his actions.

Michael hunched lower in the thinning foliage, squinting into the shadows. The hair on the back of his neck stood on end.

In the back of his mind, a desperate mantra ranted: it's only a dream—a dream of a memory. *Wake up!*

The clouds raced across the sky, driven by the warm, humid air of the jungle behind them. It was when the clouds temporarily obliterated the moonlight that the ground under their feet attacked.

Even with his instincts on full alert, his dream-self startled when the giant alien appeared. It came from out of nowhere, a huge, six-limbed creature taller than a horse emerging from a bush the size of a small dog. It brandished an enormous sword, one with a reach easily twice that of his. He felt the air of its passing as he ducked beneath its swing, flinging himself sideways into the foliage. The sword tip caught on the pack, and he experienced a moment of panic as he squirmed out of the arm straps to free himself.

As always at this stage of the dream, time seemed to speed up, borne on the wings of his adrenaline. The whine of the few lasers Michael's unit possessed lit up the night sky. He dodged another swing of the Gryphon's mighty sword, only dimly aware of other big aliens fighting their way into his unit's ranks. He heard the Fang commander through the slave collar: *Attack! Kill!*

Regardless of how he felt about it, Michael had no choice but to fight. As a slave soldier in the Fang war, there was no opportunity for negotiation. Gryphon were the Fang's enemy. Michael knew if he didn't attack the giant in front of him, he would die at the hands of his own commander.

When the Gryphon stepped in closer on its next swing, Michael saw his chance. Even then it was dicey. The edge of the giant sword opened a cut on his arm as he ducked under the swing. He surged forward from his crouch and used the momentum of his straightening body to drive his sword deep into the Gryphon, piercing to where the great heart beat.

He heard the air rush out of the big alien, and as the Gryphon collapsed onto Michael's blade, time seemed to slow once more.

Wake up, wake up, Michael's dream-self chanted. *I don't want to relive this again. Wake up!*

Ignoring his pleas, the dream—or rather nightmare, continued.

The Gryphon collapsed slowly, forelegs first, followed by the hind end as its strength flowed away with the blood. The huge sword dragged the arms and torso down until the point buried itself in the earth.

With its barrel lying flat on the ground, the creature's long head was level with his own. Colorful feathers held stiffly erect wreathed its head. The deadly looking hooked beak was only inches from his face. Michael looked past the beak and the long jaw to match his gaze with that of the Gryphon.

Although the feathered mane and beak were reminiscent of a bird of prey, the Gryphon did not have the cold, indifferent golden gaze of an eagle or hawk. Instead, the eyes reflected only a gentle wisdom.

They were beautiful, fringed with thick eyelashes, glistening dark violet in the moonlight. As Michael's heart pounded, the long, tufted ears came forward, and the beaked snout opened. Michael heard the tortured rasp of its breathing, and something that sounded like soft words whispered beneath the gasps for breath.

He couldn't help himself. Michael leaned closer, close enough to see the moon's reflection in the Gryphon's eyes and to smell the slightly spicy aroma of its feathery fur. He could also smell its life blood flooding the soil at his feet.

Wake Up! His mind was screaming. *Oh God, wake up!*

Michael shook all over. Trapped within the dream, he heard himself stammering, trying to explain, "I didn't mean to, I had to, I had no choice . . ." But not one clear word came out of his mouth.

The liquid eyes blinked as the long head on the graceful neck sunk lower to the ground. Michael now needed to bend over to get close enough to the Gryphon's lips to make out what it was saying.

The softest of whispers, given on the last hint of breath. Then the creature fully collapsed, the weight driving its own sword into the earth.

Michael's vision was blurry as he blinked away tears. "I'm sorry," he said, standing over the body of the dead alien.

His dream-self seemed suddenly isolated from the surrounding battle. The dream night reclaimed its silence just as the clouds unleashed the rain. The water poured on the plants below, dripping softly off the leaves, running down his face, and over the still body of the Gryphon.

As Michael awoke, the creature's last whispered words echoed through his mind. Three little words in a human language it should not have been able to speak.

"I forgive you," the Gryphon had told him.

AFTER ALL THEIR STEALTH WORK, it was unsettling for the Healers to disable collars with the slaves staring at them. Michael obviously briefed them on the procedure, and the soldiers did their best to comply. Still, there were a few that Lianndra eased off to sleep before she could go ahead with the deactivation.

She worked as fast as possible, sneaking up to the men in the darkness, touching them on the shoulder to announce her presence before working. Lianndra squeezed each one's shoulder when finished before melting into the shadows of the underbrush, heading for her next subject.

This was their third night of work on Michael's unit. Michael seemed to have more allies than enemies, and they weren't all human. The Zraph she worked on the first night was the Bradley Michael referred to. It didn't surprise her that Michael had no biases when it came to friends. It made her ashamed. She'd worked so long with the men in her division yet barely made it to a first-name basis.

Since the early days of the FHR division, Lianndra believed the men thought of her as more animal than human; it built a wall between them. She now recognized her isolation as self-imposed.

I am the biased one, she thought.

Looking around with new eyes, she knew the two soldiers in their rebel group treated her with nothing but respect. She'd put up impenetrable barriers, giving no one other than Hannah a glimpse within the walls.

Both of the remaining soldiers worked hard during the day hunting for meat with their small, powerful crossbows. When they ran out of arrows, the men created new ones from branches. The proximity of Michael's unit hindered their activities. They shadowed it during the day, coming in close at night when the Healers did their work.

Lianndra knew Drake's group could not stick with Michael's for much longer. Michael's unit was headed for the closest Fang supply barracks. They were now only a few days out from it, and the increased Fang presence was putting their plans at risk.

With her dappled coat of hair mimicking the surrounding shadows, Lianndra kept one eye on the fire. She crept along the jungle's edge to the next nearest soldier. The clearing Michael's unit chose tonight was smaller than usual. This meant there were more soldiers sleeping near cover, but it also meant the commander tent and fires were closer to where the Healers would be working. Drake almost pulled the plug when he'd seen the camp from the canopy above. Only the prospect of missing a full night's work convinced him to let the women go ahead.

Lianndra spotted a bedroll pushed right into the undergrowth, disguising it from the light of the fire. As she approached, she caught a familiar scent and her heart started to pound.

When she crept alongside, Michael reached out a long arm to gather her into his bedroll, pulling up the covers to hide her. His warmth and scent engulfed her. Soldiers seldom had the opportunity to bathe. Over time, Lianndra had become accustomed to the various odors of unwashed humans. Even so, there was something pure about Michael's scent.

I just don't think I could ever find anything about this man gross. Lianndra gave herself a mental poke. *I'm like a schoolgirl with a crush.*

Michael lowered his head until his mouth was near her ear. His breath made the hair on her neck quiver. Lianndra realized she hadn't retracted the hair from her face and arms. She wondered if he'd noticed in the darkness as she worked to remedy the situation. When her tail twitched beneath the covers, she wound it around one of her legs to curtail its involuntary movements.

"Hi," he said. White teeth flashed in the reflected firelight.

"Hi." Her voice was shaky. Space was tight in the bedroll. Lianndra couldn't help but have her full length up against him. She could feel he'd changed from the skinny young man she'd first met. The hard ridges of his chest and abdominal muscles were obvious beneath his thin shirt. She found herself suddenly breathless when his hips and thighs pressed against her.

Michael clasped her hand to raise it closer to his eyes. Long fingers explored her sensitive finger pads and claws. Lianndra flinched as she tried to pull her fingers away.

He respected the movement, releasing her hand. "I guess we're both different from when we last met." He smiled again. "Bet those come in really useful in the jungle."

Lianndra averted her gaze before nodding. "They do."

Michael stared at her for a moment. A log crackled and shifted in the nearest fire pit, bringing them back to the matter at hand. "We're two days out from the northernmost barracks," he whispered to her.

"If we're going to make a move against the commander, tomorrow's it. Can you get the rest of us done in time?"

Lianndra considered before answering. Drake calculated the numbers before they'd moved in tonight. It would push it as some might be too close to the fire for either she or Hannah to reach. They never managed to get every person in a unit, but as long as they got most of them, any mutiny should have an obvious conclusion.

"Most of them. Those closest to the tent are too Fang friendly and aren't good candidates anyway," she said.

Her heart thumped from more than just the closeness of Michael's body—she was now afraid. Afraid of what he planned to do and the risk it involved. Like all fighting units, the commander of Michael's unit had a direct comm link to the nearest barracks. If they didn't take the Fang commander out fast, every Fang within range would be on top of them.

The commander's bodyguards were three of the lithe aliens known as the Bernaf. Although they were also slaves, Lianndra was not sure of their true allegiance. Getting to the Fang commander meant getting past his bodyguards. At night, the commander remained protected within his tent. During the day, the Bernaf were still present, but the logistical realities of moving through the jungle might make the Fang more vulnerable.

Michael seemed to think along the same lines. "Daytime presents us with the best opportunity. Surprise and speed are essential. The main obstacles are those bodyguards. They move like lightning and are lethal even without weapons."

Lianndra thought hard. "I think you need a distraction. The jungle is full of them. I'll talk to Captain Drake and the other Healer, Hannah. Perhaps we can whip something up for you. If the Fang thinks it's a natural thing, he won't be in a hurry to report to headquarters."

"I don't want you helping with this." Michael's voice rose, his fingers digging into her arms as he forced himself to speak more quietly. "This is our gig. You have done enough."

"Don't be stupid, Michael." Lianndra placed two fingers on his lips to stop another outburst. "We're in this together. This is a rebellion. No one stands alone. There is too much riding on each effort."

His mouth formed a grim line. She felt the tension along the entire length of his body. Ignoring his physical proximity as best she could, she continued. "We'll be close to you tomorrow. Tell everyone to wait for the distraction before going after the Bernaf and Fang."

"The jungle is a busy place. How will we know when it's your distraction?"

Lianndra smiled and said. "Don't worry, you'll know. I have an idea. It depends on what jungle secrets lurk nearby but it will seem like an animal attack. It should keep the Bernaf unaware of the real threat until it's too late."

Michael's fingers tightened on her arms and she thought he would argue further. Instead, he lowered his head and kissed her. Every bone in her body melted against him as he groaned softly beneath her lips. His hands shook. His body was hard against her and he held her so tight she could barely breathe. They were both breathless when he reluctantly pulled away.

The Michael I knew on Earth wouldn't have been so bold. Lianndra's thoughts whirled. *I think I like this new Michael even better.*

"Be careful." He interlocked his long fingers with hers. "Please."

Lianndra couldn't trust herself to speak after that kiss. She merely nodded as he raised the cover to allow her to slide out of the bedroll and into the shadows. As she moved into the dense foliage, she felt his eyes on her. She headed for the next nearest soldier.

An eruption of the firelight reflected off the claws on her hand. Her heart pounded and fingers trembled when she reached the next slave. She forced herself to smile into his worried eyes. As she worked, her thoughts stayed on Michael. *If only we could live in darkness forever. These kisses might be all I ever have of him. At least I can free him, and maybe he can go home. Everything hinges on what happens tomorrow. I will free him. Tomorrow.*

FIGURES—LIANNDRA CAUGHT HER LIP between her teeth—*when you're looking for them, they're never around.* Her eyes scanned the jungle canopy. It was a quiet morning. *Too quiet. Where the hell are they?*

She sighed, shifting the rodent carcass to her other hand. She'd found a plump one so she wouldn't run out of reptile bait before she got to her target.

Finally, she heard Hannah whistle. *She's spotted them!*

Her heart, which hadn't been too steady all morning, pounded as her adrenaline surged. She took to the air, swinging to the next tree with her skrin. Hannah whistled again, using the call of a common jungle bird to help Lianndra zero in on her location.

Lianndra swung to the branch alongside Hannah. The redhead pointed to a group of tall trees. "They just flew in there." Her forehead creased in a frown as she touched Lianndra on the arm. "Are you sure about this? Maybe we should go with Drake's idea. This seems too risky."

"It has to appear like a natural accident or the Fang commander will pull every nearby unit down on us. That's why Drake agreed to this plan." Lianndra smiled at her friend. "It'll be fine. Just make sure you guys are in place. Staying undetected might be tricky if many slaves are loyal to the Fang and fight for him. We're lucky Michael is Mr. Popular. It gives us a good read on how most of the slaves stand."

Hannah nodded, her face creased with worry. "Be careful," she said as Lianndra extended her skrin, using it to bind the carcass to her torso. She then felted the skrin's controller to her waist, adjusting the rodent body to cover her back. When it felt balanced, she nodded to Hannah, who slit the body open along its back. Lianndra felt the rapidly cooling blood running down her ribcage. *My skrin will never be the same.*

Lianndra leaped into the nearest tree and headed for the area housing the reptile birds. As she moved, she grew a tuft on the end of her tail, a long brush of hair that might save her skin.

Flashes of brilliant iridescent color darted through the canopy. Lianndra heard the click and whir of the stiff feathers on the four-winged creatures. She paused on a high branch just upwind as she ground the tuft of her tail into the gory carcass on her back until it soaked up the blood.

The activity in the tree seemed to increase, and Lianndra took a deep breath. Then she swung out on a sturdy vine, moving in a large arc that almost carried her to within touching distance of the target tree. At the farthest reach of the arc, she flicked her tail, splattering gore everywhere.

A loud buzzing hum rose from the tree. Then they were after her, following the blood trail with small fangs bared.

So much for the easy part. Lianndra released the vine and flew through the air to a nearby tree trunk. She barely touched the trunk before launching herself forward with only the tips of her claws. Out of the corner of her eye, she saw the flock swirl in a rainbow of color as they pursued.

She concentrated on staying just one step ahead of them. If they caught up with her, they would descend like a school of piranha to rip her to shreds. *That is the reason I didn't tell Michael the details of what I planned and why Drake objected to the idea.* But Drake hadn't been able to offer anything better, and they'd run out of time.

Lianndra knew the rough location of Michael's unit; she relied on Hannah to guide her more precisely once she was close. The Healers had traveled beyond what was ideal to find the flock of flying lizards. Now she would have farther to go to get to the target.

The only way to stay ahead of them was to dole out the occasional morsel to the flock. She did so now, yanking out a segment of intestine with her tail to toss it into the crook of a tree as she flew by. The flock hesitated in its forward progress just long enough to devour the morsel before they took up the blood trail once more.

Lianndra was winded by the time she saw Hannah swing into full view ahead of her. Sweat ran with the blood across her body. She'd doled out most of the innards of the rodent by then, relying on her speed and agility to keep ahead of them. She was ahead, but only barely. Leaders of the flock came into view along her flanks.

Hannah moved up to full speed with Lianndra following as they dropped lower in the jungle foliage. The flock was well and truly committed, or they would never have followed her so low; they were creatures of the upper canopy. She felt a small body bounce off the carcass on her back, carving out a mouthful for itself. Several others followed. Then they were hitting her so hard they forced her lower and lower. She winced as one missed the carcass, biting into her shoulder. Another caught the back of her leg. She started using her blood-soaked tail to beat them off as she sailed through the air.

Hannah whistled as she swung up and away, signaling that the unit was ahead. Lianndra fought to stay above the lowest plants. She touched down on a branch and the flock descended on her, obscuring her vision. She wiped a couple off of her head as she launched for a vine, snagging it with one hand about twenty feet off the ground. With the other, she hit the skrin control, retracting the cable and releasing the carcass from her back so she could hold it dangling by one leg.

She saw the shocked face of the perimeter guard as she flew just over his head, fighting to stay on the vector Hannah had given her. The flying reptiles were all over her.

Hannah's aim was dead on. Lianndra catapulted without warning through the center of the marching unit between the Bernaf bodyguards. With a sodden smack, she clobbered the Fang commander in the chest with the carcass. Bright bodies obscured Lianndra's vision as she barreled into the undergrowth on the other side of the path and disappeared.

MICHAEL STRODE ALONG THE PATH, the Zraph he nicknamed Bradley stomping behind him. He'd positioned himself within easy striking distance of the Fang commander and was tense from the exertion of appearing nonchalant when every nerve was on fire.

Desperately worried about Lianndra's plan to distract the commander and his bodyguards, Michael remained on edge all morning. Knowing this jungle was full of dangers, some hidden, some not, he hoped Lianndra and her small group of rebels were not in over their heads.

Even though he was ready for something to happen, when it did, it paralyzed Michael with shock. The form that crashed through the unit bore no resemblance to anything familiar. Something bloody and torn hit the Fang commander, knocking him flying. Colorful reptiles swarmed above him in agitation before following the trail of blood to his prone form. He yelled in his coarse voice, causing the Bernaf bodyguards to leap to his assistance. They grabbed the small winged bodies to crush them in their elongated fingers.

As distractions go, it was perfect. The bodyguards assumed the surrounding soldiers were moving to the defense of their leader. Caught off guard, they died when the soldiers ran them through with their weapons instead. The Fang commander was then summarily torn to shreds by a vengeful Bradley. Bits and pieces better off not identified flew through the air, eagerly pursued by small, bright bodies.

The few soldiers who hadn't been in on the plan stood in baffled confusion as the tide turned on them. Michael ignored them. Frowning, he turned from the carnage to survey the torn leaves on the far side of the path. Mentally retracing events, he realized something had blasted straight through the marching column, plowing into the undergrowth. Something covered in more of those ravenous reptiles.

His heart lurched as he pushed his way through the underbrush. A few weakly flapping reptiles clinging to the bushes told him he was on the right path. Their distended bellies rendered the creatures temporarily unable to fly.

"Lianndra!" he bellowed, fear adding volume to his call. He imagined her shredded to pieces by those vicious creatures. "Lianndra!"

"Over here," an unfamiliar female voice answered him.

He burst into a trampled area and saw a dark-haired man he didn't know. Leaning over a crumpled form on the ground was a woman with red hair and a tail. Hannah? Surrounding them were mounds of the flying reptiles.

The crumpled form was Lianndra, but she was barely recognizable through the blood. Everywhere Michael looked he saw raw bite marks.

She isn't moving. As he fell to his knees beside her, he choked on his words of denial.

"She's alive, but she took a beating from those things." The dark-haired man tried to sound reassuring but Michael could hear distress in his accented voice. "Hannah will set her to rights. You must be Michael. I'm Drake."

Michael nodded acknowledgment and sensed the man's dark eyes assessing him. Uncaring, he only had eyes for Lianndra's prone form. He noticed Hannah's lips moved wordlessly as she worked over her friend. The shallow cuts had already stopped bleeding and the deeper ones were barely oozing now.

Michael picked up one of Lianndra's hands and sat holding it, feeling helpless.

Hannah sighed before sitting back on her heels. "She's lost a lot of blood, but I've stopped the bleeding. I'd like to wash her before I finish the healing. It will make it easier for me to see where I'm at"— she stood to look around— "there is a small runoff creek over this way. I spotted it when I surveyed the area this morning."

Drake moved to help lift Lianndra but Michael waved him off. "I've got this. You've got a rebellion to organize."

Drake hesitated before giving a brisk nod. He moved off toward the verbal confusion Michael heard building in momentum behind them.

Michael carefully eased his arms under Lianndra and lifted her limp form. She seemed so small. He paused long enough to reassure himself she was breathing before following Hannah into the foliage. Something brushed against one leg and it startled him to see a long tail, the bushy end saturated in blood. He'd heard some Healers had them but he'd only ever seen Lianndra in the dark. Looking ahead, he noticed Hannah had one as well, although it lacked the tuft and seemed shorter than Lianndra's.

They reached the creek, and he lowered Lianndra into the water. The clear spring turned deep red as the running water worked on the blood in her hair. With a shock, Michael realized she wasn't wearing any clothes. What he assumed was a bodysuit was actually hair—her hair, interwoven all over her body to resemble clothing. As the blood washed away, the hair caught the dappled sunlight through the water. Mottled with the colors blondes naturally have, it ranged from chestnut brown to a color so pale it was almost silver. Only her face, hands, and feet seemed bare. Her elongated toes possessed claws even longer than those on her hands. Then there was the tail . . .

He sighed, holding her head above the water with one hand and gently washing her cheek with the other. *So many changes.* His fingers trailed over her upper lip where the tips of long fangs gleamed. Where was the girl he'd rescued from the shark? She was barely recognizable.

Hannah's hands ran all over Lianndra's body, separating real injuries from rodent blood, working on each wound as she found it. Lianndra's lip curled in a grimace of pain, revealing one long, pointed fang. Then her eyes snapped open.

And there she was. For Michael, it was as simple as that. The moment their eyes met, nothing else mattered to him. Lianndra was there, battered and bloody, changed—but alive.

He smiled down at her and she smiled back. For a moment, all was well with the world.

Hannah was too busy to notice Michael and Lianndra having a moment. She pulled at hair matted with blood, her fingers probing too deeply into a wound.

"Ow!" Lianndra said, struggling to sit. Her eyes widened as they slid from his face to his hands supporting her. Michael saw her expression turn to one of horror as Lianndra focused on Hannah, who was still working on a wound on her tail.

In an instant, Lianndra was on her feet, yanking her tail out of Hannah's hands. Michael rose with her, reaching out a hand to her elbow as she swayed. Hannah grabbed her other arm.

With a strength she shouldn't have possessed, Lianndra shook them both off, spinning in a circle, swinging her tail in a flying spray of water to back them away. Then in a flash of wet golden hair, she leaped for the nearest branch to disappear into the canopy.

"Lianndra!" Michael called but received no answer.

Hannah shook her head. "Don't worry, I'll go after her."

"What was that about?" Michael sounded so hurt and confused Hannah turned back to him.

He saw her hesitate before she said, "She has some issues with the way she looks."

Michael was even more confused. "What?" He shook his head, staring up at the branches where Lianndra had vanished.

"I've gotta go. She won't get too far. She's too weak." Hannah turned away from him. "Don't worry," she said over her shoulder. Then she leaped for the closest branch to vanish in Lianndra's wake.

Michael got an eyeful of shapely butt disappearing into the canopy before he remembered Hannah was essentially naked even if she appeared covered in red hair.

This will take some getting used to. He shook his head before walking back toward the unit.

The chatter had died down. He assumed it meant the man, Drake, was having success with organizing things. He pushed through the foliage, following the sounds of activity.

It turned out Drake was supervising the chopping up of the Fang commander and his bodyguards. A gory, disgusting task, but if they were to succeed, all evidence of their rebellion needed to disappear into the jungle. The easiest way to do this was to ease the transfer of grisly bits into the bellies of some of its more disgusting inhabitants.

Welcome to the rebellion, Michael thought. He felt very far from home.

SWEAT RAN DOWN THE HUMAN'S face as his shaking fingers pushed buttons on the communications equipment balanced on a large rock. The reason for his fear was obvious: the stocky Farr commander leaning over him with swirling red eyes. The Farr had already tried to contact the errant unit with just his ear comm, but without any success. Now they were using the bulky box reserved for longer distance communications. Yet try as he might, the equipment remained silent in response to the human's repeated calls.

"Is the comm down?" The commander's thick tongue tangled in the simple English words.

"No, sir. Interference is at twenty-five percent, which is good." The slave forced himself not to babble. "There is just no response to our summons." His back muscles tensed. He felt the hot breath of the Farr on his shoulder. "Perhaps the comm is disabled at their end."

"Contact headquarters," the commander hissed.

These days, reporting a lost unit wasn't for the faint of heart. *The war coordinator is not tolerant of mistakes.*

The slave hurried to comply, not wanting any of the Farr's bad mood to spill over onto him. Slaves were valuable in this war but the commander had no qualms about activating the pain nodes in their collars. He loved to see them squirm.

THE MESSAGE FROM THE FARR commander came in to one of two techs on duty at headquarters. Sar%kan%bane acted quickly to pick it up; her peer was busy trying to get in a midday snack.

She listened carefully. The tech's responsibilities included the summarization of message details before forwarding them to the war coordinator. As messages swamped the coordinator on an hourly basis, this process helped to streamline the incoming information.

Sar%kan%bane asked for the last known location of the missing unit, and then checked with the Central Intelligence Processor. It registered that the missing unit failed to report in as scheduled, although they were still within the time period allowed for error.

"We require more information," she replied to the voice on the comm. "You are authorized to investigate further."

The gruff voice of the Farr signed off and the Fara tech switched modes on her console. Her clawed fingers tapped out a quick message before sending it off.

Communication between the Motherships and Tarin was difficult; the shield interfered with most wireless systems. The admin office possessed only one channel, reinforced by a special satellite which permitted such communication.

One channel that they know of. Sar%kan%bane knew of one other, on a special frequency that penetrated the shield, set up by allies of the Tlo%m rebellion. *After all, it is their shield.*

The message she sent along this secure channel was short and to the point: *We have reached Level Three. Detection is imminent.*

14

DRAKE HAD A MILITARY BACKGROUND, and it showed. The enlarged rebel group moved so efficiently through the jungle that anyone watching would have sworn they'd been training together for months. For the first few days, Michael watched as Drake assessed the men, moving them around until they fit into suitable roles. The captain assembled small parties for hunting or gathering food, sent the most focused out as perimeter guards or scouts, and assigned the strongest to break trails through tough underbrush.

To Michael, it was obvious Drake possessed the qualities of a good leader, and the freed slaves seemed to agree. The efficiency of strong leadership enabled them to quickly increase the distance between them and the barracks. With the high concentration of Fang units moving through the jungle, there was only one direction for them to go—straight toward the front lines, and then beyond to the grasslands.

Their numbers were now too large to hide. As a result, Drake put a moratorium on freeing any more slaves until they found a secure home base for the rebellion. That meant they had to get out of Fang-occupied territory; the group headed out of the jungle and toward the grasslands with all possible speed.

Michael understood the need for a home base if their rebellion was to survive. It was unfortunate that to find it, they would enter Gryphon-occupied territory.

Lianndra proposed they trade on the relationship they'd developed with the smaller Gryphon who'd given her the amulet. They knew connecting with one particular Gryphon in an army of thousands would be problematic. As nobody came up with any better ideas, Lianndra's was the one Drake put forward.

Many of the men in Michael's unit pointed out that the Healers were coming from a different perspective. As part of the healing division, they had spent their time well behind the front lines rather than fighting. This meant they hadn't fought and killed Gryphon. The freed soldiers killed many Gryphon during their enslavement. They doubted the Gryphon would forgive such actions to forge an alliance.

Drake held a meeting to address these concerns. Each person stated their thoughts and ideas. Michael had enough faith in Lianndra to accept her idea outright. Lianndra came forward to tell them what the little Gryphon had said. The small Gryphon's speech to the humans carried a great deal of weight, particularly her words about the slaves not being responsible for their actions during the war. Lianndra conveyed how she was confident the Gryphon would consider collaboration. When Michael and Drake backed her, everyone conceded.

Lianndra then showed them the carved winged Gryphon, pulling it from a felted hair pocket and passing it around. Michael handled it thoughtfully before giving it back to her for safekeeping.

"You know, it looks a lot like a dragon," Michael said. He stood as close to her as he dared, leaning against a tree.

Lianndra just glanced at him. She was becoming so elusive that some of the unit nicknamed her the Ghost. She wouldn't speak to Michael and rarely to anyone else. Unless someone suffered a bug bite or sprained ankle requiring treatment, she spent her time scouting in the trees with Hannah.

Michael spent most of his days on sentry duty. He'd volunteered for this hoping to come into contact with Lianndra, but Hannah was the one who dropped by to update him. The ground sentries doubled as hunters and gatherers for the group. It took a lot of food to keep this many people supplied, and they hunted while on the move. While Sean was an expert marksman, Michael was better at tracking, and they formed an efficient team for hunting. For big men, they moved silently when tracking through the jungle.

As the days passed, Michael's frustration with Lianndra increased. He wanted to tell her the changes in her appearance didn't matter to him. When Lianndra became even more elusive, he recruited Hannah to pass the message along. It changed nothing.

Hannah was exactly the opposite. It was obvious she was becoming the heart of the unit. During the day, she was in the trees. The minute they set up camp, she moved through the soldiers, checking them for injuries, talking with them, and assessing their mental and physical status. If Drake could accompany her, he did. Hannah fostered respect within the unit, even among those considered previously loyal to the Fang.

The Healers deactivated the collars of the few soldiers with dubious loyalties the first night; Drake wanted them considered part of the rebellion. For the most part, they had made the transition smoothly. Michael noticed, however, that Drake placed them in positions that didn't risk the integrity of the unit.

The days were a blur of activity, and each night Michael retired exhausted. Yet he seldom slept well. He remembered the feel of Lianndra inside his bedroll, a curious mixture of softness and strength. Michael longed to get closer to her, to familiarize himself with the changes in her. Her elusiveness tormented him.

When he spotted her talking to Drake, Michael's first reaction was always one of frustration. *Why does she talk to him but not to me?*

He noticed the way some of the guards looked at her. Even though she never seemed to return their interest, he still struggled to contain himself. One day, he stumbled upon her talking to a guard. When she glanced at him before doing the usual vanishing act, he felt a surge of anger and barely restrained himself from hitting the poor guy. Michael shocked himself with the intensity of his anger. *This is ridiculous. I've got to get a grip.*

It wasn't easy. It would be different if he didn't think something existed between Lianndra and himself. *She has a right to decide whether she wants to connect with me.* Michael couldn't believe she felt nothing when a single sideways glance from her made him weak at the knees. *The way she responded to me kissing her . . . could I be wrong?*

He squelched his anger and did his best to get over it.

Despite his friends in the unit, Michael was no stranger to loneliness. It was part of being a soldier, regardless of whose war the soldiers were fighting. The Fang set the units up as single gender outfits and the men needed to escape the pain and fear that filled their daylight hours. It was only natural to seek solace in companionship once they struck camp every night. Sometimes, the friendships went deeper. For some this was a natural connection, for others it fulfilled a need, helping them to cope with their loneliness and fear. Although

Michael had no problem with what others did in the dark of the night, for him, it just wasn't how he rolled. He'd coped with the loneliness in a sane and balanced fashion until Lianndra reappeared in his life. Now, things were different.

Every night he struggled to relax; he did it a muscle at a time, trying to get as much rest as possible. It didn't seem to matter what he tried. His mind, regardless of his distraction efforts, kept returning to one tortuous theme. Michael would awaken in the morning bleary-eyed, filled with a frustration for which he'd no solution.

During the day he found himself watching the canopy for any sign of a golden blur. When he caught sight of her, his heart would leap. But when he gave the whistle the soldiers used to call the Healers in for information, it was always Hannah that responded.

Things were easier before I knew she was alive, he thought. *I don't know how much longer I can go on like this.*

THE FARR COMMANDER STOOD IN the center of the chaos. All around he saw trampled foliage, bent leaves, and small trees pushed over. His slave soldiers canvassed for any signs of the missing unit. So far they'd discovered nothing but crushed vegetation and a few random bloodstains.

The jungle was full of natural dangers capable of decimating a unit, even one relatively well-armed. In his experience he'd never seen a unit suffer a natural calamity and vanish, leaving not even their equipment behind. Few such events wiped out the entire unit without a trace.

It wasn't unheard of for a unit to lose its commander. The collars held the slaves to a confined area until another commander or controller took over. Something about this situation had gone awry. He should report to headquarters. Yet to report in with no further information was galling and humiliating.

If only there were traces of what had happened, like a chewed collar or body bits.

A winded scout ran up to him. The commander nodded to the slave, bringing his full focus to bear on him.

"There is a trail, it is narrow, but it looks like there may have been survivors." The slave gasped.

The commander made his decision. In a moment, he shouted terse directions. The unit reformed, the scouts heading out along the trampled trail.

He would contact headquarters—when he had more information. First, he needed to find the slaves. Then he would get the answers he sought by making the humans squeal.

TO LIANNDRA'S GENETICALLY ENHANCED HEARING, the jungle was never silent. The soft darkness of the night was alive with exotic flora and fauna. All around, she heard and smelled them going about their nocturnal lives.

Although she was no longer fully human, her enhanced senses were one of the things she appreciated. *Humans rely so much on their eyesight they ignore their hearing and sense of smell,* she thought.

Lianndra sat in a massive tree two hundred feet above the jungle floor. Through a break in the leafy canopy, the stars twinkled at her. Every night, she left the camp after supper and climbed as high as possible. She slept high in the huge jungle trees, only dropping to the men below when they were preparing the morning meal.

Lianndra told herself she liked the isolation, but she knew, deep inside, she was avoiding human contact. Self-imposed it might be, but she couldn't bring herself to reach out to anyone other than Hannah. Nothing changed the fact she was no longer truly one of them.

Even though their physical wounds healed, the freed slaves were not in the best mental shape. The Healers could do little except coach them through their nightmares, and after only a few nights the women felt the strain. Lianndra needed isolation to rejuvenate, so she convinced herself she enjoyed being alone with the jungle, using her natural camouflage to blend with the trees.

One person could always find her. A soft sound announced the arrival of Hannah from below. Her friend cradled a large, round fruit, which she then handed to her.

"Eat this," Hannah said. "You're losing too much weight. Drake noticed it today, although he barely sees you these days."

Lianndra obediently took the fruit and bit into it, the tart juice dripping down her chin. Unlike the cloned fruit the Motherships served their slaves, the fruits of Tarin's jungle did not lack for flavor. Hannah stared at her friend until she finished and then handed her a leaf to wipe the juices off her face.

"So, how long are you going to keep avoiding him?" Hannah asked.

Trust Hannah to get right to the point, Lianndra thought. She shrugged, not bothering to deny anything. "Until he loses interest."

"I don't think that will happen." Hannah settled herself on the branch, wrapping her tail around it. "He seems interested and you two have history."

Lianndra leaned back against the tree trunk, looking up again at the stars. "Michael can go home, Hannah. I can't. I don't want him making connections that may hold him back."

Hannah snorted. "Who says he'd want to go back? We don't even know if it will ever be possible. We could die tomorrow and you're worried about him being able to go home?"

"I think Michael is too"—she groped for the right word—"loyal. If we get into something and it works, he might be torn apart with the decision. Besides, look at me. Kissing me is like kissing an animal."

Lianndra realized she was also insulting Hannah and her involvement with a certain very human male. "I'm sorry, I wasn't thinking. You're beautiful as you are and I'm sure Drake agrees. I just don't feel that way about myself."

Hannah didn't insult easily. Although her brows rose in the darkness, her reply, as usual, reflected her sense of humor. "Well, I wouldn't want to kiss you, but I don't think it has anything to do with your hairy body."

Despite herself, Lianndra laughed. They sat in silence for a while, contemplating the stars.

"Have you tried to reverse the mutations?" Hannah's question seemed to come out of nowhere.

Lianndra stared at her friend in shock. "What?"

"You heard me. You are always coming up with new ways to use your abilities. Have you tried to reverse any of the genetic changes the Fang made to you?" Hannah's gaze dropped to meet Lianndra's astonished expression. "I rather like my accessories,"—she gestured to her twitching tail and waved her claws in the air—"but you obviously don't. So have you tried to eliminate them?"

Lianndra didn't reply but her mind raced. *Can I reverse any of the changes?* They would leave the jungle in a few days, so the mutations made to ease their life in the trees will no longer be an advantage. *I'm so sunk in my despair that I haven't been thinking proactively.*

She could reduce the body hair to almost nothing, so that wasn't the issue. It was things like the tail, the teeth, the claws on her feet and hands; they were external changes the Fang created at the genetic level.

"Reversing the genetic mutations within my body is well beyond my ability but perhaps not beyond yours. You are always full of surprises," Hannah said.

Lianndra hardly heard her, she had already gone *within* the cells of the middle finger of her right hand. In the back of her mind she considered what she knew of her abilities. The Fang had enhanced the human brain of the Healers by developing a latent talent for telekinesis. Healers mentally entered a living body at the subcellular level to move molecules with their minds.

When injuries occur, neighboring cells trigger naturally to divide and fill the void. Healers train to use their telekinetic ability to enhance healing injured tissues by inducing cells to divide more quickly. First they find healthy cells next to the injury, then they use their abilities to concentrate oxygen, nutrients, and growth factors. The Healers find key complexes within the cells to trigger mitosis. Under an experienced Healer, the cells duplicate fast to heal a wound.

The Fang trained the first Healers to move cellular materials with their minds. By the time they created Lianndra's generation, the older ones were working at the molecular level. They showed the new

Healers how to identify the key molecules involved in cell division. Each differed in their abilities; many could go no further than manipulating the molecular materials to help healing.

Few understand the power at their fingertips, Lianndra thought.

Over time Lianndra trained first herself, and then Hannah, to go further. She'd isolated a protein within the cellular matrix that formed strands between the cell and the fluid matrix around it. These strands dictated the direction in which the new daughter cells would grow. Thus, she and Hannah deliberately grew the cells in any direction, forming bridges of tissue to more efficiently seal a wound.

Ripping existing cells apart was more difficult because the Healer had to use her telekinetic ability to destroy the cellular membranes at the molecular level, reopening the wound. The leftover debris could be recycled into nutrients for the new cells being built or be pushed along to the lymphatic system for disposal. In the case of infection, it was best to telekinetically push it out of the wound altogether, a very labor-intensive process.

Although Lianndra did not care to think about it, she knew they could use this ability to kill, by ripping apart and not rebuilding the cells. Vital organs such as the heart or brain could be destroyed at the cellular level. It would require a powerful Healer with extreme finite control over her abilities, but it was all too possible.

Most did not understand the specifics of how their talents worked. They felt their way through the process, identifying certain components, and then pushing them along with their minds. Lianndra had examined the process in detail during her meditations. Along with her veterinary training, it allowed her to understand more of the involvement at a molecular level. As a medical student, Hannah easily followed Lianndra's lead.

But can I go one level further? Can I manipulate genetic code? Lianndra wasn't sure.

The coded building plan for the body's cells, commonly known as DNA, told the cells what they were to become and how they were to work. The Fang had manipulated her DNA, inserting new coding so her body's cells would develop in a new way—tail, claws, and so on. Healers pushed components around, triggering the cell replication process by manipulating protein molecules responsible for reading sections of the DNA code. Attempting to alter her genetic mutations involved going *within* the nuclei of the cells and interpreting the coding of the DNA itself. In order to change herself back to fully human, she would have to first find the altered DNA sequences. Then she would have to find the original human genes overwritten or discarded and either reactivate them or reinsert them into the DNA strand.

Piece of cake. Right. With my luck, the alterations will give me superpowers. Although altering my eyes to emit energy beams might be useful, turning into the bride of Axiom-man won't make me any more human, she thought.

Swallowing her nerves, Lianndra cleared her mind. She isolated a single cell in her finger and gently inserted herself *within* it via a pore in the membrane. Entering a cell always reminded her of what it would be like to dive in the deep seas. With no existing natural light, she navigated by feel, painting a mental picture of the various cell structures floating around in the darkness. Her many previous pilgrimages into cells helped her to identify the basic structures including vesicles, lysosomes, the Golgi apparatus, and the smooth endoplasmic reticulum. She found the nucleus so well protected it would be difficult to penetrate without damage. Lianndra entered carefully via the cellular back door of the rough endoplasmic reticulum, zeroing in on the chromosomes.

Chromosomes contained the DNA strands, and the normal human cell had forty-six of them. Each chromosome inhabited its own territory within the nucleus, nature's way of keeping the genetic materials pure. The chromosomes only came together when they were ready to duplicate.

Lianndra had no way of knowing which chromosome contained the DNA the Fang had modified. Genes were sections of the DNA strand; characteristics such as eye color could be affected by more than one gene.

Who knows how many genes they changed to do this to me? I guess I'm hoping for a flashing light saying, "These are the genes you are looking for," Lianndra thought.

She fine-tuned her mental eye to scan the DNA strand of the nearest chromosome. She strained to find the gene sequences. Beads of sweat formed on her skin, dripping down her face.

After failing multiple times to identify gene sequences along the DNA strands, let alone the modified ones, she tried something different. Lianndra concentrated on the claws themselves. By pushing with her mind, she coaxed the cells to multiply and lengthen a claw. She shrank the claw to the merest pointed stub by tearing the cells apart. No matter what she did, the DNA code within the nail bed of her finger would still tell the claw to regenerate exactly as it was before. She couldn't tell it to return to a normal human fingertip without changing the gene sequence.

Try as she might, finding the gene sequence that said to grow the fingernail as a claw and emerge at the tip of the finger was just too difficult.

Lianndra was gasping when she pulled out, her body soaked in sweat.

Hannah watched her with a concerned look. "Are you okay?"

Lianndra shook her head. "I can't do it." She felt exhausted. "I can't find the code they altered let alone determine if the original human coding is still kicking around."

"It's okay, Lianndra." Hannah looked distressed, as if she regretted even suggesting her friend try such a thing.

"No, it's not. Not really. But it was worth a try." Lianndra leaned back and closed her eyes. After a moment, Hannah's warm hand touched her arm. Then she heard the other Healer slip away, heading back to camp.

Lianndra sat and watched the stars until her breathing slowed. Then she leaned forward, staring at her fingers. Invisible in the darkness, she knew her pupils were expanding until they almost swallowed her irises. She sank within, and the beads of sweat formed on her forehead to drip slowly down her face.

Where there's a will, there has to be a way.

IT WAS A BEAUTIFUL, SUNNY afternoon as Lianndra watched Michael weave through the jungle beneath her. She enjoyed the play of his muscles under the ragged slave's clothing and the fluid way he moved through the underbrush. Even though he had matured into a big man, Michael moved with agility and was light and balanced on his feet. It wasn't something she remembered about him from their time on Earth. It must have resulted from his Fang training, or perhaps he'd grown into his frame, reaching the perfect balance of muscle and bone necessary for grace. His muscles weren't bulky but smoothly joined to the bones, like a cat's.

And cats are graceful. Observing him like this made Lianndra feel guilty. *I have to stop doing this. I've become a stalker.*

She knew she was being unfair by not talking to him. In truth, it was torture having him so close and not being with him. But this was the way it had to be. If the rebellion resulted in the defeat of the Fang, there was a chance Michael could go home to have a normal life.

Whatever the future holds in store for me, it won't include going home, she thought. *Not unless I make progress in reversing these changes.* This had yet to happen, despite working at it every spare minute. Lianndra took comfort in the fact she'd freed Michael from Fang slavery. He could make going home a reality.

A soft scuffling noise announced Hannah's arrival on a branch above her. Her friend remained silent until Michael disappeared into the thick bush. An embarrassed Lianndra braced herself; she knew what was coming.

"Michael doesn't care about the changes to your body," the redhead said in exasperation, repeating knowledge she seemed to impart to Lianndra daily. "He's the real deal, Lianndra. Who knows what the future holds in store? Live now. Love now."

Lianndra ignored her, leaning back against the shaggy tree trunk. She pulled the little Gryphon amulet from its hiding place, letting it dangle between her fingers.

Hannah sighed again as she sat astride her branch, firmly wrapping her tail around it for extra support. She contemplated the figurine from her higher perch. "You know, when you turn it a certain way, it almost looks like the dragon pictures back home."

Lianndra grabbed the little amulet to examine it in more detail. What she'd first seen as simple bird's wings along the back were actually the middle set of legs extended to form bat-like wings. With the long neck and head, it did indeed look like a dragon. *Michael mentioned it, didn't he? Dragon mythology with a Gryphon connection? Hmm.*

She wondered if the winged Gryphon existed on Tarin, or were they just fanciful interpretations on the alien's own form?

The concept had obviously lost its hold on Hannah. "Lianndra, I mean what I say about Michael. I won't lie to you, I do worry whether Drake would want to go home if the opportunity arose, but a lot could happen between then and now. Seize life, make the most of each moment. Don't worry about something that might never happen." She tossed her hair out of her face and repeated, "Live in the now!"

"I know you believe in living in the moment," Lianndra said as she tucked the amulet away, "but I have to believe we will find a way home when this is over. Otherwise, what are we fighting for? What is freedom if we are trapped on an alien world? I want Michael to return home. I don't want him tied to this place, or to me. As things stand now, going home is something I can never do."

She shot one tortured look at Hannah before launching herself into the foliage.

Day after day Lianndra ghosted through the trees, reporting only to Drake and Hannah, ranging as far from the unit as possible on the pretense of laying down the best routes for them to follow. She ate and slept in the trees. Yet she couldn't help herself, she had to see Michael daily. Lianndra snuck up on him, watched from overhead, telling herself it was just to see he was safe but her heartbeat always betrayed her. Sometimes the desire was so strong it made her knees buckle. *It's only loneliness. Something I can control and resist.*

FATE HAS A WAY OF leveling the playing field, of insisting certain destinies come to pass regardless of individual wishes and desires.

The group's progress slowed the day Hannah discovered the remains of what must have been a wicked battle.

As he was on forward sentry duty, Michael was the first man on scene. He guessed the battle site was a few days old. Despite likely

Gryphon casualties, there were no Gryphon bodies, only those of the human and alien slaves left to rot at the edge of the jungle. It was the appalling smell that alerted her.

While Lianndra and Hannah stayed in the trees near the battle zone, using the height to keep an eye out for trouble, the other men joined Michael and Drake to survey the bodies.

They were quick to assess the site, and the men started scavenging. Although the survivors of the battle had removed most of the weapons, Drake's men gleaned small arms such as knives and the occasional old sword. Plates, cups, and the packs to haul them were also valuable salvage.

Michael hefted a second pack to his shoulder, his eyes skipping over the mauled bodies before fastening on Lianndra. The blonde Healer stood on a branch fifteen feet above the soil. To accommodate the midday heat, her hair only covered the essentials for modesty's sake. Her tanned skin was golden brown and beautifully complemented the mottled colors of the thick hair covering her breasts and hips. She'd grown the hair on her head long and kept it in multiple braids, interwoven with fine vines, wooden beads, and various bright feathers. The braids hung around her shoulders, reaching to her waist. Her natural beauty made Michael's heart beat erratically; he had to force himself to breathe.

If Lianndra was aware of the heat of his gaze, she didn't let on. She seemed to refuse to look directly at him, gazing well over his head and across the clearing. Michael felt a stab of annoyance. He turned full on to her, unabashedly staring at her, daring her to do something.

HANNAH WAS JUST DROPPING OUT of a tree at the other edge of the clearing when she thought she saw movement in a clump of dense foliage close to the men. She grabbed a low branch and hung in midair to squint and sniff the air. Even over the odor of dead bodies, she caught a whiff of something familiar.

Vloxx, she thought. The smell of dead bodies must have attracted one of the jungle's more repulsive denizens. Sometimes predator, sometimes scavenger, the Vloxx was a lizard-like creature standing as tall as a grown man. It closely resembled the dinosaurs of ancient Earth if one wasn't fussy about counting limbs. The Vloxx possessed six of them, all armed with vicious claws. It crawled rapidly on all its appendages or ran even faster upright on just two. The long snout contained many sharp teeth as well as a hooked horny beak at the tip for ripping into flesh. Shiny, elongated, razor-sharp, serrated scales covered the skin, reflecting its surroundings, making it difficult to see until it moved.

Vloxx had temperaments to match their looks, and they were territorial, particularly when it came to food.

Hannah's eyes widened as she caught another glimmer of movement, and her mouth opened to shout out to Drake. She didn't get the chance. With only a snort as a warning, the Vloxx barreled out of the thicket straight at Michael.

No one was given any time to react, least of all Michael. It hit him full force, tearing claws through fabric and muscle, ripping him wide open. Its momentum carried it right on past him to the man scavenging ten feet from him. The man died instantly when the razor claws separated his head from his body.

Drake barely got his laser up in time as the blur of claws and teeth bore down on him. He fired point-blank, the close shot penetrating the metallic scales. Mortally wounded, the creature ran right into him, its scales slicing into Drake as it collided.

It was over in a microsecond, and silence fell over the clearing.

LIANNDRA DIDN'T REMEMBER HER FEET hitting the ground, but she was at Michael's side within seconds of him being hit. That was fortunate as his life blood was shooting from him in great spraying arcs from a torn aorta. Far too many of his insides were in a jumble around his prone body.

It was a miracle he was conscious. Blood seeped from the corner of his mouth as he tried to speak.

"Hush." Lianndra struggled to talk through tears, her fingers reaching inside him, finding and pressing on the huge blood vessel running the length of his torso. *Concentrate, damn it.*

His blood covered her, hot against her naked skin. She forced herself to focus, sealing the tear as fast as she could. *So much damage.*

She'd never worked on anyone with this kind of injury and had them live. She pushed the thoughts away, reaching for another, smaller vessel pumping his blood skyward. His body cavity was filling with blood far too rapidly for her to keep up. *No! You will not die, not after everything we've been through!*

Suddenly, Hannah was beside her.

The other Healer moved to Michael's opposite side and started sealing blood vessels. Obviously thinking clearer than Lianndra, she said, "Recirculate the blood. Quick!"

Her words snapped Lianndra out of her panic. She redirected her efforts, using a large blood vessel as a vacuum, pushing the blood cells back into circulation before his entire system collapsed. Dimly, Lianndra heard Drake shouting orders and a part of her acknowledged, with relief, the captain had survived the collision.

She got as much of the blood reclaimed as possible before sealing the vessel, and then the two women worked on repositioning and repairing his other organs. There was extensive damage to the liver and pancreas along with his intestines.

The healing required several hours of painstaking work. The cells of organs and nerves were naturally reluctant to divide. It took a concentrated effort to induce the cells to fill in such large gaps. Michael's heart quit on them three times, and each time, they had to restart it. Finally, they'd done all they could. The organs were back where they belonged and reconnected to their various nerves, arteries, veins, and ducts. They had cleaned and repaired his guts and put them back in place. They worked together to heal the viscera and muscles. It was even a challenge to replicate enough skin cells to seal the gash, they resorted to scar tissue past a certain point since those cells required less nourishment. If he lived, he would forever have scars to tell the story.

Lianndra trailed blood-soaked fingers over Michael's face. At a point early in the process, he'd mercifully lost consciousness. He was breathing and his heartbeat was weak but steady.

He might live, she thought, *but it's far from a sure thing.*

Lianndra was reluctant to take her hands from him. As long as she touched him, she felt the reassuring thump of his heart. He was alive. Despite her exhaustion, she went *within* his body one more time to trace the energy meridians. They were full of snarls and eddies in the flow of power; a couple were almost totally severed. She used the last of her energy to reestablish natural order, bolstering some nodes while soothing others. She couldn't repair them all. It would have to wait until she regained her strength.

Both Healers felt stretched beyond their limits. As Lianndra finally sat back, Hannah nodded and Drake gestured two men forward with a makeshift stretcher. The captain's body was crimson with cuts from the creature's wicked scales.

Lianndra appreciated he'd forgone healing so both women could work on Michael. *It's taken all we could give to save Michael's life.*

Drake helped Hannah to her feet, waving away her feeble attempts to heal him. "I've had worse cuts from my razor," he muttered, supporting her with a well-placed arm. He and the other men had spent the hours digging graves for the dead slaves. They stood for a moment of silence over the mounds, thinking their own private thoughts.

Lianndra sagged against a boulder. She couldn't take her eyes off Michael, lying so quiet on the stretcher. *He is so close to joining those just buried. He is supposed to go home, not die on this planet.*

Her heart was leaden within her chest. She'd never been a person of faith, and even if she was, who should she pray to on this alien world? She closed her eyes. *Please. Please let him live.*

XOE%SAN%KRIN JUMPED WHEN THE ARRIVAL tone sounded even though she'd been waiting for Ewt%mit%fnsk. She clutched her wrap closer to her body, shivering in the cold permeating the ship's lower levels. Just beyond where she hid in the shadows, the lift door opened and her friend disembarked.

Ewt%mit%fnsk walked off the lift with the businesslike stride of someone who belonged where she was. It amazed Xoe%san%krin that her friend had embraced the subterfuge necessary for the rebellion with ease. It was a deception she'd yet to master.

Xoe%san%krin shuffled her feet in the darkness, and Ewt%mit%fnsk walked around a large conduit before sidestepping to join her friend in the shadows.

"Have you received the latest message?" Xoe%san%krin's voice came out strained and squeaky.

Ewt%mit%fnsk nodded. "They must have planned for such a contingency. It was an obvious strategy to take out the planetary shield."

Xoe%san%krin shivered. "My contact told me they expected an attack on the shield but not something this extensive. The intelligence reports indicate the shield is more resilient than anticipated so it requires a tremendous amount of power to take it down." The heavyset Fara paused, glancing around nervously. "A group of our best engineers came up with an ambitious plan to route the combined power of multiple Motherships to a single cannon. The modifications are complex, but they have already begun alterations to the power grids on the four Motherships in orbit. The proposed cannon will need power from five ships, so the *Arb%tz* will arrive in the next rotation."

Ewt%mit%fnsk looked troubled. "Five ships! What if it backfires and damages the power grids?"

"If it damages the grids on all five ships, our people will only have three functioning Motherships remaining and they are far away. They might not get here in time to save us. This plan could kill thousands of Tlo%m."

Ewt%mit%fnsk's color had paled to lilac across her face and neck. "What is so important about this planet to risk such a catastrophe? Do the rebels know what is driving this?"

"The primary rebel leaders know. It is a closely guarded secret. Yet this latest level of commitment surprised even them." Xoe%san%krin couldn't get warm. She shuffled her feet again, shivering in her wrap.

"Do the rebels have a plan for stopping the cannon?" Ewt%mit%fnsk started to tremble.

"They are working on it. The level of coordination required with all five ships makes it difficult. The rebellion does not have any members confirmed on the *Arb%tz*." Xoe%san%krin's voice shook. "The rebellion's best chance is to hold position to see how the Gryphon respond to the shield being attacked. Assisting the Gryphon with their battle plan is less likely to show our hand."

"Are they so sure the cannon will take down the shield?"

Xoe%san%krin hesitated before answering. "The cannon will have the power of five Motherships. There is no recorded history of such a powerful cannon ever being built."

The power of five Motherships . . . what has become of us? Xoe%san%krin thought. *What could be worth that kind of risk? If the power grids on the ships go down, we will have to evacuate. The three remaining Motherships can't take us all even if they get here in time.*

Ewt%mit%fnsk reached out to lay her hand on her friend's shoulder. "We have to trust the rebel leaders will think of something. Their plans have served us well to date. They will find a way through for us."

Xoe%san%krin nodded but didn't meet her eyes. Everything they'd worked so hard toward could be rendered useless by this latest development. *If the shield goes down, it will be a bloodbath. Even the ingenuity of the human species won't save the Gryphon from the full military might of the Tlo%m.*

15

THE REBELS COULDN'T STOP MOVING for anyone or anything. They carried Michael's feverish body on a stretcher between two of his huge Zraph buddies as the group pushed on through the jungle. The bulky aliens moved Michael without effort, but it meant the rebels were short of vital muscle at the head of the column for breaking the trail. Luckily, with the jungle thinning around them, it wasn't crucial to their progress.

They didn't even stop for Michael's frequent treatments. Lianndra would just hop right up onto the stretcher as it rocked along between the Zraph.

The claws of the Vloxx contained virulent bacteria she constantly needed to battle. Lianndra lost track of the times she had to reopen his wound to drain the infection away. Michael swam in and out of consciousness, living in a world of hallucinations with rare periods of lucidity.

His raging infection made it impossible for him to eat. In desperation, Lianndra gave him nutrients directly through blood to blood contact. By opening veins in both their arms, Lianndra pushed her blood, with its nutrients, into him. This was messy for both, as well as risking further infection for him, so one afternoon she modified her right index finger.

From her recent trials, Lianndra knew there were limitations to what she could achieve when altering her body, she was only able to duplicate cells or destroy them. So she enlarged the artery supplying her fingertip by duplicating the cells of the artery wall and then enlarging the vessel, creating a channel to the base of the claw. Modification of the claw itself was tougher. She destroyed cells to hollow out a channel along the underside before growing cells around it to make the claw longer and finer.

Once completed, she could use the claw as a primitive hypodermic, feeding him the nutrients from her blood along the modified channel.

The gene sequences within the cells of her nail bed would cause her claw and the blood vessel to grow out normally, but it should last like this for long enough to do the job.

More than once, she caught Drake watching her with an amazed expression. When Hannah pointed out Lianndra was rapidly losing weight supporting two bodies, he removed her from scout duty and onto full-time Healer for Michael. He also made sure she had a steady supply of food. Refusing to leave his side, Lianndra ate and slept on Michael's stretcher.

It was a testament to Michael's popularity that no one protested or claimed he put the entire unit at risk by slowing them down and keeping Lianndra's valuable talents tied up. At least not out loud. Even if they did, Drake left no doubt where he stood on the issue.

Their sacrifice was obviously clear to Michael. During one of his rare periods of clarity, Michael begged Lianndra to let him die. She was so disgusted with him that she telekinetically shoved him back into a feverish sleep without answering him.

You will not die, she silently promised him. *Not after all we've been through. Dammit, you will live.*

THE FARR COMMANDER'S TWIN HEARTS were pounding hard, a sure sign of his agitation.

In front of him stood his scouts, four of his human slave soldiers. Stiffly at attention, they did their best to ignore the waves of anger coming off the Fang.

The jungle was thinning. Already the trees were getting smaller and grassy plants more common.

Littering the surrounding ground were fresh mounds of earth. The commander stood over one he'd ordered dug up. They were graves for human slaves. A Vloxx lay off to one side, clearly shot dead by a laser.

A trail led straight ahead, out of the jungle and into the grasslands.

The commander hissed in anger. There was no longer any doubt. *These slaves are running free. How did they deactivate their collars?*

To find out, he had to follow them. Grasslands meant Gryphon. To continue to follow the trail meant the possibility of running into an enemy Gryphon troop was strong. Caught out in the open, the Gryphon's mobility would spell disaster for his slave soldiers.

The commander was now far outside the regular patrol zone for the missing unit. He was also well beyond his own perimeters. He was fortunate there hadn't been any Gryphon raids along his stretch of the front line while he'd been pursuing the mystery of the vanished unit.

Unfortunately, he'd not caught up with them before they left the jungle. With the increased threat of Gryphon contact, he could not continue tracking without reporting in.

He gestured to the slave carrying the portable comm equipment. The human scurried to set it up on a nearby stump.

Being impatient, the commander gave him a short burst of pain stimulation to promote better performance. It didn't soothe the humiliation of not completing his mission to capture the missing slaves. It did serve to get the comm unit up and running in record time.

SAR%KAN%BANE WAITED FOR THE CALL. When she saw the frequency, she nodded to her fellow tech and took the message herself. It wasn't unusual for them to take the calls preferentially; it helped with the continuity of information if the same tech handled related messages.

She listened to the Farr on the line, feeling her hearts race within her torso. When he finished, Sar%kan%bane responded. "Follow trail. Report back on results."

Technically, there was little new information shared on the matter. *Except they might be following a trail made by slaves that should be frozen in place by their collars the moment their commander died.*

Terminating the transmission, she prepared a datachrys for the war coordinator, informing her that the Farr commander was following up on a missing unit. She then contacted the commanders of the neighboring zones, asking their units to cover the gap until his return.

This was still within her jurisdiction as it was passing on relevant information.

Finally, she tapped in another message on the secure channel, sending it before deleting it as before.

Sar%kan%bane sat back, hoping the pounding of her blood wasn't as obvious as it felt. At worst, she could be criticized for not recognizing the seriousness of the situation or for not passing enough information on to her superior. Unless they uncovered the last message she had sent—then her fate wasn't the only one teetering on the edge.

ALL AT ONCE, THE JUNGLE disappeared. It had been petering out for some time, but when Lianndra next looked up from the stretcher they'd left the giant trees behind. What remained was shorter, scrubbier stock, with sections of thick bush broken up by grasses.

The grassy plants seemed determined to make up for the lack of trees. In places, the spikes were taller than a Zraph, growing in dense tufts with huge seed heads. The rebels circumvented the grasses rather than beat their way through them. Hannah no longer gained enough altitude to safely guide the group. Instead, they relied on the decrepit navigation equipment scrounged from the Fang unit to keep them from walking in circles.

Eventually, the trees disappeared altogether. The rebels wove their way through giant grassy mounds and rocky outcrops. It made everyone feel as though they were miniaturized, mere ants crawling among a giant's scruffy lawn.

The soil beneath their feet was sandy in places, stony in others. Younger grass tufts sprang up around the periphery of the giant grass mounds. Small, tough leaved plants speckled the rocks protruding from the ground. Lianndra noticed blooms on some of these, tiny spots of color in the arid landscape. It reminded her of the dunes of Bodega Bay, which made her think of other things she would rather not remember at the moment.

When they reached the rocky cliffs rising from the grasslands, Drake's priorities changed. The risk of running headlong into a Gryphon scout troop was now high. He couldn't take a chance the Gryphon would shoot first and ask questions later so he needed to find the rebels a safe, defensible place to hole up for a few days. Drake sent scouts out to scour the cliffs for a site meeting his criteria.

After much searching, they found caves suiting their purposes. It was a fair climb, especially for those carrying Michael. The top of the cliff provided an excellent panoramic view. The inaccessibility would buy the rebels time should they be discovered. Drake didn't think it suitable for a permanent base, but it would do for now.

In the night, Michael's fever broke. He fell into a deeper, restful sleep, and Lianndra breathed a sigh of relief. Hannah forced her to eat while she watched over him. Lianndra slipped into a bedroll and passed out.

Michael was still sleeping when Lianndra checked in several hours later to give him another nutrient feeding.

Hannah promised to stay with him, shooing Lianndra off. "Go relax. Michael will be fine."

Lianndra felt guilty about her preoccupation with healing him. The rebels' food stores were so low they were at risk of running out. The natural biodiversity of the jungle provided a ready source of food, but most of it was too perishable to store and too bulky to carry any distance. If the rebels were going to set up a more permanent camp, they needed to find a reliable local food source—or starve. The Healers were ideal food testers. Their ability to take everything to a subcellular level to heal themselves meant they easily screened potential food for toxins.

After several hours of sleep, Lianndra was still tired but the grass seed heads she'd noticed along their route might be an important food source for them. She could have sent a couple of the men to collect, but the grasses weren't far away and she would test the seeds. No one needs to waste effort or risk injury bringing back useless samples.

Lianndra felt weak but buoyed by Michael's improved health. She followed their tracks toward the jungle before she ventured off of the path. She searched among the grass-like plants, leaving a scent trail so she would not get lost.

The plants grew thicker as she got farther away from the cliffs. She finally spotted the giant seed heads. Using the knife she'd hidden in a hair sheath along her hip, she chose stems from as deep within the clumps as she could reach. Lianndra worked to cut the tough, fibrous material off at the base. She was careful not to leave obvious signs of her foraging where passing Fang or Gryphon units would see them.

The Fang seldom come this far out of the jungle but I'd rather be safe than sorry, she thought.

The seeds had a thick outer coating but were powdery inside. She cracked them between her teeth. Lianndra didn't detect anything toxic. They should grind up into a paste and bake into an edible biscuit.

She collected enough seed heads to hoist over her shoulder and then started following her trail back to camp.

Focused as she was on retracing her scent trail, Lianndra smelled the Gryphon before she heard them. Their spicy aroma swirled past her on the merest breath of a breeze. For a moment she panicked and thought about running. Although she smelled them, the breeze was erratic, so she couldn't determine which direction the Gryphon were coming from. Hiding was not an option either; the tufts of grass were too thick to penetrate without leaving an obvious trampled path.

The only sensible thing is to not surprise them into an attack. After all, Drake wants us to make contact with the Gryphon. Lianndra swallowed her fear and walked to where she would be visible. She stood still, her heart pounding. Memories of the Gryphon in the jungle spun through her head, their huge size and fierce weapons. She almost gave in and ran, but then the image of the little Gryphon took over, her insightful words and her gentle eyes. *I have to do this. The rebellion won't survive on its own, we need the Gryphon's help.* She planted her feet firmly in the dirt and braced for the worst.

Considering their size, it was amazing how quietly they rolled into view. They stopped before her in a swirl of dust. It was obviously a scouting party or a small border patrol. There were five Gryphon, their bright bodies marked with stripes and spots that worked surprisingly well at blending them in with the vertical shadows and highlights of the surroundings. Lianndra's eyes followed the outlines of their bodies, but she had problems focusing on parts of them. Their chests and hindquarters appeared blurred.

If it surprised the Gryphon to see her they gave no sign. But they did encircle her with their weapons drawn, looking down with their long feathered crests and neck spikes fully erect. As they settled to a halt, Lianndra noticed the blurred outlines were due to capes of reflective material. It was a very effective camouflage.

Up close, she marveled once again at their size: the biggest of them could see above the grass when they stood on their back legs. This provided them with a clear advantage in these grasslands. She also noticed differences among them. Two were larger and rather than a feathered crest they had full manes of feathers shining with brilliant colors in the sunlight. They weren't as large as the ones she'd seen during the rescue of the little Gryphon.

Young males? Lianndra wondered. *Then the ones with just a crest must be females.*

She worried they'd been following her scent trail, but if so, hoped it wouldn't lead them straight to the cliffs and the rebel camp. Lianndra bent slowly to lay the grass stems on the soil at her feet before raising her empty hands in the air in the universal signal for surrender.

Lianndra wasn't sure whether to show them the amulet or not. Any movement to fetch it from her felted pocket might be misconstrued at this point. Her gesture of surrender seemed to work. One of the Gryphon handed an abused laser rifle to her comrade before pacing forward. Pulling a short rope from the leather container strapped to her torso, she bound Lianndra's hands but seemed unsure how to handle her tail. She settled for strapping it to one of Lianndra's legs before picking her up. The Gryphon slung the Healer across the back of one of the other scouts.

A male, Lianndra thought, as he possessed a full mane of deep blue, had a bulkier build, and his body coloring was brighter than the others. With their fur and feathers, it was difficult to see any other features that verified her assumption.

As soon as they'd secured her, the Gryphon headed back the way they'd come. They picked up their pace, flying over the dusty ground. At a full run the Gryphon didn't land flat-footed but used only their toes up to the first joint. Their claws provided them with a hoof-like structure that allowed them to attain great speed.

An army of these coming at you full speed must really be something, Lianndra thought as she bounced uncomfortably.

From her upside down position, it was difficult to determine in which direction the Gryphon headed. She was pretty sure they were carrying her far away from the rebel base. Lianndra tried not to think of what might be in store for her if she couldn't connect with the small Gryphon as they'd planned. Drake had hoped to send out a scouting party once the rebel group settled in the cliffs. He had no idea how close they'd come to running straight into a Gryphon patrol. If the rebels had marched for one more day in the grasslands, the Gryphon might have run right into them.

The prone position was intolerable. Lianndra jounced along, fervently wishing she was riding astride. Her breasts and belly hurt fiercely, and she was sure she would end up bruised from stem to stern.

Lianndra had headed out on her quest for food late in the day so night descended on them as they traveled. As darkness closed in, the group slowed. The gait became even more jarring, and it proved her undoing. She lost her last meal, keeping it clear of the side of her mount only by sheer force of will. The male Gryphon seemed to take pity on her and moved into a collected version of their gallop, which was smoother but possessed a rolling sensation reminiscent of the ocean. Just when she thought she would lose it again, the entire group settled into a walk before coming to an uneasy halt. They drew their weapons. Something was up.

Lianndra wondered how close they were to the jungle's edge and the Fang units within it.

Two of the group stood up on their hind legs to survey over the grasses then came back down to hiss something to the others. The entire group launched into a gallop. These were not the distance covering, slower strides of an endurance runner, but the rapid gait of an all-out sprint.

It became obvious at least one Fang unit was close when the grasses behind them lit up with laser fire. Strapped facedown, Lianndra fought panic. She was safe as long as the Gryphon were safe, but she felt vulnerable tied like this.

Hours of bouncing on the Gryphon's back had shifted the rope binding her, loosening it in some places, tightening it in others. As they flew over the ground with laser fire raining down around them, she worked on getting her tail free. The tightest knots were the ones binding her hands to her feet around the belly of the Gryphon. Her tail snaked free easily, so she slid it up her side, tilting her body to allow it access to the knife she'd concealed at her hip.

She'd have to time this with care if she wanted to avoid a dangerous fall from the charging alien. Lianndra got a good grip on the Gryphon's fur with her fingers and toes, wrapping her body as tightly as possible around the alien's heaving barrel. Then she braced her tail against her legs and sliced through the rope. If the Gryphon felt the sudden loosening of the bindings, he was too busy running and returning fire to do anything about it. Lianndra dropped the knife and used her tail to grip the leather pack on his back, giving her a pivot point to swing her legs astride him. He must have felt her legs close around his barrel because he leaped into the air and gave a small, startled buck before resuming his all-out run. Then the female Gryphon next to him lit up with laser fire, falling with a scream in a cloud of dust and smoke.

With her hands still bound together, Lianndra lost her grip as the big body beneath her skidded to a halt, wheeled, and cantered back to his fallen comrade. Her riding experience stood her in good stead. She clung with her tail until almost all his forward momentum disappeared, and then let go, rolling to absorb most of the impact. Her Dancer training kicked in as she continued the roll to an upright stance before running back to where the Gryphon had disappeared into the smoke.

The laser had torn open one of the female's powerful hind legs. The male Gryphon tried to help the smaller female, but the hind limbs were an important part of Gryphon mobility. She only hobbled painfully forward.

Laser fire lit up the grass around them as the other three Gryphon returned to help. Lianndra pushed her way past their furry torsos unnoticed until she stood beside the injured one.

One of the Gryphon hissed at her and moved to push her away, but another put out an arm to block her fellow scout. Lianndra looked up into her violet eyes. The Gryphon cocked her head sideways before moving back to give Lianndra more room.

Lianndra saw recognition in the large eyes. *She must have seen Healers before. She knows what I am.* Lianndra held out her bound hands. The big Gryphon hesitated only a second before pulling a knife to slice her bonds. Lianndra put her hands on the injured alien. The Gryphon panted in pain but twisted her torso around to watch the Healer work. Supported by two of her fellows, she stood with the limp leg dragging in the dirt. If they stayed with her, they would be killed or captured unless Lianndra acted, and fast.

In the darkness, Lianndra slid her hands along the curve of the rump until she touched the smoking hole in the hind leg. Laser wounds were tricky because the heat of the laser burned the flesh. The wounds bled less, but the intense heat damaged tissue more extensively. Lianndra tried to ignore the fire blazing around them as well as the shouts of a Fang slave unit moving closer. Her imagination portrayed every shadow as a Fang soldier wielding the bulk of a long-range laser. She gave herself a mental shake, putting herself *within* the wound. It was only her second injured Gryphon and there couldn't be a less ideal situation in which to heal.

The lasers howled and whined back and forth around them as she focused on the big muscles. She sloughed the cells damaged by the heat of the laser before calling on the undamaged ones to fill in the gaps. Lianndra didn't have time to repair the nerve endings but reconnected the more important, deeper ones. If the Gryphon's skin was numb over this section, it would be a small price to pay.

She closed the skin, trusting the resealed blood vessels and lymph to carry away the cellular debris on their own.

Lianndra had barely finished when one of the Gryphon grabbed her and slung her astride the big female leader. They were off again at full speed. Lianndra clung to the heavy spikes along the Gryphon's torso, wrapping her legs around the furry barrel and leaning back against the pack. She was glad she had the pack to wrap her tail around, and she wished she had her skrin to tie herself down. She'd left it with her gear in the cave as it was of limited use on the grasslands.

The next few moments were chaotic, ducking and diving through a living hell of burning grass and exploding bushes. Lianndra clung to the spikes in front of her. Whatever served as a backbone for the aliens was more elastic than a horse's, which meant it flexed substantially underneath her as the Gryphon moved. Powerful muscles heaved and bunched as they maneuvered. It was all Lianndra could do to hang on.

It's more like riding a lion than a horse, she thought.

In the end, the Gryphon's speed and knowledge of the terrain won them their freedom. Safe from the Fang lasers, the Gryphon slowed to weave a twisting path through the grass clumps, hoping to confuse any pursuit. They descended a steep decline and entered a fast flowing creek, working their way upstream at their equivalent of a brisk trot. Their clawed feet easily handled the mossy rocks rolling beneath them.

Lianndra had no idea how far they'd come. She only hoped the Fang unit didn't head toward the rebel's makeshift camp. The poorly armed rebels couldn't stand against that kind of firepower. The rebellion would be over before it had even begun.

She tried not to think of Michael, who was just past the crisis stage and would easily relapse without expert care. Hannah was an excellent Healer, but when it came to innovative methods, Lianndra always led the way. Hannah likely couldn't make the changes allowing Lianndra to feed Michael. She only hoped he was able to eat and drink on his own.

Either way, she was in no position to do anything about it now and might never be again if she didn't form a bond with these Gryphon. It seemed she was off to a decent start because they hadn't replaced the rope bindings.

This could be the start of a trusting relationship, she thought. *For the rebellion to succeed, we need to form a working partnership with the Gryphon. The human rebellion won't survive long without it.*

The Gryphon traveled on into the night, settling into their ground devouring pace. Lianndra marveled at their endurance. Who knew how many miles they'd traveled since they last rested? Even with the extra weight she carried, the female Gryphon she rode seemed inexhaustible. As the night sky lightened with the approaching dawn, Lianndra got a closer look at the breastplate so cleverly reflecting their surroundings. With some surprise, she recognized the long, serrated scales of the Vloxx.

Not handmade, but hand skinned, she thought. She fingered one of the, sharp scales as they rolled along, thinking of Michael.

Lianndra lost track of time and came back to reality when the spike beneath her hand grew so hot it forced her to let it go. She became aware of the heat radiating from the spikes along the neck and shoulders. With a quick glance, Lianndra noticed the other Gryphon's spikes were fully erect, allowing the moving air to carry the heat away. As they crossed a small creek their claws turned the water into steam. Lianndra recognized the spikes and their claws as part of their cooling mechanism. The long tails possessed shorter spikes performing a similar role. She felt their heat as the tails slowly waved from side to side in rhythm with their movement. In the blackness of the night, they almost glowed.

Certainly, they didn't seem to sweat to keep cool. The body beneath her was warm, but it should be soaked after this activity. *Must be an adaptation to the drier climate of the grasslands*, Lianndra thought.

It meant they could go long distances without a drink.

Their sudden deceleration took Lianndra by surprise. She appreciated the way her Gryphon flattened her spikes and braced her torso to cushion Lianndra's body. If only some of her horses had been so understanding. She remembered more than a few unplanned equine dismounts. Lianndra almost gave the feathered torso a pat of appreciation but stopped just in time, lest it be considered rude.

The Gryphon walked between tall rocky cliffs, looking around as if they were expecting something. With the slower pace, the heat coming off the spikes threatened to become uncomfortable for Lianndra. She pushed herself back from them, bracing herself against the pack.

A voice hailed them from the deepest cliff shadows, and at their response, a large Gryphon trotted forward. Bulging muscles, big bones, a thick mane of feathers, plus a heavier structure to the neck and head identified this one as male. The darkness muted his color but with her enhanced night vision, Lianndra made out the stripes and spots of his coat. He looked at her in what was clearly surprise.

After a swift exchange of information, he turned to look beyond them, and Lianndra knew the scouts had told him about the Fang unit they'd encountered. The guard nodded and then whirled to canter into the darkness. The scouts continued on, picking up their pace again.

They passed several other checkpoints, each staffed by a large male Gryphon. Lianndra upgraded her impression of an army of Gryphon bearing down on them. *If the army included the big males, it would be pure hell in motion.*

They moved into a valley and the vegetation changed again, the tall tufted grasses giving way to shorter, lusher species covering more of the ground. The trees grew larger, but the terrain remained more open without the dense undergrowth of the jungle. Obviously, more water was available in this valley than in the grasslands.

A good spot for a permanent outpost, Lianndra thought.

The group split up. Two male scouts cantered off ahead of them into the darkness while the rest continued on at their slower pace. Watching the males leave, Lianndra wondered if they were young or belonged to a different subspecies from the big guys since they didn't have their bulky build.

Her thoughts jumped to her fate now that they were approaching the Gryphon home base. Lianndra did not know whether to be flattered they hadn't blindfolded her before their arrival, or frightened they didn't care to.

She swallowed before reaching into the pocket just below her collarbone, popping the little amulet free and slipping its cord around her wrist. *I'm betting a lot on one little figurine.*

Dawn was just breaking as they emerged into the heart of the valley, and Lianndra caught her breath at what the sun's rays revealed. She'd expected a traditional army style camp which in her experience to date seemed to survive species boundaries. This was something totally different.

The trees of the jungle were tall, but the valley ones were broad, with enormous spreading branches. Smaller plants covered the shaggy trunks, similar to the epiphytes on the redwoods of Earth. Strange, fuzzy vines climbed up the trunks and hung from the branches.

Most amazing were the structures created from living plants. Woven saplings formed buildings on the valley floor, their walls painted with the natural vivid green of new and old leaves. Over time, the saplings grew to massive trees forming the walls and ceilings of the structures. Banks and platforms led to caves carved into the rock. Ramps made of interwoven, living branches, plants, or roots scaled the rocky valley walls. Campfires burned within the caves. Lianndra saw movement inside the structures. It seemed as though the valley was just awakening from its nightly slumber.

In places it looked as if smaller, younger braided vines created privacy screens across cave entrances and hanging seats under the trees. Everything was so green and leafy that the structures blended in with their natural surroundings. Their outlines were almost impossible to trace in the early morning light.

The Gryphon were everywhere, both the full-sized versions and the smaller ones. Many stopped to stare at her with wide eyes and their feathers erect. Their multicolored coats of feathery fur sported stripes, spots, and swirls with no two being exactly alike. The valley filled with the low murmur of Gryphon voices speaking in their native tongue. It sounded like a series of musical notes, full of trills and whistles.

The most impressive buildings were those in the more open, central area. At the heart of the valley was an enormous hall created by woven pieces of polished wood. Closer inspection revealed ancient trees created the building, so cleverly interwoven they appeared as one solid surface. Plants thicker around than Lianndra's body formed arched entryways. The massive circumference of the vines and trees spoke to a history and a state of permanence reminiscent of the architecture of the most ancient cities on Earth.

The smaller entrances to the building featured intricately woven curtain-like vines. Lianndra saw Gryphon touching them, which swiftly pulled aside to reveal openings. The large main entrance had two huge doors that swung open as they approached. Two big male Gryphon paced forward to stand guard at either side of them. The building was obviously open for business.

It didn't surprise Lianndra that her Gryphon escorts brought her toward this large structure. A short distance from it, her mount halted, and she took it as a cue to dismount. She slid down the furry side only to discover her legs couldn't bear any weight. A well-placed Gryphon leg supported her until she got a good grip on one of the pack straps. One of the other females paced forward to assist. Her legs were on fire as the feeling slowly returned. Supported by Gryphon, Lianndra wobbled into the heart of the Gryphon colony.

Her first reaction was one of complete awe. The hall was full of life and light. Small native creatures flitted through the woven network of branches overhead. The woven branches let light in at regular intervals. Once her eyes dropped from the heavens to focus on the corridor, she noticed something else.

The small Gryphon were everywhere. They carried platters of food, tended to the living structure around them, and gathered in small groups. Many stopped to stare at her.

A raised area dominated the far end of the hall. Lianndra realized it once was the trunk of a truly giant tree, carved down and leveled before being polished to a brilliant sheen. As they approached, a group of the small Gryphon stepped onto the raised area from an archway behind them.

Lianndra frowned in confusion. The children were perfect miniature Gryphon. Much like the small Gryphon captive she met, they carried themselves with a dignity foreign to the young of any species she'd ever met. She examined them closely. Most immature creatures had heads and extremities that were larger in relation to their bodies than those of an adult. The proportions of the little Gryphon were too perfectly balanced for them to be children.

Lianndra thought back to the two times she'd seen the smaller Gryphon: in the Pit and in the jungle. Then she remembered the poise of the prisoner and her ability to speak perfect English.

She mentally smacked herself, feeling incredibly stupid. Size meant nothing. These Gryphon weren't children any more than the bulky males were elders. They were the adults of another race of Gryphon. Judging by the number of them within the hall, they were an important part of the Gryphon culture.

Her prospects for forming a bond with them suddenly seemed more promising. If she told them about the captive small Gryphon and the healing she'd done, perhaps they would see she meant no harm.

The Gryphon on each side of her dropped their crests flat, crossed their arms, folded their forelegs, and bowed to the smaller Gryphon on the raised platform. She needed no further confirmation the small Gryphon occupied an important place in the overall hierarchy.

As the larger Gryphon straightened, Lianndra stepped hesitantly forward. *I certainly don't want to offend anyone with improper protocol!*

Lianndra stopped in front of them and slowly extended her arm. The amulet dangled from her wrist.

She heard a hiss of surprise. A small pale blue Gryphon paced forward, her hands rising to untie a colorful band of fabric from around her neck. The fabric tugged free, revealing a familiar slave collar gleaming against her throat.

The small Gryphon approached Lianndra and extended her hand to slip the amulet off the Healer's wrist. Then she looked up into Lianndra's eyes.

"Welcome, Healer," she said in perfect human English. The violet eyes danced with flecks of pink as the edges of the long nostrils curled with what Lianndra interpreted as the Gryphon equivalent of humor. "I think we have much to talk about . . ."

MICHAEL'S FIRST ATTEMPT TO OPEN his eyes did not go as planned.

He heard a familiar voice nearby. *Female.* Groggily, his mind groped to connect the voice to a name. It wasn't Lianndra. *Hannah, right?* Hannah was talking. *Something about broth. And me. Getting me to drink it.*

As he opened his eyes to tell her he wasn't hungry, a kaleidoscope of color assaulted him, stabbing into his brain, causing him to raise one arm to block the light. It got tangled in cloth—a blanket. Michael thrashed it free but lost control of his arm and smacked himself across the face. He clobbered himself hard enough his nose throbbed and his eyes flooded with tears, which resolved part of the original issue by whitewashing the painful sunlight.

"Michael!" Hannah grabbed the errant arm to settle it back against the blanket. "You're awake!"

I never thought Hannah had a habit of stating the obvious. Michael opened his mouth to speak, but the only sound that emerged was a hoarse croak. *Is nothing working properly? Where the hell am I and what the heck happened to me?* He struggled to remember but all he gleaned were scattered, blurry images that didn't seem to connect together. Michael's last clear memory was of Lianndra standing on a tree branch, her hair glowing gold in the sunlight.

"Lianndra." The name came out as a whisper.

Was there a slight hesitation before Hannah responded? He wasn't sure. "She's not here now." Hannah's voice was brisk. "Can you drink some of this? We've got to get fluids into you."

Strong arms slipped beneath his shoulder as Michael tried opening his eyes to mere slits.

Drake smiled at him . . . at least, he thought it was Drake. "Welcome back, mate," his familiar voice said, confirming Michael's suspicion.

Michael tried to sit up, but to his dismay, he was as weak as a newborn kitten. Drake helped, propping him against a couple of packs.

Wincing against a twinge in his abdomen, Michael cautiously opened his eyes a little wider. He sat in the sunlight at the mouth of a cave. This time, things went more smoothly, enabling him to look around. He saw Bradley standing on guard not far from the cave entrance. Past the Zraph, the rebel camp bustled with activity. Try as he might, he couldn't see Lianndra's distinctive form anywhere.

Michael got distracted when Hannah wove into view, holding a mug of liquid. He didn't have the strength to refuse her and he let her feed him the broth one spoonful at a time.

By the time the mug was empty, he shook with exhaustion. Drake helped Hannah ease him back down on the blanket. Although he wanted to express his gratitude, Michael was out cold before he could whisper a thank you.

TAR%TOSK%RASK LEANED CLOSER OVER THE shoulder of the technician as if her mere presence encouraged the transmission to come in clearer.

If the war coordinator intimidated the technician, she didn't show it. Her fingers, with clipped claws, flew over the console before her, trying to reduce the heavy interference within the message.

Decipherable Tlo%m words suddenly pierced the static. The technician gave a grunt of satisfaction and then sat back as the Farr commander's message played out over the comm.

The voice of the Farr commander gurgled and crackled as he spoke in his native tongue. He'd discovered three slaves with collars that seemed unresponsive to his commands. They were part of a unit that recently lost its Fang commander and most of its members in a frontline assault. He'd discovered the defective collars while questioning the slaves about the attack.

When the message ended, Tar%tosk%rask straightened. Her Fara technician had been correct. This message required an immediate reply.

"This requires explanation," Tar%tosk%rask said. "It could be a new Gryphon strategy or a technology glitch we have never run into before." The coordinator's eyes narrowed. "He is authorized to use whatever means he deems necessary to explore this issue. Tell him to send two of the captives immediately for analysis." She paused. "No, change that to two of the defective units. We do not need living hosts to determine why they are malfunctioning. It will be more efficient to just send the heads and collars."

The technician nodded before beginning the return transmission. "It will take time to reach him through this interference." She gestured to include the other technician in the room, who was sipping quietly on a beverage. "We have been having trouble all morning."

Tar%tosk%rask turned to Sar%kan%bane, who put down her drink. "Wasn't there a message a short while ago about a missing unit?"

"Yes, coordinator," Sar%kan%bane said. "I have a commander gathering information."

"Have him check the collars," Tar%tosk%rask said, "and report back to me."

Sar%kan%bane nodded and turned to initiate contact on her console.

Tar%tosk%rask turned her back on them and walked to her office, hiding the unease this latest message had instilled in her. The collars had always been a reliable means of controlling not just humans but most captive species. There had been minimal complications with them over their many years of use on slaves. To have faulty collars showing up now was troubling.

Never had they engaged in a war that neutralized so many of their strengths. *Have the Gryphon found a way to affect the slave collars with their shield?* The thought made her hearts leap. If the collars became ineffective, the ground war was over. They would be lucky to get the Farr component of their army back to the safety of their Motherships. The few primitive projectile ships they employed within the shield held only a fraction of the Tlo%m still on the planet.

Not only did the Gryphon's shield prevent them from using the battle technology that would have ended the war in the Tlo%m's favor a long time ago, but it made communications over any distance tricky.

Never mind. This is soon to end, Tar%tosk%rask thought, soothing herself as she entered her small office. She walked to her window to gaze out at the lush jungle, grimacing at the midday rain in progress. *All this water.* She shook her body as if shaking off raindrops. *As soon as the Motherships have the last modifications made, we will destroy the shield once and for all.* Her lips opened, and the tips of three long, pointed blood-teeth emerged. *Then we will see how their primitive weapons stack up against our war machines.*

MICHAEL AWOKE TO DARKNESS AND chaos. All around him, people rushed about in semi-organized confusion. He barely had time to blink before hands grabbed him under his arms and heaved him to his feet.

Michael struggled to stand and swayed even with the support of a person on each side of him.

Drake appeared out of the darkness, a tiny light sheltered in one hand. "You've got him? Good. Take him to the top of the cliff, follow the others." Then he strode off.

The two men threw one of Michael's arms over each of their shoulders and dragged him out of the cave.

Once out in the night, Michael made out the bulky bodies of two Zraph. They stood as still as statues, silhouetted against the moonlight, just beyond the cave entrance. Both the Zraph stared out across the grasses far below them. Out on those grasslands, Michael saw lights moving toward them. Danger permeated the surrounding air.

"Fang," one of his escorts hissed.

They turned him away from the silent giants to struggle up a steep rise. The loose shale beneath their feet made the going treacherous, and Michael struggled to help them while forcing his legs to work. After only a short distance, he was sucking in huge amounts of the cool night air, his body drenched in sweat.

Ahead of them, others made their own way up the cliff's side. Near the top, they squeezed through a series of narrow crevices. Michael navigated some of these on his own as it was too narrow for the others to help him through. His arms felt leaden and useless but he muscled his way along. Past the crevices, two new recruits took up their posts on each side of him.

Michael had nothing left. "Look, just leave me." He gasped. He didn't want them to risk themselves. *I'm slowing everyone down.*

"Don't be ridiculous." Hannah came from behind, her face lined with worry. She pulled out a hypodermic salvaged from a Fang med kit.

There was a brief sting as she shoved it into his arm.

"Adrenaline and a painkiller," she said. "Now, let's get moving."

She took up position just ahead of them, lighting the way in the darkness with a small handheld torch. Their progress was faster after the adrenaline kicked in and Michael managed more cooperation from his legs.

Behind them, the night sky lit up with laser fire. The Fang had found them.

MUCH TO LIANNDRA'S AMAZEMENT, THE party of thirty Gryphon made no more noise than the smaller troop. They traveled in pairs side by side, which confused their numbers for anyone tracking them. The pair of scouts kept a fair distance ahead, communicating via whistles and clicks with those in the forward part of the column. It was an effective system. The long, tufted ears picked up the communications above the muffled thumps of their feet. The party moved swiftly over the ground, weaving through the tall grasses with ease.

Lianndra rode on a large female in the center of the column. Her former scout partner volunteered to carry her again. The Gryphon's name was unpronounceable but Lianndra shortened it to Kaye which seemed acceptable. Lianndra was grateful Kaye had no biases against being a beast of burden. She wondered if all of them would be so generous considering the extra weight involved in carrying a human passenger.

A fast Gryphon is a live Gryphon, Lianndra thought. Their speed, strength, mobility and knowledge of the terrain allowed them to fight a better armed and larger army. Those skills and their planetary shield were all that stood between them and slavery or annihilation. The Gryphon obviously counted on the shield to deter invaders. It seemed they did not have weapons more advanced than aged hand lasers; swords, knives, and spears armed most of the scouts.

It was surprising the Fang would go to so much trouble to acquire the Gryphon. Lianndra theorized the Gryphon's obvious physical advantages made them a valuable species to enslave. An army of them could move heavy artillery over many kinds of terrain. They would be a strong addition to any ground war. Still, it seemed the Fang were paying a high price to capture this particular species for slaves.

Lianndra didn't have a chance to discuss things with Virra, the mini-Gryphon she connected with while they were in the Fang's custody. It turned out the little Gryphon she healed possessed the designation of shiev of the principal valley.

Sort of like a prime minister, although she apparently reports to the Gryphon Council. Important captive, indeed, she thought.

As soon as Lianndra mentioned the rebels, Virra wasted no time in putting a rescue party together. The mini-Gryphon explained she had plans for the rebels and was concerned about their fate. Virra wanted them brought back to the Gryphon valley as quickly as possible.

They soon left the lush valley that Lianndra had nicknamed Gryphon Acres. She now knew there were many permanent bases contained within natural canyons and valleys. The real Gryphon name of the valley was unpronounceable to humans. Virra seemed amused by Lianndra's choice of name. Lianndra wondered just how deep Virra's knowledge of humans, and the English language, ran.

Most of the large Gryphon spoke little English since it was a difficult language for them to master. Virra told her that, much like the Farr, the bigger Gryphon had a jaw and tongue structure too heavy to allow proficiency in some languages, including English. They managed single words, carefully chosen to communicate as much as possible. The mini-Gryphon were the language experts.

With their smaller, more refined features they spoke many alien tongues quite well.

Lianndra found it remarkable that the Gryphon selected English as a language to learn, but she didn't get a chance to ask Virra about it. She'd tried to ask Kaye, but the big female had too limited a vocabulary to answer. They would likely get better at speaking with more exposure, but right now a full conversation was beyond them. Instead, Lianndra concentrated on picking up on some of the Gryphon's communication. The human talent for mimicry proved useful. As they traveled, Kaye trilled or whistled to her, pointing to various geographical features and plant life. Lianndra soon learned a smattering of Gryphon words for things like grass, rock, and water.

The hours slid by, each one seemingly longer than the one before. Kaye's spikes heated up. Lianndra noticed the tails of the Gryphon became more active as they encouraged air movement. Sweat trickled down Lianndra's body; to cool off, she grew a truly impressive tail tuft and took turns fanning Kaye's spikes as well as her own face. Her mount shook her head and rattled her head spikes; Lianndra took it as a sign of appreciation.

There were no big males in the party. Lianndra assumed this was a sign speed was more important on this particular venture than power. She was getting better at distinguishing between the immature genders. There were a few smaller males in this group, only slightly heavier and taller than the females. Their manes were still rudimentary, mere tufts in some cases, but the feathers were as bright as their bodies. The females' crests were often vividly colored but their bodies were more subdued. Kaye's body fur was pale yellow with chocolate brown spots, while her crest was bright yellow. Lianndra assumed the males were small because they were young, so they'd yet to attain their full size. She remembered her error with the mini-Gryphon and decided to find a way to ask sooner than later. Lianndra didn't want to risk embarrassing herself or offending them.

As they neared the site where the Fang had ambushed them the previous night, Kaye fell silent, and the entire troop was on high alert. The forward scouts signaled all clear as they passed through the scorched grass tufts. It looked different in the daylight. Tension in the group was palpable as they trotted through the burned landscape.

The scouts trilled something sounding like a query, and Kaye broke ranks to canter ahead to a swath of trampled ground. The Fang unit had obviously passed through here. It was clear which direction they headed. They were on track to the rocky cliffs, where the rebels were hiding.

Lianndra's heart clenched. *Michael, Drake, Hannah . . .*

Kaye said something in their musical language, and the scouts exchanged looks before turning to follow the unit's path. Kaye resumed her place in the column but no longer seemed in the mood to continue teaching Lianndra their language. Lianndra's mood was also dark. She tried to estimate how far the Fang unit had traveled in the past thirty-six hours. Had the Fang found the rebel camp? Would the Gryphon get to the rebels in time?

The party resumed their forward trek at a reduced pace. Their progress seemed agonizingly slow, but Lianndra knew they were making the best time possible. The Fang unit could be quite close; there was no way to tell for sure. Ahead of them, the scouts moved in bursts to keep as long a distance between themselves and the column as possible. Periodically, they stopped to stand up on their strong hind legs, surveying ahead before dropping down again to bolt forward.

Over one hundred pounding feet potentially generated a lot of dust. Watching them, Lianndra noticed the Gryphon were careful to snap their feet up with each stride, minimizing the dust displacement. She scanned the horizon for a similar cloud raised by an entire unit of foot-dragging Fang slaves. After a while, she noticed she wasn't the only one observing. The Gryphon around her constantly scanned ahead. Lianndra also noticed their spikes raised and lowered often, a sign she was learning to recognize as uneasiness. Kaye was being careful not to poke Lianndra with her torso spikes, something she truly appreciated.

Shrill whistles split the air and the entire column slid to an abrupt halt. Lianndra's heart pounded. She only just stopped herself from nudging Kaye with her legs to encourage her forward to where the scouts nervously stood.

She is not a horse, she reminded herself.

It took Lianndra a moment to realize what she was looking at. It was a large campsite complete with fire pits. Lianndra recognized the layout. A Fang fighting unit camp. The trampled area had a wide trail circling around a clump of scraggly trees before heading for the cliffs—straight for the rebel camp.

"How old are the tracks?" Lianndra asked the scouts. Their spikes rustled as though they were uneasy. Lianndra pointed to the tracks, the fire pits, and then traced the path of the sun in the sky. "How old?"

Kaye seemed to understand and queried the scouts. After a brief discussion, one of them answered in broken English. "Night 'fore."

Last night. Many hours ago. While the Gryphon had carried Lianndra safely away, the Fang unit picked up the rebel's trail. *This is my fault. If it wasn't for me, the Gryphon would have found the Fang unit before it progressed this far into the grasslands. They could have called in their warriors to deal with the Fang on their turf. Instead, they found me.*

She looked up to the cliffs which loomed close. It couldn't have taken the Fang long to reach the rebels. Lianndra's group would be too late to do anything but regret they hadn't been there faster. She felt her throat close with tears, but she forced them away. *Act now. Cry later.*

"Camp. That way!" Lianndra pointed along the tracks, her entire arm shaking with urgency.

Kaye whistled and moved forward at a long gallop, the rest of the Gryphon joining her. Lianndra realized her new friend had picked up on her anxiety.

Drake is smart. He would see them coming. Her heart pounded in rhythm to the beat of the Gryphon's feet. *Drake would know what to do. He would get them out of there.* Lianndra closed her eyes, trying not to cry. *Michael is alive . . .*

EWT%MIT%FNSK CLUTCHED THE ANIMAL SKIN closer to her as she hid in the shadows of an enormous generator. There had been a time when she couldn't stand in one spot for more than a few moments without seeing a maintenance slave. Now, the war had called upon so many, her only companion in the depths of the ship was silence.

Soft footsteps alerted her to the arrival of her friend. Xoe%san%krin appeared, warmly wrapped while nervously looking around. Ewt%mit%fnsk gestured, and her friend joined her in the darkness.

Xoe%san%krin looked rather pale. "I'm sorry to ask you down here again," she said. "I didn't know who else to talk to."

Ewt%mit%fnsk felt the surge of fear she had been stifling ever since her friend sent her the clandestine message. "What is wrong?"

"I have some news from the war, passed through the usual channels." Xoe%san%krin didn't have to say what channels she was talking about: *the rebellion*. The phrase still made Ewt%mit%fnsk's hearts pound.

Xoe%san%krin seemed to take her friend's silence as an indication to continue. "One of our operatives found information on the war coordinator's computer."

Ewt%mit%fnsk's eyes widened in surprise. She had already determined the rebellion must have some well-placed operatives to have come this far. To have someone within the war coordinator's office was as well-placed as it got, with the possible exception of having someone on the Chamber of Elders.

"I am surprised too." Xoe%san%krin's eyes were swirling red. "It is privileged information—do you understand?"

Ewt%mit%fnsk nodded, too shocked to speak. *More privileged than a plasma cannon powered by five Motherships?* Since learning of the plan, she had received only generic information on the rebellion's progress. She guessed that was about to change.

Her friend continued. "I know why the elders are so determined to pursue this war." The skin of Xoe%san%krin's face flushed red with anxiety. "There is a species on this planet whose ability, with only minimal modification, can place us as a dominant force in the universe. This species is a ready-made weapon just waiting for exploitation."

As the new information sank in, a lot of things made sense. Ewt%mit%fnsk's hearts continued to pound but now her brain throbbed right along with them. She had recognized the war was all about power, but she hadn't understood it was power on this level. She wondered if this information should change anything. Ewt%mit%fnsk wanted success for her species. But what did success really mean? For whose success were they fighting?

Xoe%san%krin watched her. She had taken a huge risk in telling Ewt%mit%fnsk about this. If Ewt%mit%fnsk decided the rebel forces were wrong to interfere, and their people should push ahead to acquire this new species, she would bring the entire rebellion down.

Power. Ewt%mit%fnsk envisioned the Tlo%m as an interstellar powerhouse and not just an esteemed species producing valuable slaves for the universal markets. *The kind of power that would enable us to dictate and conquer as we pleased.*

Most advanced beings progressed through a so-called primitive phase where they made significant mistakes on a species-wide level. The Tlo%m were no exception: they lost their home world long ago due to a struggle for power. Fang should have advanced beyond such mistakes; the genetic manipulation of their embryos was designed to decrease the likelihood of such irrational behavior from ever happening again.

Ewt%mit%fnsk recognized there had been a subtle shift in her species' behavior during her lifetime. She thought of the disparity already appearing within their political structure. The Tlo%m relied on a balanced society to exist because they lived within the boundaries of the giant Motherships. Could her species survive another power struggle?

Ewt%mit%fnsk sighed before voicing her question to her friend. "Do you think our species would survive having that kind of power?"

Xoe%san%krin shook her head slowly. "The rebellion feels this information only strengthens the rebel cause. My informant is adamant that offering more power to a system already out of balance leads to further corruption." Her eyes still swirled red, showing her distress. "I agree our species needs to rebuild from the core. We have seen the decline in the quality of our offspring in the last few generations. Acquisition of this species will only give more power to the highest levels of our structure, where we have already seen the imbalance at work. It could create a permanent chasm between the policy makers and those of us providing the information."

Xoe%san%krin folded her chilled arms into her cape. "The rebellion calculates that if we acquire this species and the power it represents, we would quickly devolve into a primitive, class-based society. Or, even worse, the Fara could devolve to behave like the Farr, concerned more with blood and battle than science and intellect."

This philosophy made sense to Ewt%mit%fnsk. The females of her species had always been proud of their enlightenment, even as they worked to preserve the primitive instincts in the males since those instincts were useful in battle. The Blooddances and Pitfights were a means to an end: keeping the Farr's thirst for blood quenched and under control.

How many Fara enjoy the bloody contests from the concealment of their own quarters? Ewt%mit%fnsk thought. Most Fara did not like to admit the hearts of a primitive predator beat within all the Tlo%m, not just the males. Ewt%mit%fnsk felt those hearts beating now and recognized her instincts wanted her species to succeed at all costs. *What imbalanced genes are within me?* How often had she succumbed to the animal part of her, the part wanting to dominate other species? How often did she react without thinking to external stimuli? *Imagine if all the Fara behaved like the Farr?*

Discussions about such primitive feelings once seemed like an intellectual exercise, something civilized beings discussed over a meal. Ewt%mit%fnsk believed the Tlo%m were a civilized race. She wanted the Fang to be known for their intellect, and not merely for the physical ability to dominate.

"I think the rebellion is right," Ewt%mit%fnsk admitted. She looked into her friend's eyes and saw acceptance.

"Then let's hope," Xoe%san%krin said, "the rebel's plans will work. The elders have given the cannon priority and work on the power grids continues. The procedure is unprecedented and not assured of success. There have been glitches slowing the process down. The elders have our best and brightest on it. They are confident the cannon will operate as planned."

Ewt%mit%fnsk gave her head a slight shake. "The rebellion might be running out of time."

DRAKE IS SMART, LIANNDRA THOUGHT. *He is wily. They have the high ground. He would have held them off for a while.* As the Gryphon ran, Lianndra chanted the captain's assets off to herself and tried not to think of how vulnerable Michael was. He couldn't be moved quickly. If the attack was a surprise, he wouldn't have stood a chance.

What had taken her an hour to walk took the Gryphon minutes at a gallop. When the cliffs were close, the column, and the forward scouts, slowed to a halt. The cliffs were silent. If there'd been a battle, it was long over.

No, no, no . . . The repetitive chant echoed through Lianndra's brain.

At a nod from the column leader—an old female with broken spikes—the scouts vanished into the rocks. The Gryphon's claws were superior to a horse's hooves when navigating rock but she still expected them to make some noise. Lianndra heard nothing as the scouts moved higher even with the loose rock beneath their feet.

They were back too quickly. The entire troop moved into the cliffs, following the scout's lead.

Close to the cave where the rebels sheltered lay a hulking form—Bradley. The tough alien had fought bravely; black blood and scorched laser wounds covered his huge form. The second Zraph lay inside, almost cut in two by a laser cannon. They were the only bodies. The cave showed every sign of being hastily vacated. The blanket where Michael had rested remained on the floor, the logs of the nearby fire strewn across the dirt.

Fighting her tears, Lianndra dismounted to walk to the mouth of the cave. After a moment, she turned so her back was to it. Kaye moved to stand beside her. The rest of the troop waited on the rocks below. Lianndra looked away, her gaze tracing the line of rock. If not killed outright, the rebels were either captured or had escaped along the cliffs. The Zraph couldn't navigate the narrow passages Lianndra saw ahead of her. Was that why they'd chosen to stay behind? The tears washed across her eyes and flowed down her cheeks.

She turned to Kaye. The Gryphon stared at her, head tilted in question. Then she reached out one of her hands, touching Lianndra's cheek with one elongated finger. Her finger dampened by a tear, she brought it to her lips. Her ears twitched.

"Trail?" Lianndra asked, pointing along the cliffs to where the rebels must have fled.

Kaye turned and whistled to one of the scouts who whistled back.

Kaye picked her way along the cliff. Lianndra followed. The other Gryphon fell into line behind them. Their progress was silent save for the occasional scrape of a claw on rock.

Lianndra made out the barest trace of a retreat: rocks rolled out of place, the faintest track of a boot step in rock dust. The rebels had made a run for it. The Fang unit couldn't have had any big aliens such as Zraph in the group or they would never have been able to follow the rebels. Only the streamlined shape, grasping toes, and amazingly flexible bodies of the Gryphon allowed them to pick their way over precarious rocks and through the narrow openings.

They rounded a huge outcropping and saw scorch marks of lasers on the opposite rock face. Heart in her throat, Lianndra continued to pick her way between cliffs so close they posed a serious navigational challenge for the Gryphon.

Beyond the narrow cliffs, the trail opened to a flat stretch of rocky slab. There were laser scorches everywhere, and in the middle lay a small pile of bodies. As Lianndra rushed forward, she identified two of the mangled forms as having come from the rebel group. The rest must have been from the Fang unit.

Michael's not here, she thought with guilty relief.

A Gryphon spoke rapidly in its native tongue as Kaye guided Lianndra away from the bodies to the signs of many footsteps creating a new trail down the cliff face.

"Capture," one of the scouts said, gesturing to the tracks. The Fang had obviously taken their captives out of the cliffs on a direct line back toward the jungle.

Captured. Lianndra's heart froze at the thought. *No telling how large the Fang slave unit is.* She stared out across the shale to where the cliffs met the grasslands. They were out there somewhere, likely within the rocky outcrops. *Are they still alive? Are they being tortured? It wouldn't take much to kill Michael at this stage.* Her thoughts raced.

She heard soft footsteps behind her as Kaye moved to lay a humanlike hand on her shoulder.

Lianndra hung her head and more tears slipped down her face. She felt overwhelmed, unsure of what she could do alone against an entire Fang unit. *Of course, I may not be alone. But do the Gryphon want to take such a chance?* She'd never had the lives of so many hinge on her actions. *Michael, Drake, Hannah, Sean. Why would the Gryphon help a bunch of humans they don't even know? Do I have the right to ask this of them? To risk their lives for the lives of the people I love?* Lianndra squared her shoulders. *Drake wouldn't hesitate. He'd be organized and plan an effective assault, reducing the possible risk to those involved. He would make a proposal to the Gryphon and have a backup plan if they refused to help. Then he'd put himself right into the middle of everything.*

On the wings of desperation, a plan began to coalesce in her brain. She turned to look up at the tall alien beside her. *The only way I will know if they are willing to help,* she realized, *is to ask.*

MICHAEL'S EYES FELT LIKE THEY were full of sand and his face ached all the way to the roots of his teeth.

Strange. I can still feel my teeth ache on top of everything else. Michael turned his head to spit out blood. He only saw out of his right eye as the left had swelled shut. His ribs ached and every breath sent stabs of pain along his left side, where he suspected splintered ribs poked into sensitive lung tissue. With hands shackled behind Michael's back, every breath pulled at his ribs and sent pulses of pure agony through him.

He rolled his eye up to meet the maddened stare of the Fang commander looming over him. The Fang was remarkably tolerant—

for a Fang. He'd let Hannah heal Michael three times so far, bringing him back from the blessed blackness of oblivion. The redheaded Healer sat in one corner of the tent. Her bloodshot eyes and strained face focused on Michael. She'd yet to cry, even when the brute backhanded her after the last healing episode. Michael admired her fortitude.

He felt like crying himself. *I'm just too damned stubborn.*

Frankly, he didn't know why he was holding out. Drake's freed slaves constituted the slave rebellion in its entirety. With them captured, the rebellion was essentially over.

Except there are still slaves out there with deactivated collars, including Lianndra, he thought. *And I'll be damned if we'll make it easy for the Fang to figure out how we did it.*

A heavy boot crashed again into his exposed left side and Michael bit his lip to keep from crying out as the ribs gave way completely. Blood trickled down his face from where his teeth had lacerated his lip, which he knew was likely nothing compared to what was happening inside of him. He wondered if the Fang would let Hannah heal him this time.

The reptilian commander snarled before turning to where Hannah crouched in the corner. Moving quickly for such a large creature, he grabbed her by the hair to drag her toward Michael. Instead of letting her heal him, the Fang slugged her hard. Hannah's head snapped backward and blood spewed from her nose.

Faster than thought, Michael launched himself with an animalistic snarl off of legs that, mere moments before, had refused to hold his weight. He slammed the shoulder of his uninjured side into the Fang's body, clobbering the blocky alien. Caught off guard, the commander released Hannah, who rolled away from him, hands to her face. Michael and the Fang hit the ground with a crash that brought the Bernaf bodyguards running from outside. With his arms shackled behind his back, Michael could not shield himself from the blow that knocked him off of the commander. The shattered ribs penetrated deep into his lung. The resulting agony became a wall of blackness rolling over him like a tidal wave, taking him under.

EPILOGUE

THIS HIGH IN THE MOUNTAINS the air was thin but crisp, and on a sunny day, the details of the surrounding lands could be seen from a distance. Even the dense jungles were visible as a dark smudge on the far horizon. Between them and the mountains to the east lay the pale green of the grasslands. They stood out in contrast to the deeper greens of the valleys the Gryphon called their home. Swinging westward, the grasslands gave way to the deserts of the great Vertraax, a giant creature with a snakelike body whose scales were all but impenetrable by sword or laser.

Sunny days in the mountains were rare, especially this high. The norm ran to dense clouds of fog or mist spinning their way through the mountain passes, leaving the cliffs dripping with moisture. For parts of the year, this moisture fell as snow that left a thick, frozen blanket over every flat surface.

The cliffs seemed lifeless this close to the clouds, and for the most part, they were. Life was stubborn and loathed leaving a usable biological niche unoccupied. Creatures with wings traveled to the valleys below to gain sustenance, returning to the caves in the sides of the cliffs for shelter. Barely visible through the fog, small dark forms dove in and out of the cave entrances, moving so quickly they were simply blurs against the rock.

As part of nature's eternal balance, where one form of life exists there was always another designed to prey upon it.

One such creature emerged out of the mist. It raised its leathery nose as it searched the air for its quarry. Fur of various shades of gray covered most of the predator, the mottled coat helping it to blend into the surrounding cliffs. It had six legs ending in long toes, with curved claws adapted to finding the cracks in the rock as it clung to sheer surfaces. Although its eyes were tiny, its ears and nose were huge. Its secret weapon was its ability to echolocate its prey, sending high-pitched clicks up the mountainside as it read the evidence of movement in the caves.

It slunk upward, pausing only to listen to the clicks rebounding off the movement above. Soon, it hunkered just below a ledge, its claws dug deep into crevices in the rock.

Just above, winged forms darted around a small cave in the side of the mountain. With a flick of dark wings, one of these swift creatures landed on the ledge, tilting its head to watch its companions.

The winged creature had a narrow head that was mostly jaw, with a beaklike tip to the snout, and a crest of stiff spikes that continued down the center of its long graceful neck. It had six legs, with the middle two modified into wings with delicate membranes between elongated finger bones. Its body was slender; it crouched on attenuated fore and hind legs which had long toes ending in sharp claws. A whippy tail also sported a row of spikes.

The little creature made a trilling noise as it crouched to launch itself back into the sky.

Waiting under the ledge until its prey leaped and made the first downstroke of its wings, the predator unleashed its main weapon: a long, sticky tongue. Perhaps thrown off by the obscuring fog, the strike was not a good one. It missed the head of its victim but attached itself to just one wing. That was the predator's first mistake.

The intended victim shrieked, flapping its free wing. Then the predator made its second mistake. Rather than releasing its hold and retreating, it held on to its prize, fighting to pull the struggling creature toward its eager mouth. This earned the prey a precious few seconds. That was all it required.

The creature's shrill shrieks brought its friends pouring out of the cave. Too late, the predator recognized the danger and tried to disengage its tongue. Rather than attacking the predator with tooth and claw, the tiny winged avengers hovered above it, long noses pointed with their spiked crests erect.

A blast of something intangible vibrated through the air. The predator didn't even have time to scream as an invisible energy penetrated its flesh, ripping it apart cell by cell.

The winged forms swirled in a dark cloud, emitting excited chirps, before returning to their daily routine. One sat on the ledge to preen its wing, working to remove the sticky slime from its surface. Other than a smear of blood on the rock, the slime was the only sign the predator had ever lived.

The winged creatures were known as Darkon, and they were the greatest secret Tarin had to offer.

One their foes, the Tlo%m, would kill to possess.

One their friends, the Gryphon, would die to protect.

A biological Weapon.
A Monster unleashed.
A final, desperate Battle.

Plagued by personal demons as Tarin threatens to burn, Lianndra must harness the power of the ultimate weapon. Even if it kills her.

On the other side of fear lies Freedom . . .

www.thegryphonsaga.com

Learn more about the
Gryphon Saga characters with
Tales from the Gryphon Saga!

Tales from

L.E. HORN

Heart of a Warrior

A young Gryphon fights an unexpected battle with the enemy. Alone and afraid, she discovers the warrior within.

The Turning of the Tide

Just as the scales of war tip to favor the Gryphon, the Fang introduce a new weapon. One which has dire implications for the planet.

Sleeping with the Enemy

To the Fang, humans are no more than animals to be enslaved. One man proves he is more than just a collared beast.

Double Jeopardy

A genetically modified human rides the fine line between the enemies within and without when he is injured in a battle.

A Shot in the Dark

To kick-start the rebellion, one mini-Grypha must make the ultimate sacrifice.

www.thegryphonsaga.com

ACKNOWLEDGMENTS

NO BOOK IS PUBLISHED WITHOUT an army of support and this one is certainly no exception. Susan and her entire entourage remained entrenched for a much longer haul than anticipated, keeping me going when my spirits flagged. My friends Kathy, Margaret, and Wendy were indispensably enthusiastic, critical, inspiring, and insightful at just the right times. My beta readers Gillian, Stewart, Ann Marie, Phil, Pat, Larry, Donna, Autumn, Beth, Phil, Lori, Brett, Jaime, and Michele took time out of their busy lives to read and provide essential observations. Editor, A.P. Fuchs, not only helped me to be a better writer, but his creation, Axiom-man, is mentioned by Lianndra when her mind is awhirl with possibilities. Last, but certainly not least, my husband kept my real life intact while my nose was in this book. Thanks to all of you from the depths of my heart!

AUTHOR AND ARTIST, L.E. HORN, describes her childhood as, "Rich in experiential learning," since her family moved every year or so until she was a teenager. Stability relied upon immersing herself in nature and the literary works of her favorite authors. Tapping into a vivid imagination, she wrote many novels as a youngster. Even today, she remains fascinated by our often unconscious connections to the natural world; she particularly loves to explore the qualities we believe distinguish us from the creatures whose planet we share.

L.E. Horn shares her country home in Manitoba, Canada, with her husband and several other interesting species that, as she puts it, "Inspire me by pointing out what should be obvious on a minute-by-minute basis. The challenge keeps me both happy and humble."